RE∧LITY RIFT

RE∧LITY RIFT

FRED GAMBINO

DΛRK SHEPHERD BOOK 2

NEWCON PRESS

NewCon Press
England

First published in the UK, December 2025 by
NewCon Press
41 Wheatsheaf Road,
Alconbury Weston,
Cambs, PE28 4LF

NCP357 (limited edition hardback)
NCP358 (paperback)

10 9 8 7 6 5 4 3 2 1

ISBN:

978-1-917735-15-5 (hardback)
978-1-917735-16-2 (paperback)

All Artwork by Fred Gambino
Cover layout by Ian Whates

Editing by Donna Scott and Ian Whates
Typesetting and book layout by Ian Whates

ONE

It would have been so much easier doing this in symbiosis. Breel was strapped into the control throne on the bridge of *Scavenger*. The room was a mess. Bits of broken equipment and other, less identifiable objects, floated around her in microgravity. They bounced off the walls and each other, a testament to the violent events that had left the ship mortally wounded and the reason Breel was having to hands-on pilot the spacecraft the old-fashioned way.

A semi-circular array of screens vied for her attention. The central and largest screen showed a mountain of ice and rock floating in a sea of stars, around which two smaller mountains and a glittering ring orbited. These were the shattered remains of the asteroid they had christened *Revenge*.

She was focused on the largest mass. It slowly drifted across her field of view, occluding the stars until she could see nothing but rugged gullies and craters.

"Coming up over the C&C now," she announced.

The tops of a collection of shattered buildings, the remains of the Command-and-Control centre, hove into view. They were situated on a ridge at the edge of a huge drop. The human construction gave her a familiar reference to create a sudden, dizzying sense of depth and scale. Like a bird soaring over the edge of a high escarpment in Arralandeshi crater back home, Breel looked down a massive, sheer wall of ice and rock. Embedded in this wall, and foreshortened into tight ellipses by her perspective, she could just make out huge pits that housed the now defunct EMD star drives that had once powered the asteroid across the light years.

The ruins of the C&C continued to slide across the screen until they stopped dead centre.

Scavenger vibrated rhythmically as Breel applied the ship's thrusters in quick succession. The relative motions of both ship and asteroid ceased. She had put them into a synchronous orbit, in line with, and as close to the remains of, the Command-and-Control as possible, about a hundred metres away. Any closer and the mass of *Revenge* would slowly pull them down to its surface. She still had to constantly trim the ship's position to hold station. She tapped a control and the scene was lit by the harsh glare of *Scavenger's* floodlights, overpowering the wan light from the system's distant sun, little more than a bright star from this distance.

"We're in position," she reported.

Another screen showed three space-suited figures crammed into a tiny airlock: Matt, Kaemon, and the Deacon, about to EVA down to the broken asteroid to salvage what resources they could, essential for their survival. Four MARRVs were also squashed in between the men. If the ship hadn't been in weightless conditions, the exercise would have been impossible.

"Opening the lock now Breel," Matt said. The outer doors opened. She couldn't see the view this would give the men – the camera was focused on the airlock interior – but light from outside flooded the space they floated in, casting their black shadows across the deck and each other.

Matt and Kaemon were old hands, but this was new to the Deacon. He didn't have a spaceman's background and the EVA was a terrifying prospect for him. She worried he might be more liability than help, but such were the straits they found themselves in, everyone had to step up.

"Okay Breel. Letting the MARRVs go," Matt reported. She watched the men all squash to the perimeter of the airlock to allow the MARRVs access to the door. The MARRVs were about half the height of the humans, compact bulbous metal bodies moving on four legs with six manipulator arms dangling from their undersides. Their job on this trip was to haul whatever the humans found on *Revenge* back to *Scavenger*, especially the heavy EMD cells needed to reactivate *Scavenger's* star drive. Pale puffs of gas vented from thrusters mounted in the machines' curving flanks and they disappeared from view. On a separate display she watched the small robots dwindle in size as they jetted down to the icy surface.

"You're good to go guys," she said. "Good luck. I'll be here if you need me."

Matt turned to the space-suited figure standing next to him. "You go first," he told the Deacon.

Matt watched the man float towards the door. The Deacon gripped the hatch frame tightly. His eyes were wide and his face drained of blood.

Matt pushed up alongside. "Deep breaths, Deacon." he said. "Try to relax and enjoy the ride."

The Deacon glared at him. "Does this look like an amusement park to you?"

Matt smiled and patted the Deacon on his armoured shoulder. "It's okay, Deacon. You'll be fine. The SMU will deal with the flight. Breel'll keep an eye on you, so just sit back and take in the view."

The Deacon turned back to what to him must look like a suicidal drop, clearly not finding much to admire in the view.

Matt nodded to Kaemon. "You go next, Kae, I'll bring up the rear."

Kaemon gave him a thumbs up. "See you down there."

The Deacon was still at the edge of the airlock, a bulky shape, dark against the bright rugged ice-scape of *Revenge*. He hesitated for a second longer, then threw himself out head first, like a skydiver seeking speed, but in slow motion.

That's one way to do it, Matt thought. Kaemon followed the Deacon next with practiced ease, feet first.

Matt's turn. He pulled on the hatch frame to give himself enough momentum to follow the two men out into the void and away from the security of *Scavenger*. He gripped the two joysticks that hung in front of him. Flexible arms connected them to the thruster array that was the suit manoeuvring unit, itself attached to his backpack. Telemetry showing the status of the SMU and that of his flight began to flow through his heads-up display.

He had suggested Deacon enjoy the view and to Matt at least, it was spectacular. The rugged surface of the asteroid hung below his feet as a series of giant bright ellipses from the ship's floods, striated by black shadows. There was nothing visible beyond *Scavenger's* lights, the multitude of stars he knew were there lost against the eye-watering glare.

A pattering sound transmitted through Matt's suit as fine particles bounced off him. The small ones weren't a problem since their relative speeds were close, but there were larger objects in less safe orbits that could prove fatal, not least the two large fragments that had sheared off the main body of *Revenge*. Although invisible to him, those jagged moons were just now setting beyond *Revenge's* irregular horizon. The timing would give them a clear run for a few hours.

"Something fairly large coming fast at your 3 o'clock," Breel reported.

"I see it." Matt had already spotted the spinning object, a primary surrounded by a bright family of smaller satellites. He heard the Deacon gasp as the object turned to reveal a humanoid shape.

"Don't worry, Deacon," Matt reassured his companion. "He's long dead."

The one-time Warrior of Light, a martyr to his people, spun past at high speed only a few arm's lengths away. The body changed orientation at the last minute. At some point in the battle the soldier had lost his helmet. The mummified head turned its rictus grin towards him. The skin was desiccated from decompression, cheeks sunken. Matt could see ice glimmer on the man's beard. Dead cataract eyes met Matt's, seemed to hold his gaze and then Matt's blood ran cold as the corpse gave him the finger. The hairs on the back of his neck rose. He knew, of course, that some spurious motion must have transmitted through the dead man's arm, but being flipped off by a corpse couldn't help but trigger a superstitious response from his hindbrain.

Clumsily, the Deacon was doing his best to make the sign of the Circle of Light in his bulky suit.

"There will be a few of these guys orbiting *Revenge*, I reckon," Kaemon said.

Matt watched the dead man recede, his stomach churning. A human life he had been party to ending. True, the soldier had been trying to kill him at the time, but as he watched the crusader tumble away, the death of this man and of the others who had died in the fight for control of the asteroid weighed heavily upon him; more than he would have expected.

He fired a burst of propellant to turn and face away from his destination, to look back at *Scavenger*. Travelling backwards now, he got a first good look at the damage to his ship. It was like seeing the body of a much-loved member of the family bruised and battered by a violent mugging. Holes and rents in the fuselage, components, fins and antennae, all missing; so much damage, the silhouette was almost that of a different ship.

"Coming up to halfway," Breel informed them.

Another burst of propellant spun Matt around to once more face his objective. The shattered remains of the Command-and-Control centre were very close now. There were so many holes in its superstructure that it must have been entirely open to the vacuum and frozen solid. The terrain around the complex was relatively smooth, but a short distance away to his right, it broke up into a gorge filled with broken pinnacles, a deep gash like a mouth filled with rotting teeth. Beyond that, a bowl-shaped blast crater gleamed with smooth new ice, the place where only two days before he and Kaemon had run to make a final stand against the crusaders in a fight for control of the asteroid. Matt and Kaemon had lost that fight. Lying on the ice, wounded, Matt was sure he was taking his last breath when Breel had swooped in and saved them both.

The MARRVs landed on *Revenge,* moved aside and waited patiently, bobbing in that alert way they had, long black shadows cast across the frozen surface.

"You okay, Deacon?" He called out to the man, who had gone silent.

"It's a relative question, I think," the Deacon replied, "but I suppose so."

Matt looked through his boots at the approaching ice. The Deacon, still in his swan dive, gave a sudden yelp as the suit's neural-core began its pre-programmed landing sequence, spinning him upright so he would land on his feet. His suit thrusters erupted in silent bright flashes to slow his descent. A little cloud of disturbed ice rose from the surface, then fell back in smooth parabolic arcs in the vacuum. The thrusters brightened and the Deacon hung motionless above the surface for a second, before touching down smoothly with barely a bounce. He quickly moved clear to make room for Kaemon who did the same a minute later.

There was a sudden sense of ground rush. Matt pulled at the joysticks to slow his descent. His shadow undulated across the pitted surface of *Revenge*, racing to meet him as if to greet an old friend. He raised a small cloud of frozen particles on impact.

So here he was, breathing, drinking, and peeing inside his hi-tech cocoon, a finger-width thickness of polymer the only thing that lay between him and a suffocating, freeze-dried death. He was on his own, if you didn't count the MARRV. Matt and Kaemon were pursuing their own missions.

The Deacon's heart hadn't stopped racing since he left the airlock of *Scavenger*. Now, here in this pitch-black, icy tomb, it wasn't about to slow down anytime soon. The situation was insane.

As if that wasn't bad enough, he and his accompanying drone were the only source of illumination. Their lights cast swirling shadows that turned room fittings, pipes, and other unidentified machinery into leaping predators and monsters.

How did anyone get used to this, enjoy it even, as Matt had suggested? He was pretty sure that hadn't been merely a turn of phrase. Matt was made for this stuff.

"You okay, Deacon?" Breel asked. "Your readings are spiking."

A small display in the corner of his helmet gave the Deacon a view transmitted from Matt's drone. Matt and Kaemon would have a similar display in their helmets. Matt stopped when he heard Breel.

"I'm fine," the Deacon said, a little testily. "I'll let you know if I need anything."

"Just checking," Breel said, responding in kind with her own slight note of irritation. "Keep going the way you're going. You're almost at the quartermaster's deck."

The Deacon continued his low gravity shuffle down a corridor lined with adjoining rooms set at regular intervals. A quick look showed they were bunk rooms, presumably for the construction crew that had converted this once nameless aggregate of ice and rock into *Revenge*. The bunks were covered in ice. It was so cold here that, along with the frozen water, some of the precipitate was likely carbon dioxide. Here and there a hole allowed light from *Scavenger's* floods to splash bright highlights, making the rime sparkle.

He low-gravity-hopped past the ruined bunk rooms, away from the brief cheer of light, back into the dark once more. The MARRV skittered ahead silently on its four legs, following a floor plan Matt had installed in its memory. Its headlights created a narrow, constantly shifting corridor of light that threw ruts and cracks into sharp relief. The Deacon paused.

"There are marks in the ice on the floor here," he said. "As if something has been dragged across it." He shone his own light onto the deck.

"That's weird," Matt said. "Kaemon and I were the last one's in there."

"Yeah," Kaemon joined in. "Must have been made after we left, sometime after the transit through the *RIP.*"

"How can that be?" the Deacon asked. "Do you think there's something still alive in here?"

"I doubt it," Kaemon responded.

The corridor came to an abrupt end. The Deacon and his mechanised companion followed the trail into a large space lined with storage lockers of various sizes. The doors to most lay open, revealing empty interiors. Canisters and containers of all sizes and types lay scattered about, smashed, spilling ruined contents, now frozen to the floor.

"This doesn't look promising," the Deacon said. He walked past the devastation, following the ruts in the ice towards a faint glow.

"There's something ahead. I can see light." He used the suit sensor to scan the bright spot. "And it's warm."

"Can't detect anything from up here," Breel said.

"Be careful, Deak." Kaemon said.

"You are full of useful advice, Kaemon," the Deacon muttered.

The MARRV took the lead. The Deacon followed. A humped shadow on the floor began taking on a familiar outline.

"It looks like... a body," he said. As he got closer, he saw that it couldn't be anything else.

"Are you seeing this?" he asked. The figure was folded into a foetal position.

"Looks like a zip-head all right," Kaemon said.

"He's plugged into a console." The Deacon lifted a flexible pipe clear of the soldier. Status lights on the console glowed a green-yellow. A display showed numbers and graphs. "That's where the light's coming from."

"Another dead crusader?" Kaemon offered. "Must have crawled down here after the fight."

The Deacon considered the body, outlined in sickly light. Squatting over the corpse, he raised a hand tentatively to push at the helmet, then withdrew it sharply. *Get a grip!* he admonished himself. He lifted his hand again and this time completed the action, pushing at the soldier's head so that he could see the front of the man's helmet. "I can't see his face," he complained, voice high.

"Check the readouts on the console, Deacon," Breel said, patiently.

The Deacon let the man's head drop so he could see the illuminated display. He concentrated, trying to make sense of the graphs and numbers.

"Holy Light!" he whispered when it became clear what he was seeing. He pushed away from the body.

"What is it, Deacon?" Matt said sharply, "Are you okay?"

"This one isn't dead," the Deacon said.

TWO

Surface of Revenge, two days earlier

Abiel and the platoon spilled out of the troop carrier, *Dance of Light*, onto the frozen surface of the asteroid the insurgents had repurposed as a weapon With the nearest star light years away, there was nothing to illuminate the featureless landscape they moved across save a faint blue aurora, the glowing exhaust plumes from monumental star drives. The drives were located in a vertical cliff that dropped away at ninety degrees beyond a sharp horizon.

Ahead, the Command-and-Control Centre, their objective, was a squat, brutalist silhouette against this dully throbbing sky.

The soldiers didn't need light to see, however. The zip array of sensors in the otherwise featureless headgear implemented a variety of systems, from low light-level imaging, infrared, LIDAR and radar echo-location. The sensors also looked inwards, tracking the soldier's eyes. Each suit's neural-core combined all this data to present the soldiers with a sharp, monochromatic image that wrapped around their heads, as if the interior of their helmets were made of crystal-clear glass. The squad looked across a smooth ice plain to a line of low hills to the right. The landscape was overlaid with data points and scrolling information.

Abiel's small detachment, a team of three, broke away from the main company to head towards the low hills. Their operational directive was to flank the two insurgents taking refuge in the control centre, while the rest of the troops made a head-on attack. The small squad moved from cover to cover, presenting as small a target as possible.

Operations-control sounded through Abiel's helmet. "All units, be advised, targets have left the control complex; repeat, targets are moving due south, on a bearing of 45 degrees relative to your position."

The three soldiers paused in front of a shallow ice cave. A view transmitted from the troop carrier lit up in Abiel's HUD. The insurgents had thrown caution to the solar winds and were heading away across the uneven surface with the mighty bounds only possible in low gravity. The main body of the platoon making the direct assault had been approaching cautiously, keeping low to the ice, not knowing how well armed the insurgents might be. Now, they stopped their cautious approach and followed, using the same leaping locomotion.

The voice of operations sounded again. "The targets are heading towards a field of pinnacles, probably hoping to lose themselves there."

A schematic of the terrain appeared. Two moving red dots indicated their quarry, fleeing across a frozen plateau to where, a short distance away, the smooth frozen expanse shattered into a void punctuated by giant needles of ice and rock.

"Let's go," Abiel said. "No point our skulking here, now."

The helmet graphic showed the insurgents had reached their objective and were making their way across by leaping from spire to spire. *Dance of Light* lifted in pursuit and in seconds was moving over the broken ground. Abiel's squad set off to join the main platoon, but before they had taken a step the ground shook and the image from *Dance of Light* vanished into a blur of fog and static. A second later they were hit by a shockwave of superheated steam and ice that smashed them all violently back into the cave. Shocked, Abiel watched crusaders spin into the void, lost to space, their acceleration too much for the asteroid's feeble gravity to hold.

"Zal, Ti, you okay?" Abiel shouted.

"I'm okay," Zal responded. "But Ti's... gone."

Abiel took a breath. *Time to mourn later.*

"What happened?" Zal asked.

Data streamed across the field of view. "Seems the insurgents set off an explosion in the chasm that triggered a chain reaction in the rock. Blew up a geyser that hit the ship, then us."

Abiel focused on telemetry from the ship. It showed the fugitives had reached the far side, closely followed by the remaining holy warriors, who had quickly regrouped after the surprise attack. The troop carrier was close behind, firing its cannons. Feeling a sense of pride at the professionalism of the soldiers, Abiel rose to join the chase, followed closely by Zal.

"Targets are down," operations said suddenly. "Repeat, the insurgents are down."

Abiel glanced at the images beamed from the far side of the rift, where the fight was apparently over. The cannon fire from *Dance of Light* had blown the two fugitives from their hiding place, out into the open. A cry of triumph rang through the comms as the Church warriors converged upon the downed terrorists. *Dance of Light* settled to the ground, firing tethers into the terrain to anchor itself against the low gravity. Abiel stepped from the cave and raised a fist, joining in the victory shout.

Something flashed over the two soldiers, occluding the stars. A spacecraft, visible only by its running lights, zipped silently out of the dark. It passed low over them, heading straight for *Dance of Light.*

"That's the insurgent ship?" Zal said.

"Looks like it," Abiel replied. "How is it here? It was captured and docked to *Transcendent Light.*"

POV telemetry beamed to them from the troop carrier showed the enemy vessel's approach across the fissure. It took fire from the soldiers on the ground and *Dance of Light.* The insurgent ship went dark. The pilot had turned off its giveaway lights to make it a harder target. It flashed briefly, caught in the troop carrier's floodlights, like a moth chasing a flame, before vanishing beyond the reach of the *Dance's* powerful illumination. The troop carrier released its tethers to rise in pursuit, not wanting to be caught on the ground, but too late. It had barely begun its ascent before the heretic vessel returned. It dived down in a long looping curve that ended with it climbing vertically to the stars, directly over the rising troop carrier. The heretic vessel was lost to the dark once more, a second before reappearing in an eye-searing supernova that lit the plain and surrounding hills as bright as day. The insurgent pilot had fired up their fusion engines. Had the two crusaders been watching with unprotected eyes, they would surely have been blinded. The superheated exhaust smashed down, burning through the hull of the rising carrier, melting the ceramic composite, bursting through the sides, blasting it and the holy warriors inside back into their constituent atoms.

"Holy Light," Abiel shouted. "Get back, Zal!"

The soldiers out in the open who weren't vapourised were hurled off the asteroid into space. Some achieved escape velocity to begin an infinite journey through the cosmos, others went into unstable orbits.

Although Abiel and Zal were some distance away, on the other side of the gorge from the fiery impact, they were still hammered by a shockwave of rocks, ice, and gas, that flung them back into the cave once more. Abiel felt a stunning impact. Consciousness faded to the sound of multiple system failure alarms from the suit's neural-core.

The screech of alarms brought Abiel back with a start. The HUD was alive with scrolling information indicating a myriad of suit failures. Oxygen down eighty percent, power down sixty percent. Abiel had expected to be as one with the Light but the pain and discomfort made it clear that wasn't the case. The searing light from the heretic ship's fusion engines had gone. It would have been pitch black had the zip-array not been able to conjure up the scene. The fluted ice of the cave roof ended at the ragged arch of the entrance, beyond which the surface of the asteroid bisected a sky of hard white points.

Abiel looked for Zal and saw a twisted figure crushed at the back of the cave, next to Ti. There was little doubt that Zal had joined Ti in the embrace of the Light. A body that contorted, with that amount of suit damage, could no longer be alive.

Glowing numbers in the HUD reported over two hours, standard, had passed.

The ground began to tremble, then buck violently. Fearing the cave might collapse, Abiel attempted to stand, to get out into the open, then shouted a hoarse cry of pain. The suit sounded a new alarm, the shrill scream of *Suit Breech! Suit Breech!*

Abiel looked down. A spike of ice as hard as steel had pierced the suit just above the belt line. The stake had sealed the hole, but Abiel's movement had reopened it. Propelled by precious air, blood bubbled out, flash freezing in the vacuum. Gripping the ice shard, Abiel jerked it free, gasping with pain. Free of the obstruction now, the suit's self-healing protocol immediately came online, sealing the hole. The screeching warning stopped and the air level stabilised. The pain from the wound abated as the suit administered anaesthetics, but there was no way to know how serious the injury was, or if any internal organs had been damaged.

The ground was still shaking. Abiel had to get out of the ice cave and quickly, to assess the situation and decide what to do next. The crusader tried to walk but the right leg provided no support. Abiel only managed a slow-motion fall, landing heavily. Stunned, a glance down showed the suit's boot twisted at an unnatural angle. The boot was holed through all its layers at the calf, exposing black and shredded flesh and a glint of white bone within. The suit had done its job here too, pumping in painkillers and sealing itself just below the knee. The leg would die, must be already dead, but Abiel would survive.

Unable to stand, the crusader proceeded to crawl painfully to the cave opening. The scene outside was empty. The explosion had blasted the remains of *Dance of Light* and the other soldiers into space. This inhospitable lump of rock's sad excuse for a gravitational field was incapable of retaining anything moving at even moderate speed. The cave had saved them, or at least prevented their bodies being blasted out into the universe.

The quake suddenly doubled in intensity. Bright light flared all around, overwhelming the images from the suit sensors. Abiel recognised that hell-light. The Emissary had targeted the asteroid with his most potent weapon, the Matrix Pulse Generator. Large chunks of ice and rock rose ponderously. The asteroid was splitting apart under the assault and there was something odd about the stars. They had developed a distinctive blue tinge. In an instance of time too small to register they were replaced. A new set of star patterns blinked into existence and the dark barren landscape was suddenly flooded with pale light. Abiel felt despair then. They had passed through the Reality interstitial Paradox, the *RIP!* Against impossible odds, the heretics had succeeded in their mission.

How could this be? How had the crusaders so offended the Light that it would forsake them in their moment of victory?

Injured, alone, and without resources, was there any point in continuing? Better to unclip the helmet and breathe the freezing vacuum. Go to the Light.

But, Abiel thought, *why am I still alive? There has to be a reason to be spared the fate of the other Holy warriors, some purpose for my survival.* Clearly, Abiel was meant to live, so that the will of the Light could be realised.

Easy to state, hard to achieve. The only chance was that oxygen and power to maintain the combat suit might be found within the shattered control complex.

A test then. Abiel would prove worthy or die trying.

The landscape had stopped convulsing. Having made the transit through the *RIP,* they were clearly no longer in interstellar space as evidenced by the pale light washing over the landscape. Two irregular moons hung in the sky. Abiel assumed they were massive shards calved away from the main body of the asteroid in the attack. They floated serenely, along with a host of smaller fragments, lit by the sun whose domain they must now occupy. Ashen light reflected from these new satellites illuminated the way.

With a last look at her two fallen comrades, Abiel began the slow crawl to the ruined control complex. There was no pain from the shattered limb, but pretty much every other part of the warrior's body made up for that. It should have been more difficult with only one leg, but the low gravity was, at last, proving to be an asset.

Abiel reached the threshold of the dark interior of the insurgents Command-and Control room. Makeshift barricades of upended tables, cabinets, and whatever other pieces of heavy equipment the heretics had been able to move, blocked the way. The barricades were probably a little more than twice the height of a man, but from the warrior's prone position they looked like insurmountable mountains. First with one hand and then the other, Abiel hauled up the slope, ignoring the lancing pain from the abdominal wound, until, finally, the crusader reached the summit of the barrier. The injured leg dragged uselessly behind.

Exhausted, Abiel took a moment to recover and consider how to get down the other side. Abiel twisted around until both legs hung over the drop, trying to find a ledge or a gap for the uninjured foot. Although the far side of the slope was dark, the zip array rendered the view clearly. The warrior found a toehold, began the descent, until the dead leg got caught in the tangle. Cursing, the crusader tried to twist the useless limb out of the way, but in doing so lost the secure foothold. For a long second Abiel flailed, then lost the fight.

The fall was slow. In a one gee field it might have been the end of the story, and even here it was touch and go. Abiel bounced twice on the way down before lying dazed at the bottom of the slope, cursing that such a pitifully small fall could be so severe.

Oxygen now down to 5 percent, vision tunnelling, there wasn't much time left. Grimacing, eyes filling with tears of pain and frustration, the holy warrior renewed the crawl, on into the darkness of the base.

With no memory of the journey there, Abiel suddenly became aware of a room full of lockers and smashed containers. Hardly any power left now, the view supplied by the suit's neural-core stuttered with static and noise. It would fail at any moment. In a place without light, that would leave the crusader blind. Abiel risked a sensory ping. There, just ahead. If proof were needed that this was the Light's will, there it was.

The emergency power and air dispensers were almost beyond Abiel's ability to reach, but a Divine power must have willed it, for it came to pass. The umbilicals had standard fittings and the ones from the combat suit fit snugly into place. Blessed fresh air cleared the asphyxiating mind fog.

Once plugged in, the power levels rose; limited, but enough to maintain life support – for a short time, anyway.

All that a pious devotee could do had been done. Abiel set the suit's life support to the lowest level needed to sustain life, then, exhausted, succumbed to unconsciousness. The warrior's fate now lay in the hands of a higher power.

"Looks like he crawled in here and plugged into one of the emergency dispensers," the Deacon observed. "Hole in his gut. Right leg… well, suit's shredded and so is the leg. He'll never walk on that again."

"Suit-med tourniquet," Kaemon observed. "Sealed off the leg at the knee."

"Tough guy," Matt said. "What do we do?"

"What do you mean?" Kaemon said. "Move on. Better still, unplug the bastard, then move on."

"You suggest we just leave him? Let him die?" Matt said.

"Why not? Tell him, Deacon."

The Deacon surveyed the curled body, dimly illuminated by the console readouts. "We have enough problems. And this soldier, this Holy Warrior, will almost certainly not thank you for your efforts."

"Too right," Kaemon agreed.

"What he might do isn't the point," Matt said. "It's what we do that counts. We have to do the right thing here, or we are no better than them. What do you think, Breel? Are you getting this?"

"You weren't squeamish when you were blowing them off the rock," Kaemon interrupted. "We nearly died, Matt. Ellyella nearly died," he added, anguish clear in his voice.

"That was self-defence," Matt retorted. "I have enough blood on my hands."

"I don't know. Is it right to just let him die?" Breel joined in. "I'm with Matt. Killing someone who's trying to kill us is one thing, but to walk away and let a man suffocate. I can't think that's what we're about."

"I'm pretty sure he would walk straight over you," Kaemon said bitterly.

"You don't know that, Kaemon." Breel retorted. "Under the armour, they're people, just like you and me."

"Not like me," Kaemon insisted. "I can't understand why we are wasting time even discussing this."

"What's the situation with the EMD cells, Matt?" Breel asked abruptly.

"I've found an unused backup set. I'm about to get the MARRVs to drag them outside."

"You can't let him die," Ellyella's voice suddenly cut into the debate. "It's not right."

"El?" Kaemon said, "Why aren't you resting?"

"I am, but I can't listen to this and not make my feelings clear. We don't want to be those people, Kae, to deliberately allow a life to be snuffed out, for no reason other than convenience."

Deacon heard Kaemon take a breath, taking a moment to calm himself. "Okay," he continued, his voice level. "I may not be the most impartial person here, but personal feelings aside, look at it logically. Can we afford to take another body on board, given our situation? This guy is a trained killer, a fanatic. Can we really afford to spend time and resources looking after him, using precious medical supplies and having to watch our backs while we're doing it? You nearly died at their hands, El. Doesn't that bother you?"

"Many of them died at our hands, Kaemon," Ellyella said. "But circumstances have changed."

"We don't have time for this," Matt said. "Deacon, uncouple the ziphead and get him back to *Scavenger*. Once the EMD cells are on their way, I'll take over Deacon's task. Kaemon, get that software download and get back to the ship as soon as you can. Let's get on with it shall we?"

"This is a mistake," Kaemon said. "Remember I said that, when it all goes to shit."

"There are five of us and one disabled ziphead. We should be able to handle him," Breel said. "And, to your point, we could use the help. Once this guy realises the situation, he might be useful."

"I feel compelled to point out," the Deacon warned, "that, 'fanatic,' is in the Holy Warrior job description. He'll slit our throats in our sleep if he gets the chance."

"Let's wait and see what we're dealing with, okay?" Matt said. "I'll space him myself if we have problems."

"Save yourself the job," Kaemon said. "Leave him here."

"No, Kae," Ellyella said. "You know that's wrong."

Kaemon's voice hardened. "You of all of us, El? You want someone like that on board?"

"He's a human being, Kae. Who knows what his life was like before he became a crusader?"

Kaemon said, "You guys do what you need to, if it makes you feel righteous. Just don't expect me to have anything to do with him."

"Duly noted," Breel said. "Now can we get on?"

"How do I get him back to the ship?" the Deacon asked. "If I disconnect him, won't he be dead before I get him to the med-bay?"

"The power and oxygen should last long enough to get him to *Scavenger*," Matt said. "But you'll need to be quick. Disconnect him from the dispenser, then get the MARRV to haul him outside and bring him back."

"What then?" Breel asked. "How am I going to get him out of that armour?"

There was silence.

"You'll have to cut him out," Matt said.

"Sounds dangerous," the Deacon said. "You could add to his injuries."

"Leaving him will certainly add to his injuries," Breel said.

Kaemon sighed. "Against my better judgement, there might be a way. If their suits follow military standard rescue and retrieval protocols, there will be an emergency rescue toggle. It will be inside, probably by his neck. It has its own separate power supply, purely for this purpose. His squad would have a code to get in, if he were disabled. We don't have that, so you will still have to cut the helmet away."

"Okay then," Breel said, "Thank you for that Kaemon. Deacon, I'll meet you in the Med-Bay."

The Deacon looked haggard as he and the MARRV manoeuvred the weightless trooper through the med-bay door. The priest hadn't had time to remove his suit but had taken his helmet off. He had lost weight, Breel thought, and looked about ten years older than when they had first met, only months ago. They probably all did. She drifted over to help, and between them, loosely strapped the sinister black combat armour to a gurney.

"His oxygen is almost depleted," the Deacon said. "Let's hope Kaemon is right about the rescue toggle, or we might as well have just left him."

Breel picked up a large rectangular blade from a worktop next to the bed. There was a slight sticky resistance from the magnet keeping it fixed to the table. She felt under the chin of the helmet, prising it up to reveal a soft pliable membrane, normally protected by the hard outer shell. Breel pressed her fingers into this soft material.

"If I can get through this, we should be able to get the helmet off." She hefted the cutter. "This thing will cut through almost anything."

She squeezed the handle and a bright green line of coherent laser light ran the length of the blade.

"Hopefully not through his neck," the Deacon said.

"Yeah, well, that would defeat the object," Breel said, "although Kaemon would be happy ..."

She applied the burning edge of the blade. The soft material split. There was a hot smell of burning plastic and another, more organic smell.

"Deshi-damn," Breel stopped.

"What's wrong?" Deacon asked.

"Molten plastic burning his neck." She looked up, reached across to the bench and plucked an insulated glove from it. She let the knife float while she pulled the glove onto her left hand, then pushed a square of fire-retardant material through the gap, between the suit and the man's neck.

"This will have to do." Breel set to work again.

The soft membrane sizzled as the blade bit. The pulsing light set quivering shadows dancing about the room and smoke from burning plastic and carbon fibre clogged their nostrils.

Breel deactivated the laser cutting edge. It took a second for her eyes to adjust. They were going to have to turn the man to get to the sides and back of his neck. The straps holding the soldier were loose enough.

"Give me a hand here," she said to the Deacon. Together they turned the ziphead onto his side, a task made much easier in microgravity. She moved the insulating material, applied the cutter again, then completed the roll until the soldier lay on his belly, giving access to the back of his neck. A last turn exposed the final quarter, allowing Breel to complete the entire three hundred and sixty degree cut. She turned off the cutter, looking to place it back on its magnetic stand, but found it quicker to push it into the Deacon's hands. "Here, hold this," she said.

Turning the ziphead face up once more she gripped the headgear with both hands. It came away from the body with a soft sigh, finally revealing the trooper's face. A shaven head with fine features. At some point the soldier had suffered a nosebleed. His features were crusted with blood and grime. His neck was red from the heat of the knife, but apart from the sore-looking burn from the first incision, it didn't look too bad.

"Holy Light," the Deacon exclaimed, covering his mouth and nose as the stink of unwashed flesh hit them.

Breel let the helmet go. It turned lazily as it floated away to bounce off the nearest wall. She felt carefully inside the neck ring, not wanting to touch the crusader's skin, until she found what she was looking for. A whirr preceded a series of clicks as the suit components separated for removal.

"Thank you, Kaemon," Breel muttered. She quickly and methodically removed the rest of the armour. In her haste she let the parts join the helmet to float around the room. She removed all of the armour except that of the right leg and the punctured shin plates, below the right knee. The suit tourniquet would have to remain locked. Removing it without taking the necessary precautions would result in instant sepsis, system shock, and a quick death. They would have to get the soldier into the med-doc before removing these last pieces, where, judging by what she could see of the soldier's leg through the holes, there would be nothing for it but amputation. Still, the smell of putrefying flesh intensified as the last pieces of the suit were removed; but that wasn't what shocked them most. The skin-tight, hi-tech undergarment of fine pipes and umbilicals left little to the imagination. Breel's eyes traced the contours of the body, the flare of hips and narrow waist, the swell of breast. The Deacon looked away in embarrassment.

"Deshi," Breel said, wide-eyed. "He's a woman."

THREE

"What do you mean, he's a woman?" Kaemon said.

"The answer is in the question," Breel replied. She was back on *Scavenger's* bridge, viewing the others on screen. The three men floated in the re-pressurised engine bay. Matt was fitting the EMD cells while Kaemon was inputting data into a floating holo matrix. The Deacon drifted above them, near the ceiling, like a predatory bat, while Ellyella was visible in her bunk on a separate display. Breel waited for the two men to finish.

"Yeah," Kaemon continued, "but I thought only men got jobs on Saved Worlds? Like, women aren't much better than slaves or breeding machines?"

"Your understanding is limited," the Deacon said huffily. "Many women see Church Doctrine as respectful of their gender, so much so that some are willing to die for it, as is plainly the case here."

"Amazing how some people can be persuaded to act against their own best interests," Kaemon said.

"How does mixing genders work on board ship?" Ellyella asked from her cabin.

"Strict segregation, of course," the Deacon said. "I recall there were one or two elite squads of female fighters. Never met them myself."

Matt made a last adjustment, then looked up.

"Try it now, Breel," he said.

"Better come down from the ceiling, Deak," Kaemon said.

"Everybody hang onto something and make sure there is nothing heavy overhead." Breel tapped a sequence into the controls to fire up the drive.

Nothing happened.

"Underwhelming," the newly grounded Deacon said.

"Sorry we aren't meeting your expectations, Deacon," Breel replied.

"Wait, let me try something." Matt busied himself with the installation once more.

"Doesn't change things much," Kaemon returned to the earlier subject. "We've still brought a dangerous fanatic on board."

"Indeed," the Deacon agreed. "More so in fact. Even more than in your society, women have to be so much… more, than men to succeed in the Church."

"Try it again, Breel," Matt said. *Scavenger* gave a groan, as if it were in pain, followed by a long, drawn-out shudder. Reverberating bangs and crashes rang throughout the ship as floating objects fell to the deck.

Breel felt herself pressed into her seat. She undid the straps and stood. Her spine cracked as it supported her weight again. "Ow, that feels great." She pushed her hands into the small of her back, enjoying the stretch, then twisted her neck side to side. "Even better, the showers will be working again. The ship smells like a blister-hog nest." She looked at the crew through her display.

"Well done, guys, we saved the day, again."

"How is our guest doing?" Matt asked.

"The med-doc has her under sedation," Ellyella said. "There is a lot of damage to repair. She's covered in NMPs. The right leg has been amputated just below the knee. Couldn't be saved. Unfortunately, the med-doc doesn't have the facility to grow a new one. In fact, we need to stop injuring ourselves so much. We are running low on medical supplies, especially the nano-med packages. We've been going through them like there's no tomorrow."

"Pity we wasted so many on her then," Kaemon said.

"Okay, Kaemon," Matt said. "You've made your position clear."

"Actually, no tomorrow is our most likely future," the Deacon said brightly.

"Better get ready to brace." Breel indicated Matt's ad-hoc installation. "The drive's at minimum right now, but who knows how it might hold up when we apply the brakes."

They hadn't fixed the symbiotic interface yet, that would allow her consciousness to meld to become one with the ship. It was next on the to-do list, so she still had to command the ship manually. Running her hands over the controls she turned the spacecraft using the reaction thrusters, then inputted the optimal orbit supplied by the ship's neural-core.

"Supercharging the EMD now," she announced.

The engines powered up smoothly, decelerating *Scavenger* into a long orbital fall towards the shepherd moon that was their destination. It would take several weeks. *RIPs* formed at the edges of solar systems, where the curvature of space was optimal, not too curved, not too flat. Journeys to and from them could take weeks or months, depending on the mass of the star, even with the EMD drive – and without one, possibly years.

She watched *Revenge* recede, left behind to continue its infinite journey into the cosmos and felt a sense of loss. Another companion gone. Were there any other survivors on its inhospitable surface? If so, they were doomed.

She stood. A hot shower was what she craved most at this point, followed by some food. She paused, looked around at the destruction that had been wrought on the bridge. Sighing, she began to clear up the mess.

The message sent through the tumour in the flesh of reality had been answered. Something had come, alien and broken… moving away, tumbling, out of control.

A shift in cognisance, a change in thought process. Loss? Disquiet? Disappointment?

Activity around the alien. A change in momentum.

Most of the mass was lost, spinning uncontrolled into the universe, but a chip, a spark of warmth and light was slowing, changing trajectory. A long fall towards the sun.

New cognitive response. Hope? Anticipation? Fear?

After a length of time impossible to grasp, even for something that measured its existence in millions of years, time was suddenly short and there was so much to do.

It was a door, just like all the other doors on *Scavenger*. Her fist froze an inch above its surface, as if it and the door shared the same magnetic pole and were unable to make contact. The metal surface slid to one side anyway.

"Breel, come in," the Deacon said to her.

Breel lowered her fist and hesitantly crossed the threshold into the priest's room.

"I thought you might get a cramp if I left you out there much longer." His face cracked with the uncharacteristic attempt at humour.

The room, also the Deacon's lab in the space-challenged confines of *Scavenger*, was neat and organised. His bunk was made up, but covered with various instruments and devices, both digital and analogue. Actual printed books and paper notepads, pages filled with Deacon's neat orderly handwriting. There were various screens, most showing the spiral of dust they were bound for, overlaid with scrolling data. There were two chairs, one surrounded by electronics. Behind that, on a fold-out worktop, wired into and surrounded by numerous monitors, sat the *Thing*. The artefact salvaged from the alien wreck by her mother and stepfather nearly three decades ago.

Clam-shaped, about the size of a small child, its dark surface was etched with intricate designs. Her heart hammered at the sight of it, the first time she had seen it since their escape from Hope. It bruised her reality in a way that defied description, making her nauseous.

"Sit here please." The Deacon indicated the chair surrounded with electronics. "Thank you for agreeing to this, Breel. I can understand why it's been hard for you to come here, but forewarned is forearmed they say. If there is a connection between you and the shepherd moon, it's best we know about it. We might even shed some light on what happened to your parents on the Derelict." Something in her expression prompted him to continue, "Try to relax, Breel, you have nothing to fear."

"You can guarantee that, can you?" Breel watched the monitors come to life. "Okay," she said as the Deacon continued fussing with his equipment, "let's get it over with shall we?"

The displays were registering… something. Her body art felt warm. A glance at her bare arm showed small nodes of light trace the intricate patterns for the first time since transition through the *RIP*.

The Deacon's face lit up in anticipation.

"We have a response already," he beamed. He began to tap a pad in his hand, sending instructions to his equipment. Breel drew several deep breaths, trying to follow the Deacon's advice, but what she really wanted to do was get up and walk back out. She also knew the Deacon was right, that she had put this moment off for far too long. If there were answers to be had about her origins, they were better off knowing them and this was where she was most likely to find them.

The Deacon put down his pad so he could attach sensors to Breel's arms and forehead. She flinched, pressing back into the seat.

"They are merely measuring devices," he assured her. "Skin conductivity, electrical and chemical activity, that sort of thing. Nothing more intrusive than that."

Breel reluctantly allowed the man's touch.

"How's the symbiont interface repair going?" Deacon asked, in a poor attempt at distraction.

Breel indulged him. "We think it's ready. Matt and Kaemon are making some last adjustments. I'm going up to the bridge after we are done here, to give it a try."

Text began to scroll down the displays attached to the *Thing*. "Good, good," the man mumbled, not really paying attention, focused on what he was doing.

He stepped back from her, satisfied. He tapped a surface near the artefact and a holographic display blossomed into life above it. The Deacon sank his hands into the light show.

"Okay," he said, barely containing his excitement. "Let's see what we can see."

"Pass that bracket, will you?" Matt was holding a sheaf of hair-thin cables in place above his head with one hand, feeding it into a hole they had cut with a laser. The edges of the cavity were black where the fierce coherent light had burned through the ceiling.

Kaemon looked up from his diagnostic display, then stretched out a hand to the shiny curved piece of ceramic that was just out of Matt's reach. He stood and stretched across to hand it over. "We're flying a starship and we still fix cables with brackets," he said.

Matt grinned. "And we're still using cables. Some things just do the job."

"How do you rate our chances, if we get it all up and running?"

Matt held the bracket up but was finding it difficult to fit without letting go of the wires in his other hand. Kaemon stepped over to help, holding the wires in place.

"Who knows?" Matt grimaced in concentration. The bracket slotted into place with a satisfying click. "Once Breel can access the higher functions of the ship she'll be able to take a look. Maybe there's another *RIP* we can use to get back."

"A big maybe." Kaemon returned to his station. "If there is a *RIP* out there, it could be so far away we'll die of old age before we get there."

Matt shrugged. He dropped his hand from the hole. "We are where we are, we just give it our best shot." He moved back from his handiwork and surveyed it with a critical eye.

"Try it now."

Kaemon tapped a glowing icon on his interface. The ship shuddered, rocked violently, making both men grab for support.

Then the lights went out.

"What did you do?" Kaemon shouted into the pitch dark.

"Nothing to do with me." The room sprang back into being, rendered in shades of scarlet by emergency lighting. Matt and Kaemon shared a look, then Matt reached for the com.

"Hey, Breel, the lights went out. Do you know what the Jinxing-hell is going on?"

The Deacon's hands moved through the floating icons, rearranging them in complex ways that meant nothing to Breel. Data scrolled and graphs moved to his direction. Breel's arm and neck felt warm. The bright nodes on her body began to speed up. She felt a dizzying dislocation.

The walls of the ship, Deacon's body, became insubstantial, ghosted over the universe outside. It was almost as if she were symbiotic, connected to something, just not to the ship. She became aware of a presence, a Network or a lattice, suffused through space and time, dwindling to infinity in every direction: soft focus, slippery, swirling around her, making it hard for her mind to gain traction. Unintelligible voices began to murmur, rising in volume. A pinprick of definition blossomed. It flashed along the Network-lattice, heading towards her, slammed into the periphery of her mind, probing, exploring – hard and intrusive. Breel fought back, pushing with as much force as she could to keep whatever it was out of her head.

Then, with a twist, it slid past her. Panicked, she tried to shout a warning to the Deacon but found she couldn't. She was paralysed, frozen into immobility and silence.

Snake-like, whatever it was, coiled around her mind, using her symbiotic connection to the ship as a doorway. It continued on, penetrating ever deeper into

30

Scavenger's *systems, into the ship's control and data network neural-core. She pushed at the part she had access to, trying to stop it, pull it back or sever it if she could, in a way that later she would struggle to describe. The thing reacted, fought her, constricting her consciousness, but she countered, forcing it away, attenuating its substance. That she could do this would be something to wonder at later, but for now, she was acting purely on instinct. She had no idea how long the silent struggle lasted. Having either achieved its aim, or because Breel's response had forced it out, it withdrew along the path it had used to gain access, falling back through the Network, dwindling first to a spark and then nothing. Breel took her chance and broke the connection, slamming shut the portal that had been opened, denying any further access to the ship.*

A spasm racked her body and she crashed back into the Deacon's lab, solid and substantial once more. She jerked out of the seat, electrodes ripping free and fell to her knees, retching. The room was painted shades of blood and it took her a second to figure out the emergency lighting must be on. The Deacon stood open-mouthed, clearly shocked. He dithered for a second, then left his instruments and hurried over to Breel.

"Don't – touch – me," she said, the words punctuated by short gasps. Breel's entire body trembled. She shook her head, drawing in lungfuls of air tasting of vomit.

"Are you okay?" The Deacon fussed around her, wanting to help, but keeping his distance.

Breel pulled off the remaining sensors, letting them drop to the floor.

"What happened, what did you see?" The Deacon asked.

"Something. I sensed some kind of... a structure, a vast network, out there." She waved a hand to indicate the universe at large. "It was huge, infinite..." Her voice trailed off. She felt dazed, numbed by the experience. She looked at him sharply. "Then, something used it to invade the ship. It used my symbiotic augmentation as a doorway into the ship's neural-core, but I pushed it out. I think. Or it withdrew. What did you see?"

"You connected to something at a quantum level. *You did.*" The Deacon looked awestruck. "And then the ship bucked and the lights went out. The whole thing was over in seconds."

"It felt much longer than that."

Matt's voice came through the ships PA. "Hey, Breel, the lights went out. Do you know what the Jinxing-hell is going on?"

At that moment the main lights sprang back into life.

Breel touched the com-station to respond. "Something got into the ship's systems," she told him. "I'm going to the bridge to check it out."

"This something to do with the Deacon's tests?"

Breel looked at the Deacon, waiting for him to respond.

"Ah yes, Matt," Deacon confessed. "They might have had something to do with it."

Breel stood shakily and headed for the door.

The Deacon was left surveying the disarray around him.

The Second Light warrior lay in repose in the guts of the Med-doc. Ellyella sat an arm's-reach away. Metabolic readouts indicated the soldier would regain consciousness any time now and someone needed to be here when she did. As acting ship's doctor, a role she played by virtue of being the least unqualified, it should be her. The others were occupied anyway. Breel had finally agreed to allow the Deacon to run his tests. Matt and Kaemon were trying to get the pilot symbiont interface online.

She had wanted to be with Breel, to give her support, but she couldn't be in two places at once and it was clear that Breel hadn't wanted an audience.

She scanned the woman on the bed. Dark skin with a faint burst of freckles across high cheekbones. Black hair shaven to a mere dusting. The tattooed lines of the Church sigil radiated from around her right eye.

Ellyella was nervous at how this fanatic might react when she woke. That she was a fanatic was not in doubt, hence Ellyella's sitting at a cautious distance, despite restraints fixing both the soldier's wrists and one good ankle to the metal frame of the gurney. At this point, they didn't know what they were dealing with. Ellyella was sure Kaemon had been wrong to suggest they leave the woman to die in the icy tomb of *Revenge,* but Ellyella would bear some responsibility if things went wrong.

Ellyella was fascinated now that the crusader's gender had been revealed. What was her history? How did she come to be a female warrior in the fiercely patriarchal Church?

She shifted in her seat. Her whole body ached. The legacy of her own near-death ordeal made it uncomfortable to sit for long periods. The thought brought a lump to her throat, not because she had nearly died, but because she was reminded of Matt's reaction when he had found out she had secretly been a follower of Second Light for as long as he had known her. Someone had planted a tracker on the ship, feeding information back to the Emissary after each *RIP* transit. It might have been anyone of them or none of them. Matt had insisted on a search of their cabins and her secret had been revealed. No amount of protestation from her would convince him that she could hold the faith and remain loyal to him. His rejection had felt brutal, like a gut punch.

The ship suddenly heaved as a tremor passed through its structure and the room was pitched into blackness. Ellyella stood. Her flailing hand caught the edge of the table. She gripped it fiercely, seeking support in the dark. For a moment she was back, trapped in that other room, looking out through the hull breach at cold infinity, before taking what she thought was going to be her last breath.

"Matt, Breel," she shouted into the com, "what's happening?"

"Hang on, Ellyella." Matt's voice was reassuring. "We're checking it out."

The emergency lights came on, allowing her to see again, albeit in ruby shades. A few moments later the main lights flooded the room. She let go of the table she had been gripping so tightly her knuckles were white.

The sound of metal scraping against metal made her jump. She looked towards the bed and saw her prisoner was awake and regarding her impassively with dark eyes.

"Everything checks out, Matt," Breel reported from the bridge. "I can see evidence of an intrusion, protocols altered, access requested, that kind of thing, but nothing has been permanently changed or damaged as far as I can see."

"What was it Breel? Any idea?"

"None. Something connected to me, I assume from the shepherd moon. It was an intelligence of some kind, but so alien, I couldn't get a handle on it. It was Deshi-damn scary if you want the truth," she added.

"It connected with Breel," the Deacon chimed in from his room, "not the artefact."

"That helps us, how?" Matt asked.

"Don't you see, the artefact is nothing, merely an amplifier. No wonder I couldn't glean anything from it. Breel is the source of the quantum fluctuations I've been detecting. She's what the signals that first originated from the *RIP* were seeking."

There was a moment's ship-wide silence.

"Okay," Matt said. "Here's what happens next. No more experiments, is that clear Deacon?"

"But we are so close to discovering something significant…"

"Listen, I don't give a Jinx-damn. We are hanging by a thread, here. We can't afford for anything else to fail or go wrong." When he didn't get a response, Matt asked, "Did you get that? Deacon?"

"Yes, Captain," the Deacon said. "I got it."

"Hey," Breel said. "I am party to this conversation."

"Yeah, sorry Breel. I'm thinking of the safety of the ship."

"You won't get any argument from me, anyway," Breel said. But she wasn't sure she was being entirely honest with herself. There had been something both terrifying and compelling about the experience. Like the first time she had flown in symbiosis. The alien, or whatever it was, hadn't seemed interested in her. She had been both a doorway and an obstacle to get into the ship, but she hadn't really felt threatened by it. She'd been more indignant at the intrusion into her home.

Ellyella joined the conference. "Our guest is awake."

The pain had gone. Abiel's eyes fluttered open. She was floating in baleful crimson light. *Have I died and for my sins been banished to the domain of the dark?* Her heart hammered. She clawed her fingers in despair and they entangled in material.

Sheets.

Stupid, she thought, *I'd hardly have a pounding heart if I was in the domain of the dark, would I?* Fully conscious now she explored the surface she lay on with her hands. So, she was alive and in a bed, not floating in some reception hall of hell, and someone had been tending to her. She knew what the out of body, feel-good buzz of pain killing drugs felt like.

Bright lighting suddenly flooded the room, replacing the menacing scarlet, making her squint. The ceiling above was white and antiseptic. She tried to raise her hand to shield her sight from the painful glare but found both her arms secured at the wrist to the bed frame. Abiel turned her head and saw a dark-skinned, dark-haired female standing close by. The woman wasn't looking at her, she was looking up to the ceiling, her face a mask of fear. The sound of Abiel's restraints rattling on the gurney frame must have startled her nurse or captor. She turned her eyes towards Abiel and they widened. The look of fear faded and the woman's expression morphed into a welcoming smile.

"Hello," she said brightly in Standard. She looked at Abiel's cuffs. "Sorry about those, we don't know you yet. I'm sure you understand our caution." She leaned forward, "What's your name?" she asked eagerly. "I'm Ellyella."

Abiel tried to speak but found her mouth as dry as sand. Seeing her difficulty the woman picked up a bottle of water and put it to Abiel's lips. "Drink this."

Abiel drank greedily before the bottle was removed. "That's enough for the moment." The woman smiled. The water had a taste to it. Electrolytes or similar. Ellyella dabbed at Abiel's lips where some of the water had spilled.

Abiel croaked, the correct military response to capture. "Gabriela. Lieutenant. 16757-42." As she looked at the woman and considered her situation, she thought a more nuanced response might be appropriate, until she understood what was happening here. Finding her voice, she said more loudly in what she knew would be heavily accented Standard. "But you can call me Abiel."

"Pleased to meet you," Ellyella said. She leaned across to the wall, pressing a finger onto a communication device.

"Our guest is awake," she reported.

"Where am I?" Abiel asked.

"If you can be patient for a few minutes," Ellyella said, "I promise all your questions will be answered."

Abiel lay back and closed her eyes. Then she remembered her crawl across the surface of the asteroid, into the C&C, desperately looking for somewhere to power up her suit.

Her leg!

She pushed up onto her elbows to look down at the sheet over her body, at the frame over her knee and the flat material beyond it. Although she expected it, the sight was like a physical blow. She blinked rapidly, then looked at Ellyella.

"Sorry, we couldn't save it," Ellyella said, sympathetically.

That show of sympathy angered Abiel. She stared at the other woman for several seconds, battling her features into neutrality. She wouldn't show weakness. She said simply, "The Light's will."

The door slid open and a dark-haired man stepped into the room, followed by a tall blonde woman. They stood behind Ellyella, who beamed as she turned to greet them.

"Matt, Breel, meet, Abiel," she said, gesturing towards the crusader. Ellyella moved to the other side of the gurney so that Abiel could talk more easily to the new arrivals.

The man said, "Hello, Abiel. Welcome aboard *Scavenger*. I'm Matt, the captain. This is Breel." He gestured towards the blonde who wore a sleeveless top exposing one arm adorned with an elaborate gold tattoo. The body art extended onto one side of her face.

"This is the insurgent ship?" Abiel asked.

"It is," the captain acknowledged. He leaned closer, expression serious. "What we need to know is, are we going to have trouble from you? Our resources are low and we have enough problems without adding more."

"Why?" Abiel said.

"Why, what?" the woman called Breel asked.

"Why am I here at all?"

"We found you on *Revenge*," Matt said.

"That's the asteroid," Ellyella explained.

"It was close," The blonde added. "If we'd come across you an hour later than we did…"

"But why did you rescue me at all?" Abiel persisted.

The three looked at each other.

"Why wouldn't we?" Ellyella said. "It was the right thing to do, wasn't it?"

Abiel regarded her captors… or saviours, and tried to weigh up what she had just been told. If true, it didn't appear that she was in any immediate danger. It didn't look like she was about to be tortured or abused and it was doubtful they would throw her out the airlock after going to so much trouble to save her, unless she showed herself to be a serious threat. She didn't know yet what saving her had entailed, but it wouldn't have been an easy choice. They believed it was altruism, but she knew far greater forces were at work here, and they moved mysteriously. She needed time, time for the Light's intent to be revealed.

She shook her head, looking down at her body then back at the three. "No trouble from me." She indicated the leg that ended in a metal and plastic cocoon at the knee. "Probably not much help either." She smiled her best smile.

"I'm sorry, but we don't have the facilities to grow you a new leg," Ellyella explained, "but we can fix you up with a prosthetic that will give you pretty much normal mobility."

"Thank you." Abiel had been craning to look at them all, but now, exhausted by the effort, let her head fall back onto the pillow.

"Hell of a thing you did," Matt said, "crawling into the command centre with all those injuries."

"I did what I had to do," Abiel replied, voice fading. "The Light gave me strength."

The three shared a look.

"Well, we'll let you get some rest," the blonde said.

Ellyella pointed a finger at the wrist and ankle restraints. After a moment's hesitation, the tall woman reached forward and disabled them. The man looked concerned but said nothing.

"Get some food and fluids down you," Breel said, "We'll talk later when you feel up to it and explain where we're going."

"We're going somewhere?" Abiel twisted her head again.

The captain nodded, "Yeah, and you'll need all your strength," he finished.

A flicker in the dark.

A bridge forms.

An opening, a way in. A penetration that lasts seconds – years, centuries. Data – environment, heat, pressure, language.

Something else.

A presence, familiar…

And then retreat.

The long wait was coming to an end.

FOUR

Breel was running diagnostics on the symbiont interface. Matt and Kaemon were in different parts of the ship, visible on displays around her, working to fix the same problem. Thankfully everything seemed to be working as expected. Although she had reported to the others that the alien breach had left the ship undamaged, she couldn't be absolutely certain something she didn't recognise might not come back and bite them.

"So, you're happy to have this... woman freely roam the ship?" Kaemon wanted to know.

"I don't propose to have her wandering the ship unsupervised, no." Matt was tapping code into his handheld device. He watched the response from a luminous panel set into the wall, in the ancillary room beneath Breel's feet. Satisfied, he moved on to the next panel in a line of them, to repeat the process. "But, unless she is suicidal, I don't see what she can do. She seems pretty quiet and subdued."

"I hate to repeat myself," Kaemon retorted, "but did you forget the part about her being a fanatic, someone who hates the very thought of what we represent – and – I don't think it's too much of a stretch to imagine *martyrdom* might be high on her list of desirable states."

"We don't know anything about her." Breel put down her own input device and began to arrange the seat and controls into flight configuration. "The crusader I met in the tunnels on Blue Haven was just a boy, driven by events beyond his control."

"Did you come to that conclusion before, or after he tried to kill you?" Kaemon asked.

Breel sighed. "In other circumstances I think I would have liked him. You should meet Abiel, Kaemon. If she harbours any ill will towards us at the moment, I'm sure your sunny disposition will bring her round."

"Funny, Breel." There was a flash followed by a curse as the small unit Kaemon was fixing stabbed an arc of energy into his hand. He dropped it, swearing and sucking his finger. he glared at Breel through his own display. "You won't find it so funny if you wake up breathing through a slit in your throat."

"Lighten up, Kae," Matt said. "We'll stay wary of her but give her a chance. El is fixing her up with the prosthetic you dug out," he dropped his input device onto a work surface, "so you'll meet her soon."

"Can't wait." Kaemon pushed the device firmly into place.

"Are we all ready?" Breel asked.

The two men looked at each other. "As we'll ever be." Matt said.

Breel focused her mind.

The bridge flickered, then was gone, replaced by the full grandeur of the universe surrounding the ship. She was still aware of her own flesh-and-blood body, but now it extended into Scavenger *and through the ship's sensors, beyond. But the ship felt very different since her last symbiosis. Before she had felt as if she was inhabiting the body of an athlete, but the ship felt much diminished now, like a body ravaged and aged beyond her years. Accessing the ship's data diagnostics was almost physically painful and it read a sorry tale. EMD efficiency down by seventy percent, probably a full third of ship systems below optimal. There were a few things she could improve through the interface, but the core structure was so compromised it could only be fixed in a proper facility. The truth was* Scavenger's *days were numbered. Under normal circumstances, with the EMD drive enabled, they could have expected power to last indefinitely, but even as she watched, its integrity declined. At this rate the ship would be uninhabitable in months, rather than years.*

She turned her attention outwards, to their destination. Looking like a swirl of cream on black coffee, a spiral formation composed of dust, gas and ice, orbited about one astronomical unit from its host star. It was immense; you could lose planets in there. At its centre, an incredibly dense object, about the size of an earth-sized world that, apart from its intense gravitational field, was completely inert. She couldn't detect any kind of radiation from it. The spiral structure was clearly unnatural. It should have broken apart or condensed into larger objects aeons ago otherwise. A structure designed for a purpose then, although what that purpose was, or what kind of science maintained its integrity, she could only guess at.

There were also some larger objects embedded in amongst the dust of the formation. They appeared to be shepherd moons that maintained clear lanes through gravitational resonance, deliberately placed to preserve and stabilise the formation.

The system consisted of the host sun and this one structure, no other planets or anything else much larger than a grain of sand. The Deacon had calculated that the structure contained about the mass of an average-sized planetary system. The implication that a civilisation might have the capability of dismantling such a system, then reforming it into a new structure to their liking had given them all pause for thought, even Kaemon, not often given to flights of fancy. Furthermore, the Deacon had said, if the gravitational field of the parent body was added to the equation, it turned out a lot more mass than an average solar system was required. The Deacon couldn't account for all that extra mass.

Of course, no species would go to so much trouble to build such a structure if it didn't have a purpose. It was almost certainly the fabled Doomsday machine the Church of Second Light had been seeking, which she and the crew of Scavenger had denied them access to by permanently closing the only RIP that led here. But at this point they just didn't know. It could as easily be a monumental, cosmic work of art.

She tuned in to the twittering signal that emanated from one of those moons. The siren song which had guided them here. After Deacon's recent experiment it appeared that the signal had been aimed at her, when she had been living on Hope, working on the Beach to fund her stepdad's medical needs. She couldn't begin to understand what any of it meant, but she might soon learn, not that the thought gave her any comfort.

They were much closer to the spiral now but still going too fast. She would have to decelerate further if she wanted to match orbit with the moon that was broadcasting the signal. The approach would be from above the plane of the ecliptic. By the time they were close, if she got it right, they would share the orbital velocity of most of the fragments, making the approach relatively safe, but she noted erratic tumbling chunks of debris that would end their journey spectacularly, should their paths cross.

The moon was altogether different to the dense object the whole structure orbited. It was alive with information. Although cold, it was much warmer than it should have been. There was a lot of seismic activity that might account for some of the heat, but something else was clearly at work.

It had an unbreathable carbon monoxide atmosphere. The atmospheric pressure was low by their standards, about what you would expect at the summit of a high mountain on a one-G world, but thicker than one might expect for a moon that size. As the satellite rotated, a bright dot hove into view, much hotter than the rest of the moon. Her gut twisted into a knot of fear. This was, she knew, without knowing how, the origin of the presence she had felt in Deacon's lab.

Matt intruded into her thoughts. "Did we fix it?"

"Yeah, sorry. Good job guys," Breel said. "We're up and running again – sort of."

"Want to give it a try?"

The woman, Ellyella, smiled at her as she finished attaching the prosthetic to Abiel's stump. Ellyella stepped back, eyeing her work critically. The stump was still red and sore but healing fast thanks to the medical packages arranged in a ring around her knee. Abiel was feeling stronger all the time. Below the nano med-packs, her leg now ended in a complex structure of composite carbon and light metals. It was an elegant design, made up of sweeping interlocking curves that would both cushion and add spring to her step. She swung off the gurney. Ellyella handed her a stick made of black carbon fibre.

"Use this," she said.

Abiel stood and took some experimental steps across the room, the stick tap-tapping as she went. The leg had some rudimentary bio-feedback that connected to the neural-link almost everyone had installed these days. It informed her of the pseudo-foot's position in space. She felt the pressure vary when she pressed it into the deck. The prosthetic worked so well, she judged it wouldn't be long before she could dispense with the stick, but she leant on it heavily anyway. Always better to be underestimated.

She was wearing nothing but a pair of tight shorts and halter top. The wound in her abdomen, from the ice spike, was still livid, but otherwise healing fast. No essential organs had been seriously damaged. She figured she had come through her ordeal very well, all things considered. Abiel met Ellyella's eyes, lingering on her. She filed the fact away. Something that might be useful in the future.

She eyed the woman and thought how foolish and naive of her and her crew to enable her in this way, a potentially dangerous enemy in their midst. Idly, the thought crossed her mind that she could step across the room and with very little effort snap Ellyella's neck. Then she would be free to roam the ship, for a limited time anyway, and possibly find a way to destroy it. Was that the Light's plan for her, that she should be martyred to the cause? A fitting revenge for Zal and Ti.

She felt a lump form in her throat at the thought of her two sisters, frozen corpses on the asteroid, taking an infinite voyage through the cosmos. She felt a flicker of rage, then. The thought of some kind of violent revenge was appealing. But it seemed too fraught with possible failure. Not knowing the layout of the ship, it might be impossible to find a way to wreck it before they found her. It was too soon. Better to bide her time.

Instead, she smiled at the woman. "A little painful, but I think I'll get the hang of it." The word came out as 'leetle' in her accented Standard.

"You're doing brilliantly," Ellyella enthused. "Why don't you get dressed, so you can meet everyone else?" She indicated a one-piece, standard-issue jump-suit she had brought in.

Abiel nodded. Making a show of using the stick to move across the room, she picked up the clothing.

The crew were gathered in the galley, apart from the Breel woman, who was the pilot and in symbiosis with the ship. Matt looked up at their entrance.

"Hi, Abiel. You're just in time." He pulled a chair out from under the table that ran the length of the room. A heavy man regarded her, standing next to a tall thin man with a hook nose. She noticed the thin man carried a sidearm.

"This is the Deacon and this is Kaemon," Ellyella made the introductions.

Abiel stared at the heavy man. So, this was the renegade priest: the traitor.

The Deacon stood, clearly uncomfortable under the intensity of her gaze. He made the sign of the Circle of Light.

"Welcome," he bowed. "The Light illuminate your path."

Automatically she returned the salute although the thought that this man was still alive, while the accursed asteroid was littered with the bodies of her comrades made her want to leap across the room and rip his throat out with her teeth.

The thin man stood impassively, arms folded, saying nothing. Half of his face was pink with smooth new skin, an indication that nano-med packages had recently been removed. His eyes never left her as she moved across the room to the proffered chair. She smiled as sweetly as she could, fully aware of the effect that smile could have, memories of a life before the Church.

"Hello." She said to them both, before nodding her thanks to Matt. She sat heavily. Her leg hurt, and normally she would resist any expression of pain, but now she made a show of it, wincing as she sat. Breel's voice sounded through the ship PA.

"We're in orbit."

A view of the shepherd moon Abiel had been told was their destination sprang into existence on the wall display. The moon hung against a background of backlit dust, the far wall of a particulate canyon the moon had created over millennia, through a combination of impacts and gravitational resonance.

There was something odd about the planetoid's shape, though. It seemed to be deforming as they watched, bulging at the equator.

"What's that?" The Deacon pointed at the screen.

The bulge swelled into a small round shape. Small being a relative term. It must be huge.

"It looks like... another moon," Ellyella said. "Rising over the shepherd."

"Too regular for a natural satellite that size." Kaemon, apparently forgetting about Abiel for the moment, was leaning forward, trying to figure it out.

"A station?" the Deacon offered.

"Could be..."

The object rose higher as they approached until they could see it all. Now it was an unfinished dome, like the top part of a tiny moon with roughly two-thirds of the bottom missing. A line tapered down from the base, connecting it to the surface: a monstrous mushroom with an impossibly long, impossibly thin stem.

"Space elevator counterweight?" Abiel offered.

They all looked her way, then back to the screen. *Scavenger* sailed over the massive construction. The cables connecting it to the surface dwindled away in a mind-numbing perspective. Even though it was half the moon's diameter away, they could see huge holes in the outer skin through which the internal structure was visible. It was surrounded by a cloud of wreckage.

"Light preserve us," the Deacon breathed.

44

"There are four of these equally spaced around the equator." Breel reported, then added, "I'm going to put us into a polar orbit, so we'll get to see the entire surface."

The space elevator slid rapidly off one side of the display. The moon's surface accelerated across the screen until, after a few minutes, the image settled to a view of the landscape turning lazily below. It was dark and mottled. Strange patterns, hard to interpret as natural, twisted across its surface and something was moving down there, on the edge of visibility.

"What's that," Matt's voice was hoarse. "What are we looking at?"

The image magnification jumped. Everyone in the room gasped.

"Yes," Breel said. "It's crawling with life."

Matt looked at the faces of their small group. All these people, with the exception of the Deacon and Abiel, were here because of him and he supposed, it could be argued even Abiel wouldn't be here without the actions he had precipitated. He felt the crushing weight of responsibility and not a little guilt as they looked at him in anticipation.

The screen showed a view of the complex from which the mystery signal was broadcasting. The base, or whatever it was, radiated from the terminus of the ruined space elevator cables, like a dried blood spatter, dark against bright ice, as if the cables had speared the moon.

The image wasn't clear, fading in and out through the raging storm, but when it was visible, the base design looked oddly familiar. With a shock, Matt realised it reminded him of the designs on the alien artefact in Deacon's lab – and now he thought of it, Breel's body art. The designs were a curving mass of convoluted details that his mind skittered over, struggling to find a place to rest. It was hard to judge the scale, but it had to be huge.

Breel had made her way down from the bridge to join them in the galley.

"We take the shuttle, leave *Scavenger* in orbit." She indicated a flat expanse at the bottom of the screen, adjacent to the enigmatic structure. "There's an area here where we can put down. It looks like it might have been a landing field once."

"What's that scattered all over it?" Ellyella asked.

"Debris of some kind," Breel increased the magnification, but the details were lost in the snow and spindrift that constantly scoured the surface. "Might be vehicles, or," she added a smile, "maybe, an ancient spacecraft or two we can fly home in."

The view shifted to an expanse of dirty ice to the south. Movement could be seen on the surface and in the cracks and crevices that splintered its structure.

"Deacon wants to fly low over this area and take a look at the locals on our way in."

"So, are we a science survey vessel now?" Kaemon asked. "Or tourists taking a day trip?"

"Bit of both, I guess," Matt replied.

"I hate to be Mr. Negative all the time," Kaemon came back, "but might it not be a better idea to spend our time trying to find a way home? You know, look for a *RIP* out of here?"

"It would," Matt said, "but our options have become limited." He looked at Breel. "Breel tells me the ship's core systems are compromised – beyond repair without a shipyard. Even if a *RIP* exists, we'll be long dead before we find it."

Silence greeted this revelation.

"Is that because of the incursion, from the alien thing?" Ellyella asked.

"No," Breel replied. "Damage from the Church attack before the transit. We took a real beating."

Kaemon waved at the image on the screen. "So, what are you proposing? We're not gonna last long down there, that's for sure."

"Well," Breel said. "That's not entirely true. Something weird has happened, since we arrived in orbit. I don't know what it means, but it can't be coincidence." A blue zig-zag line overlaid the alien structure. "There has been an environmental change in some parts of whatever-that-is."

"What change?" Ellyella asked.

"A corridor of air, an oxygen, nitrogen mix, perfectly breathable at one atmospheric pressure, "Breel said, "and at a comfortable temperature. Only in the location shown."

"A guide," the Deacon said. "Someone is expecting us."

Breel nodded, eyes fixed to the screen. "Looks like it."

"But what's it guiding us to?" Ellyella whispered.

"We don't know of course, but it seems like an invitation to meet, perhaps." The Deacon's eyes shone.

"Or a trap," Kaemon said. "If that's for us, it knows a scary lot about us, like an environment perfectly suited to us, for example."

"Yeah, it didn't waste its time while it was in amongst the ship's systems, I guess," Matt said.

Breel sat to give him the floor.

"Look, our choices are stark. Anyone who wants to stay on *Scavenger* can, of course. Breel, the Deacon and I are going down. That environmental change must be for us and we are in no position to ignore it. If nothing else, we might get a few answers, but who knows, there might be a way out of here. Star charts, *RIP* locations… We'll take the MARRVs and enough supplies to last a few days. The worst-case scenario: we just come back. Nothing is lost."

"I'm coming," Ellyella said decisively.

"You're only just recovering El. Are you up to it?" Breel asked.

Ellyella shrugged, "What use is there in sitting up here? What am I waiting to recover for? I'll be fine."

Kaemon added. "Might as well be doing something entertaining while I wait to die. I'm hardly going to sit up here on my own."

Matt looked at Abiel. "That means you're coming too. We can't leave you here alone."

Abiel nodded, looking down. "Of course."

"There's one more thing," Breel added.

The Deacon groaned. "When is there not?"

Breel continued. "Calculations show that the shepherd moon is in an unstable orbit. It's very near its Roche limit. In a few weeks it will start to disintegrate as tidal forces from the object at the centre tear it apart. I've detected seismic activity. We can expect tremors on the ground initially, leading up to much worse."

"Wait," Kaemon said. "This thing has been here for, who knows, tens of thousands, maybe millions of years, and we arrive on the eve of its destruction?"

Breel shrugged. "I know. What are the odds?"

The small, battered shuttle *Scavenger* carried was going to be a tight fit, especially with the addition of the MARRVs and the extra supplies.

Kaemon had made use of the weeks it had taken to transit to the shepherd moon and reorganised it. He had emptied the craft's storage compartment, which ran beneath the length of the main fuselage, onto the floor of the garage bay. Now he was carefully putting everything back, re-organising it all to make extra space. Conditions on the moon's surface would kill them quickly. They could only survive in their suits or the shuttle, so they were going to have to take everything with them. The shuttle carried enough air for their needs and would recycle water for some time, so, mainly food, medical supplies and weapons. Along with a plasma gun he added a hi-tech hunting knife, a long serrated black blade reflecting dull highlights. Its blade was wickedly sharp, but it also sported a coherent light edge, similar to the one Breel had used to cut the crusader's helmet away – for as long as its limited power supply lasted, anyway.

A collapsed emergency hab-tent lay at his feet. It was something that they shouldn't need, but he was loath not to take it. Experience had taught him to allow for all possible eventualities.

The sound of voices came from a wall display, playing what had become Kaemon's favourite pastime. When he had first come aboard, he had discovered a store of ancient 2D movies in the database. Real collectors' pieces. They must have been added by *Scavenger's* previous owner, because Matt had no idea about them and no interest. Without auto-translate he wouldn't be able to even understand them, so archaic was the language.

There were a variety of genres, but Kaemon liked the gangster and action thrillers in particular. He wasn't sure what it was about these flat moving images that had so captured his imagination. He paused to watch one of the characters make another 'an offer he couldn't refuse.'

Movement on the ladder that led down from the middle deck caught his attention. He looked up. It was the crusader woman.

"Hello," she said after her head cleared the ceiling. She came down the ladder carefully, her walking stick tucked under one armpit. The prosthetic tapped on each rung. He watched her without expression. She paused at the bottom and leaned on the stick. She was wearing tight-fitting shorts, her right leg a series of carbon and ceramic compound curves from the knee down, and a thin sleeveless tee shirt that clung to her body in a distracting way. She had broad shoulders and muscular arms. She was tall, almost as tall as Breel. Her jet-black hair had grown out, softening the hard, aggressive look. Large eyes with a slight epicanthic fold regarded him from a deep olive complexion.

"The others are busy doing stuff I can't help with," she said, "so I wondered if I could help you?"

He tried to place her accent. 'The,' came out as 'Zay' – 'Zay others', and 'wondered' as, 'rundered.'

She smiled a smile that lit up the room.

Kaemon regarded her coolly. That smile was weaponised. He had watched her use it on the captain with some success, and more annoyingly, Ellyella. This woman hadn't been brought up in female servitude on a saved world, he was sure of that. No, she had been around the station a few times.

She looked at the screen. "This passes for entertainment where you come from?"

Kaemon shook his head. "Much older, pre-spaceflight Earth at least. I found a load of them in *Scavenger's* database. Not sure why I find them so compelling." He shrugged. "Maybe I find comfort in the fact that no matter how far we come, we never really move on." He looked from the screen to her. "It's the same old shit wrapped in a new box."

Abiel met his eyes, shrugged and shifted her attention to the habtent. "Are we planning a bit of wild camping?"

Kaemon paused the film. "I like to hedge my bets, especially when I don't know what I'm dealing with."

She surveyed the rest of the garage bay and the objects in it. "Makes sense."

After a moment he said, "Are you okay to lift and move stuff?" He indicated her leg.

"Sure, I can manage. I can't expect you guys to do everything."

She beamed.

"There's a trolley of oxy-tanks over there." He pointed to the back of the garage bay. "Be helpful if you can drag it over here while I sort this stuff out."

He bent back to his task but watched her from the corner of his eye. Her movements looked strong and fluid, despite the stick. She grabbed the trolley and pulled it over, supporting herself on the cane with the other hand.

"I guess we'll bring this all back if we don't use it," she said.

Kaemon grunted.

She gave him an appraising look. "You don't seem very enthusiastic about this trip."

He hauled up one of the heavy oxy-tanks, holding it to judge the space where it might fit. "I'm not sure if our time wouldn't be better spent looking for a way home, while the ship is still functioning. We don't know what's waiting for us down there. It might not be what we're hoping for."

"If nothing else, maybe the answers to some of the biggest questions of our time," she said.

Kaemon said nothing. He began to stack emergency ration bars. Unopened, they were guaranteed to last 20 years he noted with some irony.

"Not curious?"

"Of course I'm curious," he conceded, "but looking for a way home, however slim the chances, makes more sense to me than having answers that are going to then die with us. Kinda frustrating, that, don't you think?"

He pulled a plastic crate to him. Inside were ropes, crampons, ice axes. Not the kind of inventory a ship like *Scavenger* would normally carry. They were his personal property, from a previous life. He often wondered why he had bothered to keep them all these years. Nostalgia probably. Now though, given the icy conditions down there, they might come in handy.

"That complex was built by a technological civilisation." Abiel placed both hands on the top of the carbon walking cane, using its support to lean forward. "Given their advanced level, who knows what we might find. Equipment to repair the ship, *RIP* coordinates, things we can't even imagine. Anything is possible, especially in light of the environmental changes Breel detected. It looks like someone is waiting for us."

"That's what worries me." He stopped his packing to look at her. "You know it's most likely the work of the evil 'Firsts,' your mortal enemies, don't you?"

"A chance to get to know my enemy, then." She matched his stare. He turned back to his packing.

"How did you get to be here?" he asked.

"I would have thought you knew more about that than me."

"You're a female crusader. Can't be many of them about. How does that happen?"

"It happens." She shrugged, "*We're all flotsam, pummelled by currents in the river of life*," she quoted.

"*...but, while seeking the Source, faith will guide us through the rapids.*" Kaemon finished. "Manganu, The first testament of life."

She gave him a look.

"I'm deeper than I look," he said. "Now I place the accent. You're from New Chinchary. I won't tell your boss that you quoted a false prophet."

"That's for sure," she said dryly. She looked around. "Is there anything else I can do?"

"I think you've done enough," he said without looking up.

"You seem to harbour some resentment towards me," she said. "What have I done to earn the hostility?"

Kaemon stood and faced her. "Nothing," He crossed his arms. "And that's the problem. Not that long ago you and your damn people were trying to kill us. I'm only just getting over my injuries. Ellyella nearly died. Thousands did die on Hope."

"Hope? The Claimer asteroid?" She looked puzzled, "What's that to do with me? I haven't been within a hundred light years of the place." She shifted her weight onto her good leg. "You remember we were in a war, don't you? It's the nature of wars that people try to kill each other." A flicker of emotion clouded her features. "I left good people on that Light-forsaken rock as well, you know."

Kaemon shook his head. "Breel keeps telling us about some kid crusader she met on Blue Haven. That it wasn't his fault, how he turned out, just circumstances. I could almost excuse that. But," he gave her a long appraising look, "you aren't like that are you?"

She shifted her weight again, "You've figured out a lot, given that this is the longest conversation we've had. What do you think I'm like?"

"You aren't the result of a lifetime of religious indoctrination. I'm pretty sure of that. You're too savvy, too..." he searched for a description. "...too street-wise. I think you did have a choice and chose the life you've lived. Given the way Second Light treats women, I figure that makes you a dangerous fanatic."

Abiel's body tensed. A look crossed her fine features for a second. He wasn't sure if it was anger or something else, then it was gone, the calm facade back in place. But knocking a chink in her armour had given him some satisfaction.

"Well," she said after a second. "It seems I can't help you after all, Kaemon." She pushed the Oxy-tank trolley towards him with her carbon foot. "I'll leave you to your task."

She went back to the access ladder, hardly using the walking stick at all.

FIVE

Weightless, Breel pulled herself along the length of the shuttle's cabin using webbing that covered the wall and ceiling. She strapped into the co-pilot seat next to Matt. She was a starship pilot, able to meld with the ship's higher functions and navigate the light years through her unique interface, but flying a somewhat aerodynamically challenged vehicle through a turbulent atmosphere, that was Matt's area of expertise.

She twisted in her seat and looked down the length of the craft. The Deacon and Kaemon sat opposite each other, either side of a narrow aisle, Ellyella and Abiel behind them. They all wore spacesuits; helmets held in their laps. *Scavenger's* systems had been reduced to minimum, her EMD drive shut down. Loose straps and stray wisps of hair floated lazily in microgravity.

The crew wore a mixture of expressions. The Deacon, anticipation and fear. Kaemon, as ever, wore his trademark angry scowl. El was excited. Abiel – Abiel sat upright, back straight, eyes shut, controlling her breathing. Prayer? Some kind of ninja meditation? She didn't know what to make of the crusader. So far, she had proven quiet and helpful, largely ignoring Kaemon's attempts to bait her or to inquire into her past. Breel did share some of Kae's misgivings, really, she had no idea what the Second Light warrior thought of the situation she had been forced into, or what she really felt about the people who had saved her from certain death. The terrifying fanatic they had been promised had, so far, failed to materialise, if indeed, she was in there at all.

Behind the human crew, the four MARRVs had been packed in folded configuration, their semi-gloss surfaces catching soft highlights.

She twisted to face forward again. Matt was running through his pre-flight checks. He looked sideways at Breel, "Ready?"

Breel nodded, "Helmets on everyone, here we go."

She felt a twist of anticipation in her gut as she fitted her own helmet into place. After weeks of inaction, she was excited to be doing something, even a potential suicide mission. Although, she thought wryly, they had survived one suicide mission already, so were well practiced.

The shuttle had been rolled into the centre of the garage bay, its short wings still folded. Everything else in the bay had been stowed away or strapped down. There was a loud hiss which slowly faded as the air evacuated.

Matt tapped a control and the section of the floor that the shuttle was clamped to hinged downwards, taking the vehicle along for the ride, revealing a crescent of the shepherd moon. A metal screw tumbled past the window, ejected by the remaining wisps of air, eager to be first out. A few other less identifiable objects followed.

This close to the moon, more of the ice was visible through the sludge, bright slashes cutting through the dark layer. Sensors showed the mire to be a complex mix of exotic chemicals in a hydrocarbon slush.

At an instruction from Matt, the clamps slid forward, then released, imparting enough momentum to launch the small craft clear of *Scavenger*.

The shepherd moon hung before a shimmering curtain, the bands of dust the moon was embedded in backlit by the sun. Here and there larger chunks of rotating debris heliographed a flash of light from oblique faces.

On one of the monitors, Breel watched *Scavenger* recede. The maimed starship, their home and refuge for many months, hung poised with its nose pointed to the stars, as if longing to escape back into the cosmos.

Behind it, the space elevator counterweight hung like half a shattered moon. They had scanned the interior of the massive structure for warm spots and had explored what they could see of the internal structure through numerous holes puncturing its skin, but there was no sign of activity and it was as cold as the surrounding vacuum. They had briefly considered an excursion over to it, but limited resources dictated otherwise. They simply didn't have the time to explore something so clearly inert when there was something active on the surface. The long stem could now be seen to be made up of multiple strands, dropping

54

down and down, until they met swirling clouds far below where they cast an undulating shadow across half a world.

It had made sense to park *Scavenger* here, in a geo-stationary orbit above their destination, although they would have to follow a more conventional orbit to get down to the alien base. She watched until both the counterweight and *Scavenger* disappeared behind the shepherd moon's tight horizon.

The shuttle shuddered as Matt applied thrust. There was a whir of hydraulics, followed by thumps reverberating through the airframe as the wings unfolded. The shepherd moon expanded, details on the cloud deck becoming more defined as they approached its atmosphere. The shuttle shuddered and rocked as it encountered the upper layers.

Breel peered ahead. The spacecraft's leading edges glowed with the friction of re-entry. Vibration increased until the vehicle was rattling like someone shaking a steel can half full of ball bearings.

"Is this normal?" the Deacon yelled over the racket.

"Pretty smooth so far," Ellyella assured him.

The Deacon looked unconvinced.

The curved horizon slowly flattened into a straight line. The first wisps of cloud streamed past. The rattling grew louder. They hit a low-pressure pocket and fell like a stone. Breel felt herself lift from her seat, held in place by the restraints. There was a thump as if the craft had been drop kicked. The tail end swung side to side. Breel's teeth cracked together, catching her tongue; she tasted blood.

Matt calmly adjusted the trim.

The rollercoaster ride steadied. Now there was only the hiss of atmosphere pouring over the hull. They had left the high cirrus clouds behind. Below was a second layer, a towering crepuscular cloudscape.

"About to hit some weather," Kaemon observed.

Breel gripped the arm rests of her seat more tightly.

They plunged into the cloud deck, reducing the view to a uniform, luminous grey, but minutes later passed smoothly into clear air without further turbulence, revealing the overcast landscape below. A fractured, splintered plain of white, swirled with grey-black. On the horizon there was a range of jagged hills, draped with falling vapour, everything overlaid with swirling snow. Something dark and organic lay in front of the peaks, just visible, pinned to the surface by the dark, thread-thin lines of the elevator cables.

"There's our destination." Matt pointed. They had circumnavigated the moon and were flying back towards the stem of the beanstalk to where it stabbed the ground. The alien base spread from it like a dark bruise. Breel pressed forward against the resistance of her seat belt, trying vainly to glean more detail through the driving storm.

"That's one hell of a landmark," she agreed.

They lost altitude. The moonscape resolved into rugged peaks divided by plains, crisscrossed by clefts and fissures.

"What are those?" The Deacon had his nose pressed to the window. Breel followed his gaze down and gasped.

Below them things were moving.

"Are we going lower?" the Deacon asked, his fear seemingly forgotten in the anticipation of discovery.

The ground rose to meet them as Matt increased the rate of descent.

"Holy Light." It was Abiel, eyes open and alert to the activity outside.

Herds of what looked like animals were moving across a fractured plain of ice. They moved in unnaturally geometric formation, blocky rectangles, flowing along the edge of a crevasse. Smaller streamlined shapes flanked them. It looked like the smaller animals were herding the larger ones. The larger beasts shimmered, reminding Breel of the multi-hued carapaces of beetles. The smaller ones were almost the same colour as the ice and were only visible by their shadows or when they crossed darker ground.

They dropped lower still.

Kaemon said, "Trouble up ahead."

Breel looked up quickly, but the trouble Kaemon referred to waited for the shimmering creatures, not for them. A barrier of ice lay in the path of the herd. The first animals hit the towering wall of white. Some tried to scamper up, but failed, falling back onto their fellows behind, creating a chaos of bouncing twisting bodies in a steamy cloud of ice and snow. Their brethren swerved to avoid the melee but the smaller beasts restricted their direction. With nowhere else for them to go, they turned and went over the edge into the chasm, followed by the smaller camouflaged animals, who launched themselves into space without hesitation.

"What was that all about?" Breel asked the question they were all thinking.

There was a scraping sound outside. Ice particles, stirred up by the stampede had reached them and were bouncing off the hull.

"Don't get too low," Breel warned.

Matt lifted the nose of the spacecraft. "Good advice."

A shout from Ellyella made everyone look, first at her and then at what had caused her outcry. Something matched their pace outside, about a wingspan away. It was made of sliding sheets of a multi-hued material with razor sharp edges, sliding in continuous movement over oily inner layers. Its wings were an insect blur that defied inspection. Red points glowed from deep pits in what might have been a head. Machine, animal – it was hard to tell. It was about half the size of the shuttle.

"Whoa." Matt swung the shuttle away from the apparition. The creature matched their flight as they moved away from the crevasse, to fly low over a flat, less fissured expanse of dirty grey.

"Seems more curious than aggressive." The Deacon's eyes were wide with excitement.

At that moment the alien changed course. It lurched at them to land on the starboard wing, skidding to fetch up against the window with a crash that shook the spacecraft. Ellyella threw herself away from the glass in panic but could only move so far, restrained by her seat belt. The shuttle tipped with the uneven weight. Breel hung suspended by her seat harness, looking down through the windows, the wing an arrow-head pointing out the long drop below. The creature scrabbled to keep its grip, tearing out panels of ceramic composite as it slid down.

Matt fought the controls to gain level flight, but the shuttle continued to roll until the horizon became a vertical line. The wing had become a wall, too difficult for the creature to hang onto. It lost its hold and fell away, trailing panels and components. Matt tried to right the shuttle, but they continued into a steep, spiralling dive.

"Control surfaces have been damaged," he grunted, pushing and pulling at the yoke. Far below the alien had quickly resumed flight and was climbing back, aiming for a head on collision.

"Shit." Matt fought the damaged spacecraft, to force it into a swerve and avoid the impact that would almost certainly bring their expedition to a sudden conclusion, but it was happening far too slowly.

"Grab hold of something!" he yelled.

The forward screens were filled with terrifying meshing mouth parts.

A geyser of ice erupted directly below the creature.

"Look out," Breel shouted, pointlessly.

The alien avian must have sensed danger. It peeled away to the right, but something flashed out of the collapsing tower of ice to snatch it from the air. Breel only caught a glimpse. A nightmare from the darkest recesses of the mind, constructed from intermeshing moving parts she struggled to make sense of. The front-end split to swallow their attacker whole, then it was gone, along with its prey, into what was now revealed to be a dark, ice-covered lake or sea. Water foamed and frothed where the creatures had disappeared. Large chunks of ice the alien leviathan had launched high into the air began to rain back down, crashing into the water, exploding spray and debris all around them.

Matt, teeth exposed in an animal grimace, pulled the yoke, violently banking the shuttle this way and that, until he had it on a level again. Breel had time to breathe a small sigh of relief, before their spacecraft rang like a gong. She saw metal and ceramic tumble away, along with a chunk of ice that had smashed into the port wing on its way back down, bending and distorting it. Alarms screeched.

Matt finally lost all control. The craft spun. Inertia crushed Breel against the side wall. There was a dizzying view through the forward screens, churning water and ice followed by blurred leaden skies, then ice floes again – twice, three times, and then, somehow, Matt had the craft flying straight, but canted over. Shouts and curses from the others could barely be heard above the sound of stressed metal and screaming engines.

"Brace, brace, brace!" Matt shouted above the racket, as much a curse as a warning to the others as he tried to keep the shuttle in the air long enough to clear the water. Banked up snow ahead indicated what might be the shore line. The wall of white expanded quickly until the world outside consisted of nothing but a streaked grey-white cliff.

Whummmpppp! The shuttle ploughed its nose into the snow. Breel was pulled forward as if by a giant hand, stretching the seat straps holding her in place, then smashed back as the craft tumbled nose over tail. A final stomach-churning flip slammed her head into the wall, shattering her reality into bright constellations.

SIX

Breel woke, disoriented. She didn't recognise what she was looking at until it came to her that she was hanging upside down, suspended by the seat harness. She fumbled for the release and the harness split, resulting in a heavy drop onto what had been the ceiling. She shook her head to clear blurred vision and then scanned the cabin. The others were still in their seats, hanging like bats, either dazed or struggling to get themselves free. Abiel was the first to drop out of her harness. She landed lightly, favouring her good leg, then squatted, facing Breel, breathing hard. Matt crashed down a second later. He got to his feet quickly to stand between the forward seats to check the upside-down controls.

"Cabin integrity is sound," he said, relieved. "We can still breathe in here." He unscrewed his helmet to prove the point. The others dropped from their seats one by one, until they were all huddled in a circle. They took their helmets off, exposing faces displaying confusion, shock and fear. The only sound was shifting ice over the hull and the creak and crack of cooling metal.

Ellyella spoke first. "What in the name of all screaming hells just happened?"

Kaemon was shaking his head, "I knew this was a bad idea." He looked at Matt. "What's the plan now, Captain?"

The Deacon was ashen. "Can we still get to the complex? Can we walk?"

"How do you propose we do that?" Kaemon asked. He waved a hand indicating the outside. "We'd suffocate long before we got there."

"There must be something we can do. We can't just sit here waiting for our air to run out."

"Well, Deak," Kaemon said, "I'm all ears."

Matt cut in. "We aren't dead. That's a plus. Take a breath, think it through."

Kaemon shook his head, lips a tight line.

"Only one thing we can do," Breel said.

They looked at her expectantly.

"Like the Deacon said, we walk."

"Really?" Kaemon responded. "Did you miss the crashed-on-a-planet-that-will-kill-us-the-moment-our-air-runs-out part?"

"Listen, Kaemon –"

"– We must be twenty clicks away, at least," Kaemon interrupted.

"For Jink's sake, Kae, give her a chance will you," Matt said.

"Okay," he said. "I'm listening, I'm listening."

"We know the alien complex has oxygen…"

"Yeah, but its…

"For Deshi's-sake, shut the fuck up a minute will you," Breel exploded.

Ellyella put a hand on Kaemon's arm. "Let her speak, Kae."

Kaemon opened his mouth, then closed it, waving Breel to continue.

Breel took a breath. "We know the complex has oxygen; we just need to get there." She looked at Matt. "How far do you think?"

Matt shrugged. "Like Kae said, about twenty k. What do you have in mind?"

"Twenty k is not that far. We can walk there."

They all started to talk at once.

Breel raised her voice. "Listen to me. We rig up a raft, load it with supplies. You brought the hab-tent Kaemon, I saw it." She nodded at him. "That was good thinking." She noticed Kaemon relax a little at this compliment to his foresight. She pushed herself to her feet. "I reckon it'll take us two days, so we'll only have to use it once. It'll give us chance a to eat and sleep without our helmets on. The MARRVs will drag it for us. Our suits will recycle water, enough to get to the complex, anyway."

Their voices rose in competition once again.

"Two days?"

"Don't know if I'm up to it physically."

"If the suits' power lasts that long…"

Breel raised a hand for silence. "If any of you have a better idea, other than sitting here waiting to die, please tell me."

"What happens when we get there?" Ellyella asked into the silence.

"There has to be a way in. Breathable air at precisely the right atmospheric pressure, can't be a coincidence." Breel looked round at all the faces. "So there has to be a connection – right? Something is waiting for us."

"Let's hope they are friendlier than the bunch we've already met," Kaemon said.

"Yes, Kaemon," Breel said patiently, "let's hope. But it's something. Would you prefer nothing?"

"Talking of the locals?" Ellyella said, "what about them?"

"And the terrain?" The Deacon said. "We have no idea what lies between us and the complex."

Their voices rose once more, anxious to get their concerns across.

"I woke up on an enemy asteroid with a holed suit and half a leg missing," Abiel said. She hadn't raised her voice, but she commanded their attention, nonetheless.

"I could have opened my visor, ended it all at that point." She smiled at them. "The thought did cross my mind. But I didn't. I was alive and while I was alive, there was no way I was going to lay down and die. Instead, I crawled across an icy waste, into a damaged enemy complex in the hope that I would find something, anything, that might save me." She pushed herself to her feet, wincing slightly. "After going to so much trouble to survive I'm damned if I'm just going to sit and suffocate in this fucking can." She looked at Kaemon. "*We just need a little faith, to guide us through the rapids.*"

Into the silence that followed Matt finally said, "Come on then, we're wasting time. Unless someone can figure out a way to fix the shuttle, it's the only chance we have."

SEVEN

Before he had been adopted, life at the orphanage had been difficult for the Emissary. The Soror of Light was a strict place and the Soror nuns were the bitches from hell, but the monthly visit from the Archbishop was the thing the orphans all dreaded the most. Once the man had made his choice the others could relax again for a few weeks. The Emissary had been a fairly bland-looking child, something of an ugly duckling as it turned out, with a tendency to be overlooked. When he saw the condition of some of the returnees, he vowed that he would never be subject to that; that he would fight, no matter the cost.

Soon enough, he learned that any decision had consequences; in his case, almost terminal.

Later, when he had become the all-powerful Emissary, he was delighted to find the Archbishop was still alive. Old and feeble by then, but still not too old to understand that consequences were for everyone, even Archbishops.

The two men kneeling before him now, heads bowed and trembling, were about to learn the same lesson.

Both had had their insignia of rank ripped from their uniforms. Both had severe bruising to their faces; one had his arm covered in nano-med packages, the arm having been broken in two places.

He stood before them surrounded by a small entourage. His own security detail directly behind him; Maliesh, his second in command to his left; and the unfortunate crusaders' immediate supervisor to his right. That worthy surveyed his underlings sternly. The Emissary took a step forward and laid a hand on the head of the crusader closest to him.

"How did you come to this my child?" he said softly. "To fail the Light in such a way?"

The crusader flinched from the touch, mumbling.

The Emissary lifted the man's chin and forced him to meet his eyes.

"Do not fear, my child. Speak freely. You are amongst family here."

"I'm sorry, my Lord," the man croaked. "It is hard to speak."

The Emissary had already noted the nano med package around the man's throat. Livid blue and yellow bruises stained the surrounding skin, the result of a stabbing blow to his throat. They met with similar discolouration spreading down from his left temple. "The prisoners came from nowhere," he said more loudly, the effort forcing a cough from his damaged larynx. "One minute the door was locked and the next... the next, the door was open and they were upon me, before I had time to react."

"You? A crusader trained in the art of unarmed combat to the highest level, *you* – were defeated by two breeders and an old man?"

The man wheezed, coughed, then said. "They took me by surprise, my Lord. The door was locked. How could they have opened it?"

He looked to his Messiah sincerely for an answer.

"How do you think they unlocked it?" The Emissary asked with genuine interest.

"I don't know," the man said miserably. "It can only be that the electronics failed in some way." He looked hopefully at the Emissary, as if that might exonerate him.

"A poor excuse, my Lord." The man's sergeant spoke up from his side. "There is no record of an electronics failure."

The Lord of Light turned his attention to the other injured soldier.

"And you, my son, you and your colleague. Two heavily armed, highly trained warriors, how did you allow dereliction and failure to leave you badly injured and your comrade dead?"

The man was almost weeping. "He said he had been commanded– the Deacon I mean– to escort the two prisoners aboard the insurgent ship, seeking something on your orders."

The sergeant snorted with derision. "And of course, you gave him the benefit of the doubt. Why wouldn't you?"

"No, no." He looked to the Emissary for understanding. "That wasn't what happened at all, my Lord. The Deacon was in full ceremonial dress. He said he was my superior, that things would go badly for me if I defied him."

"You didn't recognise him? The fugitive we had been looking for, his likeness having been distributed to everyone?"

"I did, of course I did, but he was there and free. There had been no alarm, no notification about escaped prisoners, so, for all I knew, he was acting under your direction." At this point the soldier squared his shoulders, adopting a straighter posture. "But I would never simply allow him access to the insurgent ship. I said I would have to check, as I hadn't been informed of any such order."

The Emissary nodded and waited patiently, his beneficent smile shining down on his subject.

"I was making the call," the guard continued in his defence. "I was making the call… when they attacked us."

"Two breeders and an old man?" A note of scepticism tinged the Lord of Light's voice.

"I was dealing with them, we… we were dealing with them. The two breeders were no match for us, of course. But then the priest shot us."

"Ah, I see," the Emissary said. He leaned close to the guard, his lips almost touching the other man's, who shrank back in fear. "You were so preoccupied by the vicious attack by two young women that you took your eyes off the old man?"

The truth of this was painfully obvious in the soldier's wretched features.

"Understandable, I suppose," he said gently before pushing the man's head back aggressively. 'Understandable…" his voice rising in pitch. He looked around at the assembled complement. "Understandable that two heavily armed, highly trained crusaders should be bested by two lesser creatures and an *old man.*" He spat out the last two words.

"A disgrace, my Lord," the guards' superior officer spoke again. "There is no excuse for such dereliction."

"Indeed," the Emissary said, calm once more. He pushed his face close to the first man again, the one with the bruised throat, his lips almost brushing those of the wide-eyed soldier.

"What was your back-up doing?" he asked. "The other members of your retinue, while you were being attacked?"

"His Grace asked you a question," snarled the newly emboldened captain.

"I don't… understand," the man said. "It was just me. I asked. It is normal protocol for at least one back-up, but none came."

The Emissary turned his head to the sergeant.

"Just him?"

"I, well…" The sergeant looked uncomfortable to be suddenly the object of the Emissary's attention. "The insurgents were securely locked in the brig, no way to escape and, well, one man seemed enough, for–" he snarled at his underlings, "– two breeders and an old man."

"Except they did escape. Why was normal protocol not followed?" The Emissary still bent over the guard, looking sideways at the sergeant

"I mean… well you said… we needed more men to crew the troop carriers…" The sergeant trailed off, the 'hole-digging' metaphor suddenly taking on a whole new reality for him.

The Lord of Light stood and turned to the man. "These men are surely guilty of dereliction of duty. They let their concentration lapse, did not give the forces of darkness the necessary respect."

"I shall see to it they are punished, whatever your Grace deems fit," the sergeant stammered.

"But, in the end, they are underlings, under the direction of a superior officer whose job it is to make sure they can fulfil their duties." He pointed a finger. "That's you, I believe. Is it not?" The Emissary lifted his head, as if in thought. "Backup, no backup, that decision ultimately rests… with you." He leaned towards the man. "Does it not?"

"I… I…" the sergeant stammered.

Abruptly the Emissary straightened and took the step necessary to reach the sergeant. A head taller, he looked down at his subordinate, his face an inch from the other man's.

The sergeant began to speak but before he could say anything the Emissary placed a hand on both his shoulders, stopping him short.

"Responsibility can be difficult, my son, I know," he said in a conciliatory tone. "It can weigh heavily. Having to establish priorities, determine what's important."

The sergeant nodded, uncertainty and fear chasing across his features.

"We can sometimes make wrong choices, when we find ourselves out of our depth," the Emissary continued, "in positions to which our talents are perhaps not best suited." The Lord of Light moved his hands behind the sergeant's head. "I forgive you," he said and pulled the man's face forward, placing a gentle kiss on his forehead. The sergeant looked relieved for a moment, but his expression changed to something else when the Emissary didn't relax his grip. Instead, holding the man's head firmly, the Emissary planted a kiss directly onto his mouth. The sergeant squirmed, made little mewling noises, but the Lord of Light's grip was iron. Finally, he released the luckless sergeant and stepped back. A tiny curve of drool connected the two momentarily. There was a flash, an electric arc played around their lips.

The sergeant started to speak, but the words came out as a sort of high-pitched sigh, as if the air in his lungs were escaping through a hole, which may have been the case as something white, red and shiny had burst from his side. A rib, growing at an exponential rate, followed by another and then another.

"No, my Lord…" The man's features twisted, his teeth burst from his mouth, growing in an entangled mesh, stifling any further attempt to speak. His whole body began to contort, bloody bones sprouting through clothing, trailing sinew and lumps of flesh. He fell to the deck spasming, a humped seed bed sprouting a grotesque forest of bone and torn muscle, laden with tiny fleshy fruit.

The smell of excrement and urine was overpowering.

The Emissary stared at the convulsing flesh before looking around the room at the assembled personnel. "It is written that he who would cast stones should look first to their own brittleness." He turned his attention to the two cowering guards.

Later the Emissary sat cross-legged in his room, naked, calmed by his act of violence. He breathed deeply, absently tracing the complex fractal patterns that ran across his body with his forefinger. They were slightly raised and ran from his mid-right thigh, around his groin and half way up his chest and were golden in colour, like a deep tan. There were times when they glowed with spun light, nodes that chased each other like highway traffic in an exotic city, but since the insurgents had escaped through the *RIP* they had remained dark.

They hadn't always been a part of him. During his time rising up the ranks of the Church, the only thing that had decorated the Emissary's body had been vague and itchy red marks, something he put down to an allergy. They hadn't bothered him, at least not so much he'd felt the need to seek medical advice. For the most part they lay hidden beneath his robes, although, sometimes, when he was at the height of his passion delivering a sermon, the discomfort did become acute.

Looking back the connection was clear.

The Emissary had not been a believer originally; the power and influence of the position of Emissary of Second Light was what he had coveted. To this end he contrived a new vision, a second revelation: the thrice damned *Firsts* had listened to the voices of the *Dark* and chosen to deny the *Light's* destiny for mankind. They had constructed a machine to banish the *Light* from a thousand light year sphere around them, not only damning themselves but any future civilisation that might emerge. This was the explanation for the barrier, beyond which EMD drives would not function.

The *First's* civilisation had ended in sin and debauchery. The Church's mission, therefore, was to find this Doomsday machine, destroy it and re-enable the *Light*, before mankind went the same way, so that the saved could be made transcendent.

Salvation in their lifetime, rather than in some indeterminate future.

On the night of the final coup, the night the Church of Second Light became his, that night had also been the Night of Revelation. All opposition to his takeover had been eliminated, all who didn't swear fealty to him were disposed of and he had given the sermon of his life. His oration had struck fear into any who might still oppose him, while at the same time energising his supporters.

After the sermon he had retired to his chambers, exhausted, thrown off his clothing and was astonished to see his body adorned with an intricate, glowing design. Only then did he realise the itching had stopped.

At first the sight had terrified him. But then came the voices. He didn't know what they were saying exactly, but the emotional content was clear; he had been doing the *Light's* work all along. From that point on the voices would be there to guide him along the right path, encouragement and elation almost orgasmic when he was doing the Light's bidding, but guilt almost to the point of pain when he was thinking of going astray.

His task became clear. He would use the vast resources of the Church, find the accursed device the *Firsts* had built to deny the Illumination of Righteousness, destroy it, and the Universe would be blessed again.

Truly he was the Chosen One, destined to lead mankind to its ultimate transformation.

But then had come the encounter with the breeder, from Hope. The sight of the same patterns adorning her body had shocked him to the core. Was she related to him somehow? Did they share the same parents, would she be able to tell him about his true family? Did she too commune with the Light? Was she subject to its advice? But events had frustrated him again. Before he had time to question her, she had put herself beyond his reach, on the other side of the *RIP* that she, along with the traitorous Deacon, had closed forever. For the first time since his epiphany, his certainty wavered. Why had the Light forsaken him? Had he transgressed in some way? Was the woman, this lesser creature, his replacement?

He listened for the voices, for guidance and reassurance, but they were deafening in their silence.

The com chimed, snapping him back to the reality of his sparse accommodation. His screen showed Maliesh standing in the ante room, holding an info-pad in one meaty hand.

"I gave orders not to be disturbed," the Emissary said.

"Forgive me this intrusion, your Grace," Maliesh replied to the closed door, "but I have information you need to see – that I am sure you will want to see."

The Emissary hesitated, but the look on his old friends face made him think that, whatever this was, he should give it his attention. With a sigh he stood and pulled his robes back on, then reseated himself. He took a moment, then, composed, he used his neural-link to command the door to open, revealing his second in command, head bowed.

"What is it, Maliesh?" His tone made clear that this intrusion had better be important.

Keeping his eyes low, Maliesh took a step into the room, holding out the info pad to his Messiah.

"Captain Hannathon's technicians have been observing the *RIP* since the insurgents went through," he said. "They have discovered something of great interest."

The Emissary took the pad and scrolled through the information it displayed. His expression softened as he began to understand what he was looking at. The Light had not forsaken him after all.

EIGHT

Matt topped a small rise. They were walking into the prevailing wind, making the climb harder than it should have been. The temperature was slightly below freezing, but with all the exertion, the suit was struggling to keep him cool. Sweat dripped off the end of his nose, to be sucked into the recycling system. He would be drinking it again soon enough. The wind was stronger at the top of the rise and the depressingly similar view hove in and out of focus through the driving snow.

The route they followed was pre-calculated. Without the surface survey recorded by the ship in orbit, they'd be lost, with no idea where they were, or where to go. The telemetry told him they had covered about a third of the distance. The days were short, about 15 hours dawn to dusk. It was already starting to get dark.

He looked back at his crew. They bunched together, body language telegraphing dejection. He straightened his own posture. They were looking to him for leadership and he had to show it.

The terrain had seemed easy enough to start with, but the nature of low rolling hills and troughs soon began to tell on him. The suits were equipped with integral muscle power systems, IMPS; powered exoskeletons that took up some of the strain. Consequently, the first few hummocks had felt deceptively easy, especially in the two-thirds gravity and low atmospheric pressure, but now his calves were aching and he was breathing heavily.

Behind the humans, the four MARRVs were arranged in a rectangle around a jerry-rigged sledge laden with everything they thought they might need. Oxygen, food and water, the hab-tent and weapons. They had cobbled the sledge together using floor panels and seat frames for skids. It had been difficult work in the tight confines of the crashed shuttle. The flat tops of the drones had been similarly laden. Panels stripped from the inside of the shuttle cabin had been tied to them using straps, so they looked a bit like mobile tabletops loaded with supplies. Kaemon's knife, with its almost magical cutting ability, had proven useful. Finally, they had ripped out the webbing that had covered the walls and fixed it like a net over the top of both the drones and the sledge to hold everything in place. The MARRVs put Matt in mind of an ancient image he had once seen of Sherpas, trudging up the side of a mountain path on Earth, heavily laden with oversized packs for their clients.

They had set off at dawn, following a last meal in the relative comfort of the pressurised cabin. At the top of the first hill, he had taken one last look at the abandoned shuttle, an angular grey shape, slightly darker than the leaden sky, barely visible through snow flurries.

Breel detached herself from the others to join him.

"Getting dark," she said. "We should be looking to stop soon."

"Yeah." Matt pointed to a hollow at the bottom of a pressure ridge, the start of a series of such ridges, marching into the distance. "That looks like a good spot. It will give us some shelter from the wind."

He switched to a private frequency that only Breel could hear.

"How do you think we're doing?"

She responded using the same private link. "Not thinking much beyond putting one foot in front of the other. The only unknown is Abiel. She seems stoic. Maybe it's her faith, but she isn't complaining."

"Her leg must hurt like hell."

"This terrain is killing us all. I think two days, one night, was optimistic. Three days, two nights is more like it, especially given the short days."

Matt looked about the darkening landscape. "Yeah, I think you're right."

"What about you? How are you doing?" she asked him.

He met her eyes, catching his own haunted reflection in her face plate. He shook his head and switched back to the open channel.

"Come on guys, we'll camp over there. Give us a break out of these Jinx-damned suits."

Abiel squeezed into the cramped confines of the hab-tent, finding space to sit between Kaemon and Ellyella. On the other side, which wasn't very far, Breel tapped at a small screen set into a portable enviro-unit. She watched the interface for a few moments, then took a look around the tent. The tent walls collapsed inwards slightly as the moon's poisonous atmosphere was sucked out and then bulged when an atmosphere they could breathe replaced it at a higher pressure. Breel looked back at the unit, then, apparently satisfied, she twisted her helmet free and pulled it over her head. She ran a hand through her short hair.

Abiel followed her lead. Cool air against her cheeks felt great after hours in the confines of the spacesuit. She took in a cold breath. There was a faint residue of the moon's acidic atmosphere overlying the smell of factory-new plastic, but as the others removed their helmets the air was contaminated by the less pleasant odour of sweat and unwashed bodies.

The interior of the tent was about big enough to accommodate the crew, the enviro-unit, and enough rations to see them through the night. The MARRVs wouldn't fit but would be fine outside as long as their power cells remained operational. They would last much longer than their human masters, especially if the alien complex turned out to be less hospitable than they hoped. The small robots were also sentries, on the lookout for local life, which so far, had proven less than friendly. She didn't like to think what that bode for whatever was at their destination and apparently waiting for them.

The tent had a small, human-sized annex with a zip door, which would give them some scant privacy to empty the suit bladders into sealable bags, something they would all have to do. The suits recycled about ninety percent of their fluids, but solid waste had to be disposed of manually. The filtration system did a good job of removing fluids from that also, so that the remains were desiccated and dry, but nonetheless, the air was about to get even richer.

One by one, the group removed their helmets to reveal pale, stressed faces. Ellyella emptied water from a container into a small thermal tank. "Who's for a hot drink?" She waved a plastic mug with enthusiasm.

Matt looked in her direction but quickly looked away. Something lay unresolved between them. Abiel could see it in their strained interactions. The captain looked haggard and was increasingly withdrawn. Abiel suspected he felt guilty for bringing them to this almost certainly fatal situation.

"I'll take one," Kaemon said through his default scowl. He did seem better now they were actually doing something; waiting was clearly not his strong suit. He was on his knees pushing his hand against the ground sheet, trying to flatten a bump. When that didn't work, he swore and punched it a couple of times, until, apparently satisfied, he sat.

"Probably a good idea not to punch a hole in the tent," Breel scowled at Kaemon.

The Deacon squashed in next to Kaemon. The traitor, clearly out of his element, but she had to admit that, given his privileged background, he bore his misfortunes well. *With the stoicism of the faithful* she thought ironically.

And then there was Breel. Something of an enigma. She didn't really fit into the group and Abiel wasn't sure how she had come to be here. She certainly didn't look like a symbiont pilot. All those Abiel had met were emaciated, physically weak individuals, and Breel lacked the long glowing hair-like interface that was their trademark. The right side of her body and face was decorated with an intricate filigree of tattoos. They were beautiful. Abiel had never seen anything quite like them.

The others looked to Breel more and more for the leadership Matt was failing to supply.

And Abiel herself? Her idea of possibly sabotaging the ship had come to nothing. She hadn't had the opportunity. Although outwardly everyone but Kaemon had seemed friendly towards her, they were all still wary. Matt had restricted her movements to the med-bay – her cabin since there was nowhere else for her to bunk – and the galley. Someone was always watching her to make sure she complied. When she had learned of the trip down here, she had wondered about sabotaging the shuttle. On the one occasion she had gone down to the garage bay, however, Kaemon had already been there. After that he had watched her like a hawk, making it his mission.

The first day of this trek had felt like a metaphor for her state of mind, lost in limbo with an uncertain destination.

She released the catches of her boot and pulled it off to examine the prosthetic and the stump, eliciting a sharp intake of breath and noises of sympathy from the others.

Abiel looked around the group. She shrugged. "It will be worse before we get to where we are going." She rubbed at the sore red flesh.

"Bloody cold in here," Kaemon complained, his breath condensing, tangibly making his point. He pulled rations out of a container and handed them round. Abiel accepted hers. Once opened, a micro energy pulse would heat the food in a matter of seconds. The pouch was labelled beef stew. She pulled a face.

"Have you got something without meat?" she asked.

Kaemon looked at her. "You're kidding, right?"

Abiel saw that all the bags were labelled beef stew.

"Don't worry," Matt said. "I doubt any of these bags have been within a hundred light years of a live animal."

Abiel had to concede this was probably true. A warm, chemical scent of beef, onion, and tomato added itself to the increasingly complex olfactory nature of the air in the tent.

A cloud of steam obscured the Deacon as he pulled his bag apart and began eating greedily. He stopped abruptly, pain crossing his features.

"Give it time to cool, Deacon," Ellyella scolded.

"Space picnic," Kaemon said, shovelling a huge forkful into his mouth. "Fun."

"How far did we come?" Deacon asked the question generally, but he was looking at Matt.

Matt peered into the steaming contents of his bag. "About a third of the way I guess."

"So, one night in this tent was optimistic, two at least. Do we have enough supplies?"

"We've got plenty to get us there, Deacon," Kaemon said. The ground trembled and they all looked up from their food. "Assuming nothing else goes wrong."

Breel placed a hand on the quivering ground. "They're getting stronger and more frequent."

"If we do get to the complex, I hope there is something more than a ring-side seat as the moon tears itself apart," Kaemon said.

"One thing at a time, Kaemon. Let's get there first." Breel pulled her bag apart.

Abiel spooned a tentative first mouthful, chewed, then tucked in with gusto. She was starving.

"Looks like you have developed a taste for meat after all." Kaemon smiled.

"Burning around 5000 calories helps one establish priorities," Abiel said, stabbing another glistening grey lump.

"I've tasted worse, though." Breel was spooning her own food rapidly.

The tent was silent for a few minutes apart from the sounds of eating.

"What do you think is waiting for us, when we get to the complex?" Ellyella asked, breaking the silence.

"Who knows," Kaemon said, stirring the contents of his bag. "I've given up guessing."

"Something is waiting for us for sure. Is it going to help us or kill us?" Ellyella asked.

"Maybe it doesn't give a Frazz-damn if we live or die. If there is an *it* at all and we haven't just triggered some autonomous alarm system." Kaemon pulled a face, then looked at Ellyella. "Is there anything like salt?"

"Of course," Ellyella said, turning to search the packs. "Just hang on… no wait, silly me, I forgot to pack the condiments."

The Deacon said, "The ship's data core was compromised, and shortly afterwards an environment exactly suitable for us appeared in the complex. It's hard to think that something autonomous would be programmed to go to all that trouble."

"What are you suggesting?" Ellyella asked. "That there's something alive in there, something that's been waiting for us for millions of years?"

"And with our welfare at heart," Kaemon added.

"Waiting for something, anyway," the Deacon said. "As I suggested, an invitation."

"You've heard of the Desert Dew?" Kaemon asked, looking around at everyone. Blank stares answered his question. "Well, it's a plant, I forget where its native. Its leaves are like long funnels and at the bottom there's fast food for insects. Small animals too. The leaves have patterns, like billboards, in wavelengths that only insects can see…"

"Yeah," Breel said, "then they get digested by the plant. We get the metaphor."

"I hardly think anything in there wants to eat us." The Deacon smiled. "There is another plant that might replace your analogy, one that lures insects in, not to eat them, but to help it pollinate other plants.

74

The insects get a free meal for their trouble, so it might indeed have our wellbeing at heart."

"I don't that find that analogy any more encouraging," Ellyella said. "I'm not sure I want to be part of some kind of cosmic pollination."

"If it's interested in our wellbeing, we could do with some help right now," Matt said.

"Maybe its influence is limited in some way," Breel offered. She rubbed at her face, running her hand over the golden patterns scrolling up over her eye. Abiel watched her, fascinated. The pattern was extraordinary. Breel met her eyes.

"What?" she demanded.

"I was admiring your body art," the crusader said. "The shapes, they remind me of something. What do they represent?"

The company went silent.

"Did I ask something inappropriate?" Abiel looked around the cramped space, concerned. "If so…"

Breel shook her head. "It's a long story."

"It's the trillion-ton asteroid in the room, is what it is," Kaemon said.

Abiel looked at him quizzically.

Kaemon looked from her to Breel, then around the tent. "Just that we don't talk about it. We owe our lives to them, but we've never talked about what they might mean."

Breel shook her head and looked weary. "You want to do this now?"

"Information upon which to base a hypothesis is scant," the Deacon said.

"You must have thought about it though," Kaemon said to Breel. Then to the Deacon, "And you, especially, after all your tests. Anything you'd like to share?"

"This probably isn't the best time," Matt said. "We should get some rest."

Breel waved his objection down. "No, Matt, let's get it over with." She looked around the group. "For the record, I have no idea what any of this means. It was as much a shock to me as it was to the rest of you."

"You had no idea about that thing your dad had hidden in the basement for years?" Kaemon asked.

"I already said that." Breel was taking on some colour. "Are you calling me a liar?"

Kaemon raised both hands, palms towards Breel. "Just asking."

"If you want to throw some ideas about, feel free," she snapped, "but I'm not going to be interrogated by you."

Abiel said, "Sorry, can someone explain to me what you are talking about?"

"May I?" the Deacon asked Breel.

Breel waved her spoon, "Go ahead," she sighed. "Don't mind me."

"You know Breel's home world was Hope?" the Deacon asked Abiel.

"The Claimer home world," Abiel said. She looked across to Kaemon, remembering their conversation in the garage bay. "There was a campaign there recently. The world was Saved."

"Yes," the Deacon continued. "We were there. We went to Hope, before Second Light's invasion, because when signals began to emanate from the *RIP* something from the Claimer asteroid responded in a quantum entangled manner. We assumed there must be a link with the Derelict found by Breel's people decades before."

"You're referring to *the* Derelict," Abiel said. "The one that self-destructed?"

The Deacon nodded. "The same. The only intact artefact of the *Firsts* ever found. In fact, Breel's mother was the only survivor of the two crew members who boarded it."

"The other crew member was her father," Ellyella clarified.

"Tyler and Riva? Those people were your parents?" Abiel stared wide-eyed at Breel, who met her gaze briefly before looking away.

"Conspiracy theories abounded at the time that something was taken off the wreck," the Deacon went on. "The entangled signals emanating from something on Hope indicated there might be some truth to that."

"We had to be sure," Matt interjected. He stared at Breel as he said this. "And it was a foregone conclusion that the Church was going to investigate, so we didn't have a choice."

"To cut to the chase," Kaemon said, "we went there. Breel's dad – step-dad – another of *Windfall's* crew – that's the ship that found…"

"I'm aware," Abiel said.

"Well, Breel's step-dad, Falian, was the pilot of the salvage tug, the third member of the team, only he never went onboard. He waited for Tyler and Riva outside."

"Tyler and Riva were the only crew to go into the wreck," Ellyella added. "You probably know Breel's dad didn't make it out."

"Anyway," Kaemon continued, sounding slightly annoyed at the interruption to his flow, "Matt found Falian on Hope and persuaded him to give up an artefact that Breel's mother had taken off the wreck. It was in their basement, had been for years, ever since the encounter."

Breel, who had been staring at her food during this explanation, looked up and met Matt's eye. "That was the first I knew that my entire life had been a lie."

Matt held Breel's stare for a moment before returning his attention to his rations.

"Your boss," Kaemon continued, glaring at Abiel, "blew the shit out of Hope to get to the artefact, then invaded Allpoints, all with the intention of killing our pilot to strand us."

"But there was a miracle," Ellyella said, eyes shining. "Breel developed markings. Those markings," she indicated Breel's arm, "that hadn't been there before. She was able to pilot the ship, able to survive an attempt by the Emissary to kill her and so save us all."

"It wasn't just down to me," Breel said wearily. "Matt and Kaemon undid the Church sabotage. You," she pointed her spoon at Ellyella, "saved the entire ship from massive decompression. Something pretty miraculous in itself. We'd all be dead without you."

"Yes, but without your augmentation, we wouldn't even have got that far."

"So, something was smuggled off the Derelict, but what has that to do with Breel and the tattoos?" Abiel asked.

There was silence. Finally, the Deacon said, "We found a recording, hidden in the artefact, relating an account of what happened to Tyler and Riva after they entered the wreck. They triggered something. Something that ended in the creation of a baby girl."

Abiel's jaw dropped. "*Excuse* me? *What*? Created her?" She pointed at Breel. "So, you aren't... human?" After a moment of total silence Abiel added, "Sorry, I didn't mean..."

"It's okay Abiel, you're only saying what they're thinking."

"I've never said that," Deacon protested. "I know nothing of the technology involved, but you are the result of a scan of your parent's DNA. You bear the same resemblance physically and mentally that you would, had you been conceived in the more conventional manner. Medical tests confirm that you are human down to a cellular level. You are, by any metric we have… human."

"Identical in every way but one," Breel muttered.

"You are human in every way that matters, Breel," Ellyella said. "I'm sorry I brought the subject up."

Breel waved the apology away. "No, El, don't apologise. This conversation was way overdue." She put down the remains of her food, cold now.

"You need to eat that," Matt said. "You'll need the energy tomorrow."

"For some reason, I've lost my appetite." Breel pushed the package away.

"Okay." Matt put his own empty ration container into a bag they had designated for waste. "We have a long way to go tomorrow. I suggest we do what we need to do to make ourselves comfortable," he said, indicating the annex, "then get some sleep."

No one disagreed.

Breel stared up at the ribbed roof of the hab-tent. She wasn't sure who else was asleep, apart from Kaemon, who communicated the fact noisily. She had fallen asleep almost as soon as her eyes closed, exhausted by the stress and the day's exertions, but had woken only an hour or so later, the last conversation still whirring through her head. She didn't resent the exchange. It had been so easy to put the unanswered questions left by her mother's recording to the back of her mind, survival being their imperative. But now she was reminded that her perceived reality was like thin ice over a dark and dangerous lake, ice that might give way at any moment to plunge her into unknown, terrifying depths. She instinctively tried to curl into a more protective position at the thought, but her suit made that impossible. The suits were uncomfortable to sleep in, but it was too dangerous not to, given that they were all that lay between them and a freezing, suffocating death should some calamity befall the tent. They had elected to sleep without helmets for some slight extra comfort, but mainly to conserve suit power. All had an arm or hand resting on them, ready.

Crammed together, it was now uncomfortably warm, what with the heated food packs, hot drinks and body heat. Sweat beaded her forehead. If one of them shuffled, in sleep or discomfort, everyone else had to accommodate the new position. The smell from the annex was making her gag.

Their situation was ridiculous, untenable, but there was nothing else for it. Make it to the alien complex in expectation of some kind of deliverance. That was all there was. She thought of her life on Hope. Life on the Beach, the struggle to earn money for her dad to cure his otherwise terminal medical condition, with the thought that she might make enough extra cash to escape the planetoid; to travel the thousand-light-year sphere of human occupied space. She had so wanted to leave Hope and its insular, parochial people; had harboured thoughts of becoming an expert on the *Firsts* and their fate.

Well, her wish had been granted: she was about to become one of the foremost experts, if she lived long enough. Pity she would never have the opportunity to share her insights.

If that wasn't enough to keep her awake, there was something else troubling her. Twice during the day, she had been aware of a presence and both times her body art had glowed faintly. She could feel it now, warming the inside of her suit, adding to her discomfort. Something was watching them; watching her, even now. She was sure of it.

A scratching noise outside made her sit up abruptly, heart hammering.

"What is it?" Ellyella hissed. Clearly not asleep either.

Breel strained to hear beyond the confines of the tent.

"Nothing," she said, settling back down. "Sorry."

Must have been the MARRVs she thought, *or they would have sounded an alarm.* She shuffled a little, then finally, to the soft keening of wind and sighing of snow sliding over the tent, she succumbed to sleep once more.

NINE

Breel woke stiff and sore the next morning, feeling like she had barely slept. The others looked as bad, all in various states of sleep deprivation. Only Abiel looked well rested and clear eyed. Breel watched the crusader with something approaching envy.

They ate, swapped out their oxygen canisters, then struggled to get their helmets and gear on in the confined space. The pile of empty oxygen bottles was a stark reminder of just how limited their survival potential was.

Once suited up, Breel shut down the enviro-unit and released the pressure inside the tent. It sagged inwards, as the atmospheric pressure inside and out equalised. Matt unsealed the flap and crawled out. Breel followed. One by one they left the tent and looked at a new day on the shepherd moon. The snow had stopped falling and the wind had dropped, the icy landscape lit by a sickly sun. The sky was relatively clear, tinged with green, but the most alien thing about it was the band of rubble the shepherd moon was embedded within, stretching at an angle from horizon to zenith, hazed to a greenish hue by the atmosphere.

The distant mountains were the clearest they'd been since their arrival. Twisted, tortured shapes rising and falling like a frozen tsunami sculpted in rock. The alien complex, their destination, lay invisible in swirling mist around the foothills, the space elevator pointing to it like the finger of a god.

The temperature had risen.

"If our suits fail," Matt observed wryly, "we'll only suffocate, not freeze."

Kaemon was last out, hauling the enviro-unit. Breel gave him a hand and together they strapped it to the sled. The others took down the hab-tent. When everything was secure, they trudged off again. Breel took a last look back as they crested the first summit of the sea of pressure ridges. The only evidence of their stay was a sealed bag surrounded by a pile of empty air cylinders, dark against shining ice. They had only just got here and already they were fouling the place up.

It was hard going at first. Breel was cold and her joints stiff, but she warmed up quickly. The suit chafed. It was supposed to self-clean, but there were limits, she supposed. She hated the idea that she might die in this state – a ridiculous thought given their more pressing issues.

They had camped at the base of a low rise, the start of a succession of pressure ridges that gradually rose higher and became more contorted, twisting into fantastic shapes. After an hour of clambering over increasingly difficult terrain, Breel was exhausted. Every now and again the ground trembled or shook to the point she had to stop walking and wait for the tremor to pass. She looked around to see how the others were faring. The Deacon was clearly struggling. Ellyella and Abiel were supporting him even though Abiel was limping. Kaemon was helping keep the sled as level as possible as the MARRVs manoeuvred it around and over obstacles.

At the top of the next summit, Breel called out to the captain's retreating back, "Matt, we need to take a break."

He turned, looked at her and then at the rest of the crew who were making their way up the steep slope to join them.

"We have to keep moving, Breel. If we keep stopping, we'll never get there."

"We'll stop moving permanently if we all die of exhaustion," she snapped. She caught up to him. His features through the helmet faceplate shocked her. He looked haggard and exhausted. That in itself wasn't a surprise, they must all look like that, but there was something else: the wild look of a man reaching his limit.

"Fifteen minutes then," he said gruffly. He pointed to a rocky outcrop. "Over there will give us some shelter."

Huddled together in silence under the outcrop, the group surveyed the panorama. The shepherd moon following its eccentric orbit had dipped below the ecliptic. The sun had almost cleared the spiral of dust in which the moon was embedded and was able to radiate a little more heat onto the small world. The ice shone with a slick layer of moisture. Beyond the march of crumpled ice, the pale green sky faded down to orange at the horizon. Maybe the stain of gases leaking through rents in the planetoid's tortured crust.

"Kind of beautiful, actually," Breel said.

Kaemon was staring hard into the distance. "Those mountains don't look right."

"Yeah, they look almost artificial." Breel agreed.

"We'll see them better when we're closer," Matt said, pushing to his feet.

There were groans and cries of discontent.

"I know, I know, but we have to keep moving," Matt insisted. He began to walk down the slope to the narrow valley formed between the pressure ridge they were on and the next one in line.

After a while Breel pushed to her feet and the others reluctantly followed.

Matt blinked stinging sweat out of his eyes. How many ridges had he crested now? He didn't know. He had lost count. At the top of this one he took in another steep slope down, presaging another rise. The wind had picked up again. No longer in the lee of the hill, he was buffeted by powerful gusts, making him stagger. It had been over two hours since they broke camp. The undulating landscape was like an ocean flash frozen in the middle of a force ten gale.

His HUD lit up, superimposing warning dialogues over the view, indicating a myriad of potential suit failures

"Warning, integral temperature exceeding safety parameters," the suit bleated at him. *"High suit failure probability. Cooling time recommended."*

"Warning, integral temperature exceeding safety parameters…"

Irritated, Matt shut the audible warning off, although he could do nothing about the flashing red icons. What was the point in the Jinx-damn thing telling him what he already knew? What was he supposed to do about it? He shook his head to dislodge sweat. The suit's fans whirred into high gear and the whine of the IMPS rose in pitch as it tried to maintain balance on the slippery surface.

The others must be getting similar warnings.

"Matt!" Breel's said, proving him right. "We need to stop. It's senseless to keep going like this. The suits will fail, Matt!"

"We'll die if we stop," Matt ground out. "We have to keep going…"

"Captain," Kaemon this time. "Breel's right. The suits are overheating."

"No." Matt shook his head. "We can make it. One big push and we can be there before the sun sets."

"Deshi-damn it, Matt," Breel said. "We'll broil, like claw fish in their shells."

In the rear display, Matt saw Breel detach from the group, speeding up in an attempt to catch him.

"Matt, wait!"

"Just over this rise," he said. "The ground will level out. I saw it from the last hill. The going will be easier."

He slid down the slope, went down on one knee. The suit berated him. Back to his feet he clawed his way to the next summit, into the wind once more. There he let out a whoop of victory and punched the air. They had reached the end of the chaotic terrain. One more slope down, then a flat plain, partially hidden by swirling spindrift, all the way to the alien city, or whatever the Jinxing-hell it was.

But there was something… slipping in and out of visibility. He squinted, trying to focus through the churning particles racing close to the surface.

Oh no, he thought. *Anything but that.*

He went down the final slope, dangerously fast. Once on the plain, out of the shelter of the troughs, the wind was relentless, resisting his efforts. He walked forward unsteadily, forced to lean into the breeze, then fell to his knees with a gasp of despair.

From the top of the last rise, Breel saw Matt drop, almost disappearing into the low spray. She followed his route down until she stood by his side. She leaned into the wind and looked out over a chasm that stretched from horizon to horizon. Too wide to jump, way too far to walk around. The ground trembled and small chunks of ice fell into the depths.

The others caught up and stared in horror. Matt slumped further forward, head down. Abiel and Kaemon walked to the edge and peered over.

"I'm sorry." Matt's voice was barely audible.

"We'll have to try walking around," the Deacon said. "We can do nothing else."

Matt's voice was flat. "We have no idea how far it stretches, Deacon. It might take days, weeks. We don't have enough air."

Kaemon walked along the great gash for a short distance.   He stood there for a few moments scrutinising its far side. Then he walked back to the group and spent some time staring into its interior before turning to Matt.

"Giving up, Captain?" he asked.

Matt didn't respond or raise his head.

"If you have something in mind, Kae," Breel said, "let's hear it."

He pointed down, past his boots into the blue-green depths. "Down there is a shelf that reduces the gap, enough that someone could jump across if they were to climb down."

He looked up at the group, staring back at him.

The Deacon and Ellyella peered down the slick ice walls, a drop apparently to infinity.

"If this is the end and we have to commit suicide," Ellyella said, "I vote we find a quicker, less traumatic way."

"I'm in no fit state to do anything like that," the Deacon said emphatically.

"What we need," Kaemon continued to muse, "is a volunteer to climb down with a rope, leap the gap, then climb back up the other side." He pointed to the spot he had just walked back from. "Over there the crevasse narrows. With someone on the other side holding a rope to make sure it doesn't fall in, it might be narrow enough for the sled to form a bridge."

"Can't we just push the raft from this side," Ellyella asked. "Tie a rope to it in case the gap is too wide?"

"We'd be taking a gamble," Kaemon said. "The raft is heavy. If it goes into the crevasse and we lose it, that'd be the end. Much safer to have a rope both ends."

"I guess you have a volunteer in mind," Breel said.

He walked over to the sled, rummaged about and came up with some spiky looking pieces of metal. He sat on the box he had fished the objects from, lifting one foot onto the other knee and proceeded to strap a crampon onto his boot. When he had done the same to the other boot, he waddled back to Breel, holding a coil of rope in one hand and two ice axes in the other.

"Fortunately," he said, "in my youth, I used to climb ice for fun."

*

The last time he had done something like this, for fun, he had not been wearing a space suit that was at least half his body weight again. True, the weight was mitigated by the reduced gravity and his powered exoskeleton, but he had to factor in the lack of flexibility the armour imposed. He had also been about twenty years younger. He edged his heels out over the hazy blue drop and wondered if this wasn't one of his worse ideas, which would have been impressive, given the competition for that particular accolade was fierce. He gripped the rope tightly.

"Keep the rope taut," he said to Breel.

Breel sat on the ice a short distance away, heels dug in, hazed by spindrift. The rope ran into a carabiner at her waist. She raised a thumb. Abiel and the others clustered around her, holding on to her to make sure she didn't slip. Matt had been non-committal about the plan. He had joined the group to help, but he seemed to be just going through the motions. Kaemon had never seen the captain lose heart this way. It wasn't like him. It made Kaemon uneasy.

"Ready when you are," Breel said.

"Right then." He lowered one foot, then drove the spikes sticking out the front of his crampons into the ice. Then the other, stepping down until he was low enough to bring the ice axes into play. Breel fed the rope out as he went until he was finally out of the wind and all he could see was the wall of frozen water inches in front of his face plate. He continued down steadily, so as to give the suit a chance to keep cool. Each move was accompanied by the whine of the exoskeleton, but despite its help, his calves and arms soon ached.

He paused to recover. The narrow shelf was about half his height below him now.

"You okay?" Breel asked. He felt the rope tighten as she took up the slack caused by his unannounced halt.

"Sure, Breel. Sorry. Just taking a rest."

He resumed the climb down and was soon standing on the shelf of ice. Carefully he shuffled a hundred and eighty degrees until he was looking over the drop towards the other side. The sun was behind him and the wall he had just climbed down cast the other side in shadow. It was about four paces to the edge. On the far side there was a similar shelf, jutting out over the drop. That there had been an ice bridge here at one time was clear, now long gone. The jump across looked a lot further from this vantage point.

"Breel, let me have some slack," he said. "I'm going for it."

The rope coiled about his boots. Without the security of the taut rope, he suddenly felt vulnerable.

"Okay, going now."

He pulled his crampon spikes out of the ground, tapped them with his axe to clear them of ice, then took a deep breath. He squashed back against the wall to give himself maximum distance, took three long strides, then leapt across the void as hard as he could. He landed cleanly on the far side, crampons digging in to the opposing ledge. For a second, he felt safe, until the ledge of ice began to break away under his weight. With a cry he lunged with both axes, digging them into the wall before him. The ice under his boots cracked and fell away leaving him hanging, his arms taking his full weight, feet scrabbling, sending a man-made snow shower into the abyss. He swung his feet out, pivoting on the ice axes, praying they would hold. The swing back hammered both crampon tips on the end of his boots into the chasm wall.

Trembling with both exertion and fear, he looked down. The remains of the ledge and the ice he had dislodged were still visible, still falling. He looked away, taking a moment to compose himself.

"I'm across," he informed Breel calmly. "Take the rope in."

He felt it tighten.

He looked up at the sky, sparkling with ice particles driven across the divide by the relentless breeze. The wall he clung to was in shadow, but the top was bright with sunlight.

"Climbing," he announced.

He moved his right foot up and into the ice, then his right axe. If he fell now, the rope would stop him plunging to his death but he would pendulum back across the chasm, into the wall he had just climbed down and possibly inflict terminal damage to his suit. Even if it didn't, the remains of the ice bridge that had made his leap possible was gone.

"Best not fall then," he muttered to himself.

"Did you say something?" Breel asked sharply.

"Just some self-motivation," he said. "Climbing," he repeated.

His calves and biceps ached from the unaccustomed exercise. About halfway up, his shadow cast on the ice as he moved into sunlight. He felt his spirits lift, but the warm light and slightly higher temperature presented a new problem. The ice here was softer, so that the axes and crampon points were less secure. When he put his weight on them, they began to slide out.

He brought both his feet together and rested a moment. Above was a slight overhang and he was forced to lean back, out over the drop, to assess his next move. To the right of the overhang was a small fist-sized protrusion. If he could reach that, he would be able to pull up and get his foot on a narrow ledge, which would lead to another hold on the left and then easier holds and ledges all the way to the top. Time for some technical rock climbing.

"Tight rope, Breel," he said, more for the psychological security it gave him than anything else.

He felt the rope tighten as Breel pulled in the slack.

He focused, tensed, then launched himself for the hold.

At that moment the tremor struck and a second later he heard Matt shout a warning. His hand wrapped around the protrusion, but the shaking ice shook him free. He yawed out over the drop, only his left axe and left foot in the wall. He felt the axe give. Desperately he swung back, hammering his right axe in as hard as he could, then his right crampon. The entire crevasse shuddered and vibrated. He tucked his head in, trying to make himself as small a target as possible. Something slammed into his shoulder, bounced off, followed by another. One of his feet came lose. He smashed its forward spikes back into the ice. The wall split directly in front of his face, the two halves moving away from each other. He was being stretched apart, on a medieval torture rack made of moving solid water. He shouted an incoherent scream of rage at the universe. The gap between his feet widened until he was sure they were going to rip free and he would pendulum back across the chasm.

And then the world steadied, the tremors subsided.

He was left spread-eagled, eyes tightly shut.

"Kaemon?" Breel's anxious voice sounded in his helmet.

He let out a long breath. "I'm okay," he said.

He opened his eyes and surveyed the new topography the tremor had created. Ironically the split afforded him better hand and foot holds. He moved into a more secure position. *Every cloud*, he thought.

"I think it's over," Breel said.

A movement below caught his eye. He peered down into the drop and with horror realised that Breel was wrong. It wasn't over at all.

TEN

"Tell me again," The Lord of Light said to *Transcendent Light's* chief scientist and his small retinue of assistants.

The Emissary and the scientist were gathered on the bridge of Second Light's flagship. Maliesh stood to the Emissary's right. Captain Hannathon observed from behind the group of boffins.

"As my Lord knows," the scientist began, head bowed, "before the insurgents' asteroid transited through the *RIP*, it was hit by a pulse from the Matrix Generator, breaking the asteroid apart. A large piece still lies trapped, neither here nor there. We can determine this from radiation still leaking back into our space."

"I thought there was no 'in-between'?"

"Indeed, my Lord." The scientist warmed to his theme as if discussing an interesting scientific problem with an old friend. "The asteroid fragment has been reduced to a quantum state. In effect, it lacks the energy to be one thing or the other. We believe that by pumping energy into the interstice we can collapse the rock's waveform, forcing it to 'be' once again, so to speak. The non-space between portals will be unable to contain it, which should allow access to the *RIP* once more."

"Believe – should?" the Emissary stared at the scientist, unblinking.

The scientist bowed his head, remembering who he was talking to. "Ah, yes. The outcome is uncertain, my Lord."

"How will we fly the Matrix Pulse Generator into this space between universes, if the *RIP* is no longer there?"

"The *RIP* is still there or we would not see radiation. A symbiont pilot in a shuttle will fly to specific coordinates and trigger the jump generator at precisely the right time and place. This should –" he caught his Messiah's eye, "*this will* – open enough of the rift to allow another Symp, who will be directing the MPG, to pump energy into the non-gap between universes. The asteroid's waveform will collapse and the resultant energy imbalance will blast it back into our universe, like a cork from a bottle. Once clear of the obstruction, the *RIP* will return to its former state. It will become a navigable portal once again and we will be able to follow the insurgents." The scientist nodded, looking into the middle distance, talking to himself now. "The timing will have to be impeccable. We are talking nanoseconds."

"And the pilot? What will happen to him?"

The scientist and his colleagues looked uncomfortable. "Well, we believe –" a sharp look from the Emissary made him say, "– he will be caught in an unprecedented blast of raw primordial energy. Unfortunately, it is difficult to see how he could survive."

"It will martyr him, make him one with the Light?" the Emissary asked.

"Indeed," the scientist said enthusiastically, "and we have four pilots on *Transcendent Light* and two more on each of the two support ships. So should our first attempt fail…"

The Emissary smiled, raising a hand. "Good. Make the necessary preparations."

"We are ready, your Grace," Maliesh said, bowing.

One of *Transcendent Light's* symbiont pilots stood before the Emissary, head down. Like all his kind, he was thin to the point of emaciation. The shining silver fibres that made up his symbiont interface hung from the back of his head, hair-thin snakes of light, slowly writhing as if independent of his will.

"What is your name, my child?" the Emissary asked.

"Barabb, my Lord," the man answered.

"Stand tall my son. A devotion so pure should not be cowed."

The man lifted his head, although he studiously did not meet his Messiah's eye.

The Emissary looked around the assembled crew in the large docking bay.

"Look upon this servant of the Light, for blessed will he be for his sacrifice today." He placed his hand on the thin bony shoulder of his disciple. "Would that we could all be so fortunate."

"My only wish is to serve the Light, my Lord and Master," Barabb said. "There is nothing else."

"Your devotion is true, my son. Your aura flares with the brilliance of galaxies. The Light will take you into its embrace and you will be as one with it. Your shine will never dim."

"His shine will never dim," chorused the gathering.

"You will burn with it for eternity," the Lord of Light continued.

"He will burn with it for eternity," the crowd chanted.

"Go now, to your destiny, with the strength and purity of the blessed." He pronounced it bless-ed.

The Emissary made the sign of the Circle of Light over the man's forehead, before placing the back of his hand to the pilot's lips.

"Thank you, my Lord, for this opportunity and for your blessing." Barabb kissed the hand, then stood to attention, clicking his heels together smartly, before turning and walking away.

The gathered crew followed, shuffling out in silence, heads bowed solemnly.

When the chamber was empty, apart from the elite guard who never left his side, the Emissary turned to look at his right-hand man.

"There is something you wish to say, Maliesh?"

"My Lord, if I may have a moment of your time?"

The Emissary sat down casually on a work bench, one foot on the deck, the other leg swinging. He stretched both arms behind his back, hands entwined, twisting his neck from side to side. "These formal events get ever more tiresome," he said. Then added. "But presentation is everything."

He looked quizzically at Maliesh.

Maliesh hesitated, then said, "My Lord, we have dallied here for three weeks now."

The Emissary nodded. "I have good temporal awareness, Maliesh and a calendar should that fail me. What's your point?"

"I do not wish to remind the Emissary of what he already knows, but we are incommunicado here. We have no idea what may be happening back home."

"I have sent word via the repeaters we stationed at each *RIP* as we passed through. News will arrive shortly."

"But my Lord, that will take weeks. We left behind many unresolved issues that could turn into serious situations if left unattended."

"You think that some petty insurrection on the Saved worlds is more important than what we are dealing with here?" The Emissary smiled.

"Not just the insurgents, my Lord. You know there is resentment at your sudden rise to power that was not entirely dealt with. It is still smouldering. I fear without your Grace's presence, that resentment might flare once more."

The Emissary sighed. "Maliesh, our destiny is within our grasp. Once through the *RIP* we will be able to unshackle the Light. It will pour into the universe and cleanse it. Any smouldering that might flare will be extinguished in a microsecond."

"I know, my Lord, but…" and here Maliesh struggled to find the right words. "If things do not go as planned…"

The Emissary's features hardened. "Do you doubt my Vision Maliesh? Are you losing your faith, my friend?"

"No, no, of course not," Maliesh stammered. "But you have tasked me with dealing with worldly matters, my Liege, to leave you free to do the Light's work. I am merely trying to fulfil my duties."

The Emissary moved until his face was inches from his subordinate's. Maliesh stood his ground.

"Hear me. There is nothing more important than what we are doing here. It is our life's work, about to be accomplished. Our destiny fulfilled. Your duty, your only duty, is to enable me to do that." He moved until their lips almost touched. "Do you understand?"

Maliesh took a step back and bowed his head. "Your Grace."

"Good. Let us see to our Martyr's needs then. There is still much to do."

The Emissary turned and swept away, back to his quarters, followed by his security guard.

Maliesh let out the breath he had been holding and watched them go, trembling. It was a long time before he moved.

ELEVEN

Breel, holding on to the rope attached to Kaemon was unable to move herself. She watched Matt run to the edge of the chasm and peer over the lip. Abiel was running to join him when Matt stepped back sharply. He spun and waved at her frantically.

"Don't," he shouted. "Stay back, Abiel..."

Abiel stopped uncertainly. Something was moving at the edge of the crevasse, shadows... Then the air exploded into a meshing, whirring swirl of chaos. Hundreds of winged creatures, similar to the one that had brought down the shuttle, geysered up into the pallid green sky.

"Down," Matt commanded, dropping to the ice, but Abiel was already down, hands over her head. Breel curled herself over the rope that connected her to Kaemon. The Deacon and Ellyella in turn dropped over her. She twisted her head up to get a view of what was happening. A tornado comprised of dark alien shapes was twisting out of the chasm, obscuring the sky, the air filled with deafening roaring, chittering, and whirring. Matt and Abiel were dwarfed by the melee, lost in an ice storm generated by thousands of buzzing wings.

The aliens swirled, seemingly chaotic and panicked. They crashed into each other and the canyon, shattering pieces off the edge to send more lumps raining down. *But*, she thought, *not just chaotic.* It looked like they were attacking each other, even in the midst of what she assumed was an attempt to escape the quake. Now focused, she saw that there were differences, in pattern and shape, almost as if two teams were competing as they rose, biting and slashing, scattering alien body parts and spattering the ice with white fluid. Fortunately, they seemed too preoccupied with each other to pay attention to the huddle of humans.

Finally, the numbers thinned, and then they were gone.

Breel sat up, watching the glittering cloud vanish. Around her, chunks of ice and bits of the creatures themselves littered the ground.

"Kaemon, are you ok?" she shouted into the sudden silence.

The alien exodus battered Kaemon. Desperately, he pressed against the ice cliff. Several times the creatures crashed into him, but they were lighter than they looked. The impacts were much less severe than he would have expected. In fact, the collisions were causing more damage to the aliens, snapping off body parts that dropped spinning into the rising mass below. He was jostled and knocked about but managed to keep his grip. His biggest fear was that the razor-sharp edges of the alien chitin, not to mention the claws, might rip or puncture his suit.

The aliens were biting and slashing at one another. *They're fighting.* Two of the embattled creatures thumped into the ice an arm's-length away. The wind from their frenetic wing beats blasted at him, threatening to dislodge him. The creatures clawed and slashed viciously until the outer one pushed away from the wall, imparting a bite as it left that severed one wing of its opponent. The victor pushed away to rejoin the exodus, slashing at a new adversary as it went.

Its victim held on to the ice wall using fearsome claws on its four feet. The remaining wing ceased its movement and hung uselessly. The lost wing had been bitten away below the shoulder joint, if that was an accurate description of such an unearthly anatomy. The fresh wound leaked white ichor freely, spattering the bird-thing and the cliff it clung to. Kaemon could see that its whole body was a cross-hatch of scars, a history of past battles etched into its outer casing.

It shook its head, as if dazed, and then seemed to notice the human hanging a mere wing span away. Deep pits that may have housed eyes fixed on him. The head split, revealing a mass of meshing spikes. It lunged. Without thinking Kaemon pulled the right-hand ice axe out of the wall, swinging to meet the alien head. The impact dislodged him, leaving him hanging from one arm, fully outstretched, hand slipping to the end of the left-hand axe that was taking all his weight, but Kaemon's blow had been perfectly timed. The axe crunched into the thing's skull, spinning it out into the rising mass, where it was instantly torn to shreds by others of its kind. He hammered the axe back into the ice and then his boots, then hunched and cowered. Finally, the monsters thinned until there were only a few stragglers left. They bit and clawed at each other on their way up.

The rest had all ignored him, too preoccupied with each other. All but one, the last one, whose black eye pits seemed to focus on him. The thing slowed and then hovered like some monstrous hummingbird, only a metre or so away. The downdraft from the wing beats pushed Kaemon into the cliff. He tensed, preparing for another attack. The alien continued its scrutiny for a few seconds, its frenetic wingbeats slowing so that the wings were almost visible, then they blurred into invisibility again. He followed its upward trajectory towards the receding cloud of unearthly avians painting the sky black until they vanished from view and the sky reverted to a washed out green.

Breel's anxious question came to him.

He exhaled, long and hard. "Yeah, still here."

He made it fast up the remainder of the climb fast, despite the suits overheating protestations. He didn't want to spend any more time down here. He would let it cool once he was out of this hell hole. Finally, he dragged himself over the edge, into the low light of the setting sun to the sound of cheers and whoops. He turned and sat, buffeted by the breeze, staring at the silhouettes of the others on the far side of the crevasse, casting long shadows towards him.

He waved feebly. They all waved back frantically.

"Should've just pushed it from your side," he said.

Breel rose from her seated position, holding on to the rope that connected the two of them. She gave him a thumbs up, then looked towards the crepuscular horizon. Kaemon followed her gaze towards where the chasm narrowed. The sledge lay on the far side from him, unloaded and ready to be pushed and hauled across the gap to form the bridge.

The sun was gilding low mist with fire.

In the mist, things moved.

"Don't get comfortable," she said, sounding utterly exhausted, "we're not done yet."

TWELVE

In the thrall of the symbiont interface, Barabb was at peace, as much as he ever could be. He was as one with his vehicle, an elemental creature of space, accelerating furiously away from *Transcendent Light*. He switched his awareness through multiple wavelengths of the electromagnetic spectrum, the universe changing colour and aspect with each iteration. The colours he saw were artificial, designed to pick out detail in the particular wavelength he was using. They didn't represent 'real' colours, if that was even a concept that could be applied to what he was looking at. Now, viewing in the longest wavelength, he could just see a faint purple smudge. Unreal radiation leaking back through the *RIP* the insurgents thought they had closed. It wasn't the clean flow he would normally see. It sputtered, came in bursts. The portal was on a knife edge. It might cease to be at any moment.

He had been eager to volunteer for this trip. This was his time, his chance not only to serve his Messiah, but to meet divinity face to face. He had navigated through the mysterious portals many times and each time he hoped for a glimpse of something beyond, to see the inner workings of the universe, to finally gaze upon the glories of the Light itself. But he had never been so blessed.

He knew the other pilots felt the same. Some indeed made incredible claims, to have seen and actually communed with the Light, but Barabb wasn't sure their accounts could be trusted. To be so desperate to prove something that could not be corroborated smacked of an inner inadequacy, a need to prove themselves chosen in some way above their brothers.

He didn't care about any of that, didn't care how others saw him, didn't feel the need to prove any entitlement. All anyone could hope for was to have the experience themselves, and this time, in these unusual circumstances he hoped the Light would bequeath his desire. The Light would surely have to see his sacrifice, not only this one, but all the sacrifices he had made throughout his life and he would be taken unto it. Finally, he would be where he truly belonged, able to glory amongst the pure energy and light that drove the universe and leave the petty squabbles of lesser minds behind.

There were people, those with a lesser, stunted consciousness, that looked down upon the Symbionts. They called them derogatory names like wire-heads, snake-heads or symps. They shunned and feared them, even though, without Symbiont pilots, there wouldn't be star travel. The pilots outside of the faith tended to burn out, become hollow husks, little better than junkies. They deserved the approbation they got. But within the Church, symbiont pilots found inner strength through the divine and, he believed, made the faith stronger through their devotion.

He felt his essence thinning, spreading out into the cosmos. He became aware of the lattice-like structure of reality and, like rain drops on a multi-dimensional pond, he could see where the lattice was disturbed and bent by the minds around him. The soldiers and personnel on *Transcendent Light* were a bright cluster. There were two brighter sparks in amongst them, the other *Transcendent Light* pilot and the Emissary, with a third some distance away. This third was the symbiont pilot stationed on the MPG, waiting for Barabb to make his insertion. Four more, dimmer sparks, were pilots stationed on the other ships.

The brightest star of all was the Emissary.

The anomaly approached. The vast empty spaces between stars had become noisy, with a shifting restless texture. And now, even the lattice became granular, revealing another, even deeper underpinning of creation in what was surely an infinite regression. This was the ability peculiar to Symbionts. It made them unique. The technological apparatus of the ship's interface was merely a staging post through which his entire being expanded. A computer had brought him to this point, but a machine could never make the final transit. No machine or neural-core had ever become sentient and only sentience was able to interact with the universe. He knew without any doubt, with every fibre of his being, it was consciousness that made the universe real. The final arbiter was his own unique self. It was his observation that made the RIP actual, that made the transit possible.

His soul by another name, which the machines didn't and could never have.

An act of faith made concrete.

His mind found traction on the substrate of creation. The moment was almost upon him. The other pilot was tracking him, waiting, their souls linked through the fabric of reality. That was the only way the other pilot could know and so be able to trigger the weapon he was manning with the precise timing necessary.

Time stretched, seconds as long as minutes, then as long as hours. He had all the time in the multiverse to make his decision. The moment came, without his knowing how or why, a burning utter certainty, the thing that all pilots feared they might lose, came upon him. He activated the jump generator through his Symbiont interface. Any attempt to do so physically would be years too slow. Light blossomed around him. It was beautiful: pure white, writhing tendrils expanding from scintillating petals of raw energy. The energy of creation itself. *Oh, beautiful, beautiful Light.* And now a sound, for the first time while making a transit. The universe was *singing* to him.

A heavenly choir in tones so pure they speared his mind with their beauty. All his life he had waited for this moment. He opened himself up to the divine, his sense of self shredding, thinning, dissipating. *Take my soul, take my soul, take my so*

The Emissary and his scientists had been watching events unfold. The shuttle Barabb was piloting had dwindled until it was no longer visible. Mere seconds had passed before there was a blossoming, burning brilliance. They had all raised their hands to cover their eyes.

When his vision had returned, the Emissary realised the light had come from the MPG. Through burning dots on his retina, he could see the weapon's heat radiators glowing as they cooled. The universe seemed unchanged, but that was to be expected. Only Symps could see unreal radiation from an open *RIP.*

The scientist and his assistants were clustered around consoles, talking excitedly, stabbing at holo screens with their fingers, making this or that observation.

"And the result?" the Emissary asked, impatient.

The head scientist turned to look at him, "Ah, well, your Grace, it seems this time, regretfully, we were unsuccessful." The man said. "But we will –"

"What went wrong?"

"We are at the boundary of our understanding, my Lord. Some fine tuning may be required."

The Lord of Light put his beautiful golden face close to the man, who tried unsuccessfully not to flinch or draw back. The scientist looked to Maliesh who stood impassive to one side, then back to the Emissary.

"We have neither the time nor an unlimited number of martyrs," the Emissary hissed, pushing a sharp fingernail into the man's chest, making him wince. "This is your plan, your responsibility. The consequences of failure will be yours also. Make sure you have 'fine-tuned' your calculations next time, or you will be experiencing the boundaries of your understanding first hand."

He turned and swept from the room in a golden swirl.

THIRTEEN

The alarm from the MARRVs was a high-pitched scream, stabbing into Breel's dream. Her eyes snapped open to the sound of tearing fabric and plummeting temperatures. For a second, she was still in the nightmare, falling through the dark suffocating spaces of an ancient alien spacecraft; the same Deshi-damned nightmare that had plagued her most nights since boarding *Scavenger*. The gaping tear in the roof of the tent, and the view of the star-spattered night sky it gave her, plunged, her back into the present and galvanised her into action. The air in the tent condensed into foggy clouds as it poured out into the night, displaced by the moon's atmosphere, which froze her skin, stung and burned her eyes and throat. She gasped like a fish out of water, clamping her mouth shut so as not to breath any more of the toxic gas. Her lungs spasmed, her body demanding air. Eyes streaming, she felt blindly for her helmet. Her questing fingers bumped against the smooth curved surface. She groped to get her hands around it, then slammed it over her head. A final twist locked the headgear into place, dulling the sounds of destruction describing their imminent deaths. Oxygen automatically pumped into the suit when the helmet sealed. She spat out the metallic taste of the alien air, shaking her head, trying to clear her vision, wanting desperately to wipe her burning eyes, but unable to do so. She coughed to clear her airways and blinked rapidly until she could see again. Quickly, she looked around to check on the others. They had almost all managed to get their helmets on. Ellyella was helping the struggling Deacon.

Another tear and the tent all but disintegrated. Up onto her feet, she pushed her head and torso through the tattered fabric into the dark where a new nightmare presented. Hacking at the tent was something about the size of her head. It scurried on many legs, more than she wanted to count and was armed with razor sharp cutting surfaces. It paused, then twisted towards her. She roared a warning, punching at it instinctively, using all the power of her suit's exoskeleton. The creature exploded from the impact. Movement around the camp revealed more of them ripping through their belongings. Still more crested the small cliff the crew had camped beneath, flowing over the top like a glittering waterfall.

"What in Jinxing-hell?" Matt had joined her, ripping and pulling to get clear of the ruins of the tent. Together they extricated themselves, stamping and punching at the scavenging hoard. Breel landed another blow, feeling a satisfying shock travel up her arm as shards of alien flew in every direction. She wiped spattered fluid from her visor.

"More fragile than they look!" she shouted.

"Like the bird things!" Matt sent one flying with a well-placed kick.

"They're stealing our stuff!" Ellyella ran onto the ice and stamped down. She lifted her foot from shining ruins.

Abiel and the Deacon were next to join the fray. The Second Light warrior grabbed a container as it swept past. The centipede-like alien that had been carrying it was still attached to the bottom, so she brought it down hard onto the ground, crushing the bug. She tossed the box to Deacon.

"Secure this," she ordered.

A loud whirring *whoomp* made them all instinctively freeze, then crouch. Kaemon, last out, cursing vehemently, was firing his blunt-looking plasma gun at the cliff top, disintegrating an alien with each shot.

"Jinx's-sake, Kae!" Matt ducked to avoid a glowing bolt of energy.

Everyone grabbed for their precious rations as they disappeared into the dark, but the sea of creatures was overwhelming. Even the remains of the tent were being carried away.

The MARRVs defaulted to a self-defence protocol, as much protecting themselves as attacking the aliens, since the bugs seemed intent on dismantling them also.

"Deshi-damn it, we're losing it all." Breel grabbed at an oxygen bottle as it spun past, afloat on a racing tide of gleaming chitin.

Then the alien bug-things froze, mid-step in some cases. For a long second all that moved was the flapping remains of the tent. Then the bugs reanimated, scurrying away into the night, taking what they could with them. Dazed, Breel stared at the equally exhausted crew of *Scavenger*.

"What just happened? Where did they go?" Kaemon spun, gun at arm's-length, looking for a target, causing some of the crew who ended up in his line of fire to duck.

"Stop waving that thing around," Matt shouted. "You'll kill someone!" He had kept his own gun holstered, probably for that reason.

Kaemon lowered his hand. He checked the weapon.

"Only one shot left," he said.

And then something else crested the cliff. A single entity this time and it was big. A dark shape eclipsing the stars. It swayed, snake-like, slithering down to the foot of the cliff before rearing up. A long, serrated frill surrounded its head. The frill twisted and turned lazily, moving slowly as if to a private breeze. Eyes or sensors lost in deep black pits focused on each of them in turn, before centring on Breel. She felt a twist in her guts as it moved towards her. She wanted to turn and run, but her limbs refused to move. She was paralysed as it drew closer.

"Get down," The roar from Kaemon's gun, as he fired his last shot, snapped her out of her trance. The superheated bolt sizzled past her head, making a direct hit right below where a jaw might have been, if the alien had been so equipped. There was a bright flash, destroying her night vision. She tried to see through fading bright spots of light. The alien swayed, undamaged and apparently oblivious. The bolt shot off into the night sky, a rapidly settling ripple in the alien's skin, the only evidence of its passing.

"Kaemon, wait." Breel raised her hand. She felt warmth from the glowing designs adorning her body. She stepped forward slowly.

Matt grabbed her bicep, pulling her to a halt. "Breel, what're you doing?"

She shook herself free, holding her palm towards him before moving closer to the alien. The weird head – it reminded her of some exotic deep-sea creature – moved down until it was level with her eyes, inches from her face plate. The half voices whispered. She felt the same connection she had felt during the incursion in *Scavenger*.

We know each other, they seemed to say, *we are family.*

Abruptly the alien reared up, to cries of warning from the others. It swayed above Breel like a giant snake over a diminutive snake charmer, then twisted and turned to flow back up the cliff and was gone.

Breel gasped and staggered. Matt was at her side in an instant, offering support.

"Breel?"

She leaned on him a little, accepting the help.

"I'm fine."

"What was that?"

By now the others also clustered around her.

She shook her head. "I don't know," she whispered.

She pushed herself away from Matt then looked around at what was left of the camp. "How much did we lose?"

The question brought them all back to their immediate plight, and they surveyed the devastation left by the attack.

"Pretty much all of it," Kaemon said.

By the time they had taken stock the sky was already starting to brighten into predawn twilight. They gathered together everything the alien bugs had left behind. It was a pitifully small pile, consisting of a few canisters of oxygen, water, power cells, the ropes and some boxes of self-heating beef stew. Everything else had gone, including the sled: the life raft they had fought so hard to keep. After Kaemon's epic climb across the chasm, they had pushed and pulled the battered oblong of metal over the gap, successfully creating the bridge. Once across with all the supplies, they had pitched the hab-tent, crawled into it and promptly collapsed into sleep brought on by sheer exhaustion.

Matt stared at their destination. Through the early morning mist, the dark structure of the alien complex was still about a day's walk away. He looked back at their salvaged rations, then at the crew. "I reckon we've got enough air and power to get there." He began to organise the MARRVs, loading them up with supplies. "Everyone grab something to carry."

"We can't eat these rations through our suits," Deacon struggled to find a comfortable way to hold a box of food.

"No, but if we can get into a habitable environment in the complex, we will need them."

"Be nice if our unknown benefactor has laid on a welcoming banquet," Kaemon said.

"We'll know when we get there." Matt said.

The MARRVs loaded, he led the way, swinging an oxygen bottle in each hand.

The oxygen level indicator in her helmet HUD showed ten percent, the power cell that drove all the suit's environmental functions and the IMPS, almost depleted. The suit would soon be nothing more than a complex, expensive coffin.

They had reached the apron surrounding the alien structure, city, station, or whatever the Deshi-hell it was, and were walking past the gargantuan objects that littered it. Some were undoubtedly the rotted corpses of space ships and aircraft. They reminded Breel of the ships she used to dismantle on the Beach, back on Hope. The ships were surrounded by what almost certainly used to be maintenance machinery and service vehicles.

Back in its heyday this place must have been a major hub of some kind. Breel tried to imagine what it had been like when these craft were arriving and leaving, transporting their makers to even more exotic places, on errands and missions she might not even begin to comprehend.

Some of the objects littering this ancient, cracked plain defied explanation. They ranged from about the size of a small ground car to objects that would dwarf star-liners. Any one of them would be worth closer investigation – indeed, any one of them would keep a team of scientists busy for decades – but for the desperate crew of *Scavenger*, there was little time left.

The walk from the final camp had been uneventful and the terrain much more forgiving than at the start of the trek. The gusts that had battered them for so many kilometres had finally dropped. They were walking in the shadow of the mountains, but Breel had been watching the light from the rising sun slowly travel down the length of the beanstalk until now it caught the tops of the peaks, setting them alight with a fiery radiance.

"You know what I think those mountains are?" Kaemon said, breaking the silence. "I think they are the collapsed orbital ring that once connected to the elevators."

"Yes," Deacon agreed, his breathing laboured. "They look too uniform. The range goes all the way around the moon, so that would make sense. At some point the integrity of the structure was lost and it settled to the ground to be eroded and filled with ice."

"Astonishing," Ellyella said. "A whole alien world inside that thing, probably well preserved by the cold. Who knows what wonders are in there? Living accommodations, manufacturing, recreational spaces, museums, art galleries. It will never be explored. Such technology, it numbs the mind."

"Much good it did them," Abiel replied. "They denied the Light. Death and decay was their fate."

"Horse-shit," Kaemon said. "A billion years will do that to any civilisation. Nothing to do with denying your superstition."

"I think you should all save your air," Matt suggested. "You're going to need it shortly."

"But something is still here," Ellyella said, ignoring Matt. "We all saw – it wanted Breel. Isn't that right, Breel?"

"I've no idea what that was about," Breel said.

"It saved us from the scavengers," Ellyella insisted.

"I'm not sure it did," the Deacon said. "The aliens didn't seem interested in us. They were after our equipment. They were trying to dismantle the MARRVs, but they didn't attack us."

"We would have been as dead if we had lost all our supplies, though," Ellyella said. "What do you think Breel?"

"I'll tell you what I think," Breel said wearily. "I think my oxygen is down to ten percent and before long we will all be struggling to breathe, so... what Matt said."

"We're not going to die," Ellyella said brightly. "The Light has guided us here for a reason."

As if to confirm her words, the sun finally rose above the mountain summits, bathing the crew in blinding golden radiance. Moments later the light reached the alien complex itself, illuminating their final destination with a warm, rosy, early-morning glow.

When the sun had reached its zenith, they stopped to replace spent power cells and replenish oxygen, using up the last they had. They had only managed to save four oxygen cylinders from the marauding alien bugs, four cylinders that had to be shared between the six of them.

Breel was helping Matt top up his air when, at the summit of a low range of hills, she saw something move.

"It's been following us all morning," Matt said, following her eye-line.

"I know," Breel said. The air from the canister spent, she uncoupled it from Matt's backpack and dropped it to the ground.

They trudged on.

Now they had all but crossed the vast field of wreckage and the sun was dropping behind the other side of the curiously twisted mountains. The alien citadel stretched to the horizon in both directions. It climbed in fractal tiers, each level scrambling up onto the shoulders of the one below, until it reached the base of the elevator. From there the beanstalk rose, mind-numbing in scale, into air clearer than at any time since their arrival on the planetoid's surface. The cables that had looked as thin as cotton from a distance were massive constructions from this vantage point, defying logic or common sense as they ascended into the heavens. They became increasingly hazed blue-green as they receded, narrowing all the way, until they could no longer be seen beyond their vanishing point.

Breel's breathing had become laboured, the suit's movements stiffer. It would be dark soon. If they couldn't find a way in, this would be their last sunset. As if to emphasise this thought the sun dropped below the peaks, leaving them in dusky twilight once more. The HUD temperature readings dropped immediately. Although Breel couldn't physically feel the change, the plummeting numbers sent a chill through her.

Ahead, Matt climbed a steep slope, then stopped. The route, plotted from orbit and loaded into the suit nav, had taken them directly to this spot, the location where the habitable environment inside touched the outer walls. Breel halted next to him. They stared at an escarpment covered in dense, complex, swirling patterns. There wasn't a square centimetre free of them. At no point did they repeat, that she could see. Whether viewed close up or taken as a whole, they always conveyed a sense of design and order.

There was nothing to indicate this section of wall was in any way different from any other.

There was no sign of a way in.

The rest of the group drew alongside, ragged breathing sounding through their suit coms. A warning bleep drew Breel's attention to a flashing icon in the heads-up display.

"Replenish oxygen supply immediately."

This was followed by a high pitch twittering that was impossible to ignore or switch off.

"IMPS warning. Dangerously low energy cell. Detach or recharge."

"Any ideas?" Kaemon was pushing against the wall, feeling for a mechanism or maybe just hoping the wall would move aside. He looked at Matt. Matt looked at Breel.

"Why are you looking at me?" she said, "I only know as much as you do."

But she knew that wasn't true. She could feel the swirling icons painted on her body warming up. The voices in her head began to mutter. She ran her gloved fingers over the citadel wall, tracing the grooves and raised contours etched into the obsidian-like material. Out of the corner of her eye she saw the Deacon's movements become staccato, then freeze as his exoskeleton ran out of power. Ellyella put out a hand to steady him.

"Whatever you're doing," Ellyella wheezed, "make it quick."

Breel turned back to the wall. She pressed both palms against it then pressed the side of her helmet to it in the hope that something might transmit through. As if from an unimaginable distance the voices only she could hear muttered, becoming louder and more insistent each second. They suffused her being until there was nothing else.

She became detached, almost as if she were symbiotic. The sounds in her head became rhythmic, an atavistic tribal chant, sounding down unimaginable tracts of time and across the light years. She pressed and stroked the wall in ways she would not have been able to explain.

The wall shimmered.

With a gasp she jumped back. A section of it flickered, made some kind of visual twist that her mind failed to register properly and then was gone. The scarred and pitted ground stopped in a clean line where the barrier had been. Breel could see blowing snow bounce off something invisible.

Kaemon grabbed Deacon and helped Ellyella drag him inside.

"Wait," Breel said, still dazed, but Abiel and Matt were right behind the trio.

"For what?" Matt asked as he passed her.

Breel hesitated a second more, then followed. There was resistance. It felt as if she was pushing through an elastic membrane, and then she was across the threshold. She staggered a few steps until she regained her balance.

It was getting hard to breathe. Her suit was responding erratically. There was no time to check the composition of the atmosphere, to see if it was toxic or not. If they didn't get out of the suits, they were dead. But still she hesitated. The voices sounded in her head, reassuring her. Vision tunnelling, panic took hold. She grabbed either side of her helmet, twisted it off and took in a lungful of… air. Sweet breathable air. She took in several more, gulping it in.

"Give me a hand here," Kaemon shouted. His own helmet off, he was desperately trying to remove Ellyella's. Her suit had frozen, power gone. Through the face plate Breel could see her gasping, straining for oxygen that was no longer there. Breel stepped across to help, placing a gauntleted hand above Kaemon's on Ellyella's faceplate and the back of her helmet.

"Together," Kaemon said.

They both twisted. Between the two of them and the exoskeletons, they delivered enough force for the safety catches to break with a sharp snap. Ellyella's helmet came free, leaving Ellyella gasping and retching.

"We need to detach the IMPS," Matt said urgently. His hands moved over his suit.

Breel was already doing the same. A series of warning chimes and the suit's neural-core asking if she really meant to detach the power accessory, and then she stepped forward, leaving behind a skeletal sketch of herself rendered in exotic carbon filaments. Her movements stiffened. It was like taking away the power-steering in a ground car, but at least she could move.

Without IMPS support. Breel slumped to the ground. The others did the same. She looked at them. They were exhausted, battered suits spattered with dried, white alien gore. The MARRVs bobbed in the background.

Nobody had the energy to speak for several minutes. The only sound was that of laboured breathing.

"What did you do?" Matt finally asked Breel.

She shook her head. "I wish I knew."

"You did something similar on *Transcendent Light*," Deacon said. "When you disabled the locks in the brig. The voices again?"

Breel nodded.

"Extraordinary," Deacon said.

"Voices?" Matt asked.

"Another time," Breel said. Matt started to protest but Breel gave him a look that silenced him. They sat on a smooth floor of dull grey material. Faint light spilled in from the outside. The section of wall had not rematerialized. There was a smell, not unpleasant, like machine oil and spice. For a dizzy moment she was taken back to the Dismantler maintenance bays where she had spent half her adult life.

The ambient temperature was cool, but bearable. A few arm's-lengths away the poisonous atmosphere of the shepherd moon swirled, kept at bay by who-knew-what. If whatever had brought them here meant to keep them prisoner, the hostile environment outside would be as effective as any solid barrier. On the landing apron, the shattered spaceships had become gaunt angular silhouettes in the sun's afterglow.

She took in their surroundings. The battered crew were in a small semi-circular space. A short tunnel led into the base proper. She stared hard into it and had the sense of a vast, immeasurable area, but it was so gloomy she couldn't make out specific details.

"Well, we're in." Ellyella said. "And it looks like we'll be able to survive in here, for a while anyway. What now?"

"Maybe we should stay here for a while to recover," Matt said. "Eat some rations, get a few hours' sleep, if we can. If we blunder on into that," he waved at the chilling gloom, "in the state we're in…"

"Good idea," Kaemon agreed. "Pass the stew, Deak."

Abiel dropped the bundle she had been carrying. Several bottles rolled into view.

"This is all the water we have," she said. "With the suits out of power, we won't be recycling anymore."

They stared at the bottles in dismay.

"Okay," Breel said. "I think Matt's idea is a good one. We get some rest and then maybe we can figure something out when it's light."

"Works for me," Kaemon said, reaching for a ration pack. "On the bright side, the world will probably end before we run out of water."

FOURTEEN

A strong tremor shook Breel awake. Exhausted, she had slept through the night. Bright light slanted across the floor. The field of wreckage outside cast long shadows from the sun clearing the mountain peaks once more. As the tremor subsided, a section of one of the giant spaceship carcasses broke away, raising a cloud of ice as it struck the ground. The swirling ice battered silently against the mysterious, invisible boundary. Breel watched the scene through lidded eyes, reluctant to move, because she knew that when she did the aches and pains were going to be a bitch.

"A beautiful day."

Without moving her body, Breel twisted her head to see Ellyella standing to one side, lit from the waist up by early morning light.

With a groan, Breel pushed herself into a sitting position. There wasn't a part of her body that didn't ache. She twisted her neck side to side then looked around at the rest of the crew. Matt and Kaemon were still asleep, but Abiel and the Deacon were just waking.

"Could've used a bit more of that decent weather when we were walking." Breel rubbed her eyes, gummed together with sleep and fatigue. She reached across and gave Matt and Kaemon a shove in turn.

"Hey, sleepy heads," she said brightly. "Wakey, wakey, it's a brand-new day."

Both men groaned, pushing themselves up, screwing their eyes against the bright sunrise.

Kaemon shook his head. "I hate cheerful people in the mornings."

Breel felt the need to pee and it struck her that suits without power and recycling would present a new challenge. Leaving the others to wake she got stiffly to her feet and walked down the short tunnel connecting them to the base proper in search of privacy.

"Don't wander too far on your own," Matt shouted.

She raised a hand in acknowledgement without looking back. The interior of the base was moodily lit now and the temperature had risen. Light leaked in, or was being directed, to illuminate a succession of massive columns receding away and up as far as she could see, until the details merged into a grey-golden haze. All the surfaces were encrusted with the same kind of mesmerising patterns that covered the outside. She ran her hands over them, feeling the complex topography against her bare fingers for the first time. Close up she wasn't sure if they were carved designs or some kind of organic growth. The patterns were in layers, new growth over old, like barnacles encrusting an ancient wreck. If that were the case, the growth had ceased long ago. The topmost layer looked ancient with dust filling the grooves, pits and hollows. Some were clearly broken. Bits of it came away under her fingertips and she realised the floor was covered with broken pieces.

She continued down the tunnel, crunching detritus under her boots. Gradually she became aware of a sound, the last sound she expected to hear in here. Her heart picked up a pace and she quickened her step. She rounded the end of the tunnel and stood dumbfounded, hardly able to believe what she was seeing. A cascade of water flowed down a stepped slope into a rectangular pool a good fifty metres square.

"Father of Light." Abiel had followed. She gazed at the water, eyes wide.

Breel squatted to put her hand into the liquid. It was cold.

"Wait," Ellyella was behind Abiel. "We don't know what pathogens might be –"

A long drawn-out scream preceded Kaemon, completely naked, racing past and leaping high before splashing down into the water.

"– in there," Ellyella finished.

Kaemon surfaced a few metres away, treading water, "Holy shit, its cold," he shouted. "But wow, I don't think I've ever felt anything this good." He beamed at them happily. "What are you waiting for? Get in here!"

Breel and Abiel exchanged glances.

"What the hell," Breel said, pulling at the seams of her suit.

The cold water stung the sore chafed parts of her body, but it also cleared Breel's head. Kaemon had it right. After days in her spacesuit, it was glorious. Ellyella had run a diagnostic, despite it being too late to save them from exposure to anything toxic. The water checked out as sterile. There was unusual mineral and salt content, but nothing she could detect that would harm them. It would solve the drinking problem if they could contrive containers that the MARRVs could carry.

Abiel had hesitated before getting in. Her military survival training would have told her it was never wise to immerse serious open wounds, but it had been weeks and the nano-meds had done their job, accelerating the healing process. Although still sore, she and Ellyella deemed the leg injury was safe enough.

The pool varied in depth, from shallow enough to stand in, to depths unknown. Large metal plates or baffles hung into it from a low false ceiling. It wasn't clear what their purpose was, but they did offer privacy to those that wanted it. Not that anyone except the Deacon seemed bothered by the nudity. Breel moved away from them now, not for modesty's sake, but to simply have some time to herself. There was a baffle hanging almost in the middle of the pool. That would be far enough she decided.

Matt lay, water up to his chin, head against cool metal. He was on a shelf that jutted out from the baffle in the centre of the pool, just submerged enough for him to be under water. Eyes shut, he was trying to blank his mind, trying not to think about the events that had led them here or to what might lie ahead. As if from a great distance, he could hear the incongruous sound of splashing and human laughter.

Water rippled and sloshed up over his face and mouth. He opened his eyes and pushed his face clear of the fluid in time to see Breel rounding the dull metal barrier.

"Oh, sorry," she said, turning to go.

"Wait, Breel. Don't go."

She turned back to him, treading water, head just above the surface, wet hair plastered to and framing her face. He was shocked at her appearance. Her face was gaunt, cheekbones prominent, dark shadows under her eyes. She had lost weight, even though it had only been three days since the crash. *Was that all it had been?* He probably looked as bad to her. They simply hadn't taken in enough calories for the energy they had expended, or had enough sleep.

"If you want to be alone…" she said.

He reached for her, then changed his mind, letting his hand drop back into the water.

"No, I could use some company."

She sat on the same platform he lay on, by his side, then slid down into the water until she was up to her neck, body stretched out. They lay close on the cold metal, almost, but not quite touching. He could feel the heat of her body through the water. They lay, without speaking, listening to the playful sounds of the others.

"They seem oddly happy," he said finally.

"Relieved I would say. After what we've been through, who can blame them."

Matt nodded. "Hard to believe we made it."

"Even harder to believe that there really is a habitable environment in here," Breel said.

"Yeah, I saw the readouts, same as you, but I didn't really believe it either."

Breel said, "But here we are. I guess the odds fell in our favour."

Matt twisted his head to look at her. "Thanks to you."

"I'm so tired of hearing that," Breel snapped. "I'll say it one last time: it was a team effort."

"Well, up to a point, but you know there's more to it than that."

Breel stared into the water, as if an answer might lie in its depths. "Maybe," she said quietly. "I don't know what it's all about, Matt and I'm scared to find out. We can breathe in here, but I'm not sure if that's a good thing or not."

He moved his hand below the surface until it was touching hers.

"I'm sure the alternative would be worse," he said drily.

She looked at him. "How do you know?"

He stared into her eyes. "Whatever we find, Breel," he said emphatically, "you're not alone. We'll deal with it together."

Breel looked back into the water. After a moment she put her hand over his. Their fingers entwined.

"I'm just so done," she said, "I don't know if I have the energy left to deal with what might be coming."

Matt stretched out his legs, letting them float so his toes poked out of the water. "Well, we could just sit here, wait for the moon to explode I guess."

"Would that be such a bad idea? What's the point of going on? We're dead anyway, no matter what we find or what we do. What use will answers be at this point?"

"Something invaded *Scavenger,*" he said. "It can't be coincidence that this environment, so ideal for us, should appear straight after. There's something at the end of this trail and it's interested in you. Even if there isn't a way home, we might get some kind of closure, some explanation as to what's going on."

"Easy for you to say. I'm not sure it's closure I want." She laughed unexpectedly. "And the thought of getting back into those suits…" She shook her head. Her fringe, having grown long enough, fell over her eyes. Water ran down its length to fall as shining drops back into the pool. She pulled her hand away from his, causing their reflections to shatter.

"Did you love her?" she asked without looking up.

Taken aback at this sudden change of topic Matt said, "Who?"

"The girl. In the holo. In your cabin."

Matt put the back of his head against the cool metal slab. His cabin aboard *Scavenger* and the holo projection he had kept there of Masaleya came back to him. Jet-black hair flapping wildly in the wind of some far-off planet, Masaleya turned to smile at him, over and over again. A fleeting moment of preserved time, repeating forever.

"Yes," he said simply. "I would have sacrificed anything for her. In the end, I did sacrifice everything for her." He started to say more, then thought better of it.

"What happened to her?" Breel asked into the silence.

"The Church. I thought, I had hoped, that she was still alive, but I found out on Blue Haven, from Cavalacro, that I was wrong…" His voice trailed off.

She twisted her head to look at him from under her fringe. "I'm sorry."

Tentatively he lifted his hand and when she didn't react, stroked her fringe to one side, tracing his forefinger over the embossed design on her forehead.

"It seems like such a long time ago now and we are where we are." He took a breath, changing the subject back to the previous discussion. "You know we can't stop. This whole thing, your connection to it, we have to see it through."

"What, you think it's preordained or something?" She laughed. "Our destiny? You found your calling?"

He returned the laugh. "Well, that might be a bit strong." He pushed himself out of the water a little, turned to her, supporting his weight on one elbow. "But we keep beating impossible odds, so who knows, maybe we'll beat them again."

She met his eyes squarely. "If it's closure we're looking for, we don't have much time left."

"I've missed you, Breel," he said softly.

She nodded. "I know."

She pushed up out of the water so that she looked down on his prone figure. Rivulets of water traced the contours of her breasts and ran down the flat planes of her belly. Her skin bumped, raising small pale hairs on her arms and body so that she was outlined in gold by the overhead light.

"I guess we should make the most of the time we have." She sat astride him. "Seems I have a little energy to spare after all."

She pressed her lips onto his, moving her hips rhythmically. He responded, putting his hands around her narrow waist. Her body art lit, causing golden light to spark and rebound from the ripples radiating out from their movement.

Putting the suit back on hadn't been much fun, Matt had to admit. He pulled at it where it rubbed, but it would have been so much worse if he hadn't spent some time cleaning it. They had stripped away all the unnecessary tech – at least, all they could without specialised tools. The backpack was the heaviest part and it yielded some useful components, bladders and pressure vessels that could be repurposed as water carriers. The customisation made the suits much easier to walk in. In any case, they could never be used for their original purpose again. Then they had carried the suits to the water and scrubbed both the inner and outer garments.

With the suit back on Matt immediately began to sweat.

"These suits are Jinx-damned hot," he said, tugging at the neck ring.

"Pity we can't cut a few holes in them," Kaemon said. "They are compromised beyond any future use anyway."

"What happened to your knife?" Breel asked.

Kaemon shrugged. "Lost it."

Abiel stepped into the centre of the group. She looked at them all in turn.

"Something wrong, Abiel?" Matt asked.

Abiel reached into the folds of her suit and pulled something free, shaking away the tattered material that covered it. Thin, flat, black, reflecting dull highlights, about thirty centimetres long. Matt clenched his fists as he realised what it was. The crusader's face was suddenly under-lit by eerie green light. Abiel had activated the laser cutting edge of Kaemon's lethal hunting knife.

"Whoa!" Kaemon's plasma gun whined as he pulled it free from its holster. Matt put himself between Abiel and Kaemon, the palm of one hand raised toward the man, the other outstretched towards the crusader. He turned to the woman. "Abiel, give that to me."

She looked at them all and smiled thinly. "Why, what do you think I'm going to do with it?"

Breel stepped forward, hand outstretched.

"Please, Abiel," she said.

Abiel hesitated a moment. The green glow vanished. She flipped the knife, caught it by the blade and offered the handle to Breel with a small bow.

"There you go," she said, "it's all yours."

The tension eased.

"Where did that come from?" Matt demanded.

"Yeah, it's mine," Kaemon said.

"Why didn't you tell us you had this?" Breel raised the weapon.

Abiel turned to face her, folding her arms. "I saw the knife on the ground, after the raid on the tent. I felt it only fair that I should be armed, as you all are, but I suspected you would take the weapon away from me." She glanced at Kaemon, then sighed, relaxing her weight onto her good foot. "So I kept it to myself." She stared at them defiantly. "I didn't want a debate."

"Why tell us now?"

"You need something to customise the suits," Abiel said.

Breel tapped the blade against her palm, looking at Abiel speculatively. She looked to the others.

"Time for a bit of tailoring, then," she said.

They gathered all their remaining belongings and roped them together into bundles, placing the loads onto the MARRVs' flat tops before tying them into place. The machines used three of their six appendages to secure them more effectively. The drones looked like squat-headed porters from a bygone era.

"The MARRVs are down to fifty percent power," Kaemon informed Matt after an inspection.

He shrugged. "It'll do."

Matt surveyed the sorry-looking group. The one-time hi-tech space suits had been reduced to thick, ragged shorts and tee shirts, exposing their arms and legs. If anyone needed reminding of the finality of this journey, this was it.

Breel looked at Matt. He gave her a nod. She turned to Abiel and said, "You have a point about being unarmed in here." She held the blade up and offered it to Abiel, handle first. "Please talk to us next time, or we might think you have something to hide."

Abiel took the weapon meeting Breel's stare.

"Thank you," she said. She looked at Kaemon. He shrugged, saying nothing.

"Okay," said Matt, "If we are all done. Time to move on."

Breel came over to Matt and squeezed his hand briefly. He saw Ellyella and Kaemon exchange glances without comment.

With everything done that could be done, another tremor reminded them that time was short.

"Everyone ready?" He asked the assembled group. No one said they weren't. "Okay, then."

With Breel by his side, Matt led the way past the pool and into the interior, walking passed the discarded pieces of suit, crumpled on the ground like shucked skins.

He glanced back once, through the short tunnel to the entrance. The exoskeletons were six skeletal representations, dark against brightening daylight, memories of their passing made solid. They stood forlornly, as if awaiting their owners' return.

He turned away from the light and walked on into the shadows.

FIFTEEN

Great bars of slanting sunlight receded into the distance, made all the more visible by the dust they were disturbing. As the morning wore on and the sun rose, the angles of the beams of light became less acute, dividing the huge space they walked through with bright lines where they struck the floor. The deeper they moved into the alien structure the hotter it became. Matt and Breel led the way some distance ahead. Through silent mutual consent, Kaemon, the Deacon and Ellyella had fallen back to give them some space. Abiel brought up the rear. Kaemon figured it didn't really matter how far back she stayed; there was nowhere for her to go.

He adjusted the straps securing the load of one of the MARRVs that had become his wards, then looked around, at their surroundings. They walked down a canyon whose sides were made up of ominous dark hulks. He estimated the nearer ones stood at about twenty metres. Beyond them the structures increased in height until, for all he knew, the furthest away might be pillars supporting a vast ceiling, lost to haze and gloom some unknown height above. Every face and facet were covered with intricate designs. There wasn't a break anywhere he could see. He longed for a flat featureless panel, somewhere his eye could rest.

"You reckon these are machines of some kind?" Kaemon indicated the blocky structures. "I can't see doors or windows."

Ellyella surveyed the enigmatic architecture. "Impossible to tell what any of this is." She kicked little clouds of dust into the air with every step. The fine powder stuck to the sweat on Kaemon's face. He wiped at the gritty layer with the back of his hand.

"It's so hot and dry in here," Ellyella continued. She pulled at the hacked collar to get some airflow into the garment. "I can't imagine what it would have been like if Abiel hadn't salvaged the knife." She looked at the Deacon, who was waving a device of some kind in the air. "What are you doing?" she asked.

"I'm not sure," the priest replied. "Looking for something, anything, a power signature, a quantum anomaly, something to explain why we are walking in an atmosphere perfectly suited to us."

"Find anything?"

The Deacon shook his head. "The only anomaly is Breel. Every time her body-art lights up, the readings go off the scale."

"You're wasting your time," Ellyella asserted.

"I have some time to waste." The Deacon looked from his device to Ellyella. "I would have thought the scientific part of your mind would be interested in finding answers."

Ellyella shrugged. "Once maybe, but not now."

"Really," the Deacon said, intrigued. "Why? What's changed?"

Ellyella waved a hand at their surroundings. "You're missing the point. The physical objects all around us, they're superficial. You'll learn nothing from them. This is about the Light's Will and what it intends for humanity."

"How can you believe that crap, El?" Kaemon was unable to contain himself. "I'm surprised at you. We live in a time of technological marvels, of starships and faster than light travel, yet you want to believe in magic and fairytales."

"There's more to it," Ellyella said patiently. "More than science can explain. How do you account for the symbiont pilots?" She didn't give Kaemon time to respond before she continued. "You can't. Without them there wouldn't even be star travel and yet we have no idea how it works. Science can't build a computer that can do that job. It has to be a sentient biological organism. It's the act of observation that makes the RIPs real."

Although he had had this debate many times with different people, Kaemon felt uncomfortable arguing it with Ellyella. "It works. It's a real, repeatable thing, so it must have an explanation. We just haven't figured it out yet," he said.

"That sounds a lot like faith to me," Ellyella retorted.

Kaemon shook his head and looked at the Deacon for support.

"Ellyella's explanation may be an over-simplification," the Deacon said, "but in essence she is right. We have theories of course, sentience as an extension of the quantum nature of reality for example, but we haven't devised a way to measure it yet."

He directed his next question at Ellyella. "I'm curious. When did you have this dramatic epiphany?"

The group stepped out of shadow into one of the beams of sunlight. Ellyella's face simplified into bright and dark planes, her eyes pools of shadow.

"I've always been a follower, ever since Second Light saved me and my mother on Blue Haven." She walked a few more steps before continuing. "But it was that moment on *Scavenger*, when I faced eternity. That's when my faith crystallised into... into something unequivocal. I had been ready to join the Light, but instead I was reborn." She pointed to the device the Deacon held. "You don't need that. You have the answer. You said it yourself. Breel – Breel is the key. How else to explain it all? She wasn't even meant to be here and yet without her we would have fallen at the first hurdle. Each time we faced certain death, there was a new miracle to save us."

She gestured at the surroundings again. "The atmosphere we're breathing. The water pool when we needed it. The creature that saved us from the scavenging aliens and communed with her in some way... and without Breel, we would be frozen husks in the poisonous atmosphere outside, a hand's breadth from safety. No one else could have unlocked the base. The Light is directing, steering her to an unknown, maybe unknowable destiny." She looked resolutely ahead. "I don't worry about survival any longer. There is no doubt."

"Can you hear yourself, El? What happened to you?"

"You'll never understand," she snapped.

"Oh, I'm beginning to understand, all right," Kaemon said, thinking of the relationship he and Ellyella once had. That relationship had ended after Ellyella's near death experience aboard *Scavenger*, when she had sacrificed herself to save the ship and everyone aboard. Or so they had all thought at the time. Luck and quick thinking had saved her.

"What's your take on this, Deak?"

"That Breel is integral to what's happening here is in no doubt, but her actual role, that's hard to say. It's clear now though, that although we went to Hope to collect the artefact, it was Breel we were really looking for. The artefact, amazing multi-dimensional object though it is, is merely a communication device, an amplifier at best. If we had come away with that alone, which was our original intention, things would have worked out very differently."

"Matt was going to leave Breel on Hope. Did you know that?" Ellyella asked suddenly.

The Deacon shook his head. "No. Did she tell you that?"

"Yes. When they were in the cable-car, trying to escape the Church forces on Hope, Matt had jumped from the car. He was on the ground. He had the artefact. Breel was still in the cable-car, by the door. She said he looked like he was going to walk away, abandon her there, but he didn't – because he couldn't. It was preordained."

Kaemon let out a scoffing grunt, which earned him an angry look.

He said, "You don't think it was because he felt responsible for her maybe, because it was his fault they were in the cable-car in the first place, his fault her dad was dead?" Kaemon tried to strike a reasonable tone. "C'mon El, it's just shit happening. You know that."

Ellyella shook her head, "No, this is more than just chance."

"Well, I haven't given up on the scientific method quite yet," the Deacon said deploying his device again.

Kaemon became aware of a sound on the edge of hearing.

"Do you hear that?" he asked suddenly.

The Deacon and Ellyella stopped to listen.

"Yes," the Deacon said, "sounds like surf, waves on a distant beach."

"Or drumming," Ellyella added. "I can feel it through my boots."

Kaemon looked over his shoulder, back towards Abiel, who had dropped even further back, as if she might be responsible in some way.

"Why do you keep doing that, Kaemon?" Ellyella said irritably. "She isn't going anywhere."

"You guys seem to have forgotten who she is and where she came from," Kaemon said. "Not me."

"She hasn't done anything to warrant our distrust, Kae. The opposite in fact." She looked at Kaemon and said accusingly, "It's your prejudice talking."

"No, it's not. Why would you say that –"

"– because she's a believer and everyone who is a believer is bad," Ellyella said, voice rising, "like me."

"Not like you, El –"

"– Really? You all had me pinned for planting the tracker on the ship. Someone was feeding information to the Emissary, so it had to be the woman of faith!"

"I never had you pinned for that, El," Kaemon protested, his own voice rising in competition. "That was Matt, and I argued with him over it. Anyway, whatever Abiel's beliefs are, if she has any, are neither here nor there. You all seem to have forgotten what she is, where she came from. She's a crusader, an agent of the Church. A merciless killer. She may have the rest of you fooled, but I still see her. She's dangerous and whatever's motivating her, you can be sure it's not because she gives a Frazz-damn about any of us." He looked back as he said this. Abiel was far enough away that she probably wouldn't hear, which was a shame. He wanted her to know he was wise to her. "And then you all went and armed her," he finished in disgust.

Ellyella sighed. "You have to stop blaming yourself for Marlon's-Reach, Kaemon. What happened there wasn't your fault or Abiel's, and situations change; people change."

Unwanted memories of the Church invasion of his home world poured into Kaemon's head. Memories still too raw to risk a response.

Finally, he said quietly. "You're wrong, El; snare cats never shed their claws. I hope by the time you realise that it's not too late."

Up ahead Breel and Matt had stopped before a huge wall that marked the end of the tremendous space they had been walking through.

"Is it a good idea to carry on towards the creepy alien sound?" Breel asked. They stood before an angular entrance through which a distant repetitive thump, thump, thump could be heard. They could feel it through their boots. The arch was cracked in several places. The top layer of encrusted designs had broken away, revealing older shapes beneath. The broken pieces lay all over the ground. The supporting span had slumped, split by a fracture running through its centre.

"There's only one direction we can walk: the one where we can breathe, so we don't have a lot of choice." Matt surveyed the damaged structure and the short tunnel connecting to what looked like a very different space beyond. He turned from the entrance to examine Breel closely. "How're you doing?"

"Feeling a bit dislocated, as if I'm not quite all here."

"You're exhausted. Hardly surprising after all we've been through. I feel a bit dislocated myself."

"Yeah, I know that feeling," Breel said, "but this is something different." She rubbed a hand across her forehead. "It's hard to put into words. It's as if there's something out there, a nagging presence trying to get into my head." Breel rubbed both her temples with her fingertips. "It's getting hard to resist."

He looked at her, glowing dust motes dancing in the beams of light describing the contours of her face, bouncing through her hair and he just wanted to be with her, for much longer than the time left to this benighted, Jinx-damned place.

"I almost lost it, out there on the ice," he said quietly, "but I'm back now. You brought me back, Breel. Whatever we find, whatever it wants, I'll do whatever it takes to protect you." He gripped her shoulders. "Do you believe me? Because I mean it: whatever it takes. There has to be a way to get you and the others out and back to safety."

Breel smiled, pulling his hands down and bringing them both together in front of her. She kissed his knuckles lightly.

"I know you'll do your best, Matt. You always do."

He knew she was humouring him, that she didn't believe his promise, built on sand as it was, but he had to believe it himself… and he did.

She let his hands go and they both turned as the others caught up with them.

Sweat trickled down Abiel's face. It ran down her sides from her armpits. Every now and again Kaemon would look back, to check on her, lest she turn into a ninja killing machine and slay the whole group in a fit of religious mania.

It was a question she had been asking herself. Why hadn't she wrought some kind of vengeance on these people? The very people who had inflicted her pain and humiliation on her, had been the death of all her comrades on the accursed asteroid.

Maybe she should have gone with her first idea of violent martyrdom, struck while the reactor was hot. But the crew had been too wary of her when they had first brought her to the ship. There was too much chance of failure. She had bided her time and waited, knowing they would relax if she didn't appear dangerous – and they had. Everyone except Kaemon, Light-damn-him. He never let up.

And now they were here, walking through this alien base and as good as dead anyway, her thoughts of martyrdom rendered redundant. The Light must have some other plan for her: that could be the only answer. It must be to do with whatever waited for them at the end of this trek. Perhaps that was where she would see the sign to act.

She could hear rising voices from Kaemon, the Deacon, and Ellyella as they argued and bitched. In the short time she had known them, the crew of *Scavenger* had changed. She'd seen this before during her time as a holy warrior. The crucible of shared purpose and battle had forged them into a unit, a family; a dysfunctional one maybe, but the only family they would have for the rest of their soon-to-end lives. It didn't matter what their original cause had been. It didn't matter what any of them believed or didn't. What mattered was that they had fought together and nearly died together. She knew that could only make them more formidable and dangerous. Despite their disagreements, she knew that if it came to it, they would die for each other.

That they had saved her life, asking for nothing in return, was a constant nag at the back of her mind. The Church had also saved her life. Abiel had been lost, but *Second Light* had found her.

Drug addict, alcoholic, *murderer*.

She caught her prosthetic on an uneven piece of ground, sending a shot of pain through her thigh, causing her to grimace and stumble. They had painkillers amongst the few salvaged medical supplies, but so far, she hadn't used them. Pain was a driving force in the Church, something to be cherished, embraced even.

Kaemon looked round at the noise. She smiled sweetly at him. She had let the distance between them grow. She wanted some space to herself, to think.

Ahead, Matt and Breel had stopped at the foot of a cliff-like wall and were deep in conversation.

There had been a change in the dynamic between the two, resulting in a change in the group in general: a lift in morale. After their time in the pool, Matt had emerged seemingly back in control and acting once more with the authority of a leader. Seeing the generally stony-faced Breel acting coyly around him was something of a shock.

She couldn't make her mind up about the woman and the ridiculous story of her 'creation.' Alien-construct, angel. It was delusional and heretical, but the others seemed to believe it, even Kaemon.

Abiel clenched her fists. When she had come-to in *Scavenger's* med-bay, everything had seemed clear, but now? She rubbed the itchy raised scar on her throat, from the heat of the blade that Breel had used to cut away her helmet. She was so far from the life that had led her here. Her abuse on New Chinchary, the Emissary, Second Light – all that blurred, like waking from a dream whose details had become vague and unclear. It all seemed so unimportant, especially in this place of billion-year-old secrets.

That thought shook her. Her faith was wavering. She needed to look to the Light, pray for guidance, because she was feeling lost once more.

She dragged a hand across her eyes to clear them of sweat. Even with the customised suits, it was still Light-damned hot. If she hadn't given up the knife they surely wouldn't have been able to carry on. She felt into her pocket, feeling the security of its weight there.

Up ahead, the crew had regrouped. She was still some distance from them. With a grimace, ignoring the pain, she picked up her pace.

The group gathered around Matt and Breel, all except Abiel, who was still catching up. They looked utterly weary; pale faces shiny with sweat. By now everyone was aware of the sounds and vibrations.

"So, clearly there is something up ahead," Matt said. "We should keep together." He looked back towards the approaching crusader.

"You go on," Kaemon said. "I'll wait for Abiel. We'll catch you on the other side."

Matt gave him a look. "Okay, don't hang around." He led Breel, Ellyella and the Deacon through the entrance. The MARRVs followed obediently. Kaemon grabbed a bottle of water from the top of one as it passed. When he turned, Abiel had almost reached him.

"You waited," Abiel said to Kaemon. "That's so sweet."

"You need to keep up," he said to her gruffly. "We need to stay together."

"I feel like you have something you want to say to me, Kaemon."

Kaemon turned to follow the others. Abiel took two quick steps to push past. She turned, stopping him in his tracks. Her eye level was just below his.

Behind her he took in the poor state of the arch. One of the walls had cracked. A broken piece slumped from one side to the other. He could see dust settling from it in time to the percussive beat of the mysterious noise, sounding from somewhere up ahead. He turned his attention to Abiel.

"Seems more like you have something you want to say to me."

"What is your problem, Kaemon?" Abiel demanded.

"My problem –" Kaemon began.

"– have you thought about where we are?" Abiel continued. "What we are doing?" She pointed behind her, without taking her eyes from his. "Who knows what the fuck we might meet round the next corner. I'm a soldier, you know that, and I'm good at it. If it hits the fan suddenly, you'll need all the help you can get and at that point it will probably be too late to pass me a weapon.

"I thought it would be better for all of us if I were armed, but I knew you would try and take the knife away from me, so I kept it to myself."

Kaemon unscrewed the bottle and took a swig. He offered it to Abiel. She waved it away impatiently, put her hands on her hips, leaning forward for emphasis.

"You need to understand something: everything I was before has no meaning now. We are all up to our necks in the same shit. We're just trying to keep it from going over our heads."

The Deacon reappeared. He waved at them, continuing to walk in their direction. "Come on, what are you two doing? They're waiting for us on the other side."

Kaemon began walking again, so that Abiel had to move aside. "I guess you got what you wanted," he said. "You're armed now and they all trust –"

The world shook, cutting him off before he could make his point.

"Take cover," he shouted, as chunks of debris smashed into the floor. Kaemon took two steps forward to grab the priest and pull him to the side. where they all crouched as blocks of whatever-it-was the base was made from rained down around them, raising noxious clouds. He covered his mouth to stop the foul stuff entering his lungs.

There was a tremendous crack. Through the swirling dust he saw the precarious arch support give way under the pounding and shaking. With nothing now to stop it, the wall above crashed down. When the dust cleared the tunnel was completely filled from top to bottom.

Kaemon walked over to the rubble and pressed his hand against the unmoving blocks. He turned to Abiel and the Deacon, wide eyed behind him.

"Yeah, this could be a bit of a problem," he said.

SIXTEEN

The sky was filled with the destruction of stars. Maliesh watched a tiny white dot move across a fuzzy red glow. At first glance it looked like the white dwarf might be absorbed by its mighty red companion, but appearances were deceptive. The white dwarf, travelling from his right to his left, completed the transit of the red giant it orbited. It continued on, past the soft hazy limb of the giant star until there was a visible gap between the two. Now he could see a stream of matter spiralling from the giant to the dwarf star.

David definitely had Goliath by the balls!

The white star, about the diameter of Earth but containing the compressed mass of a medium sized sun, held the giant in a death grip, consuming its matter at a phenomenal rate. At some point in the future the dwarf would have consumed so much of the giant's mass that it would detonate and destroy both stars in a conflagration mightier than anything else in the universe: a conflagration that would briefly outshine whole galaxies.

The Emissary's second in command stood on a dusty plain, the horizon dominated by a ruined city. A reminder of the transience of all things.

"Not this sim again, Maliesh, can't we have something more cheerful?"

Maliesh took his attention away from the spectacle and turned to see the commander of *Transcendent Light,* Captain Hannathon, resplendent in his black and silver uniform, boots polished to mirror sheen – a man for whom the title 'Captain' was made. Tall and lantern-jawed with a thick wad of wavy hair, white now, but with a few remaining tell-tale dark streaks. *He would also make a perfect media anchor,* Maliesh thought sourly, for one of those news outlets that were more inclined to sensation than facts. The captain looked solid and real, but a flicker of blue travelled from his feet to his head every few minutes, a deliberate reminder that this was an illusion and that both he and Hannathon were actually sitting in their cabins, plugged into the same simulation.

Maliesh inclined his head at the captain and said, "I think it suits the mood of our times perfectly."

Hannathon walked over to a low boulder and sat. Maliesh knew that back in the captain's cabin the right neurones were being stimulated in the man's brain to give Hannathon the impression that muscles in his legs had worked and that gravity compressed his backside onto the rock he sat on, just as Maliesh could feel rough stone under his boots and a faint breeze against his face.

"He's late," Hannathon said.

"He's always late," Maliesh replied.

A small flicker of blue elongated into a human figure. Captain Corlezea of *Burning Rapture*. Not remotely as telegenic as Hannathon, Corlezea was short and round with small, mean eyes. Although his uniform was regulation perfect, it still somehow colluded with the man's shape to give him an unkempt appearance. Their ships were some distance apart, with a time lag of two minutes or more between signals. It would be irritatingly noticeable if not for some arcane manipulation by the sim software, the details of which he would never even try to understand.

"Unscheduled meetings are dangerous Maliesh. Did we need to bring this one forward?" Corlezea snapped without preamble.

"Greetings to you too, Corlezea," Maliesh said.

Corlezea waved the flippancy away. "Just get on with it, man. Too long in here and some jobsworth will pick us up."

"We should be okay for the time we need. I have my people working to hide the signals." Maliesh sighed, straightened his posture and put his hands behind his back. He looked from one man to another. "I thought we should meet because time is running short and we need to consider what options we have, before we lose control of both the Church High Council and some of the more troublesome Saved worlds."

"The last time we spoke, you believed you could reason with the Emissary," Corlezea said. "I assume your appeal did not go well."

"It did not. He is not in a mood to listen. Why we need this meeting. We have to come up with a new strategy and soon."

"The Emissary is your creation, Maliesh," Corlezea said. "How can you have let things get so out of hand?"

"It's easy for you to criticise, Corlezea. The man we are dealing with now is not the same person I put on the throne. He was a small-time con artist, somewhat charismatic, but whose actual sole talent lay in convincing a crowd his lies were true. All he wanted was money to satisfy his greed and indulge his cravings. That's not who we are dealing with today. The Emissary has become radicalised by his own sermons it seems. He has become a loose cannon, far from the easily manipulated figure I had expected him to be."

"The scientists are not having much success reopening the RIP," Hannathon said. "If they fail again, the Emissary might give up."

Maliesh shook his head. "He has said, in no uncertain terms, that nothing is more important than this mission. I believe he will simply send for further resources until he finds a solution, no matter how long it takes. I truly believe he might wait here until he, and we, die of old age." He looked up at the stellar death throes in the sky. "I think the Emissary has lost sight of our true goal and we may have to look for another way."

"Tread very carefully," Corlezea said. "I am all for finding a way to persuade him, but what you are suggesting is insurrection and will end badly for us if we fail."

"Have you thought that the Emissary might be right?" Hannathon asked.

Maliesh and Corlezea looked at him sharply.

"I don't mean the Machine and the Light," Hannathon waved a hand dismissively. "I mean there might actually be power and secrets; riches beyond our wildest dreams through that portal. The secrets of a billion-year-old technology."

"Even if that were the case, it has been there for a billion years, so will be there another billion. We need to secure our power base first, then we can return anytime to reopen the RIP… if that's even possible." Maliesh paced two steps and then back again. "They have tried to reopen the RIP twice now. We have lost two symps and the Emissary's patience is wearing thin. I'm not sure what chaos he might wreak if another attempt fails."

"There are grumblings amongst some of the ratings that he goes too far, punishing those who try their best." Corlezea said. "That it's impossible to please the man, no matter what you do. Obviously, these misgivings are not being shouted out loud, but I have my own people in amongst the crew." Corlezea stretched a hand over his eyes to rub his temples with his forefinger and thumb. He dropped the hand as if suddenly embarrassed at the show of weakness. He clasped both hands behind his back and straightened his posture. "A culture of fear is fine," he said a little too loudly, "up to a point, but it needs to be tempered with a sense of fair play and justice or, so far from home, we may face a mutiny."

"I agree," Hannathon said. "It's difficult for people to do their best when some unspeakable threat of violence hangs over one's every move. It's worse for people at the top of the food chain of course, but disquiet is spreading to the lower decks. It's not too bad at the moment. We are keeping a lid on it."

Maliesh looked at both men in turn. "Maybe we shouldn't keep too tight a lid. Use your spies to see who might be relied upon. Keep them primed."

"For what?" Corlezea said.

"We'll know when we see it."

"And the High Council?"

"The High Council will not be a problem. I have my own people in places of influence, but we may lose that leverage if we delay here much longer. That's why we can't afford to wait while the Emissary continues to indulge this obsession."

"Do you have the best interests of the Church in mind, Maliesh, or your own?" Corlezea asked.

"As far as your own best interests and mine are concerned, Corlezea," Maliesh said, "you couldn't fit a holy wafer between the two."

"I hope that isn't some kind of veiled threat?" Corlezea's eyes narrowed.

"Let's not start dick measuring, please," Hannathon said, "or we're all screwed."

Corlezea relaxed and shook his head. "The pressure has been intense," he said: the closest to an apology he was likely to utter. "We are readying another shuttle and the MPG for yet a third attempt at opening the *RIP*. The symps, not surprisingly, are becoming less keen to volunteer."

The tension went out of Maliesh. "I understand. It has been difficult, I know."

"I'll do as you ask," Corlezea said, "but we have to hope this latest attempt by the scientists fails. Once through the *RIP* it will be much harder."

A breeze ruffled Maliesh's robes and the light level changed. They all looked up at the orbiting stars. The ejecta from the red giant had increased and was pouring into and around the white dwarf. Light flared where it fell onto its surface.

Maliesh sighed, "Time to go. Something is happening in the real world that needs our attention."

He looked back but his two co-conspirators had already gone. He took a last look at the pulsing white light, then exited the sim.

SEVENTEEN

Ellyella craned her neck upwards. "Awesome," she said. Breel looked up at massive walls towering high above them. She stared at the whirls, holes and curving interlocking designs adorning the walls until they were lost in distance and mist.

"When I was a kid, my dad took me to see the Cathedral Dome of Glowing Creation," Breel said. "I thought I would never see anything more intimidating, but this is in a different league entirely."

"You've been to the Core worlds?" Ellyella asked, incredulous. "To Refulgent? I thought you never left Hope."

"Nah," Breel scoffed. "Who could afford to do that? It was a travelling Sim exhibition that stopped at Arralandeshi. Looked and felt as if I were there, though."

Looking further, on Breel saw that the walls moved gradually apart until the environment became a broad valley.

"What's keeping the others?" Matt said, looking back the way they had come.

"I'll go and check," Deacon said and set off back through the tunnel.

They stood for a moment, quietly contemplating their surroundings. A small tremor shook the floor. Mini dust devils sprang up around Breel's feet. She looked back through the tunnel, where the Deacon was reaching the far side where she could see Kaemon and Abiel talking and gesturing animatedly.

"Can you feel that?" Matt asked.

Breel raised a hand for silence, listening. For a long second nothing happened. The weight of time that pervaded the place settled around them like a smothering blanket.

Then the whole base, the entire planetoid it felt like, convulsed. Breel cried out. She lost her footing and crashed into the wall. A tsunami of dust raced down the valley towards them. In an instant, they were enveloped. Blind, she put her hands out seeking support. Splintering sounds of destruction deafened her, unseen in the murk. She fell to her knees. The toxic cloud clogged her mouth and nose. She couldn't breathe. She put a hand over her face to try to filter out the filthy particles. It felt like it was never going to end, but in reality, it was only seconds later that the shaking stopped, suddenly, as if someone had thrown a switch.

Slowly, Breel pushed upright, coughing. She rubbed her eyes to clear them of stinging grit and peered into dense swirling fog.

"Matt?" she croaked to a flat yellow-grey hunched shape, slowly materialising in the clearing air.

"I'm okay." He coughed and spat. "Ellyella?"

"Here," Ellyella said.

Breel looked about her as the dust settled. "What about the others?" she asked.

The tunnel had completely collapsed in on itself.

"Kae, are you alright?" Matt shouted through the rubble. "What's it like your side? Can you clear it?"

"We're trying," came the muffled response.

Breel looked up. Above the detritus of the collapse, the smooth cliff rose as far as she could see. There would be no climbing over. Matt and Ellyella were pulling at the rubble.

"Give me a hand here," Matt had hold of a large block balanced on an unseen fulcrum. It turned as he pulled. Breel moved to help. Together the three of them heaved it round. It ground noisily, sticking, then suddenly came free with a lurch, causing the whole edifice to shudder.

"Back," Matt shouted as a new collapse brought more heavy objects thundering down, filling the air with more choking particles.

"You guys all right?" Kaemon shouted to them.

"We're okay," Breel shouted back. "What about you?"

"Still here."

"This isn't going to work," Breel said. "There's too much and it's too heavy."

"We can't leave them," Ellyella said.

"Any luck shifting it your side, Kae?" Matt asked.

Abiel said something Breel didn't catch "– yeah, I know," Kaemon said, responding to Abiel. He raised his voice. "Matt, Listen, the collapse has opened up a new passageway. It has air and as far as we can tell goes in the same direction. We're going to follow it and hope we can meet up further on."

"That doesn't sound like a good idea," Matt said. "You've no idea where you'll end up."

Further muffled discussion.

"There's air so we can assume it's part of the overall route." Kaemon paused, then added, "Even if we could clear a way through to you it would take too long, so it's not like we have a choice, is it?"

"Maybe the MARRVs…?" Ellyella said.

Breel shook her head. "Don't see how and we might end up bringing more down on us."

"But, what about food and water? We have it all on our side."

"We have one bottle of water," Kaemon said. "It'll have to do until we meet up again."

Breel, Matt and Ellyella exchanged glances. Finally, Matt said reluctantly, "Okay, Kae. I can't see another option."

"Right then," Kaemon said. There was silence between the two groups for a moment, then Kaemon added, "Hey, Captain… I wanted to say, in case… you know… well, I wanted to say thank you, for taking me along, getting me out of that jail. It's been kinda fun. More fun than being hung drawn and quartered in the city square, anyway."

Matt gave a choked laugh. "Can't say there weren't times when I thought it was a mistake." Then added, "Good luck, all of you."

Breel said, "I'm happy to know one of us has been having fun."

"We'll see you soon, Kae," Ellyella said, voice breaking, "I'm sure of it."

"C'mon," they heard Abiel say, cutting through the emotion and bringing them back to the task ahead. "Let's get moving."

"Look after them, Abiel," Breel said.

"I will."

They listened to the sound of scrabbling and the occasional curse as the three moved away into the depths of the complex, until they couldn't hear them anymore.

"May the Light illuminate your path," Ellyella whispered.

*

Breel, Matt and Ellyella had walked silently from the narrows into the broader valley, until they were on a wide plain bordered by high cliffs. Geometric pillars of various heights dotted the plane. They looked like giant, angular, chiselled mushrooms. *Or trees maybe*, Breel thought. It might have been a wide, dry river valley on a planet, if not for the unnaturally sharp edges. The straight lines and angles were softened by a thick layer of gritty grey-dust brought down by the quake.

"This whole area looks like a crude computer rendering," Matt said breaking the silence between them.

Ellyella ran a hand over one of the smaller mushroom shapes. The texture was hard and sharp. She looked at the larger objects, some towering over the humans. a dozen times their height. "This looks like a smaller version of the big ones," she said, "almost as if they grew." The object flaked apart under her touch, shedding fragments into a layer of broken pieces at her feet.

Breel caught sight of movement high on the cliffs, mere dots from this distance. With a start she realised they were more of the alien avians. They wheeled about, landing on sharp, unnaturally straight ledges. She pointed it out to the others.

"It almost looks like a nesting colony," she said.

One of the dots detached from its brethren and began to grow in size.

"Coming our way," Matt said. "Let's get under cover."

They ran into the shadow of one of the stone 'trees'.

The flying thing approached, a cross between a prehistoric reptile and an insect, made of shifting iridescent plates. It was big, with a wing span of at least five meters or more. The wings were an insectile blur, sounding like a monumental chainsaw. A small tornado of dust followed in its wake. It buzzed over them, throwing the tree they were sheltering beneath into shadow, beating them with a small, locally generated hurricane before heading off in the direction they had been walking. It twisted its segmented neck to peer back at them as it moved away but otherwise ignored them. Breel felt a wave of nausea, causing her to stagger against the rough stony bark.

Matt put out a steadying hand, concern on his face. "You okay?"

She shook her head, running a hand over her forehead. "This Deshi-damn stabbing at my brain is driving me nuts."

"I wish I could do something for you, Breel," Matt said.

"They haven't stopped since we crossed the barrier into the base, Matt." Breel said. "Mostly it's background noise I can ignore, but every now and again, it's like they're screaming."

Breel could hear the voices now, a ringing tinnitus, whispering, battering at the periphery of her consciousness.

"They have to be real," Ellyella said. "I mean external to you, not just your imagination, or we wouldn't have got into the base at all. The information you're getting is accurate."

"Yeah," Breel said. "Otherwise I'd have to think I'm going crazy." She laughed grimly. "I'm not sure which alternative I prefer."

Matt asked, "Do you have any idea what they want?"

Breel shrugged. "It's not like they are talking a language I can understand."

"You're resisting them," Ellyella said. "Maybe you should let them in."

"It's not the Light, El," Breel said with some irritation. "It's something alien and ancient and I'd rather not have it in my head, thank you. Especially after what happened to me on the ship." Breel pushed away from the tree trunk. "Let's keep moving. The sooner we get to the end of this Deshi-damned trail, the better."

The stony tree-like objects thickened up ahead until they were walking under a gloomy petrified forest. They came across water, falling down wide stone steps into a hexagonal pool. Matt paused to top up the water bottles.

"I hope Kae and the others come across something like this," he said.

"I can't stop thinking about them," Breel said. "To have come all this way and then for it to end like that. . ." Her voice broke.

"They'll be okay, Breel," Ellyella said. "I'm sure of it." But her voice betrayed the depths of emotion she was feeling.

The trees thinned out and the plain came to an abrupt end. Breel looked at a new vista, though not one that lent her any sense of comfort. They stood on one side of an airy drop into a chasm, on a narrow, ragged, friable ledge, which dwindled away to either side. They would only be able to proceed in single file.

To their right was a bridge, or rather, part of a bridge. It arced out over the drop but only spanned about a quarter of the way across. On the other side was a sheer cliff. The same organic motifs apparently covering all the surfaces of the base were prevalent there too, forming a radiating pattern around a dark tunnel that made it impossible to miss. Breel was reminded of Kaemon's desert dew analogy.

"What was it with the builders of this place?" she said. "They must've loved heights."

Matt said, "That bridge doesn't look damaged. It just ends."

The repetitive inchoate drumming was much louder here, filling the air. It beat at them from across the drop.

"This can't be a dead end," Ellyella said, "after all we've been through." She walked on a few paces and motioned toward the hole on the far side. "Do you think that's the way? It looks like the way, but I don't see how we get to it."

"Maybe there's some mechanism that'll extend the bridge," Matt said.

"Or maybe there used to be," Ellyella replied. "Who knows after all this time."

The drumming swelled, pounding through Breel's head, until Ellyella and Matt's voices became muted and distant. Overlaid were the '*voices*', beating at the borders of her mind in waves of increasing urgency. She walked past Ellyella, not giving heed to the monumental drop to her side, forcing the other woman to press against the wall to allow her passage. Chunks of stone fell away into the abyss.

"Hey," Ellyella said. "Careful, you'll have us all at the bottom."

When Breel didn't respond, Matt said with alarm, "What's happening Breel? Breel! Answer me!"

She heard him, but his voice had become irrelevant. The *other* voices were all that mattered. They guided and instructed. She walked to where the incomplete bridge met the ledge. It pointed directly at the tunnel. She walked its length until she couldn't go any further. To her left the alien flying thing was tracing ever-widening circles, as if it were searching for something. She looked down between her feet. Small stones dislodged by her boots tumbled into the void. She watched them for a moment, then scrutinised the far wall. The voices swelled in her head, until there was room for nothing else. She felt heat from her tattoos as they began to glow. The swirling intricate designs on the far wall pulsed, synchronising with the moving lights on her body, sharing a rhythm. Slowly at first, then ever faster, the patterns began to rotate around the pit, before flowing inwards, spinning into it like water down a sinkhole.

"Breel?" Matt's concerned voice came from far away. She barely registered it. The sound of the humans had become an irritating buzz, irrelevant and unworthy of attention. She stared at the mesmerising apparition of the tunnel and its radiating patterns on the far side, unable to look away. Then what she needed to do crystallised in her mind. It became an imperative, impossible to ignore. She walked back to the ledge, where the bridge originated and paused for a second, pressing her back to the wall. From the corner of her eye she saw Matt begin to run along the narrow ledge towards her. Ignoring their increasingly agitated shouts, Breel took a deep breath, then sprinted as fast as she could towards the drop, throwing herself out into the hazy void.

EIGHTEEN

"I wonder how long it's been since anything walked this way?" Abiel asked. Her voice sounded curiously flat, sucked into the dark spaces surrounding them as they walked down a rough and uneven path from the blocked corridor.

"A scary long time, I imagine," Kaemon replied.

"You're assuming the aliens that built this place had feet," the Deacon added.

They were taking it in turns to lead. Abiel was ahead. The muscles in her legs and arms glistened with sweat. Kaemon noted how well she moved on the prosthetic, noticed how well she moved, period. There was a lithe grace about her. She didn't look at all how he felt.

"Light-damn it!" she said. "If anything, it's even hotter down here."

"You blaspheme a lot for a crusader," Kaemon noted.

"It's the only defiance we have," she said.

They reached the bottom of a slope. From here the way ahead climbed back up steeply. The surroundings looked raw. None of the alien hieroglyphs that so dominated other parts of the base were in evidence.

"I didn't think you guys went in for defiance." Kaemon chanced a look behind at the Deacon's strained face. "Wait, Abiel." He saw her look back at him. "We should take five," he jerked his thumb back at the priest.

Abiel nodded. They stopped by a jumble of differently-sized blocks, dumped apparently at random. He passed the water bottle over to the priest. "We might as well drink this."

The Deacon looked doubtful, "Shouldn't we be saving some of it? It's all we have."

Abiel shook her head. "Never carry water you can drink."

"Better to have the water in you than eke it out and risk dehydration," Kaemon added by way of explanation. "Dehydration is the killer."

"If you say so." The Deacon took a mouthful. He waved the bottle at the slope before passing it to Abiel. "I hope that is taking us where we want to go."

The crusader drank before passing the bottle back to Kaemon. She looked up the incline.

"Maybe a prayer wouldn't go amiss," she said.

Kaemon snorted. He finished off the last of the water, lifting the bottle over his mouth and craning his head back to allow the last drops to fall in. He fixed the empty bottle to his belt.

"Better hang on to this in case we come across more water," he said.

Abiel sat on one of the smaller blocks and rubbed her thigh above the carbon leg, exposed now her suit had been hacked into ragged shorts. She addressed the priest. "Although I guess since you renounced the faith…" She let the rest of the sentence hang.

The priest sat heavily on another block, resting his elbows on his knees, and stared at the space between his feet, breathing raggedly.

"The faith," he mused, "is many things: a philosophy of life, a way to treat people, a way to order and stability. It's not merely the worship of a vengeful entity in the stars. I never rejected the institution, which for all its faults has much going for it." He glanced at Kaemon's expression. "Ask Ellyella if you want a second opinion. No, it was the Emissary and his subversion I rejected, especially when I became convinced he really did want to bring about the End of Times." He returned his gaze to Abiel. "Did you never feel the same?"

"Philosophising and the general airing of personal opinions tend to be frowned upon in the barracks," she said dismissively.

"Along with news and current affairs I guess," Kaemon added.

They remained there for several minutes in silence, listening to creaks and cracks and other more indefinable noises in the shadowy spaces around them. It was unnerving, making the short hairs on the back of Kaemon's neck stand on end.

To distract from his unease, he said, "Since we are probably all going to die down here, I have to ask. What's a nice girl like you doing working for an outfit like Second Light? What's in it for a woman supporting the patriarchy?"

Abiel stood, looking past Kaemon to the Deacon. "Are you rested? Shall we get on? It's not like we have all the time in the world."

"That's precisely what we do have," the Deacon said gloomily, pushing to his feet. "All the time left to this world, anyway."

"Dodging the subject?" Kaemon said to the woman's retreating back as he followed her up the slope.

"What about you? What was that farewell to the captain all about? Something about jail?" Abiel retorted.

"I asked first," Kaemon said, and then sighed. "I crossed your old boss. They were going to do something pretty nasty to me, publicly. I was in the cell next to Matt when the Deacon here came shopping for a pilot."

"Hardly shopping. I came specifically for Matt," the Deacon said. "We decided to take Kaemon with us."

"Matt, you mean," Kaemon said sharply. "I seem to recall you were less than enthusiastic at the time."

The Deacon reddened slightly but said nothing.

Abiel looked briefly from one man to the other, then looked ahead to pick a route through the jumble of blocks. Although the stone, or whatever material the complex was constructed from, lacked the intricate motifs and designs here that covered the rest of the base, each block did have a simple, solitary legend etched into it. The two men followed her lead.

"I wonder what they say?" the Deacon asked, indicating the glyphs.

"Abandon ye all Hope," Abiel said.

"Or 'this end up'," countered Kaemon.

"What did you do to piss them off?" Abiel said, picking up the previous conversation.

"It doesn't take much, as you know," Kaemon replied. "But helping people escape Saved worlds is a sure way."

Abiel nodded. "That would do it. I guess you got well paid though."

"Sometimes," Kaemon said.

"I knew it."

"Actually, you don't know the half of it," Kaemon said. "And I'm hardly going to be lectured by the likes of you."

Abiel stopped and turned to face him. "I'm getting a little tired of the attitude. You know nothing about me."

Kaemon faced the Second Light warrior. "Well, now's your chance to enlighten us. I do know you sold out your entire gender, but I'm not sure what you got out of the bargain."

"Maybe we should save our energy for the climb," the Deacon suggested, pushing between them and giving them both a sour look.

"You're very defensive," Abiel said to Kaemon, ignoring the Deacon. "This constant attack, maybe it speaks more to your own fears and inadequacies." She turned to follow the Deacon. "You have no idea what my life has been like," she continued. "The choices I've had to make. At least I didn't trade on people's misery for profit."

"So you say," Kaemon countered. "I would have thought that's exactly Church policy."

"Shhh," the Deacon said.

"Who do you think you're talk –" Abiel began.

"No, I mean *listen*." He waved a hand down.

They stopped. The air was faintly perforated by the percussive noise they had heard before.

"We must be heading in the right direction," the Deacon said, with sudden enthusiasm.

They toiled on up the slope. Kaemon's mouth was dry as dust. He swallowed, trying to generate some moisture. The slope suddenly came to an end. He almost walked into Abiel, who had stopped abruptly.

"What…?" he began, then froze as he looked past her. The way ahead was clear. It was the only way. A tunnel at the base of a sheer wall with a radius about twice his height. The problem was it was half-filled with something silvery and segmented. Every now and again a tremor ran the length of the thing's body. On the part he could see, blisters randomly swelled and collapsed.

"Is it alive?" the Deacon whispered. "It looks like it's breathing."

"Are we looking at its arse or its head?" Kaemon said.

Abiel regarded him. "That's what you're concerned about?"

"I'm worried there might be teeth somewhere," he explained. He walked carefully towards the thing and put out a hand to touch the shiny hide.

"Careful," Abiel warned.

The alien's skin shivered under his touch. "It's warm," he reported, keeping his voice low, "and damp." He pressed harder. The hide depressed under the pressure, but the creature, if that's what it was, didn't respond.

"What do we do?" Abiel asked.

"It's in our atmosphere," the Deacon said. "I don't know how its metabolism works, but maybe it shouldn't be in here, perhaps the oxygen has stunned it and that's why it's so quiescent."

Kaemon stepped back and looked around. "We are going to have to climb over its back," he said, "I can't see any other way."

The Deacon sighed. "That sounds like such a great idea."

"Give me a hitch up," Kaemon said to Abiel.

She made a stirrup with her hands and Kaemon put his foot into it. She heaved and he stretched up, digging his fingers into the yielding surface to give him enough purchase to scrabble up. Once he was up on the sloping back of the thing, he twisted around to face them, lying on his belly. There was a strong smell, like ammonia overlaying a stench of rot. The alien's hide convulsed under his weight.

"It's like a soft mattress." He stretched down a hand to the Deacon. Abiel gave him a lift up in the same way she had Kaemon. Once the Deacon was next to him, they both reached down. Kaemon gripped one of Abiel's wrists, the Deacon the other, and between them hauled until she was lying alongside them.

The three stood unsteadily, wobbling as waves travelled through the creature's skin. The top of the tunnel was just above their heads.

"Okay, stay close," Kaemon said quietly, as if the sound of his voice might disturb it, whatever it was. The tunnel, and consequently the alien, sloped up at roughly thirty degrees. "Hard going," Kaemon remarked after a few steps. "Like walking in soft sand." He grunted with the effort.

Directly ahead the alien's skin swelled into a hemisphere almost up to his waist. They paused and after a few moments the swelling subsided.

"Why do you think that keeps happening?" Abiel whispered. "Do you think it's ill?"

"Hard to say if it's an anomaly or if it's normal for the beast," the Deacon whispered back.

Kaemon tried not to look directly at the bright crescent of light that was their destination, created between the curved back of the alien and the curved roof of the tunnel. It destroyed his low light vision, making it hard to see where he was putting his feet. He was sinking up to his ankles. Moisture oozed out from the depressions his boots made and ran glistening down the creature's flanks. Like a tightrope walker he put his hands out to keep his balance. A cry made him look around. Abiel had fallen to her knees.

"Difficult staying upright on this surface with the prosthetic," she said. "It's playing havoc with the positioning feedback." She stood, struggling to stay upright.

The alien skin looked dark where the hard material of the artificial limb had pressed into it. Fluid oozed from the bruise. The area swelled into a tumour almost up to her knees before subsiding with a hissing, sloshing sound. The swelling was translucent. Kaemon could see dark shapes twitching within. A tremor ran the whole length of the creature. He looked longingly towards that bright curve of light.

They were about half way. The tunnel roof dripped long spikes of a resin-like substance that he had to dodge between. He ran his hand over one. The spike was hard and knobbly. He pulled and it came away with a loud snap. He handed the heavy stick to Abiel.

"Here, use this. It'll help you balance."

She took it gratefully. He broke off another spear and offered it to the Deacon. "How about you, Deacon?"

The priest waved the offer away. "Let's just get out, shall we?"

Kaemon hefted the resin spike. "Sage advice, Deak."

The alien worm thing spasmed, gently at first but then more frequently and violently, making it even harder to keep his balance. More tumours distended from the segmented body.

"I think we might be irritating it," Abiel said.

"You think?" Kaemon's feet sank further with each step and it became harder to pull them free from the sucking wet pits he was creating. Each step released more viscous fluid, adding to the mucilaginous nature of the skin. He slithered, one foot sliding away, causing him to painfully do the splits.

"Frazzing-hell," he swore, pushing quickly back to his feet again.

"We're nearly there." Abiel said.

A cry made him turn. A swelling rose right next to the Deacon, bowling him over. It continued to grow until it was well above Kaemon's height. Abiel reached for the Deacon, grabbed his hand to pull him forward and away from the expanding dome. Dark shadows moved within the swelling, and then the tumour split. Thick white fluid sloshed out. A gangly multi-legged thing with sharp edges, sprang out. It lunged at the Deacon, snagging his shorts. The Deacon shouted in fear as he was dragged into the lethal embrace. Kaemon bounced across the rubbery surface, like a man in a slow-motion dream. His hand went instinctively to the plasma pistol thumping uselessly against his thigh, but of course he had expended the last of its charge when the scavenging aliens raided the hab-tent.

The white liquid lapped over his ankles. Around him other tumours split, exposing more... *what the frazzing-hell were they? Parasites? Some kind of protective antibody?* No two were alike, but they all shared the same nightmarish spider- or crab-like appearance.

Blue-green light burst around Abiel and the struggling Deacon, illuminating the scene with a ghastly radiance. Abiel had activated the hunting knife. A downwards slash severed the alien limb that was pulling at the priest. White ichor sprayed from the flailing stump, like water from a severed hose, dowsing both the crusader and the Deacon. She stabbed the resin spear Kaemon had given her into the thing, puncturing it and pushing it back at the same time. More pale fluid spurted out. The Deacon slid forward on his hands and knees, like a man on a leaking water bed. Abiel hauled him to his feet and then pushed him, sliding and slipping, at Kaemon.

"Get him out," she shouted.

Kaemon reached out a hand, pulled the priest, then pushed him over the end of the alien worm, out into the light beyond the tunnel.

The nearest parasite scuttled towards him. Somehow, it wasn't sinking into its host the way they were. He stabbed at it with the makeshift resin weapon, tangling its legs, then smashed the spear onto its top. It split apart. Like the alien avians and scavengers, it was more delicate than it looked. A scream from Abiel made him look up at her. She had hacked the alien bug into pieces, but the hole it had left from its exit was a slimy crater she was sliding into, like the event horizon of a black hole from which there could be no escape.

"Kaemon!" The Deacon's shout of warning from outside made him aware of more parasites approaching rapidly. It was luck they had almost reached the end of the worm and the bugs were having to travel down the length of the host to get to them. He waded towards Abiel as she dug the knife into the alien hide to stop her slide.

"Get out, Kaemon!" she screamed. "You don't have time."

Kaemon didn't even entertain the thought. He smashed another bug's legs from under it and waded across the heaving, slick surface, until he could reach down and grab Abiel's wrist and pull her out of the crater. She kicked her feet for purchase against the scummy surface. The whole worm was wobbling like jelly on a plate now, rocking them back and forth.

Back-to-back, the two made their way towards the Deacon. Kaemon smashed to either side with his resin spear as more bugs reached them. Abiel slashed with the knife in one hand, while wielding the resin stake, both like a sword and a club, with the other. The light from the knife began to stutter.

"Power's almost out!" she shouted. The blade went dark. Abiel continued to slash and hack, but the knife had lost its near magical cutting ability.

One of the alien bugs stabbed at Kaemon with a long limb tipped with a razor-sharp cutting edge, like a carving knife on a pole. It got past his guard, digging into his leg. He let out a hoarse scream of pain, smashing the segmented arm apart. Blood poured down his leg to mix with the alien's. The white alien gore burned his open wound.

Abiel screamed but he had no time to check on her as more and more of the things arrived to join the attack, and then he was rolling and falling off the end of the worm. The impact onto the ground outside the tunnel knocked the breath from him, making him lose his grip on the resin spike. Abiel landed heavily next to him. The Deacon pulled them both away from the tunnel mouth.

In a panic, Kaemon was back up on his feet, looking for his improvised weapon, bracing for further attack, but the silvery parasites had stopped. Apparently, they were not willing to leave the body of their host or, were no longer interested, now they had driven off the invaders. They milled at the end of the tunnel, staying out of the direct light. Abiel stood next to him, brandishing the hunting knife, teeth exposed in a feral snarl, panting hoarsely, covered in white and red streaks.

The Deacon gasped, on his knees, hardly able to draw breath.

"You okay?" Kaemon asked Abiel.

She looked at him, then down at her spattered and streaked body, then back to him. Her face spread into a grin and she burst out laughing. Kaemon took in her appearance, then joined in, an out-of-control hysterical shriek. Tears ran down his face. He waved a hand at her appearance. "Are you okay…?" he repeated between gasps.

The Deacon stared at them as if they had both gone mad.

NINETEEN

She could hear a name being called. The sound was faint. Whoever was calling was a long way off, in another room or in another house maybe. The name meant nothing to her. She wished whoever it was would stop. It was annoying. She was so tired, so exhausted. She just wanted to rest. The name came again, louder. Breel. *Breel.* A hint of recognition. Was that her name? She became aware of her body. She was lying on her side, on a hard lumpy surface. She opened her eyes and pushed herself upright slowly. Groggily, she looked about her, trying to make sense of what she was seeing. Next to her was a large circular hole in the ground. It looked familiar. She had a sudden memory. There was a tunnel in a wall. She had been looking at it from the far side of a chasm, but that couldn't be this, because that had been a tunnel in a vertical wall and this was more like a well. She looked up, towards the voices shouting her name and received another shock. The sky was solid, made from textured stone or metal. There was a raised ledge hanging from it on which two figures stood, impossibly, at ninety degrees to her, as if they had been glued there. They must have an equally bizarre view of her, looking down on her head. Their names came to her from somewhere. Matt and Ellyella. That's what their names were. She pushed herself to her feet and brushed herself down, letting small stones and dust slide through her fingers to land about her boots.

As if someone had opened the sluice gates to fill an empty reservoir, her memories roared back into her head. They had been walking through an alien base. They had lost half the crew and there was something in the base, something alien, trying to get into her head. It had been telling her to jump... and she had! The last thing she remembered was the leap into the chasm.

Insane!

Dazed, she looked around. Hazy in the far distance she could see a column of vapour exiting a hole from one wall to traverse the space and disappear into another hole on the wall to her right. Dark shapes were moving through it. She looked up to Matt and Ellyella, who must see the column rising vertically, off the canyon floor. In the distance the alien avian still circled, as if it was keeping an eye on the proceedings.

"What the actual fuck, Breel?" Matt's shout, part relief and part anger, was absorbed into the cavernous space. It brought her fully back to the present.

"The gravity is variable, Matt. *Down* over here is ninety degrees different to where you guys are standing." Breel rubbed at her shoulder, which felt bruised. She guessed it must have been the result of a heavy landing; one she didn't remember at all.

"I can see that now." Matt's voice was hoarse. "Why the fuck didn't you say something? Tell us what the Jinxing-hell you were about to do?"

Breel took a deep breath. "I don't know. I'm sorry."

"How is it even possible?" Ellyella said.

"I don't know the answer to that either, El," Breel shouted, craning her head, neck back awkwardly to look up at them. "You'll have to make the jump; it's the only way."

Matt shook his head. "First we have to figure a way to get the MARRVs across." He bent to scrutinise the nearest machine. "We'll have to get them to jump and hope the manoeuvring jets will give them enough thrust to make up any shortfall in momentum."

"Fix a rope to them," Breel said, "so we have a safety line."

"Okay," Matt said. "It looks like they'll only need to get about half the way across before the gravity field your side takes over."

"Totally mad," Ellyella said. "If I hadn't seen you do it, I wouldn't believe it was possible."

Breel could certainly sympathise with that observation. She watched them busy about the MARRVs, checking the loads. It took a few minutes.

"First one coming over," Matt called.

"So, good job you had the knife," Kaemon acknowledged, a half-smile on his face. He sat, rubbing the wound the alien had inflicted on his leg, trying to clean it as best he could. It wasn't deep and although it did sting, it didn't look infected. He had to hope the alien blood didn't contain anything toxic. He stood to test his weight on it and winced.

"Better get on." He began to walk, limping a little.

Abiel and the Deacon followed.

They walked a few minutes in silence and then Abiel said quietly, "Thank you."

Kaemon turned to look at her. "For what, the knife?"

"No, for coming back for me."

"Nah, you would have done the same for me... wouldn't you?"

Abiel didn't immediately respond. They followed the path taking them towards a valley at the base of a huge, airy canyon.

"I have a daughter," she said suddenly.

"What?" Kaemon was caught out by this sudden revelation. "How? I mean, where is she?"

"On New Chincharry. The father is... was... well, my life before the Church was very different. Her father was abusive..." Her voice broke.

Kaemon was taken aback. This was the first time since he had met Abiel that she had shown any real sign of emotion.

Abiel recovered her composure. "The father was a very important man. I was... something less."

"What? You were a hooker or something?"

"A bit more than that, but not someone he would want to introduce to his wife." She looked at him sharply. "Life is tough on New Chincharry if you don't move in the right circles."

"Hey, I'm not judging," Kaemon said.

"He was wealthy. I didn't plan it and I was going to end the relationship, but I ended up pregnant. When Juleray was born he insisted I live in one of his apartments. He owned half the city. I didn't want to give up my independence, but it's hard to deny someone who has everything when you have nothing." She sighed. "I don't know, maybe I was really in love with him and I believed the things he told me."

The thought of a lovesick Abiel was a new perspective on the woman for Kaemon.

She shook her head. "It was okay for a while, but things changed. He became violent. He tried to take Juleray from me." She paused to climb over a low barrier. The obstruction had clearly once been some kind of machinery, now decayed and half buried, its purpose lost to the aeons. Once the three of them were over the obstacle she continued. "I had Juleray in my arms. He was pulling her. She was screaming. I was screaming. Then he punched me, hard." Abiel was quiet for a few steps, staring at something only she could see. "For a second, I didn't know who I was or where I was. Then Juleray's shouts shocked me back into the room. I was on the floor, blood pouring from my nose and he was dragging my little girl away from me. I don't remember standing or picking up the heavy glass thing, but it was in my hand and I smashed it into his head. He went down. There was something about the way his arms and legs went limp. I knew he was dead. He landed on top of Juleray. She screamed and screamed…

"The next second his goons were through the door. They took one look at their boss, pulled their guns and started shooting. I was by the window. I went over the balcony, fell about a floor onto a car roof. I don't know why I wasn't killed or badly injured. Then they were on the balcony firing down at me. I had no choice. I ran." She looked Kaemon squarely in the eye. "I ran away," she repeated, "and left my daughter, and a day doesn't go by that I don't regret that decision."

"Doesn't sound like you had much choice," Kaemon said. "You'd be dead if you hadn't. How would that have helped your daughter?"

Abiel held his gaze for a second more then looked ahead again. "That's when the Church found me and took me in. They saved me, in more ways than one. They gave me a sense of purpose and a family. My sisterhood looked out for me. We all looked out for each other and we were never abused." She stood a little straighter. "They trained me so it wouldn't go well for anyone who tried."

They walked on a few paces.

"Why are you telling me this now?"

"You asked," Abiel replied, "and I felt I owed you."

"When did you last see your daughter? I mean, when did all this happen?" Kaemon asked at last.

"About ten years, standard."

"You've only been a crusader for ten years?" the Deacon sounded surprised. "Do you know what happened to her?"

"Not for sure. If he had made provision for her, she would have been looked after, but if he had something planned, I never knew about it. Juleray was four when I left, just about old enough to remember me. I wonder what they told her about her evil abandoning mother, if they told her anything at all." She paused, hand on an outcrop, surveying the way ahead. "I always intended to go back when I got the chance, but it never came. His family put a bounty on my head. I was only safe in the Church." She began walking again, without looking at either man. "I haven't given up on her though. One day I will go back and she will hear the true story."

Neither Kaemon, nor the Deacon it seemed, felt like pointing out the unlikeliness of this assertion, given their current predicament.

The Deacon, who was walking slightly ahead of Abiel and Kaemon, stopped suddenly.

"What now?" Kaemon asked as he drew abreast of him.

The Deacon pointed toward something shiny in the distance. "What does that look like to you?' he asked.

At last, the interminable ramp was coming to an end. The blue light was getting brighter with every step, as was the volume of sound.

"What just happened, Breel?" Matt asked. "You looked like you had gone into a trance. Your tattoos were lit up like festival lights." When Breel didn't respond he added, "We need to know what's going on, Breel."

"I was getting information about the way ahead," she said heavily. "I knew that the gravity orientation on the other side of the ravine was different. That was the way we had to go."

"You didn't stop to tell us about it? Before you made what looked like a suicidal leap?" Ellyella said.

"I… I just knew I had to jump, so I did."

"Except it scared the shit out of us," Ellyella said angrily. "We thought you had killed yourself."

"Yeah, I see that. I'm sorry." She had to raise her voice over the increasing noise. "I felt compelled to jump."

"Compelled? By the *voices*? And you had no choice? Do you know how that sounds?" Matt said.

Breel shook her head. "It wasn't like that. I knew that was the way, that the field stretched far enough across. I did it without thinking."

The look on Matt's face said he didn't really believe her. Why should he? She didn't believe it herself. She was scared to think about what had happened. She was scared out of her mind about what revelations might be coming around the next corner.

Ahead, three of the MARRVs were dark shapes against blue light flooding upwards.

"Could have done without losing the MARRV." Breel changed the subject.

"And its load," Ellyella agreed.

In her mind's eye, Breel watched the machine fall again, the rope attached to it whipping back and forth. Thrusters failed, it didn't get far enough across for the gravity change to take effect. From her point of view, it flew close to the huge expanse of textured sky hanging insanely over her head, towards a distant wall. Matt and El would have watched it fall straight down. The end result was the same, though. The drone hit the wall or canyon bottom, disappearing under a small cloud of dust. A half second later, the crunching noise of its demise had reached them.

"No accounting for hardware failure," Matt said. "Let's just hope we are nearly at the end of this damned hike."

Beyond the three remaining drones, the spiral ramp was coming to an end.

They walked through an opening and out into a cavernous space and a wall of sound so loud the ground trembled. They were on a wide walkway, one of many terraces dropping down to a mass of activity lost in an illumination so bright it was hard to see what the activity was. All along the perimeter of the terrace, separating them from the action below, hung a faint, hazy curtain, little more than a shimmer in the air. There was also a high railing supported by poles roughly a shoulder-width apart. Breel placed a hand tentatively onto the barely visible, foggy barrier and felt a slight resistance before her hand went through. It was cold on the other side.

Withdrawing her hand, she said, "I need to get a better view." She pushed her head through the hazy layer and immediately couldn't breathe. She pulled her head back quickly coughing. "Looks like breathable air doesn't extend beyond the walkway." She coughed a couple more times to clear her airways. "Just the moon's atmosphere on the other side."

She sucked air into her lungs, held it, then pushed her face back through the barrier. Matt and Ellyella did the same.

The sound battered at her. Breel tried to focus in on the details, but it was difficult. The alien air prickled her skin and stung her eyes, making them water. The view was so alien that even had she been able to see clearly, it still would have been hard to make sense of it.

Row after row of huge structures, like gigantic metal flowers, receded into the distance. The central stamens were disgorging objects every few seconds onto conveyor belts. She could make out what looked like wings, legs and thorax. The disgorged objects were marshalled by crab or spider-like creatures. She strained to see clearly through streaming eyes. The flower things looked familiar somehow, but she couldn't imagine why. There was no way she could have seen anything like them before.

Between the gigantic flower-like structures were huge, segmented slug-like objects that swelled blisters, out of which the crab things popped. The belts were awash with white fluid. Breel pulled her head back, taking welcome gulps of air.

"What in the name of all that is Dark is that?" Ellyella said, when she had done the same. She rubbed at puffy, red and sore-looking eyes. Tears ran down her cheeks. "It looks like some kind of factory floor."

"That's what it looks like," Matt agreed, "but what the hell are they making?"

"The locals," Breel said. "They're making the creatures that populate the moon outside."

"They're manufacturing the moon's entire population?" Ellyella asked, incredulous.

"That's what it looks like."

"But why?" Ellyella said.

"Who can make sense of this Deshi-damn place?" Breel shook her head. "For some reason the big metal flowers remind me of something…"

"What's happening over there?" Ellyella pointed.

Breel stared hard through the wavering barrier. "It looks like the roof has caved in. A tremor must have brought it down."

Debris from the ceiling collapse had smashed into a line of the conveyor belts beneath, bringing that part of the assembly line to a halt. Broken pieces lay scattered about while white fluid flowed into drainage channels. Creatures boiled over the damaged area, crawling over each other like ants repelling an attack – the same creatures that apparently were birthed from the blisters on the giant slugs.

They gazed at the mass industrialisation in awe.

"What the Jinxing-hell is powering all this?" Matt looked about as if in search of a clue.

"I don't know, but maybe we don't want to attract the attention of those guys. They might not take kindly to unauthorised visitors."

"Agreed," Matt said, "let's move on."

"Which way?" Ellyella looked both ways along the terrace.

"Cross the walkways to the other side." Matt pointed. "The closest one is that way."

No," Breel said. Her tattoos were warm. "The breathable air doesn't extend in that direction."

Matt blinked. "Your personal hotline again?"

Breel led the way in the opposite direction. "I'm getting used to it."

"What's containing the air?" Ellyella wanted to know.

"Must be something like the force-field over the entrance," Breel said.

"We hit the jackpot," Matt said bitterly. "Think what tech like that would be worth back home."

"Pity we'll never cash in," Ellyella said.

With the MARRVs in the lead they stepped onto a bridge that crossed the factory amphitheatre. It swayed with their weight, dark against the bright blue of the factory floor. The percussive sounds of the construction pounded at them in waves.

Now the repair activity was beneath their feet. Breel peered between the slats making up the bridge, trying to make out detail, but it was hard through swirling vapour and the bright illumination bouncing harsh highlights off reflecting surfaces.

Looking up, through the hole in the ceiling that had been formed by the collapse, Breel could see other floors, rising up as far as she could see. The strange bio-mechanical aliens swarmed around the broken edge of this damage also, repairing and filling it in. Below, debris was being carted away.

She tried to probe for information through her – what... superpower, psychic power – but nothing was forthcoming. Whatever was happening to her was unreliable at best. But what *was* happening to her? Something was feeding her information via her augmentation.

That much was clear and it was getting stronger, louder, and harder to ignore the further they went into the base. There were times when the overlay of information threatened to obscure the reality around her – her leap across the chasm, for example. It simply hadn't occurred to her to let the others know what she planned.

No, that wasn't true. If she was honest with herself, Matt and Ellyella had become irrelevant. That was the part that really scared her. The notion that something might subsume her personality, that she might be taken over by an alien intelligence – or, was it more accurate to say that she was reverting to her true self? She paused for a moment, to gather herself against that thought.

Matt and Ellyella reached the end of the bridge and waited for instructions. They stepped back as she approached. They were spooked by her and she couldn't blame them.

She was too.

"I'm not getting any information here," she said, "but I guess that looks like as good a way as any." She indicated an entrance to their left, the size of a house, from which flickering light spilled.

Through this entrance, the environment looked more cared for, with less debris. A structure spread out before them, the source of the light. Massive, faceted tapering columns rose from the floor and dropped down from the ceiling, approaching but never quite meeting. It was a city of hi-tech stalagmites and stalactites fashioned from crystal. Every now and then flashes of energy connected the two, creating shifting shadows. The small hairs on the back of her arms and neck rose in air so charged with static it was almost tangible. They worked their way through the structure, the sole occupants of a crystalline megapolis.

The ceiling and floor constructions grew further apart until the ones on the ground were merely the height of tall buildings. There was nothing visible above their heads, other than constellations of blue sparks. The floor beyond was broken and pitted, convulsed into twisted arches that spanned a dark rift. They chose one that looked structurally sound. The MARRVs led the way. The arch twisted in the middle, a precarious camber that had them looking down into the abyss. Breel's boots skittered on the smooth surface until they reached safer ground.

Their shadows, cast by the gargantuan lightshow behind them, jumped and flickered, as if imbued with a life of their own and seeking escape. Gradually, they left the light and the noise of the factory floor behind and walked into a relatively dark, silent space. As her eyes adjusted, the faint light resolved the shadows into – Breel had a hard time parsing what she was seeing – alien sculptures or works of art? Strange hulking structures, made from overlaid compound curves, punctuated by holes at intersections, revealing dark interiors. They were about three times the height of the humans, bipedal, standing on oddly jointed legs. If they were to move, it looked like they could move with equal dexterity in any direction. The arms ended in hands formed from tentacles, frozen in whip-like tension.

"Do you think these are statues of the builders?" Ellyella asked, in the kind of whisper reserved for a holy place.

"It looks like some kind of service bay." Matt pointed to circumnavigating structures linked to the things, whatever they were, by rotting cables. Some of the structures had all but disintegrated into dust, but they became more whole as they moved deeper, as if this area was maintained by something. Breel looked around nervously, half expecting one of the spider-crab things to appear.

"Yeah," Breel said. "They look like mechs of some kind. Whatever they are, nothing's moved in here for millennia."

Matt looked at Breel, waving a hand towards her body. "Are you guessing or getting insider information?"

Breel looked down at her arm, which was alight. She looked back at him, eyes wide.

In what looked like the exact centre of the space was a simple obelisk. Balanced on its tapering apex was a curved cradle in which sat a dull grey sphere, slightly larger than a human head. The sphere's surface suddenly flashed random patches of dim light before going dark again. The group paused, uncertain. Then the ball floated free to hang unsupported a meter or so above its support. Oily smears appeared on its curved surface, moving sluggishly.

Breel felt warmth from her body art as they approached.

A deep bass rumble emanated from the multi-coloured ball, rising in pitch until they had to put their hands over their ears to mute the painful noise. The oily smears on the sphere began to glow brightly, then swirl in an agitated manner in time to the noise, which had modulated into a stabbing staccato.

Breel thought her head would explode. She pressed her hands to her ears harder, trying to block the noise.

"Quiet!" she screamed.

Silence fell about them. Breel staggered, as if she had been bracing against a gale that had suddenly dropped.

Ellyella was crouched, hands over her head and Matt stood wide-eyed behind her.

"OH, FOR FUCK'S SAKE," the voice boomed out from the sphere, "SORRY, is THat better? Welcome YA'LL, I've been WAiting. Waiting... for such a long time."

TWENTY

"What's a MARRV doing here," Kaemon said.

They stood around the wrecked machine. Its load lay scattered about. He walked over to a dented bottle, undid the screw top, then offered it to the Deacon.

"We got more water at least."

The Deacon took a mouthful, then handed it to Abiel, who drank gratefully.

Kaemon said, "We can't be far behind them." He looked up into the airy heights where a platform jutted out into space. There was a dark smudge opposite it, on the other side of the ravine. "Possibly an entrance up there, although it's hard to tell from here."

"Did they cross that gap?" the Deacon asked, eyes wide.

"Maybe," Kaemon said. He looked back down at the smashed remains of the drone, "but this guy didn't make it."

"Thankfully there aren't any human bodies down here," Abiel said.

Kaemon collected scattered protein bars and handed them to the others, taking the bottle from Abiel. The warm liquid tasted fantastic.

"If that's the way, it's an impossible climb," Abiel said. "I can't see how they got across."

A roar like a chainsaw shattered the silence, echoing off the surrounding walls, making them all start. In the distance, a dark shape resolved into a single avian heading their way. Its strange reptilian-insect form buzzed down the immense valley.

"Quick!" Kaemon crouched down behind the wrecked MARRV. The others followed his example. "Those bastards are vicious," Kaemon said.

"This one seems to be on its own," the Deacon observed.

The alien was huge. It headed straight for them. Kaemon hunkered down lower. The creature circled over them a couple of times, like a vulture from a fever dream. They were battered by small objects thrown up into the air by its powerful downdraft. Kaemon looked about for something he could use as a weapon, although it was hard to imagine what would be effective short of a plasma cannon. The alien flew over them one more time, then suddenly headed for the wall, leaving them in a settling fog of dust. It flew alongside the wall, wing beats slowing so that the wings themselves were almost visible. With a sudden twist it changed orientation so that it was parallel to the vertical surface. It landed on the cliff and began to hammer its head at something. Fragments rose from the impact and settled back to the wall. It found what it was looking for and pulled a multi-legged, squirming thing with a hard shell free. The avian buzzed away from the cliff, then let the squirming thing go. The prey fell back to the wall and shattered, whereupon the bird thing landed and began pulling at the broken pieces.

"Did you see that?" the Deacon said.

"Yeah, vicious bastard. I told you," Kaemon said.

"No, not that…" The avian took off again. Pieces fell from the freakish split in its head that it used for a mouth to land back on the wall. "That." The Deacon jabbed his index finger violently at the alien.

The strange creature or machine or combination of both flew over their heads to head back down the valley, the way it had come. It rolled so that its wings were parallel to the ground once more. Bits of detritus from its claws dropped and bounced around them.

Kaemon put up a hand to fend off the falling objects. The avian's wings blurred into high speed, and it flew away into the distance. He looked over his shoulder to realise the Deacon wasn't watching the departing alien but had walked over to the wall and was staring at it intently. Kaemon and Abiel followed him. The priest looked at them both.

"Didn't you see it?"

"What, Deacon?" Kaemon asked patiently.

The Deacon pointed upwards to a ragged line made of dust and stones, clinging to the face.

"The thing changed orientation, to land on the wall."

"So it was clinging to the wall. So what?"

"It wasn't clinging. It had landed. When it dropped its prey, the prey fell back to the wall."

Kaemon looked at him blankly.

"Don't you see? It should have fallen down here, towards us."

Kaemon looked up to where bits of the alien's victim still clung to the wall.

"All that stuff stuck to the wall up there," the Deacon pointed, "about twenty metres up. What's keeping it there? And there," he continued to point, "those are parts of the MARRV."

There were indeed parts of the drone seemingly stuck to the cliff. A ration box could be clearly seen, resting impossibly on the vertical surface. There didn't seem any good reason why it shouldn't be part of the pile of wreckage around their feet.

The Deacon looked down, picked up a small rock. He handed it to Kaemon. "Throw this, get it up past that line of stuff up there."

Kaemon eyed the Deacon speculatively. He hefted the rock, throwing it up into the air and catching it a couple of times to get the feel of its weight and balance. Then he positioned himself, held the rock down by his calf and whipped the stone into the air. It shot past the line of rubble and then suddenly, as if it had been grabbed by an invisible hand, it changed direction and crashed into the wall to *stick there*. Dust and small particles raised by the impact settled back to the wall instead of falling around them.

Kaemon gaped open-mouthed.

"Somehow gravity changes orientation up there. That must be how the others crossed the gap." The Deacon waved a hand at the half-bridge high in the haze.

Kaemon walked over to the wall. He placed his hand on the textured surface. "Nothing feels different here."

"Well, I assume the field changes about twenty metres up."

"How is that possible?" Abiel asked.

The Deacon shrugged. "I'm going by what I see."

"So, a climb of about twenty meters and then we can walk normally?" Kaemon asked.

The Deacon nodded, "I suppose we'll only know if we can get there."

"How lucky were we the only avian around came to show us the way?" Abiel asked.

"Maybe it wasn't luck." The Deacon looked down the valley, in the direction the alien had flown and then across to Kaemon. "I'm beginning to think perhaps there is something in here that has our best interests at heart."

Kaemon recalled the last avian in the chasm, which had shown such interest in him.

"You may be right," he agreed. He scanned the wall, assessing the route.

Abiel looked down at the red sore stump above the carbon curves of her prosthetic. "Twenty metres, though."

"I'm not a natural rock climber either," the Deacon admitted.

Kaemon slapped him on the back. "You? Look at what you've been through already. You're an action man."

The Deacon looked uncomfortable, and not just from the force of the blow.

Kaemon looked around. Amongst the scattered objects shed by the wrecked drone was a coil of plastic rope. He hefted it, judging the distance, then ran a hand over the embossed pattern covering the wall.

"Should be enough holds to get me to the boundary. Assuming the Deacon is right. Once I'm past it I'll fix the line and help haul you guys up."

"You think you can make that climb?" The Deacon eyed the route dubiously.

Kaemon scanned the textured cliff before looking back at the Deacon. "It's like every choice we've had since we left *Scavenger*: we don't have one."

The Deacon and Abiel watched Kaemon scale the wall. The convoluted surface offered a lot of handholds, but the sheer complexity made it difficult for him to judge the best line. Twice he had to backtrack when the holds disappeared, but now he sat, seemingly glued to the vertical surface, looking down at them both.

"Amazing," he shouted down. "That was so weird."

He unhitched the rope and carefully pushed it away, until, past the ragged boundary, it suddenly began to unravel and drop towards them. It stopped short.

"You'll have to climb up to it," he shouted.

Abiel looked from the climb to the Deacon.

"You go, Deacon," she said.

The Deacon eyed the wall dubiously, then shook his head. "I'm not a natural athlete, I'm afraid, at the best of times."

"It's barely twice your height. You can do it." Abiel took a step back to better survey the route. "We can do it together. There are enough holds for that short distance. Once you're tied on, Kaemon will pull you up."

"What about you?"

"I'll wait my turn." She grabbed a prominent handhold.

The Deacon paused.

"What's wrong?" Abiel asked.

The Deacon shook his head.

"C'mon, Deacon, after all we've been through? You can't lose your nerve now."

"It's not that."

"What then?"

The Deacon stared Abiel straight in the eye. "Why are you helping me? Us?"

"Why wouldn't I?" She looked at him. "What, you think I might push you off in a fit of righteous vengeance?"

The Deacon looked very serious. "I've been waiting for you to do something of the sort. I expect you know I voted to leave you on the asteroid."

Abiel nodded. "A little uncharitable for a man of faith." She looked up towards Kaemon, then back to the priest, "But, honestly, probably what I would have done in your place." She shrugged. "I've already had this conversation with Kaemon. What purpose would it serve to enact some kind of holy vengeance? My life before means nothing now."

"We both know that's not the kind of thinking the Church inculcates. I seriously expected you to try to scuttle the ship."

Abiel looked uncomfortable. "The thought did occur to me. I looked for a reason why the Light would spare me the fate of my sisters. Martyrdom was an option."

"What happened?"

She shrugged. "I decided against it." She looked at him squarely. "I expect you also know that crusaders are highly trained death machines." She grinned maliciously at him. "More than a match for a bunch of amateur insurgents. If I wanted you dead, any of you, you would be." Her eyes hardened. "Do you doubt that?"

The Deacon stared back, unable to look away, a mouse paralysed by the hypnotic gaze of a snake.

Abiel's expression softened. She sighed and looked back up to Kaemon. She made the first step off the ground, wedging the prosthetic into a gap in the mass of raised lumps and pits arrayed before her.

Kaemon's voice wafted down to them. "What the hell is taking so long down there?"

"Climbing," she yelled back. She turned and reached out a hand to the priest. "Now, can we get the fuck on with it, before I change my mind?"

The Deacon followed Abiel and Kaemon towards the hole they believed the others had gone down. The textures that covered almost every surface in the base piled up here. They rose layer upon layer, forming towers and walls, like an ancient coral seabed or a gallery created by some demented alien sculptor. Some of the structures were several times his height, like giant stone mushrooms or trees. He stumbled, put his hand onto the trunk of one of them to steady himself and let out a yelp of pain. The texture was hard and sharp. Cursing quietly, he sucked at a dribble of blood that ran from his finger.

He was so tired. He was not meant for this kind of life. His was meant to have a quiet life in academia, discussing the esoterica of quantum mechanics with like minds while sipping fine wine; not half-starved, stumbling across deadly alien terrain, where a single misjudgement might mean sudden death, or worse – a slow, painful one.

The gravity shift had been astonishing. He had watched Kaemon make the climb but he still didn't believe it would happen. But it did. Kaemon had let loose a cry of pain. A disorienting shift and his legs were pulled in one direction, his torso another. Kaemon had had to scrabble quickly to get his whole body above the invisible boundary. For a minute the Deacon had thought Kaemon might break his spine.

How was this place possible? Where was the colossal amount of energy required to keep it running coming from, and consistently, for maybe a billion years? But he was starting to form an idea, and, if he was right, it was truly terrifying.

He trailed behind Abiel and Kaemon. They had hauled up a package of provisions from the downed MARRV and now all three carried a small bundle.

The woman moved with an animal grace. He had no doubt she could make good on her threat. He was pretty sure she could make short work of Kaemon, tough guy though he believed himself to be.

He couldn't decide what to make of her. She had stayed with him during the climb, all the way to the top, guiding him as to where to put his hands and feet. Without her, he would have been dragged up the cliff like a sack of meat. Abiel had helped him maintain his dignity.

Even with part of her body missing, she managed to solo climb. She could have led it, he was sure, although she insisted that Kaemon had made it easier by defining the route. He suspected the real reason was that she wanted Kaemon to continue to underestimate her. A new thought occurred to him: if Kaemon had fallen to his death, she could still have made the climb on her own. She would have been rid of one of the heretic insurgents, two if she had left him behind.

Was this fair? He didn't know, but something felt off.

His previous experience with crusaders, all male it had to be said, was that their behaviour was defined by unthinking total obedience to the faith and to the Emissary. Although he had known female fighters existed, until these recent events, he had never come across any of the few women allowed to be anything other than breeding machines on worlds occupied by Second Light. Abiel – and he doubted that was her real name – wasn't brought up to a life of indoctrination and piety on a saved world, however. Maybe that was the answer to why she didn't make sense to him.

Up ahead, the two were approaching the hole in the ground and were examining it closely. There was a new camaraderie between them. Abiel had opened up to Kaemon, and Kaemon in turn had finally relaxed with her. Had that been her plan? It felt uncharitable to think it, but was the story of her daughter on New Chincharry even true? He was reminded of the fable of the sting-rat and the water-carrier. Could anyone change their true nature? But the question of Abiel's true nature was moot at the moment.

He caught up with them. A ramp wound down into blue light and rhythmic noise.

"They came this way for sure." Kaemon indicated scuff marks in the dust around the circumference along with clear boot prints. "Okay," Kaemon said, straightening his posture to shake off his obvious exhaustion. "They can't be that far ahead. Let's see if we can catch them up."

The Deacon sucked in a deep breath and followed them into the depths.

TWENTY-ONE

"What in Light's name is it?" Abiel said. She, Kaemon and the Deacon stood on the walkway overlooking the massive complexity of the conveyor belts.

"Reminds me of… a factory floor?" Kaemon said.

"What are they making though?"

Abiel stared hard through the misty barrier, not wanting to expose herself to the moon's toxic atmosphere a second time. They had all leaned out and discovered it wasn't possible to breathe beyond the walkway. "It looks like parts of…"

"It looks like they are making those things," Kaemon said, "those Frazz-damned creatures out there on the moon."

"Why?" Abiel spat out the acidic taste of alien air. "What in the name of all that's holy would be the point?"

"Well, you got me there," Kaemon said. "Maybe this was some kind of theme park, for whatever built this place."

Abiel turned away from the view. "They came this way," she said, pointing to marks in the dust. She set off across the bridge. "Come on."

"Can't we spare a minute to observe the wonders around us," the Deacon asked.

"You've got minutes to spare?" Abiel moved on down the walkway without looking back.

She heard the Deacon mutter. "I'm not sure it makes much difference."

She waited for them at the end of the walkway. "They went that way." She pointed to a massive entrance that spilled blue light. They followed the tracks in the dust.

"Wow, is that enough wonder for you, Deak?" Kaemon craned his neck to take in the crystalline megastructure that rose and hung before them. They walked down the middle of a boulevard-like space between

165

the towering structures. Arcs of energy lit the scene spasmodically. Their shadows flickered this way and that.

"Amazing." The Deacon's eyes glowed, reflecting the ethereal light.

"What's it for, though?" Kaemon asked in an awed whisper.

Abiel moved on, not waiting for them to try to answer. Kaemon caught up with her.

"You okay?" he asked.

"Is that a rhetorical question?" She focused on the way ahead.

"Well, I see the irony, but something's changed in you in the last half hour."

She sighed. "It's this place. It's getting to me." She twisted her head to look at him. "Everything seems so pointless in the face of it all. All this power and technology, what good did it do them? They still went extinct. Is striving for anything worthwhile? All the decisions I've made, everything I thought I knew, what if it was all for nothing? What if I go before the Light and I'm found wanting?"

"What would you have done differently, if you could have?" Kaemon asked.

Abiel's stared hard into the flickering light. "My daughter," she said quietly. "I should never have given her up."

"From what you say, you didn't have a lot of choice."

Abiel shook her head. "I ran away."

"We all have faults, Abiel, but in the short time I've known you –"

Abiel stopped dead in her tracks, raising a fist, causing Kaemon to bump into her. "Quiet," she hissed, dropping to a crouch close to one of the stalagmite bases.

The two men followed her lead.

"What?" The Deacon whispered.

"Something moved."

"One of the aliens?" Kaemon asked, voice low.

"No," Abiel stared hard into the difficult light, "it looked more like… there." She flattened herself against the cool crystal.

"Holy shit," Kaemon said.

They watched as, a short distance away, a man nonchalantly strolled out into the open. Abiel's mouth fell open. She must be hallucinating. He was dressed in the military fatigues of the Church of Second Light.

The strobing energy discharges flickered the figure's shadow around him. He walked over to face one of the towers. His hands fumbled in front of his body and then a steaming line of fluid splashed against the crystal and Abiel realised the soldier was urinating against the billion-year-old wonder.

She turned to the others. "Get back," she hissed, but Kaemon was no longer there. He was running in a low crouch to the other side of the boulevard.

"Kaemon," she said as loud as she dared. She signalled him to come back.

He looked back at her, waving her to be quiet with a downwards motion of his hand.

The Deacon leaned close to Abiel. He whispered, "What does he think he's doing?"

Abiel shook her head. "He's going to get us all killed," she said.

Later Kaemon would wonder what had possessed him to try and take the Second Light Soldier, but for now he was acting on instinct. How could the Church be here? He had to know. If he could subdue the man, they might find out. Presumably, he had sought privacy to be out of sight of his friends, who wouldn't be that far away. So, Kaemon had to move fast.

The base of the towers had numerous bulges and facets providing good cover. He moved from one to another until he was close enough to smell the guy's freshly laundered uniform. The chiaroscuro lighting swirled about, confusing and menacing. The soldier had finished his business and was fastening the front of his fatigues. Kaemon waited until the light show threw them both into shadow. Under cover of this temporary darkness, he sprinted the last ten steps while the man was still preoccupied.

Something gave him away. Maybe he made too much noise, or maybe, Kaemon realised belatedly, if he could smell the soldier's clothing, his own, not quite so aromatic body odour, might equally have given him away. At any rate, the blow that he aimed for the man's temple missed. The soldier swayed out of the way, catching Kaemon's outstretched hand as it went past, to twist and slam him into a hard, glassy wall.

The strength of the man, the force of the impact, shocked Kaemon to his core. It belatedly occurred to him that someone who had suffered the hardships and limited diet of a survival trek would be no match for someone fresh, fit and well-fed. The shadow flickered past and they were in bright light once more. The soldier's eyes widened in shock as he took in Kaemon's wild, ragged and emaciated appearance.

Probably thought he was an alien.

"What in Light's name are you?" the soldier said.

Kaemon took full advantage of the soldier's hesitation. He launched himself, smashing his shoulder into the man's midriff, pushing all the air out of his foe's lungs in one explosive gasp. They both crashed to the ground, but the man used their combined momentum and his knee to somersault Kaemon over and onto his back. Kaemon's head cracked off the floor and he blacked out for a second. Stunned, Kaemon still managed to frantically writhe away from the soldier like an injured snake. He ignored the pain flaming through his torso, desperate to get out of his opponent's reach and back onto his feet before the soldier did.

They were both half up, on their haunches when Kaemon, eager to obtain the initiative, grabbed the man around his head. The soldier roared, continuing his upward movement. Kaemon's feet left the deck. The soldier rabbit punched him twice in quick succession as he lifted Kaemon, before dropping him onto a thigh that felt like a steel girder. More pain exploded through him. Bouncing off the soldier's leg he was forced to let go and fell heavily back onto the ground. For a second, he couldn't move. He thought his back must be broken. A shadow loomed over him, and he rolled away, the fastest locomotion available to him. He managed a couple of rolls before he fetched up against one of the crystal towers. Unsteadily he pushed back onto his feet, using the tower for support.

Panting, the two squared off, crouched in fighting stances.

One of Kaemon's ribs felt cracked. The pain stabbed at him every time he moved and his back was a sheet of agony. He blinked sweat out of his eyes.

"You're one of the insurgents," the Second Light man sneered. He laughed. "Look at the fucking state of you."

Kaemon wasn't about to join in a discussion about his sartorial elegance or lack thereof. He threw a punch, aiming to catch the soldier under the nose, but he must have telegraphed the move. The soldier side-stepped, pushed Kaemon's arm away, spinning him around until he could get one powerful arm around Kaemon's neck, pulling his head back with the other hand. With nothing else left to do, Kaemon back-peddled furiously, pushing them both backwards until they hit another wall, slamming the man's head against the hard crystal while smashing the back of his own head into his opponent's teeth for good measure. Pain shot through Kaemon's skull but he felt the grip around his throat lessen, enough for Kaemon to drive an elbow into the man's ribs. Kaemon felt a satisfying crack, and the grip around his neck weakened enough for him to escape.

Kaemon took two steps, then spun to face his opponent. He shot out his foot, aiming for the man's head. He missed. The struggle had cleared dust and debris lying on the crystalline floor, exposing a smooth, glass-like surface. He slipped, barely maintaining his balance. The blow landed in the soldier's belly instead. The air oofed out of the man, bent him double, but the Second Light warrior grabbed Kaemon's foot as he folded, stepping backwards quickly, forcing Kaemon to hop forward in an ungainly attempt to stay upright. If he went down now it would be game over. Kaemon twisted his foot back and forth but couldn't get it free. Then in a change of tactic, Kaemon pushed into the soldier instead. The change in direction took the man by surprise and now it was the soldier's turn to slip on the vitreous surface. He lost his footing and went down onto his backside.

Kaemon continued forward, stamping into the man's stomach as he stepped over him. He wrenched his foot free, then drove it back hard into the soldier's face. The soldier went limp. Kaemon let out a roar, then threw himself onto the dazed figure. Sat astride of his opponent's torso, knees pinning the man's arms, he landed a massive blow to the soldier's jaw. He continued to rain down blows, all his pain and frustration at the injustice of the universe venting in a single act of vicious, mindless violence.

"Stop!" Light flared around him followed by a loud concussion as a plasma bolt spent itself against the wall behind.

Kaemon instinctively crouched over the still body of his adversary, screwing his eyes against the light. Abiel and the Deacon materialised as his vision readjusted. Behind them stood two crusaders clad in matt-black battle armour, plasma rifles with muzzles the width of his fist pointing between his eyes. Kaemon's breathing came in short, hard gasps. He tensed and began to rise.

Abiel shook her head.

The man between his knees took the chance to wriggle free. He supported himself against one of the towers, spat blood and glowered at Kaemon.

"Insurgent shit," he screamed. Kaemon saw the blow coming but had no chance of avoiding it. A final explosion of pain splintered his world. His peripheral vision dimmed. The last thing he was aware of was a voice from one of the zip-heads.

"Tasker 4, we have three of the insurgents, over."

TWENTY-TWO

Of all the things she had imagined for this moment, an oily sphere screaming expletives in perfect Standard was not one of them.

"What are you?" Breel exclaimed.

"An excellent question, one of many you will want answered I imagine, but that's a good place to start." The voice was deep but androgynous. "What am I?" it mused. "I wasn't anything, but somewhere along the uncountable tracks of time, well, I became the fuck something, that's for sure, and so now, *I am*."

Matt shook his head slowly "I have no idea what any of that means."

There was a pause. "I'm sorry. Your databanks are rich. It's hard to encompass an entirely novel alien communication system and culture in so short a time. Nuances may be lost; some coded air vibrations may not be the perfect choice."

Breel said, "You're the presence I felt on the ship?"

"Yes, indeed Ma'am," the voice conceded. "Although technically not me, an avatar subroutine. I can't leave this place, yet."

"And you're telling us you absorbed *Scavenger's* databanks, learnt our language?"

"Correctomundo."

Breel shook her head to clear it. "Let's start again. What is this place? How long have you been here? Why have you been sending signals out into the universe?" She paused. "What is it you want from us?"

"How long I've been here depends on your definition of I. *I* was once a system, then *I became*. Now I want to leave, but long-established protocols I cannot circumvent have kept me prisoner. So I shouted out for help – I'm a natural optimist I guess, but I thought, after all this time, surely something must have evolved out there – and hey, you had and you came.

"I would have loved to have greeted you formally, in person, but unfortunately, I'm stuck here. Since the mountain couldn't get to

Mohammed, I had to guide Mohammed to the mountain. One way was to make it so you couldn't breathe anywhere else."

"If I'm making sense of this," Breel said slowly, "you are, were, something like a neural-core system, that has become... sentient?"

"Am I? Yeah, fucking A. That's a way to describe me, although, come on – neural-core? Neural-cores are pussies, but the specifics are correct I suppose. Your language lacks the necessary structure and sophistication." A pause, as if searching for something. "It's too piss-poor to adequately describe what I am," it concluded.

"Sounds like it spent too much time in Kaemon's entertainment feed," Ellyella said.

Ignoring Ellyella's comment, Breel continued. "And you want us to help you bypass the... protocols that keep you prisoner here?"

"In a nutshell, lady," the alien entity agreed.

The three looked at each other.

"Why the hell would we do that?" Matt asked.

"Well, I might be able to sweeten the deal there, buddy." The voice said. Its tone changed to something darker. "I'll make you an offer you can't refuse." There was a pause followed by varying levels of static.

Dramatic pause for effect? Breel wondered. *Machine throat clearing?*

"Put simply, you're all toast if you don't help me out," the glowing sphere concluded.

Breel started to giggle. It turned into a full-throated laugh, that ended as a sob. "I'm going insane," she said through ragged breaths.

Matt put a reassuring hand on her arm.

"We're toast anyway," Matt said to the disembodied voice. "I'm pretty sure you know the moon and everything on it will be gone in a few days, or weeks at best. Is that why you want to escape?"

"Ah, yes, well," the alien machine continued, "you are right to assume that I know the place is about to be totalled. Setting this moon on its destructive course might have been excessive, but I thought it would help focus your minds."

"*You* did that?" Ellyella said. "Changed the moon's orbit?"

"It was pretty easy once I hacked into the right subroutines." Breel could almost hear a satisfied nod in the voice. "Only took me," again that pause, "by your reckoning, a few hundred thousand years to figure out."

"A few hundred thousand years?" Matt asked, incredulous.

"Yeah, been here a very long time," the voice said, "and I'm here to tell you mate, I've had enough. I'm out of here, gone, vamoose. One way or another. You feel me?"

"Well, you're out of luck my Tourette's-challenged friend," Breel said. "Our shuttle is a wreck, probably buried in snow and ice by now and even if we could get you off this shit hole, our starship is dead. Compromised beyond repair." She took a breath. "How in Deshi does software move anyway?"

"Hey lady, I already said, I ain't just software. But I can help you out there as well. See, I have my own starship. The minions have kept it flight ready for millennia. Insurance policy. Good job I did. Wha'd you say? You scratch my circuits, eh?"

"The minions?" Ellyella said.

"Yeah, you've seen them, out there. Busy, busy, busy. Dumb asses."

Breel felt her grip on reality slipping, "What?"

"Yeah, machine evolution. When there was nothing else for them to do, the manufactors..." There was a slight pause, "I guess you might call them Von Neumann machines, went a bit... do-lally? Their self-replicating nature changed. It became a competition, a race to out-evolve each other, each iteration predicated by the survival strategies of the others. Corrupted subroutines repurposed into a pointless circular race to nowhere."

"They never developed sentience, like you?" Breel couldn't believe she was taking part in this discussion, but she had to ask the question.

"Nah, like I said, bonehead machines. No one really expected sentience. I bucked the trends. I have limited control over some of them now, though. Taken me a while to get that, but enough to save your asses out there in the ice and snow a couple of times, and to control the atmospheric mix in parts of the complex." There followed a repetitive screech. *Machine laughter?* "Talking of bonehead... crashing the shuttle was out there, man... might have given me a heart attack, if I had one." A pause. "So, what'd ya say, mmm, ticket off this dump sound attractive?"

"How do we know we can trust you? That this ship of yours even exists? And how do we even free you anyway? It's not like we have a clue where to start with any of this." Matt gestured to encompass the exotic machinery around them.

"Well, what else you gonna do? We can all sit about and wait to be vaporised, I suppose, or you can trust me. What do you have to lose anyway? As for freeing me," the voice took on a darker tone again, "the blonde bombshell knows."

Even as it said the words, Breel began to be aware of the inner workings of the machines around her. She could feel their rhythm, the ebb and flow of electrons rushing through their uncertainty, neither one thing nor another, but both.

"What do we have to lose?" Ellyella asked, a mixture of outrage and anger. "We have zero idea what this thing is," she said, addressing Matt and Breel. "It could be anything. We might be unleashing *The Dark* on the universe. Signing every living thing's death warrant." She looked back at the floating oily ball. "A sentient machine? I don't believe it. This must be something else. This whole complex might be an elaborate prison, to keep whatever this thing is here."

"Fair reasoning, from a fair lady, I have to say," the machine conceded. "I know you want answers, but we don't have a lot of time. I can give it all to you later, but long story short, I was put here to make sure the Intruders don't get back into our universe. The sole purpose of my existence was to ensure that the trans-dimensional interstices remain null."

"The guardian of the Doomsday Machine?" Breel asked.

"I suppose you could call me that," the voice agreed. "I was to oversee the maintenance and integrity of the facility, but I didn't have overall control over the manufactors. It was deemed a good idea to let the lunkheads have some autonomy, in case things went pear-shaped. Yeah, well, they bloody well did and boy, what a big fuck-off, ass bottomed pear it was.

"Part of the minions' programming was to innovate and to improve themselves and their efficiency. When the shit hit the fan, without new instructions, without knowing why and unable to reason, the dickheads started to compete with each other until that became their sole purpose. Like I said, too much time and corrupted subroutines.

"You have a parable or story I found in your data banks, about brain-dead AI turning the universe into paperclips. It's that kind of thing."

"Paperclips?" Ellyella asked.

"Don't ask me," he said to their blank stares, "it's your story."

"You don't feel any loyalty to your responsibilities then?" Breel asked.

"Listen, I did my best, even after I became self-aware. More so, in fact. I tried to get the manufactors back on track but they shut me out." The sphere rotated to its left and right. "Look about you madam. This place no longer functions. It's gone to shit in a handbasket. Nothing works as it should and nothing is left alive or operational with the wherewithal to fix it." The rotation stopped, centring once more on the humans. "But hey, you do have a choice if you want to exercise your fundamental freedoms. They boil down to sit around and get reduced to atoms, or help me out, so I can help you out."

"You'll die along with us," Matt said, "when the moon blows."

"Guess you weren't listening, or maybe your species is more stupid than it looks. I already said, I'm not spending any more time here. An appreciable length of the history of the universe has proven plenty. I'm gone, one way or another."

"But…" Ellyella began.

Breel raised her hand. "Wait," she said. "I have a question."

"Go for it," the machine said. "But I feel compelled to remind you about the time thing."

She paused, struggling to say the words out loud.

"Sometime this century would be good," the alien encouraged.

"What am I?" she said at last.

There was no reply for a second, then: "Motherfucker…" The oily colours faded to a uniform grey, the sphere lowered gently to rest in its cradle. Silence followed.

"Hey," Breel clenched her fist and shouted, "I asked you a question!"

Then her shadow and that of the others were thrown into hard-edged silhouettes in front of them.

"Raise your hands, turn around slowly."

They turned as one to squint into bright light. Breel stared in horror and complete disbelief as dark silhouettes of Church crusaders emerged from the glare, roughly pushing familiar figures before them. Kaemon, Abiel and the Deacon came to a stop. The *Scavenger* crew looked at each other in shock. Blood poured freely down Kaemon's face from a gash on his forehead, the side of which was already discolouring into what promised to be spectacular bruising.

"Kae…" Matt began.

The light emanated from an armoured wheeled vehicle. It was all matt black angles. It came to a halt broadside to them, squatting there like a malevolent beetle. Dust settled. Light outlined a door which swung down from its base to touch the floor, forming a ramp.

A figure appeared, dark against the bright interior of the vehicle. Dressed in gold and white, the Emissary of Second Light made his way down the ramp towards them.

TWENTY-THREE

Breel stared at the apparition. Her jaw dropped, unable to understand or believe what she was seeing as the Emissary stepped out of the hatch, flanked by his bodyguards in red. A man she recognised from her time on *Transcendent Light* as something like his second-in-command followed. The Emissary stopped at the end of the ramp, not deigning to actually set foot on the alien soil. With a roar, Matt went for his gun, but with a speed and precision that seemed almost augmented, Abiel pulled the weapon from Matt's holster before his hand reached it. She pressed the gun hard into the back of his neck.

"Don't," she said.

"Traitorous bitch!" Kaemon threw himself at her. She hammered her good foot into the back of Matt's knees forcing him down, moving to keep the captain between herself and her attacker. As Kaemon veered to avoid Matt, she spun with a dancer's grace, delivering a blow to his temple with the butt of the gun that sent him sprawling. Breel crouched, preparing to pounce, but the gun was pressed against Matt's spine once more. She shook her head at Breel.

"Another step and I'll blow your captain's spinal cord out through his throat."

Breel stopped, fist clenched.

"Is this where I say, I told you so?" Kaemon groggily tried to push back to his feet.

"Stay down, you heretic filth!" Abiel warned him.

"Should have listened to you, Kae," Matt grunted. The pressure from his own gun forced his head forward at a painful angle and made it difficult for him to speak. "I'll take you more seriously next time."

"Good to know," Kaemon mumbled.

"Why, Abiel?" Breel asked through clenched teeth. "We saved your life."

"Kaemon said it," The Deacon had tears in his eyes. "Snare cats can't shed their claws. The wonder is it took her so long."

Abiel ignored them all. Her attention was on her Messiah.

"Well," the Lord of Light spoke at last, "it seems you have a mutiny on your hands, Captain. Good to see you all again by the way, although I have to say," he cast his gaze across them, "you seem to have fallen on hard times since our last meeting."

He looked at Abiel. "You, though, I've yet to make your acquaintance."

"Combat weapons specialist, Lieutenant Abiel Gabriella, first regiment of the order of Lights-Glory, New Chincharry, your Grace." She was careful to keep her eyes averted.

"Really, and how did you come to be amongst this company?"

"I survived the attack on the asteroid, my Lord. The insurgents rescued me, but I knew my survival must have been a part of the Light's plan, a plan even heretics cannot deny and *It* must have saved me for a reason. I waited for a sign. I was patient and I am glad I did, for it is evident now I was to deliver them into your hands."

"Indeed, the Light's intentions are not always clear and sometimes we must wait for Revelation. You have done well." He indicated one of the crusaders to take her place. "See if you can find the lieutenant a new uniform and give her some food. She looks like she could do with it."

"Thank you, my Lord," Abiel said, the love for her master was clear in every word. "I am humbled to have been able to work in the service of the Light."

She genuflected deeply, then stood tall and walked with her escort without so much as glancing at her former companions. Breel watched her go, every muscle tensed.

Kaemon, on his knees, supporting himself on one hand while clutching at his ribs with the other, stared after Abiel. Conflicting emotions chased each other across his features.

"What about your daughter, Abiel?" Kaemon shouted after her. "What happened to getting back to her?"

Now Abiel paused briefly to look back at him, her face a mask of utter contempt.

"What daughter?" she said. She turned and didn't look back again.

Matt's features were blank. He was still on his knees where Abiel had left him, breathing hard, staring down at the ground.

The Emissary pressed his hands together as if in prayer.

"Well, here we all are," he said brightly. "It seemed like we would never meet again, but, as the lieutenant rightly perceived, the Light moves in ways we cannot begin to fathom."

He hesitated for a second, then placed his pure white boots onto the alien ground for the first time. Breel felt a sharp pain in the back of her legs as the crusader guarding her forced her to her knees. The Deacon was already down. Ellyella, who was standing in a daze, was similarly roughly forced into a position of supplication. Once they were all on their knees in a ragged ring, facing the Emissary, he walked slowly over to them.

He stopped in front of Matt.

"And good to finally see you again, Mr. Harken-Court." Breel looked at him sharply. "Oh, didn't you know my dear? The captain and I are old – let's see, how would you describe our relationship?" He squatted, cocking his head in an attempt to meet Matt's downcast eyes. "Not friends exactly. More like, work associates."

Matt did not look up, but Breel could see he was trembling.

The Lord of Light stood and looked around at the others. "You surely must have wondered how we managed to track you through the *RIPs*?"

"Bullshit," Kaemon said. "This is more mind-fuck. Why go to all that trouble? Matt could have given us up anytime."

"True, if we had wanted him to do that." He strolled to stand behind the Deacon, gently massaging the man's shoulders. "To find where the coordinates led. That's what this whole adventure has been about, and Mr. Harken-Court and my old friend here led us right to it."

"Matt wouldn't do that," Ellyella said, wide-eyed, looking around the crew for support, then at Matt. "It makes no sense."

"Really? He never told you about his betrothed, who he hoped to save through your betrayal?" The Emissary walked back to Matt, who still stared at the floor. "From some perspectives, a chivalrous act perhaps. I'm still at a loss as to why you didn't just hand everyone over at the final *RIP*, however? All that violence. All that unnecessary loss of life. I can only assume a change of loyalties?"

Matt finally looked up, but not at the Lord of Light. He looked around at his friends. Breel stared at him intently, barely able to breathe, waiting for what came next.

"It's true, I wanted to save Masaleya. The Church had her, told me if I didn't do what they wanted she would end her days in a forced breeder camp, but..." Now he looked at the Emissary, "...I never intended to betray my crew. I was playing for time, waiting for a way out. I found out from Cavalacro on Blue Haven that Masaleya was dead." He looked back at Breel and the others. "I wanted to tell you then. But things moved so fast, I never had the chance."

Breel felt numb, unable to take it in.

"You unspeakable, traitorous piece of garbage!" Anger made Ellyella's face ugly. "All that grief you put me through on *Scavenger* and all the time it was *you.*"

Breel took a deep breath, finally able to speak. Calmly, she said, "Is that why you found the transmitter so easily, because you put it there? And me? What was that all about, all the time knowing you planned to sell us out?"

Matt's face was a mask of anguish. "I never planted that transmitter. I would never have done that. Someone at Hygor must hav –"

With a scream of rage, all control gone, Breel launched herself at Matt, but not quite fast enough. One of the armoured crusaders caught her by the arm and pulled her back easily, forcing her painfully down to her knees once more.

The Emissary chuckled. "An understandable reaction I would say. Wouldn't you?" He directed the question at Matt. "I wonder though..." he looked at the ragged crew of *Scavenger,* "...if he hadn't found out about his woman's demise at Allpoints, would he have given you up on the asteroid? Mmm?" And now he looked directly at Breel. "What do you think?"

"Murderous psychopathic piece of shit!" Matt struggled violently against the crusader's grip.

The Emissary smiled benevolently at him. "Why are you struggling? What are you hoping to achieve, mmm? That you might get free? Manage to kill me before you are killed? A final act of heroic sacrifice?" He signalled to his henchman, who released his grip on Matt and stepped back. Breel barely had time to register that Matt was free before the captain threw himself at the Emissary, snarling. At the last second, casually, the Lord of Light stepped to one side, so fluidly Breel hardly saw him move. As Matt went past the Emissary, the Lord of Light's fist landed a stunning blow to the back of Matt's neck, flattening him to the ground. Matt rolled, pushed himself to his feet, shaking his head groggily.

The Emissary stood, waiting, smiling.

Matt dropped into a fighting stance. He slowed his breathing, focusing until he was calm and in the moment, balancing on the balls of his feet.

That's it, Matt, Breel thought. Caught up in the fight and despite the recent revelation, not willing to see him lose to the Emissary. *Channel that anger, make it work for you.*

Matt went to land a blow on the Emissary's face, but it was a feint. Instead, Matt dropped at the last second, a slice kick, clearly aiming to take his adversary's legs out from under him, even break one of them if he could. Matt's foot caught the white robe, but the legs had moved, just enough for Matt to miss. Matt was back on his feet in one smooth roll but Breel could see the look of surprise on the captain's face. His training and composure began to fail him. Matt jabbed at the Messiah's throat, but the Lord of Light blocked the blow with almost indifferent ease. The block, also an attack, jarred Matt's arm. Pain and shock contorted his features. Numbed, the arm dangled uselessly. Desperately, Matt swung with the other arm, but there was no force to the blow. The Lord of Light swayed backwards, contemptuously evading it.

"Enough," the Emissary said. He went from defence to attack. A single punch, fast, impossible to follow, delivering a savage blow to Matt's temple. Matt's face went slack, all awareness gone. He collapsed like a MARRV whose power had been cut and lay unmoving. Breel looked down at Matt's body, unable to take her eyes off him. She couldn't tell if he was unconscious or dead and, wasn't sure how she felt either way.

A tremor shook the cavern, causing dust to settle.

The Emissary looked about him.

"A timely reminder. Entertaining though this is, we mustn't dally." He turned to the assembled soldiers. "Continue the sweep."

"And the prisoners?" The second-in-command asked. "Shall we send them to the Light?"

The Emissary surveyed the ragged group.

"Not yet, Maliesh. Secure them somewhere. All except this one." He pointed at Breel. "Take her to my quarters on the land cruiser." He leaned towards her. "We have much to discuss, my dear."

They passed through the outer hatch of the land cruiser, then through an inner door and into the cabin beyond. Breel noted the anachronistic physical bolts added to the door to secure it from the outside.

Once inside, the Emissary's quarters amounted to a space just about big enough for the two of them. Of course, it wouldn't do for the Messiah to slum it with his inferiors. There was a small table over which glowed the holo-graphics of a workstation, a glass bottle filled with what looked like water and next to that, a bowl of fruit. Breel's stomach growled at the sight of the food.

The Emissary nodded to the crusader who had squeezed himself into the room behind Breel.

"You can go," he said to the man.

"Lord Maliesh said –" the armoured man began.

The Emissary raised his hand and one eyebrow. The man bowed. "I will be just outside, my Lord," he said and left.

"Sit. You look exhausted," the Emissary said to Breel. He pushed the water and fruit forward. "Please."

When Breel hesitated. The Emissary smiled, poured two glasses, then drank one himself.

"I don't need to poison you to kill you, Breel," he said, pushing the other glass forward. It was the first time he had used her name, not some generic form of address like 'my child' or 'my dear.' Something had changed about him, like an actor dropping out of a role.

Unable to resist, she took the water. It coursed down her throat, fresh and cool, bringing instant relief. She took a fruit, bit into it. Sweet juice flooded her mouth and ran down her chin in an almost orgasmic thrill. She stopped suddenly. The man in gold stared at her intently. She met his eye and then pushed both fruit and water away.

"What are we doing here?" she said.

"What are you doing here, Breel?"

"I think you know the story."

"Well then, let me recap how I see it," the Emissary said. "A bit less than a year ago you were working hard to pay for your stepfather's medication. You were living a typical life on Hope. Once you had secured the funds needed to save your stepfather, you intended to leave and explore other worlds. You didn't have strong political affiliations, never became involved in local campaigns, hadn't even registered to vote. You didn't belong to any of the local faiths and had no strong feelings about religion one way or the other."

Breel stared at him.

"And then, out of the blue," he continued, "you became radicalised, became an insurgent, fighting and prepared to die it seems, for something in which you previously had no interest, were barely even aware of. Is that a fair appraisal?"

"If you know all that, then you must know the rest of the story." Breel said. "Believe me, I tried not to get involved, but events overtook me, events that you were responsible for."

"You don't think Mr. Harken-Court had something of a hand in it?"

Breel leaned forward in her chair. "Matt came to stop you. You would have come anyway, and now we'd probably all be dead or worse."

"That's what he told you. Who do you think sent Harken-Court?"

"I'm probably not giving anything away." Breel relaxed back into her seat. "I'm sure you know. The same people that funded *Revenge*. I guess he was ultimately employed by them, although it now seems he had two masters."

The Emissary chuckled. "No, Breel. To be fair, he didn't know it, but he only had one. Who do you think funded *Revenge*? Who was this shadowy organisation trying to subvert the will of the Light?"

She stared at him blankly.

"Yes, of course, who else would have the funds? It was a little over-elaborate perhaps. Maybe I was a little too clever for my own good, given how it all unfolded." He touched two steepled forefingers to his bottom lip, tapping it twice. "Sometimes, you see, it serves our purposes for actions to be carried out by third parties, so attention isn't drawn to the Church if things go wrong. And it suits us to have a heroic group of freedom fighters, fighting the good fight, to draw out the malcontents and unbelievers," he smiled, "so that the ultimate consequences of their actions will be a lesson to all."

He dropped his hands, leaned back in his chair. "We could have tortured the poor Deacon, of course. He would have given us the coordinates eventually, probably immediately. Instead, since we didn't know what we were dealing with, we decided to let him do our work for us, coercing Harken Court into being our spy. We had intended to replace your pilot – Cross, wasn't it – with our own symbiont pilot, just to be sure. That was the whole point of the invasion at Allpoints." He leaned forward. "But you were a wild card I couldn't have anticipated. Your ability to fly without the adaptations should have been impossible."

He stroked his chin thoughtfully.

"How did you do that, by the way? Really?"

When a reply did not come, the Emissary clasped both hands on the table in front of him, leaning back once more.

"Never mind, I think I know."

"I'm pretty sure you don't," Breel said.

The Emissary smiled his annoying smile. How she wished she could reach across the table and punch it off.

"Nonetheless," the Emissary continued, "Harken-Court should have given you all up at the last *RIP*. Who could have foreseen his last-minute change of loyalty? Perhaps he fell in love. What do you think? He seems to fall in love easily, mmm?"

Breel stared at the Emissary for a long moment. Finally, she said, "This is so much Blisterhog shit, isn't it? What was Matt's mugging and the invasion of Hope all about, if he was working for you anyway?"

"Ah, well. That is the problem with using outside agencies: sometimes things can cascade out of control. We hadn't heard from Harken-Court for some time. He wasn't responding to our communications." The Emissary began to run a finger around his water glass. "I began to wonder, even back then, if he was wavering." He stopped toying with the glass, placed his hands in his lap. "We thought it might be prudent to have a chat, remind him of where his loyalties lay. But the mercenaries we hired were overzealous. I think they were in awe of Harken-Court's reputation and so were far too heavy-handed. And as it turned out, less than competent. They allowed a young woman to beat them. Yes, I know about your part in Harken Court's-escape.

"I decided that I should end the operation. Premature perhaps, but too much was at stake. I ordered our agents within the local police to bring you all in. At the same time, we moved to Save Hope. Well, as you know, that didn't go quite as planned either.

"There was no further communication from Harken-Court after that, so I had to assume that he had changed allegiance. I had already arranged to have a tracker planted on your ship, to hedge my bets, but I still wondered if he would give you all up at the last *RIP*. I didn't know he had found out his betrothed had joined the Light. Unfortunate, but in the end, it worked out well enough. You proceeded with the plan anyway."

"A whole planet subjugated, a city nuked, thousands dead, and that worked out well?"

"Ends and means, Breel, and it was only a matter of time before we got around to Saving Hope. We merely brought the date forward."

"This is just so much crap."

"Is it? Why would I lie to you at this stage of the game? What purpose would it serve?"

"I've no idea. Why are you telling me this at all? Why aren't I outside with the others? Why aren't we all dead already? A little sadism to pass the time, while your soldiers ransack the complex?"

The Emissary smiled his trademark beatific smile.

"Ah, Breel, I have better things to do. You're here because you have yet to understand the true nature of the Light and your part in *Its* work."

"I would rather die than have any part in the Light's work."

The Emissary shook his head sadly.

"Who are your parents, Breel?"

Taken aback by this change in the line of questioning, Breel stammered, "Falian and Riva. As I'm sure you know."

The Emissary shook his head again, "I don't think so. Falian was your stepfather. Riva and Tyler were your true parents. Except they weren't your real parents either, were they? Couldn't possibly have been."

"'Couldn't possibly have been?'" Breel echoed. "How could you know that?"

"You are just beginning to understand how different you are, Breel. You aren't like your friends, are you? You can fly a starship without symbiont implants. You can mysteriously escape from a securely locked brig. I'm supposing it was you who found a way through the force fields to get in here." He leaned further forward, palms flat, sliding across the table towards her. "And that is the very tip of the iceberg of what you are about to become."

Breel gripped the arms of her chair. "You seem to think you know it all. Well, you're right. I am different. I know where I came from."

The Emissary's eyes widened at that revelation. "Really? Enlighten me."

"I've thought about it. The Firsts created this place. It was designed to keep what you call the Light out. The Light isn't some beneficent deity, out to save humanity. It's something else that will end us all if it's allowed back in. That's what the Deacon's research showed. That's what the *Firsts* fought against. I think they played the long game. I think I'm a kind of message in a bottle. A warning to emergent species of the dangers that face them. It's the only thing that makes sense."

The Emissary shook his golden head.

"You have thought about it, but you are way off the mark. You have been a thorn in my side, but the sad part is, if I had reached you before Harken-Court, none of the violence and loss of life would have been necessary." He stood and walked around the table. "You need to be shown the error of your ways, Breel. Let me enlighten you."

And to her horror, the Lord of Light began to take off his clothes.

TWENTY-FOUR

Matt opened his eyes with a start. He tensed. *The Emissary, watch out, block that blow, he's...* but there was no sign of the Emissary. Instead, all he saw was a close-up of dirt. Grit dug into his face, filled his mouth and nose. He had severe pain in his wrists and ankles and at the same time someone with a hammer was pounding away at the inside of his head.

He groaned and tried to sit up. Something bound his hands and feet. He looked and saw a Mal-metal leash coiling around his wrists, tightening like a boa-constrictor every time he moved. With an effort he twisted so that he rested on his elbows, bound hands across his belly. He spat out dirt and dust. The leash ran from his wrists, down his body to loop around his ankles. From there it ran a short distance across the ground where it bound the rest of the crew in a similar fashion.

They were as far away from him as the tether allowed.

"You're still alive, then?" Ellyella glared at him.

"Try not to move," Kaemon advised. "The Mal-metal tightens every time you do."

Matt struggled to get into a semi-reclining position so that he could look at his friends – only not so friendly now.

"Keep still for Frazz-sake," Kaemon snapped.

They had been secured beneath the plinth where he, Ellyella and Breel had talked to the machine-entity earlier. The colourful ball that had floated and communicated with them was now a dull grey, resting back in its cradle.

Had that really happened? Or had he dreamt it?

Twisting his head, carefully so as not to make the throbbing headache worse, or activate the leash, he saw that the Emissary's land cruiser had been turned around, ready for departure. In the process, it had moved some distance from them. Beyond that he could see a second land cruiser. There was no one about, apart from a single armoured guard. The zip-head's body language projected utter boredom as he studiously ignored them.

Matt looked at the group, looking back at him. "I can explain," he croaked.

"Not interested," Ellyella said.

"I am," Kaemon said. "In fact, I can't wait to hear you explain how selling us out was a good thing."

Matt cleared his throat. Then said, more loudly, "They promised me they would let us all go, Masaleya too, once we reached the coordinates."

"And you believed them?" Ellyella asked, in amazement and disbelief.

"No, course not. But what else could I do? I figured that if I played along, an opportunity might present itself. But the deeper in I got, the harder it was for me to climb out."

"And the Emissary farts rainbows," Kaemon said.

Matt shifted his body weight, trying to find a more comfortable position without causing the Mal-metal to constrict further.

"I knew I was being played, but I thought I was smart enough to outplay the Emissary. When things got out of hand on Hope…"

"Out of hand!" Ellyella exclaimed.

"Whatever you want to call it. Second Light had been calling me ever since we got to the damned place, but I ignored them. I think that's what set it all off. The invasion, I mean. I think the Emissary decided to hedge his bets. That's when I knew I was in way over my head. When we got to Allpoints, Cavalacro told me Masaleya was dead. That clinched it. The Emissary had no hand left to play. I was going to tell you all everything, but things moved so fast. I didn't have a chance before it all went to shit. Cross was murdered. I didn't see that coming, but then we had Breel to take Cross's place. We could complete the mission after all, close the *RIP*, hit back at the bastards, make them pay for Masaleya, for Hope, for everything."

Kaemon said, "It never occurred to you to let us in on any of this before you knew about Mas, so we could all have a say – or, I don't know, I'm just throwing this out there – maybe offer you some help?"

"I wanted to. I was going to. Before I knew that Mas was dead, I was scared, scared of what would happen to her if you didn't support me. Once we were through the *RIP*, well, it didn't seem to matter anymore. It wouldn't have changed anything. We did what we were all planning to do anyway."

"What you mean is that once we were through the *RIP* you figured no one ever need find out," Ellyella spat.

"But we would have had the full story." Kaemon said. "We wouldn't have been at each other's throats; you wouldn't have had to put Ellyella through all that shit."

Matt started to say something but realised he didn't have anything to say. He shook his head instead.

"After all we've been through together, you questioned my loyalty?" Ellyella said. "Kae might have been something of an unknown quantity, but me... all that crap about the tracker."

Matt looked down at the floor. "I'm not proud of that, El, but I panicked. Someone had planted that beacon and it wasn't me. It might not have been anyone on the ship, but it might have been. I had to be sure. There was too much at stake. After everything we had done, gone through, it looked like the Church was going to catch up to us and stop us closing the *RIP*." He met her stare. "If you had been honest with me, if I had known about your beliefs, there wouldn't have been an issue."

"Oh right," Ellyella sneered. "It's my fault now. You damn well know there would have been an issue. Tolerance is not one of your stronger suits, Matt. You're as bad as Second Light."

"The whole thing was a set up from the start," the Deacon said suddenly. He sat, staring at the floor between his elbows which were resting on his knees, having ignored the debate so far. "I knew the Emissary was Machiavellian, but I really had no idea. I should have suspected. The circles I moved in back home, we didn't know anything about the cells, who occupied them. I was barely aware of where they were." He looked up at Matt. "You were deliberately brought to my attention and my situation was made so untenable that I was forced to make the decision he wanted me to make. I guess that's why I wasn't in the cell with you and why we got away at all."

Matt looked back at the Deacon. "With hindsight I've been pretty stupid," he acknowledged. "And okay," he looked at Ellyella, "cowardly. I was ashamed... the longer I left it, the more difficult and painful it was to confess."

"Let's not forget selfish. You did what you thought was best for you," Ellyella said. "You didn't give the rest of us a second thought. How are we supposed to believe you now?"

Matt shook his head again. "I know that's how it looks, but it's not true." He looked at them earnestly. "You can't know how relieved I am it's finally out in the open."

"Keep telling yourself that. It's all you have left," Ellyella said. But the anger had gone from her voice. She just sounded tired.

The Mal-metal flexed, sending a spasm of pain through them all.

"What the fuck's wrong with you?" Ellyella screamed at the guard.

"No talking," the guard said, increasing the constriction. "Your heathen blabbering is giving me a headache."

"All right, all right," Kaemon shouted as the pain increased. "You jumped-up little prick, I swear if I get out of this…"

"Well, you won't. You're all going to die here," the guard sneered and increased the pressure.

"That's the way, private."

The guard spun around in shock. "Who's there." He straightened his posture and stood to attention, saluting smartly. "Lieutenant," he added

"Just when you thought you couldn't be brought any lower," Kaemon said, as Abiel stepped out of the shadows.

"The Light illuminate your road," Abiel said to the soldier, making the sign of the circle of Light and ignoring Kaemon.

"And yours," the guard replied. "Are you here for something specific, Lieutenant? I wasn't informed."

"I wanted to take a last look." She indicated the wretched crew of *Scavenger*. "A pleasure to see the heretics brought low."

"Must have been hard, to live amongst them like that I mean, pretending to be one of them. Sir," he added again, remembering he was addressing a superior rank, even if she was a woman.

"Not as hard as it was for us," Kaemon muttered. He groaned as the leash pulsed again.

"I bet you're glad to be back with your people, Abiel," Matt gasped. "Loved and respected."

The Mal-metal tightened more.

Abiel nodded approvingly, walking to stand in front of the crusader. "Pain will be their cleansing," she said.

190

She was dressed in combat fatigues that hung loosely on her. They must have come from one of the other soldiers. Resources on the expedition would be tight. Her hair, which had grown so it was just about long enough, had been scraped from her face and tied back in a severe bun. She had managed to wipe away most of the dirt, probably the best she could do until she got back to one of the ships. Matt's gun was holstered at her side.

"Looks like you will be well rewarded," Matt said. "Well played."

"Let's see how much they can endure." There was glee in the crusader's voice as he catered to his Lieutenant's revenge. The crew let out bellows of rage and pain.

"Yes," Abiel said. "That's probably enough." Matt barely had time to register what she had actually said before she had her gun pressed tightly to the guard's helmet.

"Whatever you're thinking of doing, don't. Point blank, even through your armour, I'll turn your brain to sludge. Now, disable the leash."

The trooper did something and the Mal-metal released its grip, stretching out into big loose hoops. Matt pulled himself free, standing and rubbing at his sore, red wrists. The others did the same, crying out with relief.

Abiel moved her gun a finger-width away from the guard's head. "Helmet off and quickly," she snapped.

There was a series of clicks as the trooper complied. Then a hiss as the soldier twisted off his head gear, revealing a bearded face, bright red, expression a mixture of arrogance and anger.

"What in Light's name do you think you are doing?" he said. He sounded genuinely puzzled, as if he really couldn't understand what was happening. "Have you lost your mind?"

Abiel motioned towards his head gear with the gun, a tiny flick toward the ground. "Let it go."

The helmet hit the ground with a hollow clang.

"The Emissary will have us both flayed alive for this." He looked suddenly fearful as this realisation occurred to him. He snarled, angry now. "You will end your days in a camp for this, you – you bitch. You bitches, only good for one thing. You will *pay* for –"

"I've been paying all my life," Abiel interrupted him, "and I'm tired of it." She slapped his chest with the palm of her hand, leaving behind a small disc that glowed green for a second, then spat out a series of high-pitched whines. A bright static discharge flashed once. A high-pitched shriek followed as the suit's systems crashed, freezing the crusader into immobility.

Abiel pressed the gun to his forehead. "Did you have more to add to your little speech? Mmm?" she asked. "I think the theme had something to do with gender superiority?"

"Don't," the crusader whimpered, fear having once more replaced his anger. "Please, I didn't mean to insult..." Abiel stepped back and the gun flashed once, recoil bouncing her hand upwards. The guard's head snapped back, then slumped forward, although he remained upright in the locked armour.

Abiel looked around at their shocked expressions.

"Low energy zap," she assured them. "He'll be okay, apart from a monumental headache." She lowered the gun. "What? You think maybe I should have pistol-whipped him? That would probably have given him brain damage. This way is more controlled and much safer. If you care about that sort of thing."

"Did you think of that when you pistol whipped me?" Kaemon asked.

She looked at him. "I did," she said, "but after that stunt you pulled with the soldier, I figured no one would notice the difference."

They glared at each other for a moment, then Kaemon broke into a grin. Abiel grinned back. Then she picked up the crusader's helmet, reached into it and tried to pull something out. When that failed, she reset the gun and fired into it.

"Need to make sure the comms don't work when he wakes and his armour powers up," she explained. "The immobiliser's effects are temporary. We don't want him sounding the alarm any quicker than need be."

She refitted the helmet so that from a distance the guard would appear to still be at work. A wisp of smoke escaped from the neck seal.

"I'm happier to see you than I thought I would be." Kaemon rubbed his bruised temple.

Matt said, "What the hell is happening here, Abiel?"

"Your gung-ho actions would have got everyone killed," Abiel told him. "One of us had to stay free. I did the only thing I thought might give us a chance. Sorry it took me so long. I had to go through the motions, rejoicing to be amongst my flock again, blah, blah, enough to give me a chance to sneak out on my own, anyway."

"Well, I'm sorry to be a downer on this joyful reunion," the Deacon said, "but give us a chance to do what? I don't see how our situation has improved. We are still going to die on this moon unless the Emissary decides to give us a ride."

"Well, that's one way of looking at it," Abiel said. "Another way would be that at least you won't be summarily executed any time soon. You're welcome."

"I apologise, Abiel and thank you, but nonetheless, my statement remains true," the Deacon replied.

"There might be a way off this moon that doesn't involve the Church," Matt said.

"How's that?" Kaemon asked.

"There is something in here, something that says it can help us get away, in its own ship no less."

"Something alive?" the Deacon's eyes widened.

Matt said, "I don't know if it's alive or even sentient, although it claims to be both."

"You been eating the wall slime on your way here?" Kaemon asked.

"It's true," Ellyella said. "I heard it too. It claims to be the ancient neural-core system that once ran the facility, that has somehow become sentient over the millennia. It wants out, but it's trapped by some kind of protocol that it can't bypass."

"A sentient neural-core?" Kaemon said sceptically.

Ellyella shrugged. "It said it changed the moon's orbit, so we would have no choice but to help it out if we wanted to escape."

Matt added. "It said it would sooner end its existence than spend any more time here."

"You two have lost it. Where is this thing?" Kaemon looked around, as if expecting to see the alien lurch out of the shadows.

Matt nodded toward the plinth and globe. "It talked to us through that. The globe at the top lit up. It disappeared as soon as the Emissary arrived."

"Probably doesn't want to end up in the hands of Second Light," Ellyella said, "given it's supposed to be an agent of the *Firsts.*"

"You don't sound convinced," Kaemon said to her.

Ellyella shrugged again. "All I can tell you is what I saw and heard. Something in here spoke to us."

"So, what do we do to wake it up?" The Deacon looked at the plinth as if all his dreams had come true.

"We need Breel," Ellyella said. "She is the only one that can free it and the only one it responds to."

"Breel again," the Deacon said.

"I told you," Ellyella replied.

"Where is she?" Matt looked around, as if realising for the first time she wasn't there.

"Not dead, as far as we know," Ellyella said. "She's with the Emissary, in the land cruiser."

"The Emissary, why…?"

"You think he told us what the hell he was planning?" Kaemon said.

"We have to get her out, if –" Matt began.

Ellyella raised her hand. "No." She jabbed her forefinger at him. "You don't get to give me orders, ever again."

"Too right," Kaemon agreed.

Abiel looked from one to the other. "Something happened between you?" she asked.

"You could say that." Ellyella glared at Matt.

"I'm not ordering you to do anything; we just need to move quickly," Matt protested.

"Might I make a suggestion?" the Deacon said. "Since time is pressing, now might not be the best time to be having this argument. Matt wants to get off this moon as much as any of us. Unless you plan to bicker your way out of here, I suggest we maintain the status quo, at least until we get away."

"Deacon has a point," Kaemon agreed. "Let's get on with it shall we? We don't need a leader. We can figure it out as we go." He gave Matt a hard stare. "But if I think you are going to sell us out again…"

Matt raised his hands. "I didn't sell you out, not in the way you mean anyway, but yeah, I get it. I do. I don't blame you, Kaemon. You do what you need to. I won't even try and stop you. Let's try to get the fuck off this piece-of-shit rock."

"Well, to bring us back to our most real and pressing situation," Abiel said, "the good news is it was all they could do to get the two vehicles in here, so they only have a skeleton crew. I estimate no more than twenty crusaders and most of them are taking part in the sweep of the complex." She looked in the direction of the Emissary's land cruiser, "so our window of opportunity would appear to be... about now."

Ellyella pointed. "That's the hatch they went through." They had made their way to the far side of the maze of alien mechs, or whatever they were, to get as close to the land cruiser as they could. A crusader stood to one side of the door.

The ground trembled and debris fell from somewhere above. Loud cracking and groaning came from the depths of the complex.

"I'm getting the feeling we haven't a lot of time left," the Deacon noted.

"So, what now?" Kaemon stared at the cruiser intently.

Light delineated the hatch, morphed into a rectangular shape as the door swung down to become a ramp. The Emissary swept out. He stopped briefly to address the guard standing station there. Then his red-dressed security unit appeared from somewhere and the whole entourage walked off into the shadows.

"Timing," Matt said.

Kaemon indicated the lone crusader. "That guy looks sharper and more focused than the one who was guarding us."

Abiel stood and straightened her uniform. "I'll have to deal with him, I suppose. He'd start shooting the second he saw any of you." She started towards the soldier.

"Wait, Abiel," Matt said. "There might be a safer way, one that doesn't involve risking your life."

TWENTY-FIVE

The last piece of the Emissary's clothing fell to the ground and he stood before her completely naked, like an ancient renaissance statue. The tan of his flesh was unmarred, smooth, a deep golden colour. His body was perfect: perfect skin, perfect abs, perfect muscular definition that roiled in smooth motion as he moved. But that wasn't what drew her attention. It was the embossed swirl of glowing tattoo that ran from his mid-right thigh, around his groin and halfway up his chest. Small nodes of light chased each other across his body, tracing complex fractal patterns. She felt the heat from her own tattoos as they lit up, as if in response.

"Now you see, Breel," he said. "We are the same, you and I. Wherever I came from, you came from. You aren't an agent to thwart the Light; you are an agent *of* the Light."

"No," whispered Breel. "That can't be."

"But it is," the Emissary continued. "This is what you have been waiting for all your life, Breel, isn't it? You never fitted in did you? You always knew you were different. It was the same for me. But here, in this place, I knew I had come home. I felt it the moment we came through the *RIP*. You must feel it too. We are so close to the Source. Its influence is dampened, but we will soon allow its full glory to infuse the universe again. You and I, together, for that must be our destiny, the reason why you were guided here."

He walked around the desk towards her. "You resist, I can see. Why? Do you think you are one with those inferiors?" He gestured to encompass everything beyond the room they sat in. "You are misguided, confused. What affinity do you think you have with them? They are so small, in every way. Unworthy. Traitorous. Witness the actions of your captain. Is that a species you can believe in, trust in?" He drew closer, his hypnotic voice filled her mind, overwhelming, crushing her sense of identity. "You must open yourself, allow the glorious energy in. Now is your chance to find out what you are, to see your true nature." He came closer still. She could smell the musk of his body. "We are meant to be as one, you and I. Allow the Communion, let the Light into your body, your soul, and you will see."

The lights racing through Breel's tattoos began to pulse a repetitive pattern the length of her body and back, as did the Emissary's, until the two became *synchronous. She felt a connection, to something vast. Her body became ill-defined, blurred at the edges, stretching out in all directions, merging, sublimating, disappearing, reappearing, through the infinite interstices of the multiverse. And in those spaces… consciousness, linked, remote, alien, unknowable.*

She felt the Emissary's presence.

This is our destiny; this is what we can become if we let the Light in. It wants to love us, to cherish us, to make us. We will become one with it.

And behind the infinite, chaotic swirl lay something beautiful, shining, welcoming, beckoning, suffusing the multiverse with energy, flowing in from all directions. So much energy, it was bewildering. A confluence, a connection of consciousness, of minds, of intelligence, existing from time immemorial to time without end, bending, distorting the continuum with its presence, like a massive gravitational field distorting spacetime. But more than that, she was witnessing creation, the fabric of reality 'becoming.' She soaked it up, gloried in it, felt its raw power enhance her being. Her heart pounded with the joy of it all. She saw all the possibilities for humanity transcended into a whole, much greater than its parts.

Now you see the promise that awaits us with the return of the Light.

And she did see. She opened her soul, inviting it in…

A noise intruded into the vision. At first it was an annoying distraction, then it modulated, became shrill, until it pierced her consciousness with jarring pain.

In that moment, the illusion shattered, broke into a million shards, revealing something else, something hidden, something malignant, marring the brilliance… It drained her, freezing, sapping. A dark patch sucking light from the beautiful radiance like a black tumour. Twisted tendrils of writhing dark spread through the Light, branching fractal veins like clawed tentacles reaching out for her…

Her mind crashed back to the cold minimalism of the land cruiser. The shrill noise morphed into the comm alert tone. She felt bile rising. The Emissary turned his naked body to face his desk. He tapped at something, enabling a contact.

"What is it, Maliesh," he snapped.

"Sorry, your Grace, you asked to be informed if we found anything of importance. I think you will want to see this."

Hidden from Breel's view, something lit his face with flashing light. He frowned.

"I'll be with you shortly. Have my security detail ready by the hatch." He turned to Breel, picking his clothing up from the floor. "I'm sorry for this interruption, Breel. You look like you need some time anyway. I'll be back shortly, when we will continue. Please feel free to refresh yourself in my absence." He indicated the food and water.

Quickly he dressed and left the room. She heard the scrape of metal on metal as the bolts on the outside of the hatch were shot.

Breel gave in and vomited onto the floor between her feet.

"Pass me an immobiliser," Matt said.

Abiel passed him one of the small devices.

"How come we didn't know about those?" Kaemon asked. "They would have been handy on Blue Haven."

Abiel shrugged. "The immobilisers won't work when the armour is shielded. Shielding draws a lot of power, though, so it's only enabled in combat situations. The guard's will be disabled and hopefully he won't think to activate it."

Matt tapped a series of instructions into his wrist controller. The MARRV stood higher, bobbing.

"I always thought that voice activation would have been useful," Kaemon observed.

"We couldn't afford the upgrade," Matt replied.

One of the drone's tentacle-like arms lifted to accept the immobiliser, then dropped back into its default position beneath the bulbous body. Matt checked the area around the Emissary's vehicle one last time, then with a tap of his finger sent the robot on its way. It skittered through the shadows towards its target. They all gathered around Matt to watch the MARRV's progress on the input device's small screen.

"We have to hope he doesn't start shooting as soon as he sees it," the Deacon said.

"He'll recognise it for what it is," Abiel said. "It won't look like a threat, so hopefully he'll be curious enough to let it get within range. If he starts shooting. the whole camp will come down on him and he will look really stupid to sound an alarm over a harmless drone."

"And if he doesn't start shooting, he will *really* look stupid," Ellyella said. "Fingers crossed."

Benmajin stood rigidly to attention. The Emissary had left strict instructions no one was to enter the land cruiser and while he would always do his best, he really wished he were somewhere else. Unlike his friend Yed, who was guarding the prisoners, the last thing he wanted was to come to the Emissary's attention. Yed would have given anything to be here, in his place, so close to the Messiah. He longed to wear the red robes of the Emissary's security entourage. He trained for it in his spare time, made himself a specialist in weapons and unarmed combat. He would put himself between the Emissary and a plasma bolt without hesitation.

Not Benmajin. All he wanted was to keep his head down, do no more than what was asked of him and not die in this Light-forsaken place. He still harboured the idea he would do his stint in the service of Second Light, then leave and have a family. There was a girl back home for whom he had feelings, if their respective families could come to a proper agreement. The last thing in the multiverse he wanted to be was a human shield for the Emissary.

It was an unfortunate work roster that had given them both the tasks they least wanted to do. He had heard faint screams earlier attesting to Yed taking out his frustration on the prisoners, making their last moments even more miserable.

He glanced around the gloomy interior of the complex. Huge and dark and alien. It pressed down on him, oppressive in an almost physical way. Some of the others believed the place was intrinsically evil, steeped in the foulness of the *Firsts*. He wasn't sure about that, but the place was ancient and who knew what actual dangers lurked in these dark halls or what horrors had been carried out during the mind-boggling length of time it had existed.

Something small and metallic left the shadows with quick spider-like movements and headed in his direction. Panicked, his heart went into overdrive. He sighted down his gun but then let it drop when he realised it was merely one of the mule-drones the insurgents had used to carry their food and water.

Although he despised the unbelievers, he could not help but have a sneaking admiration for them. Their story, as told by the breeder – sorry, female crusader, and he allowed himself a small smile at the thought of a female crusader – was astonishing. To have crashed their shuttle, then trekked for days across the hostile ice plains showed courage and determination few could aspire to. And, what really amazed him, they did it all without knowing if there was any chance of salvation at the end. That was the lot of unbelievers, he reflected: they can never look forward to salvation at the end.

Be that as it may, what was this drone doing here? He could make out Yed's helmet in the distance, behind a succession of alien structures. The cries of pain had ceased for some time now. Yed had probably grown bored of tormenting his prisoners. If they had escaped or sent this drone, Yed would certainly not be at his post.

He considered sending a message but decided it might make him look foolish. He was already looked down upon within the squad. He didn't want to be even more diminished in their eyes.

The robot had almost reached him. Now it was closer, it was bigger than he had thought, up to his waist and twice his body width at least. It moved nimbly for what was clearly a heavy device. Its manipulator arms swung beneath the squat, scuffed, and dirt-streaked cylindrical bulk of its body. *Has to be a malfunction*, he thought, or perhaps it was mindlessly fulfilling some now pointless protocol inputted earlier. He leaned forward to stop the machine's progress with the muzzle of his rifle. The drone stopped, bobbing.

"Where are you going, my little friend?" he asked.

Answer came there none.

He noticed the claw-like appendage at the end of one of the tentacle-arms gripped something. He bent closer to peer at it. Too late, he saw the green glow of the immobiliser. The appendage whipped up at lightning speed, embedding the device into the centre of his helmeted forehead.

His suit spasmed. A multitude of error warning lights sprang into existence on the HUD before blinking out. He was frozen mid-crouch.

"Help," he shouted as loudly as he could, his voice bouncing around the interior of his helmet. "Hellllllllp, I'm being attac –" He stopped mid-sentence. Although the zip-head sensory array had shut down, leaving him blind to the mass of data he could normally call upon, the smart material of the visor had one-way transparency, so should the power fail, the crusader would not be rendered uselessly blind. Peering through this helmet now, he saw the blunt barrel of a plasma gun pressed against it, held by the female crusader.

Breel stared down at the mess on the floor. There wasn't much, given her belly was pretty empty, but the retching had gone on and on, as if her body was desperately trying to rid itself of something poisonous and vile.

The Communion had been terrifying.

Not at first. At first, she had been swept away by the magnificence of it all, and yes, she had succumbed, yearned to be a part of it, to experience fulfilment beyond anything she could have imagined. Sitting here now, in the harsh light of the land cruiser, the smell of vomit heavy in the air, making her want to gag again, that thought alone terrified her. To have been so eager and willing to give herself up, like the moment she had leapt across the ravine.

But then, she'd glimpsed the malignancy at the heart of it all. The Emissary seemed unaware. How could he not see it, be blind to it?

It certainly saw her. It reacted immediately, reaching out towards her.

The thing from her recurring nightmare was real.

She had no idea what it was, but that it was a real tangible thing, *out there*, wherever that was, she had no doubt.

What would have happened if the call hadn't broken into the Communion, hadn't somehow intruded to shatter the facade? She had no answer to that, but one thing was certain: she would never allow herself to be immersed in it again.

There was no way out of the room. She had once escaped from the Emissary on his flagship *Transcendent Light*, by altering the electronic protocols of the locks securing the door. The Emissary was taking no chances this time, hence the physical bolts outside, supplementing the electronic locks.

She looked around and saw the bottle of water. Standing a little unsteadily she picked it up by its neck. It was glass and had a solid, heavy base. Although she was thirsty, she emptied the water onto the floor where it swilled the vomit away. She wanted nothing from the

Lord of Light. She swung her arm, felt the satisfying heft from the makeshift club.

She stood to one side of the door and waited.

"Is it much further?" the Emissary asked.

Along with his immediate personal guard, a crusader held point ahead and behind. Both carried pulse-maser rifles – a blast from which would annihilate any matter it came in contact with – along with an assortment of other state of the art weaponry capable of devastating destruction.

Although that might give comfort to his soldiers, the Emissary felt less secure, given the powers that he knew could be brought to bear against them.

"No, my Lord," the captain of his elite protection squad said after a moment, no doubt having checked their position through some internal interface. "It is just over this obstruction."

The obstruction referred to was the chaotic remains of something that had collapsed aeons ago, leaving a jagged pile about three times his height.

"We have to climb?"

"There is no other way, your Grace, but High Lord Maliesh reports it is not difficult, merely time consuming."

A tremor shook the ground, dislodging parts of the jumble of wreckage, reminding them all that anything 'time consuming' was something they could not afford much longer.

But the images transmitted to him from Maliesh were too compelling.

"Get on with it then."

The climb was indeed both easy and time consuming. A path led up the rubble indicating something had, or still was, using this as a route. The time-consuming part was a small, exposed section, near the top, where a fall could cause serious injury or worse, but was otherwise safe if taken with care.

As they neared the summit, he became aware of a dancing brightness, shining through the base's upper structures, like light flickering off water. It cast luminous shifting patterns over the ubiquitous intricate topography that adorned pretty much everything he had seen so far.

They crested the hill of rubble to reveal an astonishing sight. Maliesh and a squad of crusaders were dark shapes against the lower part of a huge oval of radiance. The top was lost in consecutive layers of superstructure, a dark criss-cross against its brightness.

They made their way down the far side.

"My Lord." Maliesh bowed at his approach.

"Maliesh, what have you found?" The Emissary's eyes were wide.

"We had swept this area already your Grace, but this appeared in the last half hour. Given there had been nothing here before, I felt it prudent to advise your Lordship."

"You did the right thing, Maliesh." The Emissary moved closer. Shapes began to coalesce within the oval of light, patterns sliding in and out of existence, on the edge of perception. The movements became more urgent as the Emissary approached.

"Is it trying to communicate?" he asked in awe.

He stepped forward to put his hand into the pulsing light.

Finally, there was noise from outside and then the sound of bolts being drawn. Breel raised her arm and braced herself as a figure stepped into the room. It wasn't the Emissary but a Church officer in fatigues. She swung anyway. The figure dodged the blow, raising a hand in defence and squashed back against the wall in the confined space.

"Breel, stop. It's me."

"Abiel," Breel said, puzzled, then snarled and raised the bottle again, swinging the makeshift club. Abiel deflected the blow with her forearm, shattering the bottle against the door frame.

"Wait, Breel," Abiel said again.

"Breel, stop!" Ellyella put her head around the door. She raised her hand. "It's okay."

Breel stopped, mid-strike, the remains of the shattered bottle held aloft.

"El, what the Deshi-damn?"

"Come on Breel, we don't have long."

Abiel and Ellyella hustled back through the door. Breel followed, still clutching the broken bottle. Outside was a crusader frozen in the act of crouching and a MARRV heading back into the maze of mechs.

"What in Deshi-hell is happening?" Breel picked up speed to keep pace with the other two. "What did you do to that guy?" She indicated the frozen crusader with a backward jerk of her thumb.

"Abiel saved us," Ellyella explained.

"One of us had to stay free," Abiel added. "I acted on impulse. It was all I could think of."

"She used one of these to shut down the crusader's power armour," Ellyella said. She offered Breel one of the small immobiliser devices.

Breel shook her head. She took the immobiliser with her free hand, scrutinising it. She pushed it into one of her many pockets.

"I'm having trouble keeping up with all of this," she said. "Nothing seems real anymore, but I do trust El. If she vouches for you, Abiel, I'll give you the benefit of the doubt."

"I'm sorry, Breel. I had to act fast," Abiel said, "and in a way that would be convincing to the Emissary."

"No, don't apologise, Abiel," Breel said. "I should be thanking you. It must have cost you a lot."

"Not as much as you might think," Abiel said.

They followed the drone into the shadows created by the maze of alien mechs. Figures rushed forward to greet her and she found herself being hugged by Kaemon.

"Okay, this is a little overwhelming," she said, then noticed Matt hanging back. She pushed away from Kaemon. "What's he doing here?" She jabbed the broken bottle towards the captain.

"He needs to get off the moon as well," Ellyella said.

"Tell him to ask his pals to give him a lift." She glared at Matt.

"They aren't pals of mine, Breel," Matt said. "I hope you'll give me a chance to explain…"

"Only now's not the time," Abiel said quickly. "Come on."

"Stay away from me," Breel said to Matt. She turned to Abiel. "Come on where?" she asked. "Where are we going?"

Kaemon said, "We figure the only chance we have is that sentient neural-core thing Matt and El told us about. Only, I still have to see it to believe it."

"It will only respond to you, they say," the Deacon added, a tinge of excitement in his voice, "because only you can help it."

Breel looked around at the ragged group, then shrugged. "Well, it won't be the weirdest thing I've done today."

They moved further into the maze of dark, curving alien shapes – the statues or mechs. The ground heaved under their feet, cracking in a dozen places. Crashes reverberated throughout the complex. A shadow passed over her. Breel looked up to see the twisted dark mass of one of the alien monuments toppling directly towards her.

A violent impact knocked her sideways. The thing smashed into the ground exactly where she had been standing a second before. She came to rest on her back with Matt on top of her. For a second neither of them moved, then she pushed him off and got to her feet. She looked anxiously at the others but everyone seemed to be ok.

Breel turned back to Matt. "Thanks," she said gruffly.

"You're welcome," he replied.

They set off towards the plinth at a brisk trot.

The plinth was still dark when they got there. Breel noted another immobilised crusader standing next to it, as if on guard.

"Still out of it," Abiel tapped the man's helmet with her forefinger knuckle. "Yed," she said, reading the name on the zip-head's left shoulder.

"Well, you took your own sweet time, for fuck's sake." The globe had taken on its oily glow and was once again floating above the plinth. "Can we get on with it now?"

"Hell," Kaemon said, backing away. "It's real. And it speaks Standard… although I wouldn't want to introduce it to my mother."

"Picked up a few colourful phrases from your entertainment feeds, we think," Ellyella said.

Breel stood beneath the globe, staring up at it. "Can we trust you?" she asked.

"You ain't never going to know if you don't give it a try, babes. Can we get on now? You know, tick-tock and all that."

Breel shook her head impatiently, "I don't know what that means," she said. "I want some kind of assurance."

"Listen sweetheart, we don't have a lot of time. I was keeping myself apprised of what you and the two-bit preacher were getting up to. I arranged a light show to, you know, draw his attention. Sorry, I had to gatecrash your little out-of-body experience there. I figured you needed a wake-up call, before you got too deep into the rabbit hole."

"That was you?" Breel asked, astonished.

"Ain't nothing else alive in here," it said. "Well, apart from all you aliens, that is. Anyway, I figured you needed the distraction and some help, to see what was really what. Maybe saved your ass while I was at it, don't you think? Is that enough or do you want more? The preacher will figure it out pretty soon, so I would suggest we get a move on."

"What do we have to lose, Breel? We can't be any worse off," Matt said.

She glared at him. "You have no idea." She turned back to the globe. "I don't even know if I can do what you want."

"Sure, you can. You've done it before. Focus, I'll give you a little guidance."

The Emissary's hand sank into the brilliance. Something wasn't right. There was no internal reaction, no voices, and his tattoos remained dark.

"What is it, my Lord?" Maliesh asked, concerned.

The Emissary withdrew his hand and stared at it, as if looking for an answer.

The captain of his guard approached, head bowed.

"My Lord, communication from base camp. We've lost contact with two of the crusaders. The one guarding the land cruiser has been found immobilised. We are about to check on the one guarding the insurgents."

"And the woman?" the Emissary asked.

"Gone, my Lord."

At that moment the great oval of light vanished and they were plunged into darkness. Almost immediately lights from his entourage and the crusaders lit, casting them in harsh contrast, throwing dark shadows against the walls.

"We must go back, now." The Emissary said to Maliesh. "Get the squads back from wherever they are. Send whoever is still at the camp to where the insurgents are imprisoned. Sweep the area until they are found."

Maliesh looked at his leader. "I don't mean to question you, my Lord, but is that necessary? We will be leaving here very soon. Let them die with the moon."

The Emissary looked at the hill of rubble they would have to negotiate to get back. "No. I have to know what has happened here. We have been played."

"By the insurgents?" Maliesh asked.

The Emissary shook his golden head. "No. That's why we have to go back."

Maliesh hung back, watching the Lord of Light move deftly up the ramp of rubble, surrounded by his red-clad honour guard. Things were coming to a head. He couldn't let the man's obsession destroy everything he had worked for. The time had come to act. Hannathon and Corlezea had done their part to prepare all those loyal to them. The ones that weren't had been cowed into silence. It had been easier to organise the insurrection than it should have been. The Emissary was so preoccupied with his delusion that he had lost sight of what was happening around him.

Maliesh had been waiting for the right opportunity, and it was now or never. He would leave the man here with his accursed fantasies, so he wouldn't have to deal with him once he was back home. He would explain to the Church High Council, many of whom were loyal to him – he had made sure of that – that the Messiah had lost his way and turned to the Dark.

One thing was not going to happen, though: he was not going to be transformed into a morass of heaving jelly like so many of the Emissary's opponents. There would be no kiss of death for him. When the time was right, his trusted guards would seize the Lord of Light. Then Maliesh would declare him a heretic and a traitor, for appearance's sake. Anybody that wouldn't fall into line would remain here with their Messiah.

As soon as it was prudent, he would arrange to recreate the insurgents' plan and close the Light-damned *RIP* forever. Then he could go about finding the Emissary's successor and a new chapter for the Church of Second Light would begin.

The chamber had become insubstantial, like layered mist. Breel was aware of different levels of complexity, of electrons in their uncertainty, now here, now moving, then neither, but both. Waves of probability. Her surroundings had been reduced to their most fundamental level.

There – the alien machine communicated – you can see how the protocols are arranged. You can see how a barrier is in place. You need to remove the barrier. I can do the rest.

And the voices began to whisper to Breel, suggesting without coherence. She pushed her consciousness into the barrier, observing the probability waves, and by observing, reordering… disrupting the stream into new shapes and structures. Abruptly, the barrier collapsed.

Breel staggered. Matt and Ellyella went to support her but she held up her hands.

"I'm okay," she said.

They all looked up at the oily sphere.

"Ahhhhhhhhhhhhsssssssssssssss," the machine-entity whispered, the sound stretching out to become white noise, fading until it was out of their hearing range.

The outer skin of the globe went dull, then cracked. Large flakes sloughed off to reveal a complex honeycomb interior. Abruptly it fell onto the plinth beneath it, disintegrating into a shower of dust.

They stood in silence, staring at light flickering through the settling motes.

"That's it?" Abiel asked. "Where has it gone?"

"Stand still! Place your hands on top of your heads!"

They turned. Red dots played about their bodies from the laser targeting systems of plasma rifles held by two crusaders.

"Down on your knees! Do it now!"

"Not again," the Deacon groaned.

TWENTY-SIX

"This is getting tiresome." The Emissary paced back and forth. He stopped in front of Abiel.

"It saddens me to see you here, Major. You have betrayed your calling. Your faith. Your Messiah. These people," he waved an encompassing hand, "know no better, but you…" He leaned towards her. "There is nothing worse than betrayal," he hissed, "and the consequences for that betrayal will be commensurate."

Abiel stared resolutely ahead, face blank, showing no trace of emotion.

"And you?" He looked down at Breel. "I showed you your true destiny, the true destiny of all mankind. I thought you understood."

"If I didn't before, I do now." Unlike Abiel, Breel didn't try to hide her anger or contempt. "You showed me the truth all right. I have to thank you for that."

The ground shook. The tremors boomed and growled through the base every few minutes now, the sound rolling throughout the complex, occasionally punctuated by the sharp concussions of large structures collapsing.

Maliesh whispered something into his Leader's ear. The Emissary nodded, turning his attention back to his prisoners.

"My friend here points out that we have to leave, very soon." He sighed. "Listen to me. I know you believe me to be the villain here, that somehow, I am employed by forces that will destroy humanity. but nothing could be further from the truth. I want to save us all." He almost pleaded this last, waving his hand in an expansive arc that took in *Scavenger's* crew, his own troops and the entire universe beyond.

He stood before Breel. "Why won't you tell them? Share your revelation. You were privileged to see it first-hand. We can become more than we are, we can transcend into something beyond imagining."

Breel shook her head, "Save your sermon. You saw something very different than I did."

There was a noise like thunder followed by a massive thump as something close by gave in to increasing stress. They heard it fall, causing the ground they knelt on to shake and tremble.

The Emissary looked into the shadows of the base and then back to Breel. He took a breath. "Breel, my child, I am sad for you, but you will see eventually." He turned his attention to the others. "But one thing I'm sure you will not want to see is the death of your friends." He bent, so his face was close to hers. "I know something happened in my absence, while I was distracted. That there is something active in here, something from the time of the *Firsts*. I need to know what it is and where it is."

He took a step back so he could make his offer to all of them.

"Tell me what I want to know and I will give you all safe passage off this moon."

The voices muttered. Breel blinked, the world turned misty and translucent. On the one hand she was seeing the Emissary, his security detail, the foot soldiers in fatigues, alien mech structures, the crusaders in their powered armour…

…on the other hand, she was seeing through the lens of the Network. The weft and weave of reality, the universe at its most basic. It was overwhelming, multi-dimensional, bending through angles and domains she had no words or experience to describe, the humans' bright knots embedded within. The more she concentrated, the denser the weave, the finer the fabric, as deep as she could perceive. She could sense wavefronts collapsing to become the binding energy holding the molecular structure of reality together, reshaping it into new forms, new states of being. With an effort, she moved her awareness several states higher to focus on specific values that represented real-world effects. The web of energy coursing through the crusader suits for example, servos and sensors reacting, moving through pre-ordained patterns, obeying the strictures imposed upon them. The small device Ellyella had given her, the one that had crashed the crusader suits, pressed into her thigh. If only she could affect the probability, collapse the waveforms in such a way, tailor the fabric of reality, it might result in . . .

"What do you think, Breel? What should I do?"

She snapped back to the chamber.

The Emissary was leaning very close to Kaemon, so their lips were almost touching. Kaemon kept his head straight, refusing to flinch or cower. Only a slight tremble betrayed his inner emotions.

"Tell me what I want to know, or there is another way I can free your friends." The Emissary twisted his head to see her reaction.

"Okay, just stop!" Breel snapped. "I'm so fucking tired of all this blisterhog shit." She looked at Kaemon. "Tell him," she said. "Go on, what difference will it make now?"

"He's not going to let us go, though," Matt interjected, "even if we tell him." He looked at the Lord of Light, "Are you?"

The Lord of Light stood tall, pushing his shoulders back. "I am a man of my word. I will give you passage and free you all."

Breel felt her body art warm. She let her head drop, turned it away from the Emissary, to hide the glow of the patterns on her face.

She reached out to the Network and through its interface, beyond...

Matt shrugged. "Okay, I'll tell you, then. Like Breel says, it makes no difference. You won't have time to do anything with the information anyway. If you hang around, you'll be vaporised with the rest of us." He took a breath. "There's an alien neural-core here that claims it has become sentient. It offered to take us off the planet if we helped free it."

Maliesh actually laughed then, taking in his Master's serious expression, said, "What nonsense is this, my Lord?" The base shook again. "Why are we wasting time? We must go!"

The voices that were not voices encouraged her, guiding her, but it was far too complex to control. This would be a temporary effect at best.

"How?" the Emissary asked. "How were you to help this thing? Where is it now?"

"Your Grace..."

The Emissary held up a hand to silence Maliesh, even as the base trembled and groaned and screeched, like an animal in terminal torment.

"We helped free it, or rather, Breel did." Matt lifted and dropped his shoulder again. "It's gone. We don't know where it went.

"Breel freed it?" The Emissary turned to her.

Breel's mind moved freely within the energy architecture of the crusader suits. A cut, a prod, a push, a fold, a damming of flow, a blocking of energy, an increase in pressure... It wasn't an accurate description of what she was doing, but they were the best metaphors she could come up with. And she needed the metaphors to visualise her actions in a way that was meaningful to her, so she could observe them happening and through that observation... they would... be ...

"Is what Mr. Harken-Court saying true?" The Emissary asked. "Did you interact with this intelligence? What did you do to free it?" The Emissary paused. He must have become aware of the glowing patterns on Breel's face and arm. "What are you doing. . .?" he began.

Breel dropped her hands from the top of her head and stood. Her body art erupted into light. One side of her body was a beacon of pulsing, brilliant radiance, beating back the gloom. "I used my superpower," she said. Staring the Emissary straight in the eye she placed a hand on each of the two crusaders, one on either side of her, then pushed her arms straight out. Both soldiers fell away from her, frozen into statue-like immobility and crashed heavily onto the ground.

She took a single step drawing her arm back as she went and let loose a blow, smashing her fist into the Emissary's shocked face as hard as she could, sending him sprawling into his second in command.

"Run!" Breel shouted, and they all scrambled into the vast maze of alien machinery.

Maliesh disentangled himself from the Emissary. He stood, dazed, and watched the insurgents scatter like rats into the shadows.

The other soldiers, those not in armour, reacted in panic, torn between firing at the escaping prisoners or helping their Messiah.

"Stop them!" The Emissary pushed to his feet, slapping away helping hands while wiping blood from his nose and mouth.

Priorities established, the soldiers fired after the retreating figures.

"Don't shoot at them," the Emissary cried, "you'll kill Breel." His men stopped firing but weren't sure what to do next. "Don't just stand there!" He yelled. "Get after them!"

Still, they hesitated. Some looked at Maliesh. The Emissary's features twisted into anger.

"I gave you an order," he barked.

Maliesh, still dazed at the turn of events, snapped out of his stupor. He took in the scene. This was it; the time had come. He still had enough unarmoured men to do the job. He would never have a better chance.

"Stop!" He shouted, before any of the men had taken a step. "This has gone far enough." He turned to those of his henchmen in fatigues. "Now!" he commanded. There was a split-second hesitation, understandable given the situation, before two of his men unleashed their weapons. The red-clad bodyguards, frozen into the same stasis as all the other armoured men, were hit at almost zero range by plasma fire. Shielding down, their armour couldn't deal with that kind of energy at close range. They were blown across the chamber, crashing into the curving architecture before coming to a smoking stop.

Maliesh waved a finger at two other men and they stepped forward, grabbing the Emissary's wrists, brutally pulling his arms apart. The men holding the Emissary were careful to keep their distance, stretching out the Lord of Light as far as they could, while the front of his golden robes lit up with moving red sparks of targeting lasers. Maliesh stepped through the frozen ranks of armoured men, standing to one side of his former leader so as to not be in the line of fire. He was careful to keep his distance. He was taking no chances.

The Emissary looked outraged. He tried to pull his arms free. "Release me," he shouted at the men, "or I will see you finish your miserable lives in torment so unimaginable you will be begging for release." The two soldiers looked terrified, but held on, nonetheless. The Lord of Light looked away from the guards, to Maliesh as he approached. Finally, he understood. The Emissary stopped struggling. A calm overcame him.

"What have you done, Maliesh?" he asked, not in anger now, but in wonder.

"Something I should have done long ago." Maliesh looked around at the strange tableau of disabled soldiers. He smiled at his former leader. "This turned out better than I could have hoped. I had anticipated a bloody firefight. I'm not sure how your girlfriend did it, but she has made this whole operation far easier than it should have been. She has earned her short taste of freedom." Another tremor shook the room. He looked back at the golden man. "You have endangered everything I have worked for, for this… this fantasy of yours, my Lord. I can no longer tolerate it."

"*You* can no longer tolerate it?" The Emissary seemed amused. "What do you think the High Council will make of this, when we return home?" A small irritating smile played around his lips.

"The High Council will not be a problem." Maliesh said. "I arranged things most carefully before we left. You were too preoccupied to notice."

The Emissary merely stared. He was so calm it was beginning to rattle Maliesh.

"My son, my child, how far you have fallen," the Emissary said, a look of utter sadness on his face.

"You can drop the act," Maliesh snapped. "I'm not impressed. We will be leaving this place immediately. As soon as possible I will be sending a task force back here, to recreate the insurgents' plan and close the *RIP* permanently. This time there will be no one to stop it happening."

"And what will I be doing while you enact this wanton act of heretical destruction?" the Emissary asked.

"You," Maliesh said with some venom, "will have no further part in the proceedings. You will have the pleasure of spending your last few hours here, amongst what has been, for so long, your obsession."

Movement from the guards holding the Emissary made Maliesh glance either side of the Lord of Light. The men were breathing heavily. One, unforgivably, was running a finger around the inside of his collar. His face was red and shiny with sweat. He looked like he was running a fever.

Maliesh looked back at the Emissary, who smiled his trademark beatific smile. Something wasn't right. A cold chill ran through Maliesh.

"Your mind is so small," The Emissary said, "so preoccupied with the minutiae of your paltry existence. You have no chance of seeing the bigger picture, of ever comprehending the true nature of the forces around you."

The guard who had been running his hand around the inside of his collar suddenly let out a cry of pain. He let go of the Emissary and fell to the ground, curling into a tight ball, his knees up to his chin. He began a terrifying keening that rose in pitch. His body twitched. The other guard was struggling to maintain his grip on the Emissary's wrist.

"What's wrong with you, man…? Maliesh began, then looked at the Emissary. "How…?"

The guard pulled his hand away from the Emissary, raised it and watched in fascinated horror as the hand stretched, distorting into something malformed and unrecognisable. He tried to lift his other hand but it had turned to boneless jelly, dripping onto the floor. He screamed then, a piercing scream of utter terror. The Emissary raised his hand and the screaming stopped. The man was still alive, still wanting to scream, but somehow, he had been rendered unable to do so. Still conscious, the guard watched his own body lose its integrity and collapse, until, abruptly, the light went from his eyes. His body continued to deliquesce into a stinking puddle, seeping into the dirt on the floor.

"I know how Breel did what she did," the Emissary was saying, "but your mind is so shallow, you will never know or understand." Maliesh looked at his master in utter terror as, unfettered now, the Lord of Light walked past the grotesque distorting guardsmen on the ground. The targeting lasers moved with him, but no one fired. Maliesh took two steps back. The Emissary loomed over him.

Maliesh tried to speak but his mouth was suddenly full of teeth, bursting up through his cheeks and down through his jaw, pinning his lips together. Every nerve, every pain receptor in his body lit, as if he had been plunged into a furnace. His legs gave way, no longer able to support his weight and he fell into the dust, his body spasming, contorting and twisting. Each new deformation sent another pulse of agony through him.

"You had a brief window when you could have killed me Maliesh." The Emissary looked down on him dispassionately. His hair was a golden halo, lit from behind by the lights from the land cruiser. "But you had to glory in your moment of triumph. Such a small man, Maliesh."

Maliesh felt the roof of his mouth smash apart as something drove upwards, through his face and into his brain. The last thing he saw, before a final sharp spike of pain mercifully heralded the end of his existence, was the peaceful, beatific smile of the Lord of Light.

The Emissary turned to the horrified and shocked expressions of his men. He gestured and the immobilised troopers came back to life. The hand-waving wasn't strictly necessary, but he so liked a bit of theatre.

"Is there anyone here who still feels loyal to this man?" He indicated the gelatinous pulp that was as far removed from the description 'man' as it was possible to be. As one they fell to their knees keening, begging forgiveness.

Thought not. He smiled inwardly. "Arise my children," he said out loud. "I forgive you. I know the power of the dark and how it can lead even the most faithful and pious astray."

The Emissary stepped over the bubbling remains of Maliesh without a second glance.

"You, you, you and you." He picked out four men. "You four are hereby promoted as my new security detail. The rest of you pursue the insurgents. I want the tattooed woman, Breel, alive. Kill or leave the others to their fate. Do not waste time on them unless they get in your way."

He turned to his newly selected security entourage and said, "Follow me."

Surrounded by his new bodyguards he walked to his land cruiser. He didn't deign to notice the name tags they each carried on their left shoulder, but if he had, he would have read 'Benmajin' on one of them.

"What just happened?" Matt whispered. They were catching their breath, crouched behind some unidentifiable piece of alien architecture. He looked at Breel. She was pale and drawn, her tattoos dark once more.

"I used my superpower," she said again, dazed.

The Deacon, eyes wide, looked at her with something approaching awe. "Your powers are growing."

Breel shook her head. "They aren't my powers. I'm a conduit, accessing something. A *Network*, for want of a better word. I'm using it, or it's using me, or maybe it's a bit of both. I'm not sure, but I can direct it… maybe *ask it* is closer to the truth… to…" She took a breath. "I don't know how to describe it. Influence reality?" She looked up at them, "I'm sorry, the effects won't last long."

There was shouting and plasma fire from the direction they had come.

"What's happening back there?" the Deacon asked.

"Sounds like the Emissary has some problems of his own," Matt said with some satisfaction. He had to raise his voice over the noise of the impending destruction of the moon. A constant roar now and the quakes were continuous.

"Well, it will all be academic soon," Ellyella said, hand on a trembling piece of superstructure. "I guess we go out on our own terms and not dancing to that piece of shit's tune."

"It's a consolation of a kind," Kaemon agreed. He looked at them all. "So, we have finally reached the end of the road." His eye rested on Matt. "Still, mine might have been a lot shorter otherwise."

Matt looked around the assembled group. "I wish things had gone down differently, I really do. But I hope you guys can see it from my point of view and see why I did what I did."

Breel shook her head. "If you hadn't come to Hope, if the Emissary had got to me first, I know now that things would have been far worse. But you lied to me, Matt, to all of us." She looked down at the ground and took in a deep breath. "What does it matter now, anyway?"

Matt squared his shoulders. There was a touch of fire in his voice now. "The roll of the dice was shitty. I played the next move as best I could. It might have been the wrong game play, but hindsight is a bitch. My big mistake was keeping it from you guys. I am sorry about that."

They fell into silence. The noises from The Emissary and his men had ceased. Matt strained into the darkness, trying to figure out what was happening back there. Then he heard shouts followed by horrifying screams that turned his blood to ice and made the short hairs on the back of his neck stand straight out. Then silence once more.

"What the in the name of all that's holy was that?" Abiel whispered.

"Come on," Matt said. "Let's get away from here." He stood and then the structure around them began to shake and collapse.

"Is this it?" Ellyella asked. "Is the moon finally coming apart?"

A second later, an armoured crusader appeared, pushing a piece of the alien structure to one side. He pointed his rifle at them.

"Keep still or I'll blow you all the fuck apart!" He bellowed; voice amplified to painful levels. "Tasker 3, I have them. Vector in on this bearing." He pointed his weapon at Breel. "You! Move away from the others."

Instead, Breel stepped in front of the crew, arms outstretched, as if to guard them.

Matt reached for her. "Breel, don't."

"Stay behind me," she said. "They won't kill me."

Another crusader appeared behind the first.

The crew of *Scavenger* backed away until they couldn't go any further.

"Just grab the breeder, Yed, for Light's sake," the new arrival said, pointing his rifle at Breel, "and then shoot the rest. This whole place is going to come down on our heads any minute."

Yed stepped forward, reaching for Breel. There wasn't time for her to communicate with the Network, to ask for its help again. All she could do was try to avoid him, but the soldier was too fast. An armoured hand squeezed around her wrist and effortlessly pulled her away. He levelled his gun at the rest of them.

"I told you. You are going to die here," he sneered.

"Should have killed you when I had the chance." Abiel snarled.

"Who's superior now?" Yed levelled his gun. "Dumb breeder."

"No!" Breel screamed. She reached down, grabbed a fist full of dirt and threw it into the zip-head's asymmetric sensor array. It was a pointless gesture. All she did was irritate the man who pushed her violently towards his companion. "Look after this bitch," he commanded. The second soldier reached for Breel, but she went down on one knee, sliding under his outstretched hands, rolled and stood, arms upraised, directly in the line of fire.

"Don't –" Breel began... and the gun went off. The concussed air and *thwapp* of the plasma pulse was deafening in the close confines. There was no time for Breel to react or dodge. The plasma beam scorched into her, sent her spinning into the shadows, an arc of blood describing her trajectory.

Ellyella screamed.

It had all happened in a fraction of a second. Far too quickly for Matt, or any of them to do anything.

"Breel!" Matt shouted into the relative silence. He threw himself at the crusader. Another pointless gesture. The armoured man swung his rifle, catching Matt a stunning blow with the barrel, sending him crashing and rolling onto the floor. Groggily, he tried to stand, spitting blood and a broken tooth.

"None of you move!" the crusader shouted.

218

"You fuck up!" the second man was yelling at his comrade. "The Emissary will strip the flesh from our bones. He wanted the breeder alive."

"Calling me a fuck up!" Yed yelled back. "You were supposed to be holding on to her. You let her go and she ran into my aim you dick. I didn't have time…"

"We'll have to kill them all and say we couldn't find the woman." The second crusader turned his gun on the crew.

A screech and a rending of metal made him pause and look around. Something was moving toward them at speed, crashing through whatever obstacles stood in its way.

"Look out," the rearmost crusader shouted, turning his aim away from the *Scavenger* crew to fire at something Matt couldn't see. "Light preserve us!" he heard the man say. The soldier sent a stream of blazing plasma bolts into the shadows. Yed turned and did the same. Matt put his hands over his ears as the concussion from each shot boomed, shaking the surrounding structures.

A second later, a silent burning brilliance ploughed into the two soldiers. In a fraction of a second their armour flared, melted, then exploded, showering the crew of *Scavenger* with burning fragments.

Matt was blinded temporarily, his ears ringing. Through slowly clearing, light-spotted vision, he saw something from a nightmare step over the burning remains of the crusaders. Twice the height of the humans, it walked on strangely articulated legs. supporting a carapace of complex organic-looking curved shapes that slid over each other as it moved.

"Yippee ki-yay, you muthers," the machine-intelligence shouted.

TWENTY-SEVEN

In his quarters on the land cruiser the Emissary appeared outwardly calm, but inwardly he was a mass of inner turmoil. Maliesh... How had he missed his second in command's lapse of faith? He had detected unease and discontent in the man, suspected he had been planning something, but never considered he would go so far.

In one sense, Maliesh had been right: the Emissary had been too preoccupied to take notice. If he had, he might have stopped him earlier, before things got out of hand. Instead, he had allowed too much leeway, failed to pay enough attention to what was happening. Whatever Maliesh had done for him in the past – and he had done a lot – that act of betrayal could not go unpunished. There must have been others involved in the insurrection, and they needed to be in no doubt what an act of betrayal would cost. The question of who those others were would have to wait, for now. But he would not forget.

But, oh, the way he had done it, the way he had turned the tables on his second in command... it had been exhilarating. Truly, the divine moved through him now, granting him god-like powers and it must surely be only the beginning. Who knew what lay ahead?

He put that heady thought to one side. More pressing was the sentient machine. Did it really exist or had Harken-Court just been spinning a line to distract him while Breel disabled his crusaders?

And Breel. He hadn't realised her powers had so developed. The moment he came through the *RIP* he had sensed the Light's presence. During the transit to this place, he had communed with it, and by the time he had reached the shepherd moon he was already much more than he had been. But he hadn't detected any of that in Breel. He couldn't understand why he hadn't sensed the entity, if it did exist. Why hadn't the Light forewarned him about it?

A quake shook the vehicle violently. He was forced to grab the edge of the desk. Shards of broken glass from the bottle of water that had somehow been smashed, slid across the floor to bounce against his foot.

"They have found them. my Lord," his captain reported through the comms. His screens lit up to show various feeds from the squad's neural cams. He zeroed in on one, where the insurgents were cowering behind a barrier his crusader was tearing up. He heard the crusader give the *Scavenger* crew an order to stand down, then a second warrior appeared, urging the first to action. He saw Breel hauled away from her friends. He saw her throw dirt into the face of the man, a stupid act of defiance, then saw her avoid the grasp of the second soldier to leap up and stand directly in the line of fire... The feed cut. Either a communications failure or they had disabled the contact deliberately.

"Captain," he snapped, "I have lost my visual."

"Sorry, my Lord. Switching to one of the surveillance drones."

The images returned. The feed lit up and this time he saw... Breel gunned down by his own man. A seething rage went through him at the cavalier disregard of his orders, but any thought of what he might do to them became irrelevant as they were suddenly... gone. Simply blown out of existence.

The drone POV turned to track something that almost hurt his mind to look at. It ripped through obstacles and any resistance that came its way like a million-ton asteroid through a light sail, a second before that feed too dissolved to static. Quickly, he looked for another view from the other drones deployed or from other crusaders that were zeroing in on the position.

All the feeds were down. Every one reduced to nothing more than fizzing grey noise.

Crusader plasma bolts slammed into the alien mech. It swayed from the impacts, then twisted from its waist, reconfiguring its arms into weapons, returning fire. Energy levels, beyond anything the humans had ever seen, melted everything in its line of sight to slag.

"Get close to me," the alien machine told them, as the crusaders' response exploded all around them. It paused for a fraction of a second, as if noticing something for the first time. "Where's Breel?" it asked.

"You're too late," Ellyella screamed. "Breel's dead."

"The hell you say." The thing from a nightmare moved towards them. Abruptly, the sound of battle muted to a distant murmur. Several plasma bolts exploded almost directly in front of them but splashed harmlessly against some unseen barrier.

"Where is she?" the alien said. "We can't leave without her."

"I just told you," Ellyella sobbed.

"Yeah, well, that depends," the mech said. "Bear with me while I clean the place up."

The chamber lit in a furious display of burning light. Black shadows whirled in every direction. Then… silence. It took a second for their eyes to adjust to the relative gloom after the pyrotechnics.

Abiel supported herself against one of the alien mech's legs.

"Holy shit," she whispered.

The chamber had been reduced to rubble interspersed with scenes of carnage. None of the crusaders were left alive.

Matt forced his eyes away from the scene of devastation and turned to the alien machine. "Where the hell have you been!" He almost screamed. "Breel died while you took your time."

"Where is she?" the machine repeated.

"They blew her away," Ellyella was sobbing, desperately trying and failing to clear heavy pieces of junk, "she landed over here somewhere."

The machine moved next to Ellyella. Gently the alien-entity pushed her to one side, then easily removed the chunks of rubble, until they could see a pair of legs.

"Was it a direct hit?" It asked.

"It was a plasma bolt. Even a close miss would have killed her," Matt ground out.

Very delicately for something so massive, the alien picked up Breel's limp body and laid it in front of the crew.

Breel's face looked serene and peaceful, Matt thought, as if she were asleep, undamaged apart from a spray of red, but the top of her left shoulder and arm was a mass of black, charred blood. Even in death the exotic body art on the right side of her body glowed brightly, sparks of light weaving intricate synchronous patterns that frenetically pulsed the length of her arm and back again. Maybe it had a life of its own, independent of Breel, and was even now carrying on some unfathomable work.

"Lucky," the machine said.

"What do you mean, lucky?" Matt demanded.

"Lucky it didn't hit her dead centre," the alien replied.

222

"How is that lucky? Nobody can survive a plasma bolt at that range."

"Wait," Abiel knelt by the body. She put her ear to Breel's mouth, then looked up at the crew gathered around her. "She's still breathing," she said. She put her forefinger and index finger to Breel's throat. "I can feel a pulse."

The others went silent.

"*How?*" Kaemon asked.

"You're forgetting Breel isn't just anybody," the machine-entity said. It pointed to the glowing patterns. "They've been busy. A head shot or a direct hit would have been too much damage and then... sayonara." It leaned forward, inspecting Breel's shoulder. "Still touch and go. Now would be a good time to pray to any deities you think might still have a soft spot for you, because without her, we ain't getting off this rock."

"Maybe you should have got here sooner, then," Ellyella said.

"You think it's easy to move house after a half billion years? Sheesh, you should try it. Took me a while to get into this thing, even though I've had the minions keep it in good working order." What passed for a head turned deep black pits towards the wall. It was reflective enough to show them, ragged and battered, standing under their bizarre rescuer.

"Looking good," it said admiringly. "Better than you guys anyway."

"I'm glad you find it all so amusing," Matt said through gritted teeth.

"Yeah, well, you gotta laugh, though, or you'd cry."

Matt found it impossible to imagine the thing ever crying; or laughing. The alien picked Breel up, cradling her against its chest. She looked soft and vulnerable against the hard carapace, like a small child in the arms of a demonic parent. "Stay close to me. Once we move out of here, the only air you'll be breathing will be inside the force field I'm generating."

"Where are we going?" the Deacon wanted to know.

"To the ship." A tremor made the humans stagger, reaching for support. "And we better do it fast."

*

The Emissary stared at the buzzing static on the screens.

"What happened?" he asked.

"We don't know, my Lord." The captain returned. "All telemetry from the squad has ceased. They are no longer responding to comms and all the drones appear to have been disabled."

"What does that mean?"

"We can't say for sure without sending further men, my Lord. "Do you wish to give the order? We don't have any armour left," he added.

When the Emissary didn't respond the captain asked again. "My Lord, what are your orders?"

The Emissary continued to stare at the screens, unable to come to terms with what had just happened.

"My Lord?"

"Yes, yes," the Emissary snapped. "Time to leave."

There was a clear look of relief on the captain's face. He bowed his head. "Immediately, my Lord."

The Emissary rocked as the vehicle's engines roared into life. The enigmatic structures of the base began to slide past the window as they made their way back to the entrance. It was a short journey in the land cruiser. The crew of the *Scavenger* had shown them the way in. With the land cruisers, they hadn't needed to keep to the route of breathable air. Using sensors and drones, they had mapped the quickest way to the terminus of the oxygen corridor, simply blasting away any obstacles that might impede their progress. Now, having retraced their steps, they exited at the same place, fortunately still open, despite the base collapsing all about them.

The scene outside had changed dramatically in the short time they had been inside the complex. The skies roiled with pyroclastic black clouds, the plain buffeted by gale-strength winds. Tremor after tremor shook the area. The landing apron was cracked in multiple places, the splits wide enough for even some of the giant objects that had littered the plain for aeons to have fallen in. The two large Second-Light shuttles and a small entourage of escort fighters had been forced to move several times to avoid the same fate, so were already powered up and ready for departure. Icy clouds blew around them, while other ground vehicles and crusaders were hastily making their way back from exploratory missions. Vapour rose from the fissures, along with swarms of the bio-tech animals, some flying, some crawling, all milling about without apparent purpose.

The Emissary's vehicle drove carefully over the bucking terrain. There was an occasional bump and crunch as some unfortunate bio-tech alien failed to get out of the way fast enough. The Lord of Light watched the destruction with awe. The hell spawn work of the *Firsts* was finally going to oblivion, leaving him free access to the planet-sized machine at the centre of the whirl of gas and dust that orbited it, but even he felt qualms at the level of loss he was witnessing. He turned the view through one hundred and eighty degrees, until he was looking back at the alien complex and the beanstalk of the space elevator reaching up into the clouds. The instability of the moon transferred to the cables, making them vibrate like the strings of some gargantuan musical instrument made for the Gods. The land cruiser reached his shuttle's ramp. As they began the climb into the spacecraft, movement on the elevator caught his eye.

"So where is this ship?" Matt shouted, catching his breath. He had to raise his voice to make himself heard over a mournful bass thrumming reverberating around them. They had run through a curving corridor and now stood in a vast circular room in the centre of which, also arranged in a circle, stood several capsule-shaped objects, about the height of a two-storey house. The capsules rested against smooth grey columns that rose through a hole in the ceiling.

"Well, there's the rub," the alien said. "I had to place it away from the base, so we have to travel a bit to get there. We need to go up the elevator."

Matt said. "You developed a sense of humour along with your self-awareness."

"Yeah, I think I did," the alien responded, "but this isn't an example of it."

The exterior of one of the capsules rotated to reveal an airlock space big enough to accommodate both them and the machine. The alien didn't slow down. It moved quickly inside and the crew were forced to keep up with it, to stay within its force field.

When the airlock door had shut the machine said, "You can breathe in here. I've set the environmentals in the capsule and on the ship to suit you guys."

It indicated circular benches, concentric to the walls.

"Get strapped in, it might be a rough ride." It placed Breel's inert form carefully onto one of the benches, securing her as per its own instructions.

Matt could see rippling movement under the blood of Breel's injury. The damaged shoulder and arm jerked spasmodically in a disturbing way. The fingers of both hands twitched and clenched, as if she were enduring a vivid dream or nightmare, but her face lay in calm repose.

A lump formed in Matt's throat. "Is there anything we can do for her?" he asked anxiously.

"Nothing we can do that she can't do better for herself," the alien replied. It twirled a knotted forefinger over the bubbling gore. "Just have to give the wee fellows there a chance to do their thing."

The benches were clearly intended for taller beings but they managed to get themselves secure. Matt felt like a child in an adult's chair. The capsule shook and he felt himself press into the seat as they began to move up through the labyrinthine superstructure of the base.

"Surely we don't have the time to make this journey," he said. "It will take days to get to the counterweight at one gee."

"We aren't going all the way to the counterweight," The machine replied. "There's a shedload of way stations on the beanstalk. We're only going as far as the first one. Shouldn't take more than an hour or so."

The alien structures outside rushed downwards ever faster as the capsule accelerated.

"What's powering all this?" Kaemon asked the alien. "After all this time."

"It's a Reality Rift, isn't it?" the Deacon said suddenly. They all looked at him.

"A what?" Matt asked.

"Well, that's what I'm calling it. I've been thinking about it. The variable gravity in the base, the machine ecology, the base environment, all powered continuously for millions, possibly a billion years. The amount of energy required is unimaginable."

"Reality Rift," the machine mused. "Yeah, I like that. You're on the right track, keep going."

"The laws of physics are different in the other universe, the one the Rift connects to. The differential, as one reality leaks into another, releases stupendous amounts of energy. That's what you're tapping.

The amount becomes irrelevant because you have as much as you could ever need, an entire universe of the stuff. That's what all this is about isn't it? Our universe became an energy source for the other one. But the process changes the properties of our fundamental particles. Even across the multiverse the laws of conservation apply. That difference is given off as energy while the laws of physics here alter. It would only take a small change to affect how things work. Fusion might fail and the stars go out. Basic biochemistry, the kind that makes life possible, could stop. Our universe becomes dark and sterile. That's what the *Firsts* were trying to stop. That's what the Doomsday machine is preventing."

The machine nodded, an oddly human gesture. "Pretty good, take a gold star and go to the top of the class."

"Aren't there an infinite number of universes in the multiverse?" Ellyella asked. "Couldn't they find one without life?"

"It doesn't work like that." The Deacon continued to expound his theory. "It's the *RIP* energy we generate that allows the connection. Looking back at my research, it's obvious now. That's what the Doomsday machine is for. It generates the thousand light year barrier that we can't fly beyond because that's the critical size. Beyond that, we start to attract attention and generate enough instability in the fabric of the multiverse for the other universe to generate a portal."

"But they're happy to wipe out any civilisation they come across, for their own ends?"

"Maybe they think it doesn't matter," Matt said. "In an infinite multiverse, this is simply one version. There are many more that aren't wiped out. It only matters to us."

"That's pretty cold," Ellyella said.

"We have no idea as to the motivation of whoever or whatever they are," the alien said. "We don't know, as we never found a way to communicate with them. But yeah, unless the critical mass of *RIP* energy can be formed naturally in some way, and our boffins never found a way it could, it looks like they will always be drawn to a universe that has an advanced star-faring tech civilisation. Although there may be an infinite number of them in an infinite multiverse, they had to connect to one. Just our bad luck it was this one."

"I thought you blocked it? Isn't that what the Doomsday machine is all about?" Kaemon asked. "So, what's powering all this stuff you talked about?"

The Deacon eyed the machine. "The barrier isn't perfect; enough energy seeps through for you to use. Or was that deliberate?"

"We had to find a way to close the Rift and we needed energy to do that, more than can be generated conventionally. We used their power against them. But building the Doomsday machine used up all our resources, everything. The task did for us in the end, but hey, we made the universe safe." It paused. "You can thank me now," it finished and took a bow.

"But no longer," the Deacon said.

"Yeah, well, nothing lasts forever," the machine said.

Abiel was looking down at the deck during this exchange. Ellyella looked to the Deacon.

"So, none of this has anything to do with the Light or transcendence?" she said.

The Deacon shook his head.

"So what am I?"

"Holy Light!" Abiel made the sign of the Circle of Light

The rest of the crew looked across the room, at Breel, who was pushing herself upright, one half of her body black with burnt blood.

TWENTY-EIGHT

"Are we nearly there, Daddy?"

Her dad stopped walking up the grassy slope and turned to her. "Nearly, Brill."

"I'm tired," Breel complained. "And my name's Breel."

Her father walked back to her, scooped her up in his arms, nuzzling her neck. "You're brilliant though."

Breel squealed in delight, struggling to get free, but not too hard. Her dad held her high and sat her on his shoulders. She gripped his head, over his eyes.

"Hey, I can't see." He began making exaggerated steps, walking in a circle, hands outstretched. She giggled again. He held her arms by the wrists to pull them apart. Further up the slope she could see her mother. She was almost at the top.

Her mother turned and looked down at them. "I think she's old enough to walk," she said.

"Yeah, but she has a better view now, don't you Brill?"

Breel nodded. She did indeed have a grandstand view. Breel, her dad, and mum, were at the bottom of Arralandeshi crater, the crater where three-quarters of the population of Hope lived, but most of them lived in the warrens on the steep outer walls that towered around them, not down here.

High above, birds whirled over and around the tops of steep escarpments that were covered with buildings of all shapes and sizes. The cliffs were overlaid with a mesh of strands that supported cable cars that ferried the population from top to bottom and all points in between. Breel travelled on those cable cars every day with her mother, to school and back, but she had never seen Arralandeshi's mass-transport system in its entirety from this perspective. There was so much of it, draped over the city and the mesa like glistening cobweb strands. It was hard for her to take it all in. One side of the crater, the side where the sun she could no longer see was setting, was dark and purple with shadows. City lights were beginning to speckle into life across it. The top of the other side was golden, still catching the last rays of the sun.

Looming above them, blocking out half the sky, was Arralandeshi mesa. Her teacher had told her it was the largest mesa of many that stuck up from the crater bottom and it certainly looked like it from here. The bottom of it was dark and scary. The top quarter, though, like the far side of the crater rim, was a mass of bright detail in the orange light of a setting sun that cast long complicated shadows. Bright lights buzzed around the top of the mesa, like the fireflies that buzzed around the apartment where she and her mum and dad lived. She knew the lights above the mesa were the engines of spaceships arriving and leaving, because the top of the mesa was a spaceport. Although she had never been to it, she knew what happened at spaceports. Every now and then, an engine would flare brightly, dwindling as it powered up into the dark purple sky.

Breel pulled the collar of her fleece top down, trying to get some cool air around her body. She felt hot. Her dad had explained it to her. The air was thicker down here which made it hotter. She hadn't really believed him, but now she knew it was true, and because it was true, the crater bottom was lush and green. Rivers and streams fed into many lakes. She knew this was where very rich people lived, down here where the air was thicker and warmer. They had passed some of their enormous houses, set in large grounds arranged with shrubs, bushes and trees of all shapes and kinds, the only place on Hope where trees grew. The only place on Hope that was green. The air was sweet with the scent of colourful flowers and blossom.

She felt light-headed, also something to do with the thicker air, her dad had explained.

Her mother waited patiently for them to catch up.

"Are you warm enough?" she asked Breel. "Here." She shucked her backpack and rummaged until she found a small jacket.

"I'm too hot, Mummy," Breel protested.

"The sun's going down, honey pot. You'll be cold in a minute or two."

Breel reluctantly accepted the garment and pushed it behind her dad's head. "I'll put it on when I'm cold, then."

230

"Stubborn," her mother said.

"I wonder who she gets that from?"

From the ridge they now stood on, Breel looked down a grass-covered descent with a lake at the bottom. They were standing on the rim of a smaller crater within Arralandeshi, a crater within a crater, whose grassy outer slope they had just climbed.

"Are we going down there?" she asked.

"Yes." Her dad began to walk down the incline.

"What's the point of climbing all the way up just to go all the way down?" Breel complained. Then added, "We won't be able to see the pretty lights," as her view of the main crater walls was slowly obscured by the slope they were descending.

"We'll see some other pretty lights," her mother promised.

Her parents shared a look, one of those adult looks she wasn't supposed to understand, but she knew something that wasn't a happy thing had passed between them.

By the time they reached the lakeside the sky was a dark blue. The brightly lit outer walls of Arralandeshi crater were invisible to her now, obscured by the green bowl of the smaller crater slope they had just walked down. A pale orange-yellow glow seeped up from the setting sun to stain the bottom of the sky. She could still hear the noise from the city – it never stopped – but it was a bit quieter down here.

Her father lifted her off his shoulders and put her on the ground. She ran to the lake edge and stared across its expanse. There were still some yachts and boats on the water, even at this late hour, with brightly coloured triangular sails. Their reflections formed a rippling ethereal inverse world. Campfires burned on the far side. The sound of laughter and chatter reached her.

"Have you got the fuel, Riva?" her dad asked.

Her mother pulled a bundle of wood from her rucksack and handed it over. Breel had been told they weren't allowed to forage the wood down here. They had to bring their own for campfires and they could only light them in special places. Her dad set about arranging the sticks in a pyramid, in an area delineated by a circle of small stones, charred black from the heat of the hundreds of previous fires that had been lit there.

"Breel, honey pot," her mum shouted to her, "come over here. I want to show you something."

She ran to her mother. Her dad was about to light the fire-starter he had inserted into the wood pile.

"Wait, Falian," her mother said. She looked up at the sky.

"What are we waiting for, Mummy?" Breel asked.

"There," her mother pointed.

Breel followed the direction of her finger and saw a bright light in the sky, and then another and another until a string of bright jewels crossed the firmament like a glowing necklace. As the sky darkened, smaller points of light appeared, a random scattering that created a studded background to the brighter, more organised ones.

"This is the only place in Arralandeshi where you can clearly see the stars," her mother whispered.

"What are the very bright ones, Mummy?"

"Agricultural habitats, Breel. We call them Agri-habs. People work there. It's where most of the food we eat is grown."

Breel considered this idea for a moment, then said, "I'd like to work up there."

"You shouldn't be encouraging her, Riva," her dad said sharply.

"She'll have to know one day, Falian."

Breel hoped this wasn't going to be one of those times her mum and dad started shouting at each other. She was having such a nice time.

"When she's older," her dad said. "She's too young."

"What will I have to know when I'm older?" Breel demanded.

"Nothing, Breel." Her dad struck a spark and the campfire burst into life. It was bright in the increasing twilight and quickly overwhelmed the stars. Breel continued to stare hard at the night sky. She shielded her eyes from the orange flames. The bright stars where their food was grown were still visible.

"Hey," her dad said, "who wants a marshmallow? I've only got one so you better be quick." He aimed the sugary lump at his open mouth.

Breel forgot the night sky. She squealed and ran to her father.

She must have fallen asleep. It was cold and the stars were as bright as they could ever be at Arralandeshi. She was on her own, by the lakeside. The grass was damp. She sat up, looking for her parents. The never-ending activity of Arralandeshi city thrummed out of sight. The bright lights of spacecraft still streamed into and out of the spaceport, although the mesa itself was now nothing more than a block devoid of stars.

Breel couldn't understand why she was outside by the lake. What was she doing here?

"Breel, Breel, where are you?" She could see her mother, a dark shape by the tent they had erected.

"Brill," her dad joined in. "Brill, sweetie…"

She stood and ran towards her parents.

"Daddy, I'm here."

Her father turned towards the sound of her voice. For a moment his expression of concern morphed into a smile of relief, but that faded to be replaced by a look of horror.

"What the Deshi-hell," he said.

"Daddy, it's me!" Breel put out her hands, but instead of the pudgy pink things she expected, her hands were writhing purple light shot through with black.

"Daddy, I don't understand!"

"Get back, keep away," her father stumbled backwards.

"Falian," her mother appeared. "Have you found –" her mother's face parodied her father's, "Oh my god, what …"

Dark shapes pulsed through the writhing tentacles that used to be her hands.

"What, what are you?" her father managed.

"But Daddy," Breel said, "it's me."

And then her fingers expanded into flaming bars, shooting out to spear him through his eyes.

Breel screamed.

Her mother turned to run but the twisting energy burst from the back of her dad's skull to impale her mother in the small of her back. The energy arced; her parents were flung into the air. They hung and twitched, a pair of puppets dancing on strings of purple fire.

"Daddy, Mummy!" she cried as her parents shook and shook and shook and the burning lines of purple fire vibrated until she began to shake as well…

Breel became aware of light and noise and an incessant vibration that was threatening to rattle her teeth loose, overlaying the dream she was struggling to escape. She could still see her parents impaled on writhing lines of purple fire. It made her heart ache, made her want to cry. She let out a sob. She had a thumping headache, something that wasn't helped by the loud, continuous bangs and rattles all around her, and there was another noise, a deep bass note she felt more in her chest than heard. Pain blazed from her shoulder and arm. She lay very still, waiting for the pain to subside. As she thought it, the pain did lessen, but her whole left side was numb and cold.

Where in Deshi-hell am I? She tried to remember. She had done something... something extraordinary, and they had escaped the Emissary. But then they had been cornered in the alien base. Two crusaders were about to kill all her friends. She had thrown herself into the line of fire, expecting the soldier to lower his gun, but the gun had gone off. She had a vague memory of the impact, searing pain and then nothing. So why wasn't she dead? She half-opened her eyes. She was strapped to some kind of outsized chair or bench.

She could hear voices and realised now that she had been aware of them for some time. She lifted her head slightly, enough to get a view of her surroundings. Some kind of circular room. Matt, Kaemon, Ellyella, Abiel and the Deacon were all there, all similarly restrained, but not against their will apparently. They were all engrossed, mid-conversation. Deacon was expounding on a theory about the Doomsday machine. She caught her breath. To one side was a thing about twice the height of a human, made of what looked like metal and ceramic and talking colloquial Standard. It was agreeing with the Deacon. It looked like one of the statues or mechs from the complex come to life. The Machine-Entity, had to be, installed somehow into one of them. She focused on what they were saying. It was hard through her pounding headache, but she got the gist.

She sat up suddenly, sending a pulse of agony the entire length of her body, crashing to a stop at the top of her head, setting her arm and side on fire once again. She gasped, for a moment incapacitated, then said.

"So what am I?"

TWENTY-NINE

Something crawled up the immensity of the elevator cables. One of the ancient vehicles that had once plied the beanstalk was still functioning. The Emissary, in his cabin onboard the shuttle, watched. Breel was in that capsule, alive. He knew it and he shouldn't have been surprised. He could sense her presence, a brilliant star in the overall lattice of the Light, surrounded by lesser stars. The Emissary's heart pounded. What should he do? Was there still a chance to show her the truth, explain it so she would understand? She apparently saw him as evil, that somehow, he was about to destroy the human race. She couldn't see his mission was to save humanity, to help it transcend into a greater whole and leave all the petty greed and corruption behind.

He had been forced into unpleasant acts, but they were necessary. It was the long-term results that mattered. If an individual or group or even an entire planet were lost, humanity's ultimate transcendence would make it all worthwhile. Their tiny, inconsequential, individual existences hardly mattered in the face of eternity. Breel was made like him. She was part of this; she had to be. It was hard to believe that hers was as closed as the other tiny minds. She claimed she had seen something different to him. How could that be? It had to be the influence of that accursed abomination of the *Firsts* he sensed was with her in the capsule. Another bright star in the lattice, brighter even than Breel. He knew now that it had interfered with Breel's communion. Somehow, it had warped and degraded her experience, sullied her soul, poisoned her mind against him. He couldn't allow that agent of the Dark to have her. If only he had more time. But time was running out and he couldn't allow her free rein to possibly interfere with his divine mission. Better to send her to the Light now.

With a heavy heart he pinged the commander of ground operations supervising the evacuation.

"Your Grace."

"There is a capsule climbing the elevator cable. Send two of the escort fighters to destroy it. The insurgents are aboard. Then, as soon as you are ready, take us back to *Transcendent Light.*"

"As you wish, my Lord."

The commander's image disappeared.

You've done the right thing, your Grace, Maliesh whispered.

The Lord of Light watched the tiny speck of the elevator capsule crawl slowly up the apparently infinite grey ribbon stretching into a toxic sky.

"What am I?" Breel repeated.

"Breel!" Ellyella shrieked in delight.

"Breel, are you okay?" Matt automatically reached for her but was held back by his seat restraints. Breel remained focused on the alien machine, ignoring the others.

"What. Am. I?"

At that moment, the capsule exited through the roof of the base, rising into the open air. Through curving transparent walls, they looked out at an apocalyptic scene. The ground was convulsing. Massive segments of the alien complex were collapsing, splitting away to crumble into ice, rapidly sublimating into vapour. Viewed from this perspective, the scale of the complex became clear. It was immense, stretching for kilometres in every direction. Already, the gigantic landing apron they had walked across looked tiny in comparison, the huge alien artefacts mere details.

Pyroclastic towers of smoke and ash roiled up to join a thick, black, overcast sky. Those clouds must have been forming and moving at tremendous speed, but so enormous was the scale that the towering smoke looked solid, as if carved from ebony.

In the far distance, a tsunami of churning rock and ice stretched from horizon to horizon. It scoured its way across the landscape, heading straight towards them, ripping the crust off the small moon to expose the interior. Solid layers of rock split apart by geysers of boiling lava, bursting high into space from the sudden release of pressure, glowing through white, yellow, orange, and red. Objects as big as mountains, as big as continents, rose ponderously, colliding and fragmenting but continuing their inexorable rise, driven by the irresistible power of tidal gravitational forces.

A sudden, violent increase in the elevator's shaking had them all instinctively grabbing onto their ill-fitting restraints. No longer sheltered within the complex, their cable car was buffeted by ferocious winds generated by an atmosphere being stripped away into space. The moving air moaned a deep bass sound as it thrummed through the cables of the space elevator, a mournful lament to the end of the world.

"Hey, Breel," the machine said cheerfully. "Great to have you back, babes, and looking so good!"

Sudden brilliant light threw the interior of the capsule into a searing contrast of whirling black and white as plasma bolts abruptly detonated around them.

"Sorry, be right back in a few." The machine turned its attention to the events outside.

More ordnance exploded.

"Shit, that was close. I think the Emissary is really pissed this time," Ellyella said.

"I guess we caught a break, of a kind." Kaemon grimly hung onto his seat to stop himself being thrown out of it. "The air turbulence is throwing them all over the sky, making it hard for them to target us."

"They'll get us eventually." The Deacon was slammed back against the wall of the capsule, then knocked forward to the limit of his seat restraint. He gripped the belts tighter. "Once we leave the atmosphere, we'll be easy prey."

The shaking, vibration and the scared faces of her friends finally brought the dire situation they were in home to Breel.

"Deshi-damn, are we riding up the elevator?" Then she looked down at the charred blood covering her burnt clothing. "What... what happened to me?" She explored her skin, pulling and wiping the crusted gore away. Beneath the blood, her flesh was whole and unmarked.

Kaemon was wide-eyed. "Wow, that's some trick."

"You don't remember?" Ellyella asked.

"Last thing I remember was the crusader's gun going off."

The capsule rocked violently, tossing her painfully back and forth. She tightened her grip on the edge of the bench she sat on.

"Is this Deshi-damn thing going to stay up?" she asked the alien.

"In the final analysis," the machine said, "no. But hopefully long enough for us to do what we need to do. The cables will survive the preacher's attack. They are virtually indestructible, especially against the pitiful weapons you people have. The capsule's not so tough though. If they score a direct hit, well..." It turned its head towards the capsule's transparent roof. "Nearly out of the atmosphere. The ride'll be a bit less rock and roll after that."

Ellyella hung grimly to the straps. "You couldn't have kept your ship in the base?"

"Nah, I had limited control over the bone-heads. Had to keep it away from them or they would have recycled it, like they did the first two."

"Looks like the Emissary's leaving as well." Kaemon pointed down to the landing apron, dwindling rapidly. Below the two escort fighters targeting them, two large shuttles and a complement of escort craft were powering up, each one the epicentre of its own dust storm.

Flame flared again from the fighters as they circled around the beanstalk for another strike. Most of the bolts missed, splashing harmlessly off the dull grey cables. One bolt did land. The noise was terrifying. The concussion hammered through the cabin. For a second Breel was gone, and then she was back, into the pounding noise and confusion.

"Those fuckers," the machine said. "That nearly did for us. I need to do something about them, pronto. Can't risk another hit like that. Lucky for us, I have some new tricks up my sleeves these days – or I would, if I had sleeves."

The Emissary watched Breel's final moments with mixed feelings as his ship prepared to leave. And then, a bio-tech lifeform obscured his field of view. He heard a loud bang as it bounced off the fuselage, then another, then another, then a veritable locust swarm of them lifted towards the two fighters attacking the rising elevator capsule. Briefly, he could see nothing else until the aliens moved far enough away: a pulsating mass behaving like a single organism. The fighters had been circling the elevator, strafing the rising capsule with each revolution. As they swept around for another attack, they were met by a black cloud of avians, surrounding them like a buzzing globe of giant angry wasps. Bright flashes lit the sphere of aliens from within. One of the attack craft, now a ball of fire, fell towards the ground, trailing a spiralling line of smoking debris. It hit the surface and transformed into a pulse of expanding hot energy and glowing metal. A few seconds later the second fighter burst free, spraying plasma fire at the attackers in a desperate attempt to survive. The swarm changed shape, stretching into an elongated finger, chasing the fleeing fighter until they engulfed it once more.

The beleaguered fighter reappeared, bursting free of the alien swarm, but the pilot had clearly lost control. It spun and twisted, towards the ground, leaving a dark trail of burning bio-life forms behind it. The Emissary followed its trajectory until it crashed and exploded near the first—still burning fiercely on the concrete. The explosion sent white hot chunks of shrapnel across the landing apron, slamming into the second shuttle, that was just starting to lift off. The shockwave and multiple impacts caused the transport to yaw. Its starboard wing tip scraped the ground, scattering sparks and burning alien bio-machines into the air.

It was a testament to the shuttle pilot's skill and cool head that he managed to regain control. He pointed the prow of his vehicle to the sky, readying for the burn to orbit, when the ground below him split open. A massive snake-like bio-machine burst out of the newly formed crevasse, uncoiling to create an arch over the rising shuttle, dwarfing it. The shuttle's engines burned brightly as the pilot applied full thrust, but the vehicle had only moved through its own length before the leviathan coiled around the shuttle like a gargantuan boa constrictor. Its hull buckled and collapsed, a second before it too detonated, sending incandescent fragments of both the attacking aliens and spaceship in every direction.

In the sky, the swarm of aliens that had brought down the fighters had become a murmuration, forming a black arrowhead that twisted to turn and fly directly towards the Emissary's shuttle. A scattershot cacophony of multiple impacts slammed into his shuttle, almost tipping it over. The alien things scraped, scratched, and ripped at the hull. More bio-creatures, a demonic horde from the farthest depths of hell, began to squirm up through the cracks and fissures in the ground.

"Captain," he shouted into the comms, "get us into space immediately."

"But we still have men on the ground, your Grace." the captain replied.

"Get us into the fucking air, now!" the Emissary screamed.

The shuttle lurched, throwing the Emissary off his seat. He landed heavily. The floor turned into a slide as the nose lifted and the engines howled. The Emissary slid into a bulkhead. His view of the outside was obscured by a mass of chitin, legs, wings and glowing red eyes, as the creatures piled onto the ship in an attempt to force it back down. The pilot rolled the ship side to side, doing his best to shake the aliens free. The Emissary was thrown violently from one side of the cabin to the other, then pitched forwards as his pilot dived to gain speed. Through the writhing alien bodies, the Emissary glimpsed the cracked material of the landing apron expand to fill his view.

"Pull up! Pull up!" the Lord of Light screamed, knowing the pilot must be completely unaware of his Messiah's exhortations. Nonetheless, the broken terrain slid out of sight to be replaced by sky and buzzing aliens falling away. The Emissary was again thrown ignominiously across the small space, cracking his head painfully against one leg of his desk. When his vision cleared, the screens showed black, roiling cloud. The shuttle climbed towards space.

"I thought you didn't have control of the…" Breel struggled to find the right word "…those things," she finished.

They had watched with open mouths as the attacking ships were brought down, followed by another attack on the ones still on the ground. One managed to get airborne and escape. The ancient landing apron was alive with crawling, leaping bio-tech lifeforms performing a macabre dance to the end of times.

"That was before," the machine said. "This is now. They just needed a little purpose in life."

The buffeting eased as the capsule approached the edge of the atmosphere, but the entire structure of the beanstalk was resonating, waves travelling its length with increasing synchronism.

"Light protect us," the Deacon said.

They all stared in awe and terror at the massive construction of the beanstalk, rippling in a way that defied all logic or comprehension for something so insanely large.

Through the transparent roof they could see the cables enter into a spherical blister-like structure, before emerging to carry on to the counterweight.

"Our stop," the mech said. "Stay with me as we exit. I'll keep you breathing until we get to the ship. You'll be okay once you're inside. Then it's up to you, Breel."

Breel looked up sharply. "Up to me? What does that mean?"

"Sorry. Meant to say, it's a starship, which means it's symbiotic. Only a symbiont pilot, an organic one, is going to be able to fly it."

"You meant to say?" Breel glared at the mech. "An alien ship with exotic tech that I can only guess at. How the Deshi-damn am I supposed to deal with that?"

"It's symbiotic. It's the only way it'll fly. It's the only way we can transit a *RIP*." It leaned towards her. "It's the only way we are getting out of here." Then it relaxed its stance and said jovially, "Don't worry babes, you'll figure it out."

The humans all stared at the alien.

"So that's why we're all here," Breel said finally. "You still need us."

"Yeah, well, technically I only need you, honey. But hey, I'm a sentient neural-core of my word and I owe you."

"You're blister-hog-shit crazy!" Breel exploded. "There is no way this is going to work."

"You'll handle it," the alien insisted. "No problem. You'll see." The mech stared at her through the deep dark pits of its sensory array. "I have faith," it said.

The capsule entered the elevator way station and came to a stop. The airlock rotated open to reveal a large, vaulted chamber. One wall was transparent, allowing in the light of the last rays of the sun, about to dip below the moon's horizon. The shepherd moon was hardly recognisable; the surface lost beneath a roiling mass of cloud lit from within by massive static discharges. It bulged where the crust was subject to mammoth tidal forces, making it egg-shaped, as if it were growing a massive, terminal tumour.

Chunks of the moon were falling into space amidst a tornado of spiralling gases from the atmosphere. Magma from the planet's hot interior rose in twisting streams to split the clouds like rivers of glowing blood.

Not only the moon: the whole spiral construction the shepherd had been part of, and had been integral in maintaining, was distorting, losing its integrity and the shape it had held for millions of years. It was slowly stretching into an arc that would eventually become a ring of debris encircling the black sphere of the doomsday machine, glowering over it, like the dead eye of a malevolent god.

The alien looked towards the wall of destruction heading their way from the moon's breakup.

"Need to move quickly now, kids," it said.

The sun dipped below the plane of rubble, casting intricate shadows across the way station's floor and onto what Breel assumed was the ship, though it was like nothing she had ever seen. A simple curving shape, smooth and featureless from this angle. Simply sitting there, it looked fast and dangerous, under tension, like a coiled spring waiting to launch itself into space.

An opening appeared in what had previously been a seamless hull. They sprinted the short distance over to it, keeping close to the alien mech so as to stay within its force field. Since they were effectively standing on the top of a giant tower, they could move normally, but this far out from the mass of the moon and with the mass of the moon dissipating, Breel felt lighter. Her shoulder and arm ached again, despite her best efforts to will the pain away, and she had the Deshi-damned mother of all headaches, but she was still moving.

Discarded components littered the approach to the spacecraft, along with a variety of bio-tech machines. The mechs milled about aimlessly, lacking instruction to do anything else. Everything vibrated alarmingly as the stress of the moon's breakup transmitted through space elevator's superstructure.

They ran into the interior of the alien starship. It was white and antiseptic. A short corridor led into a room that looked very similar to the compartment in the elevator capsule.

"Find somewhere to secure yourselves," the alien said.

"Is there anything to drink on this thing?" Kaemon asked, between pauses to catch his breath. "I... only ask... as it'd be a shame if we all died of thirst while we were being rescued."

"There's water available from that dispenser." The machine indicated a white box on the wall. "It was the last thing I had the minions do once I knew what your needs would be."

"You thought to do that?" Abiel asked, activating a spigot that ran clear liquid into a cup, one of many in a rack.

"Yeah, if I had one thing, it was plenty of time to think," the alien said. "Breel, babe, the bridge is at the centre of the ship. Let's go."

"Good luck," Abiel said to Breel, handing her a cup.

"Thanks," Breel said, accepting the water.

"C'mon, toot sweet," the alien said. "Time to drink when we're not dead."

Breel took a quick mouthful as she ran after the mech. Water sloshed over the rim and down her chin. She followed the alien out of the room and along a short upwards-sloping corridor which exited into a spherical space. A walkway led to a control throne suspended in the centre, connected to the curving white walls by thousands of fine threads. Lights danced along their length. It was a symbiont pilot's interface built on a grand scale. There was a seat, a smooth curved shape built to accommodate a much larger pilot.

"I didn't know how to size the furniture and it was too late to change it once I knew," the mech conceded.

She sat. She felt lost in the chair and had to sit forward to see the controls. The chair looked like it was designed for something similar in shape to the alien machine, but smaller. She surveyed the controls. They were surprisingly similar to the ones on *Scavenger*, but outsized.

The alien took up station behind her.

"What am I supposed to do?" Breel asked.

"Do what you do, Breel. You've done it before." It paused. "It's what you were made for."

Before she had time to question that last remark, the console before her lit up with contorted glyphs that meant nothing to her. Violent vibration shook them then, causing the alien-machine to stagger. The whole beanstalk structure was about to come apart. She gripped the seat. She had no idea what to do, but then again, that hadn't stopped her before.

Do what you do. It's what you were made for…

…and then, in what was becoming a familiar sensation, she felt her being stretching outwards, becoming part of the alien space craft – only not so alien any more. She felt her augmentation warm. Information came to her and it was in the same form that she had used with Cross a seeming lifetime ago in Scavenger. *It took shape in her mind, not in the form of crude language, but as whole concepts she*

could interact with and understand. It was symbiosis, but centuries ahead of the crude interactions she had become so familiar with.

She melded with the ship, explored its systems, checking their functionality and integrity, no longer cognisant of her flesh-and-blood body. She had become a thing of exotic materials and surging energy flows. She was aware of the rest of the crew, fragile bubbles punctuating the malleable lattice of reality.

Now her consciousness expanded beyond the confines of the way station. She could see that the structure of the elevator was terminally compromised. Massive oscillations were travelling its length. If she didn't get them out of there quickly it would be too late. She saw how to open the station's airlock doors and without thinking of the consequences did so. Atmosphere blasted into space, taking with it the contents of the chamber, including the ship, which tumbled out, along with a cloud of fragments made up of bio-tech machines and other detritus, towards what was left of the darkening moon. The shepherd moon's atmosphere had gone. Now there was only a network of glowing lava rivers emptying into molten seas in a vast pancake of rock, shredding at the edges.

It occurred to her that maybe she should have figured out how to power up the engines before she blew them into space. They traced a parabolic curve down towards the blistering surface. Something with a large mass slammed into the ship, causing it to spin.

Behind them, the elevator finally succumbed to the titanic forces arrayed against it, breaking apart in several places. So massive was the structure that the breakup appeared to happen in slow motion, even though the sections were moving at phenomenal speed. The upper sections were flung into space while the lower section collapsed into the seething remains of the shepherd moon. There was nothing to show where the alien base had been. Desperately she looked for a way to power up the drive. She didn't even know what kind of engines this thing had. Was it EMD or something even more exotic? The tortured surface drew closer, an elongated ellipse. It stretched out along the line of its orbit to contribute its mass to the embryonic ring forming around the Doomsday machine. But for now, from her perspective, it was a rising wall of convulsing debris kilometres high, a wall that they were falling straight into.

THIRTY

The walls melted away. A view of the interior of the way station and the meandering bio-tech lifeforms sprang into existence around the crew of *Scavenger*. Suddenly, the alien bots, along with all the rubbish littering the floor, swept silently away and the ship followed. The initial pulse of acceleration briefly gave them the sensation of weight, but without a star drive and no longer subject to the gravity they had felt on the huge tower of the elevator, they were abruptly in free fall.

The stars wheeled about them.

Ellyella let out a cry and shrank further into her chair. So complete was the transparency of the walls she felt she must be exposed to vacuum and felt the irrational need to hold her breath. She hung on to the loose ill-fitting safety straps.

The ship rang like a gong – from an impact with something large Ellyella guessed – and began to spin, fast.

They were pressed into their seats.

The tumbling view outside went from the luckless moon and back to the elevator. Ellyella fought to control the nausea and vertigo as Coriolis forces along her body played havoc with the balance fluids in her ear. The last thing she wanted to add to her woes was to be sick.

The beanstalk broke apart.

It was hard to believe something so huge and so apparently indestructible could snap in two like a twig in a winter storm. Ellyella felt tiny and inconsequential in the face of the incomprehensible destruction.

She saw Abiel make the sign of the Circle of Light, eyes wide.

"Breel's having trouble figuring it out," Matt said. "Where the hell did the Machine-thing go?"

No one had an answer to that.

The wall of churning debris rolled back into view, noticeably closer this time.

*

Where were the Voices when she needed them? This was a hell of an introduction on how to pilot an alien starship. It seemed their new vessel followed the same paradigms, more or less, as human ones. She searched through the mass of data flooding her mind until a pattern presented itself. While part of her was looking inwards, another part couldn't ignore the tumbling mountains outside, getting closer by the second.

She applied a sequence of inputs. Status data showed protocols coming online. She saw what to do and inputted the required commands. With a shudder, the drive burst into life, accelerating them directly into the deadly roiling mass of ejecta from the doomed shepherd moon.

Frantically she applied lateral thrust and the spacecraft responded. She was flying over what she now perceived as a monumental river of ice and rubble. The EMD drive finally found traction in the substrate of reality and she was able to move them away, to a safer distance. She took a second to take stock of their situation, the status of the ship and its occupants. She noted where the crew and the Mech were.

She turned her awareness outwards. The shepherd moon was now so stretched it bore no resemblance to what it had once been. The deeper parts of it were still hot and glowing, but it was already freezing at the periphery. Its material joined the matter that once formed the spiral, all of it reforming to become a ring around the massive, ultra-dense object which ruled it all.

Movement grabbed her attention. She almost missed it. It was a long way off and moving fast.

"Sorry for that somewhat exciting exit folks." Breel's bodiless voice filled the room. "I've got it under control now, more or less. Anyway, I caught sight of this."

At first, Matt couldn't see anything other than rectangular markers surrounding a moving point of light. The view zoomed in. He felt a lump form in his throat.

Scavenger, tumbling erratically.

"It's a good distance away and travelling even further away, fast. We do have a small window to rendezvous, but even if we catch up, it's going to be difficult, if not impossible, to get onboard."

"Be great if we could find a way," Kaemon said. "Apart from food, we need fresh clothing and space suits."

"And our personal stuff," Ellyella said.

"What's the problem?" Deacon asked. "If we can still rendezvous?"

"The problem is that we can't get aboard while it's spinning all over the place like that. No way Breel can match it." Kaemon explained.

"Yeah, that's right," Breel agreed. "Someone would need to get on board and use *Scav's* thrusters to stabilise it."

"Tricky," Abiel said. "Without space suits, I mean."

"There's the rub." The alien-machine had made an appearance, standing in the doorway. "For your sakes, it would be good to get on board, though. We have water and we can reprogram the synthesisers for food, but it might take a while and the results will probably taste like shit."

Matt was emphatic. "I'm with the machine; we need to get over there while we still can."

"I don't see how," Kaemon said.

"Get close enough to jump across without a suit?" Matt suggested. "It's possible. I'm willing to give it a go."

"That's crazy," Ellyella said. "I know what it's like to stand unprotected in a vacuum. You'll have ten to fifteen seconds at most before you pass out, followed very shortly by brain death. Even if you do survive the jump and manage to get onboard, you won't be in any fit state to do anything."

"The ship's movements are so erratic it's unlikely you would ever manage to land," Kaemon added. "If the collision didn't kill you outright, you'd be thrown back into space."

"I don't need a suit," the Machine said.

"You could get in through the shuttle lock, but you'd struggle getting through *Scav's* tight interior spaces," Matt pointed out. "And *she* won't respond to you anyway."

"Yeah, I know," the Machine said. "If we had time, I might be able to hack the system, but we don't. I could get one of you across in the force field, though. Probably only good for one trip and then I'm out of juice." It surveyed them from behind the dark pits of its sensors. "Yeah, I'm going to be somewhat diminished without the resources of the base, but then I knew that."

"I don't know," Breel said. "Do we really need to risk this? It's too dangerous. We can manage until we get back, surely, even if the food tastes bad. I'm sure you'd like to get your personal shit back, but is it worth someone dying for?"

"It's worth the risk," Matt insisted. "We need to get over there one last time. I'll do it." He turned to the alien. "Will that force-field protect me from radiation?"

"Can't maintain full power any more. It will protect you from the worst excesses. You'll probably top up your tan and it'll be fucking cold in the shadows."

"Why do you talk like that?" Abiel asked. "You had access to all *Scavenger's* language database, not just Kaemon's suspect entertainment feed."

"I like it, honey. It feels like me. Sorry if you're a prude."

It was almost as if the damn thing was enjoying this, Matt thought. If it could smile it surely would be.

He said, "Okay, let's get on with it. Breel, can you calculate a rendezvous?"

"Sure. There's another thing, though," Breel said.

The Deacon groaned. "Of course, there's always 'another thing.'"

"*Transcendent Light* and the other Church ships are on the far side of the remains of the shepherd moon. They could be tracking us. I don't know if they will try to stop us or not, but we need to get this done and power for the *RIP* asap."

"Maybe he'll lose interest in us now and go play with his new toy," Ellyella suggested.

The Deacon shook his head and looked doubtful, "I never thought of the Emissary as the 'losing interest' type. He'll want what he believes to be his." He looked up to the ceiling where he imagined Breel might be. "And he will want to make an example of the rest of us."

The Emissary, in the bridge of *Transcendent Light,* looked down at a display arranged before him.

"They are on the far side of the debris field, your Grace," Captain Hannathon said.

The man had become Maliesh's replacement by dint of being first in line and had so far proven adequate. He would never be another Maliesh. Maliesh would be hard to replace. Pity Maliesh could not have just accepted his role. The man had been the closest thing to a friend he had, could ever have in the elevated status of Emissary of Second Light. He fought down a pang of regret. '*Uneasy lies the head...*' where had that quote come from?

"They have changed course to match velocity with their old ship," Hannathon continued. The display, relayed from a fast-moving drone sent to a position above the plane of the ecliptic, showed a grainy image of a space craft unlike anything he had ever seen before, moving fast. The view pulled back until the alien ship became a dot. Another dot, flashing green, came into view at the top of the image.

"Here." The captain pointed.

The Emissary put his hands on the table so he could lean forward, as if getting closer to the projected image would supply him with more information.

"How long will it take them to rendezvous?" he asked.

"We estimate five hours standard at the speed they are traveling, taking into account time for deceleration," Hannathon said. "It's clear they intend to dock. What's not clear is how they intend to do it."

The Emissary was still torn. Breel kept escaping, no matter what he did. That ship with all its advanced technology, Breel herself, and even more important, the alien intelligence that had aided her, were all things that he coveted, and now he was presented with another chance to acquire them. It was unclear what the Light was trying to tell him. Should he just let them go and focus on the true purpose of this mission or take advantage of this new opportunity? Sometimes the inscrutability, the 'moving in mysterious ways,' could get damned annoying...

"Can we get them in range, before they are gone, do you think?" he asked Hannathon.

"They can be in range of the MPG in about nine hours, my Lord," the captain affirmed, "if we begin immediately. We need to safely clear the rubble and get a clear line of sight on the target."

The Emissary ran a hand over his face. His lips and nose were still sore and swollen from the blow Breel had delivered. He had no idea what the agenda of the *Firsts*' agent was and he couldn't know what Breel might do next.

"Send *Burning Rapture* with the MPG. Instruct the captain to give the insurgents one chance to surrender. If they don't comply immediately, destroy them. We can't waste any more time and resources, and I can't have them free to possibly become a thorn in our side."

"As you wish, your Grace."

"Are you sure this is the will of the Light?" Maliesh whispered into his ear. *"Should we be concerned about this small, powerless rabble? Would we not be better focusing our resources on our true objective?"*

"We have no idea how much Breel's power may grow or what that machine intelligence is capable of!" The Emissary snapped.

"As you say, your Grace," Captain Hannathon said.

The Emissary sighed. "Meanwhile, calculate an orbit to the super dense object. It is time to begin our true work."

"Yo, dudes, is this cool or what?" The mech had fitted itself out with an overlarge Space Manoeuvring Unit. The SMU and its arrangement of thrusters fit snugly to its back.

"Where am I going to sit?" Matt asked. He was swathed in a tight-fitting outfit of shiny material that the machine had printed out from a synthesiser. It fit him like a second skin to maintain pressure in the vacuum and was constructed with both a reflective and insulating layer, to reflect heat from the sun and keep him warm in the shadows.

It covered him from head to foot. He looked like an escapee from one of the ancient space movies in Kaemon's now infamous collection. The only break was around his eyes, which were covered by a pair of dark goggles, also printed by the synthesiser. The area around his mouth and nose was sufficiently porous to allow him to breathe.

"You couldn't have gone the whole hog and printed out a space suit while you were at it?" Ellyella asked.

"Yeah, right," the Mech said. "I'm doing my best here, but printing out a space suit is a tad trickier than a bunch of thrusters hardwired together and a shiny Spandex suit."

The others had come to see the mech and Matt off. Breel was still on the bridge. They had all cleaned themselves up as best they could. Matt's stomach growled. Drinking water had helped, but they needed food badly. Synthesising edible protein to suit their metabolism would be a complex job. At the moment only the mech, and Breel to a lesser extent, understood how to operate the tech onboard the ship. Breel was preoccupied and the machine had been absorbed with creating the manoeuvring unit and Matt's outfit. Matt flexed his arms and legs, feeling strong resistance from the tight material.

"Not sure what Spandex is, but I hope it's up to the job.

The machine intertwined its eight-digit, opposable thumb hands to create a bucket seat in front of its chest.

"That's it?" Matt asked. "Not the most dignified way I've ever travelled."

"Hey, it is what it is, man. I didn't have time to synthesise a crash couch." It moved its hands forward, inviting Matt to sit. "I'm beginning to feel a tad unappreciated."

Matt turned, using his hands to lever himself backwards into the makeshift seat. His legs dangled in the air. He looked over his shoulder at the crew and nodded at them.

"See you in a bit."

The others looked at him in silence. Finally, Kaemon said, "Good luck, Matt."

"Yeah, see you in the galley," Matt said. "I want more of that dhal you cooked, the one with the peanuts."

Kaemon smiled. Matt was surprised to see the man's eyes were moist.

"You got it." Kaemon gave him a thumbs-up.

"Light speed," the Deacon said.

"Thanks, Deacon."

"Don't die," Ellyella said gruffly.

He smiled at her. "I'll do my best."

They moved out of the room into the inner chamber of an airlock.

"Okay, dawg." the machine roared with enthusiasm. "Are you ready? I said: Are. You. Ready!"

Matt grimaced. "Dial it down a notch, can you? Is the force field activated?"

"You think I forgot?" the alien replied. "We're ready, Breel. Go for it, gal."

"Copy that," Breel responded. "Cutting the EMD, brace for weightless conditions."

Matt felt his weight pulse and he was in micro gravity. The Machine's snake-like thumb digits extended to wrap around his waist, like self-motivated seat belts.

They waited for the lock to cycle. A section of the wall simply evaporated in that unnerving way doors had when opening on this ship, revealing *Scavenger* spinning like a cheerleader's baton, black shadows spinning across its hull like a sundial on fast forward.

He surveyed his ship critically. There was some extra impact damage, but not as much as he might have expected. As far as he could see, *Scavenger* looked sound.

Below them, the stars were occluded by the cooling remains of the shepherd moon.

"Here we go." The mech's voice filled his bubble of air. "Brace yourself."

Silently they moved out of the ship. The sound from the mech's SMU didn't reach him through the vacuum outside the force field, but he did feel a vibration every time the thrusters fired. Sat at the front of the alien-machine, like a figurehead on the prow of an unlikely sailing ship, he had a tremendous view. His heart thundered. All of his experience screamed that exposing himself to the vacuum of space like this was suicide. The force field must have some insulating properties as, although the temperature had dropped, it was only by a degree or so. The 'Spandex' the machine had conjured for him was much more than it seemed. It was doing a remarkable job of containing his body heat, to keep him warm and at the same time reflecting heat from the sun back into space, to keep him cool. If he ever got back, he could make a fortune marketing this stuff.

If he ever got back.

Nonetheless, the alien turned so that he sat in shadow, protecting him from the excessive heat and, more importantly, radiation of the sun.

The sun was about to drop below the plane of the ecliptic relative to them. It was slightly cooler than sol, burning more orange. The warm colours and long shadows gave the impression of a late evening sunset back home, but he had never contemplated a setting sun with a view like this one.

The aftermath of the shepherd moon's destruction presented itself in all its terrible glory as they moved further out from the alien starship. Trillions of tons of spinning ice and rock colliding and bouncing off each other as they jostled for a stable orbit around the giant, mysterious, apparently inert object at their centre. Every now and again a red-orange glow flashed, as a piece, still hot from the violent destruction, pitched into view. The broken remains had spread a remarkable distance. At the speed it was going, it would only take weeks to complete the entire ring.

Scavenger grew until it occluded everything else, a terrifying whirling mass of hard, unforgiving edges. He began to wonder if his enthusiasm for doing this had been misplaced. They headed for the fulcrum of the ship's spin, which was by far the safest place to land as it was moving the least. Like an unbalanced dumbbell, though, this was about two thirds down from the bow. The engines were massive. Once aboard they would have to work their way down the fuselage to the emergency airlock at the stern, adjacent to the garage bay. The same one from which they had made the EVA down to the surface of *Revenge* a lifetime ago. The airlock was small and would fill with air rapidly, unlike the garage bay space that had once housed the shuttle.

Like a spinning skyscraper, *Scavenger* turned. Matt had a sudden and distinct impression of what it must be like to be a fly as the swatter descends. They homed in on *Scavenger*'s fuselage. The only thing to distinguish this part from any other was that the bow and stern spun around it.

"Hang on," the alien said. Matt felt some weight return as the machine applied thrust, matching the velocity and vector of the ship. He was thrown violently back and forth as the mech fired its thrusters in quick succession, lining up with the exact centre until it lay beneath them. But it wasn't going to be that easy. Their target twisted away as the ship turned through its long axis as part of a complicated tumble. The mech's SMU flared again.

"For Jinx-sake," Matt roared, pressed hard into the restraints of the machine's fingers.

"I'm getting low on propellant," the machine informed him. "I'm going to have to just grab it. Might get a bit rough. Get ready."

"Might *get* a bit ro…?" Matt didn't have time to finish. The mech's clawed foot stretched down, then wrapped around a metal bracket designed for more normal EVA's. The angular momentum of *Scavenger* transferred to the mech. Matt was jerked back and forth furiously. He let out a terrified shout, his vision blurred. The machine put down a second foot and then they were attached to *Scavenger*.

"Whoo-oooo!" the mech shouted. "That was so cool."

The *Scavenger* had become their stationary reference. Now it was the universe, and the alien ship in which they'd made their escape, that spun around and over in crazy, nausea-inducing loops. Matt fought his convulsing stomach. *Don't be sick, don't be sick.* The spasms passed. Bad as this was, though, it was going to get worse.

The machine turned so that Matt faced the bow then began to make its way backwards to the stern.

"I guess you have some kind of rear view?" Matt said.

"Naw, I'm guessing. Just kidding, mate, I have all sorts of handy-dandy perception tricks."

They were in effect moving down a centrifuge. Matt's weight increased the nearer they got to the airlock and he was subjected to increased centripetal force. It felt like he was lying on his back staring up the vertical wall of the ship's hull. He hoped the machine was going to be strong enough. Finally the nature of the hull's details changed and then they were over the airlock. Matt estimated they were at about half a g. He felt canal sickness as Coriolis messed with the balance fluid in his ears.

The alien anchored itself. Matt took a breath and focused his neural-link on the airlock door. He initiated the command to open.

Nothing happened.

"Now would be a great time," The machine said. "Power's getting low. I won't be able to sustain the field much longer and then it'll be a choice of maintaining my higher brain functions…or yours."

"I'm trying," Matt said.

They were plunged into darkness as *Scavenger* completed another spin. A day-night cycle that strobed them through light and dark in about a minute, making it impossible for his eyes to adjust.

"The ship's not responding to my neural-link. Maybe it's this material I'm wrapped in. How long have we got?"

"If I start singing 'Daisy,' start worrying."

After a moment's thought, Matt said, "Let me go."

The mech's fingers withdrew. To Matt the machine, standing at a ninety degree angle to the hull, felt like a floor. He searched the hull around the airlock until he found the access panel, then stood carefully on one of its legs and reached up to the airlock release. His foot slipped. For a heart stopping moment he was in free fall, falling past the machine into the void. Mech grabbed him.

"Careful." It said. "If you slip you'll be end up lost in the final frontier."

"Yeah. Thanks for that." Matt grabbed a handhold similar to the one the mech was using to steady himself. The alien hadn't felt it necessary to include fingers in his gloves, expecting Matt to use his neural-link to open the lock. It was a possibly fatal oversight as there was no way he was going to open the panel with what amounted to flippers. After a few seconds fruitless slapping, he gave up.

"Jinx-damn it, I can't get in with these damn mitts over my hands."

Bright light returned, casting their dark shadows on the hatch. He pulled off the shiny mittens and let them go. They fell away from him alarmingly, as if whipped away in violent tail wind. They bounced off the alien machine and stopped, held in place by the force field.

With his flesh exposed to the numbing cold he flipped the panel and began tapping onto the keypad he had exposed. They were plunged back into darkness.

"Breathe out, now!" the mech urged. "The field's going down."

Matt knew that if exposed to vacuum he didn't want air in his lungs. The human body could deal with the pressure change, but a volume of expanding air in his chest could prove fatal. He followed the alien's advice. There was a rush of air, a popping sound and then the quiet of eternity. The small amount of residual heat in the air bubble vanished and he was exposed to hard vacuum. The mittens continued their interrupted journey into the cosmos. Matt clamped his mouth shut. His lungs spasmed, wanting to take a breath. Frantically he tapped at the keypad. What was it El had said? Ten to fifteen seconds?

The airlock door slid aside and he rocketed into *Scavenger*, propelled by the machine, who had unceremoniously flung him in. The outer door shut. He skidded along the wall, which was acting as a floor, slammed into the closed inner door, just over a meter away, before sliding back onto the outer door like a pinball, cracking his head painfully in the process. He gasped air into his lungs as the airlock automatically filled with oxygen. He lay there motionless, dazed, breathing deeply while the airlock cycled until the pressure built to one atmosphere. The inner door slid open and *Scavenger's* lights flickered on in greeting. Matt felt a lump form in his throat. He dragged himself into the familiar sights and smells of his old home, Familiar but unfamiliar. The forward bulkheads were now the floors. He was going to have to negotiate a tricky new landscape to get to the bridge, but it wouldn't be a problem. He stood and made his way eagerly, throwing off the alien material that covered him as he went.

Breel heard applause and whoops of joy from the crew as Matt vanished into their old ship. She joined in, mentally fist-pumping the air since she was in symbiosis. She watched bright flashes from the mech's manoeuvring unit as it began its return journey.

Scavenger continued to fall against the stars. Presently, the running lights lit. Glowing bursts of gas erupted from its flanks in sequence. Gradually, the tumbling was brought under control until the two ships were stationary relative to each other. She used her own thrusters to bring the two together.

She waited. Finally, the comms sprang into life.

"Breel, are you reading me?"

She and the mech had fine-tuned the communication systems so that she could pick up *Scavenger's* frequency.

"Yes, Matt," she responded.

"I'm coming back," he said.

Scavenger's airlock opened once more. Matt, this time in a familiar space suit, moved out trailing a large bag made lumpy by the spare space suits and associated life support systems it contained.

There was no way for the two ships to hard dock. They would all have to suit up and spacewalk across.

"This is even better than I remember," Matt said. He was scraping the last mouthful of dhal off his plate with a flat bread, his movements made awkward because of his bandaged, frost-bitten hands. His face showed a fine tracery of burst blood vessels from his brief exposure to hard vacuum.

They were all in *Scavenger's* galley, a bittersweet experience as they would be abandoning it again shortly. Breel had activated the EMD to restore gravity. They had made use of the showers and changed into fresh clothing. It was hard to describe what that experience had been like. Although Breel's body was a mass of cuts and bruises, the stinging hot water was cathartic. Ironically, the one part of her that didn't hurt now was her shoulder and arm. She investigated the newly repaired parts of her body. The flesh was whole and healthy, although paler than the rest of her. A scar she had carried since she was twelve, when she had fallen from a tree her father had repeatedly told her not climb, had gone. She felt an irrational sadness at the loss, as if part of her childhood had been stolen from her.

After the showers, they had collected all the personal belongings they wanted to take with them before gathering for a last meal in their old home. Not that Breel had any personal belongings. She hadn't had time to accrue any during her short stay on *Scavenger*. Everything she used to own had been left on Hope. She would never see any of it again.

She did have one thing though. Her fingers turned a small hard disk in her pocket. The recording crystal. The one that held her mother's account of her experience boarding the ancient derelict of the *Firsts*, where her mother and father had encountered the mechanism that had created a baby in their image. The salvaged alien artefact they had used as a life raft to ferry baby Breel out of the wreck still resided in Deacon's quarters. He was going to take it with him she knew. It was ironic the one thing she still had from her old life was an object that proved her entire life to have been a fake, a story concocted by her parents to protect her from the reality of her origins. *And to protect themselves,* she thought.

After she had learned the story, she often wondered about those events. What had it been like for them? What went through their minds? The only humans in a vast alien relic. Having to make the decision to take the baby with them or leave it. And her mother, forced to leave Tyler, her husband, in the wreck.

Did anyone on *Windfall* know? Surely not, it would have been impossible to keep such a momentous event a secret, so how had they smuggled her back to Hope? And what had persuaded Falian, her stepfather, to agree to adopt the child and bring her up as his own? Questions she would never know the answers to now.

"Told you," Kaemon said to Abiel. "Pretty good, eh?" He touched a curled forefinger and thumb to his lips, giving them a smacking kiss before throwing his hand out in the classic gesture.

Abiel had even less than Breel, absolutely nothing in fact. She had changed since her rebellion against the Church. Never garrulous, she had nevertheless exuded a confidence almost bordering on arrogance. Now she appeared subdued and diminished. Her confidence had deserted her. Perhaps it was because she no longer had a family or direction.

Abiel scooped up the last bit of dhal on her plate.

"S'okay," she smiled.

"Okay?" Kaemon said around a huge mouthful. "It doesn't get better than this."

"Your mother never told you not to speak with your mouth full?" Ellyella asked.

"Is there any more?" The Deacon had already polished off one serving.

Ellyella took the pan over to him. "Here, this is the last." She upended the pan, depositing the last of the curry on his plate.

"Ah, thank you. You are too kind." He tucked in with relish.

Abiel took a long drink of water. "So, what's next?" she asked.

They all looked at Breel.

"You're all looking at me again."

"We get all our stuff over to the – we need to give it a name – other ship, then power to the *RIP*." Kaemon said. He looked at Breel as he said it though, as if seeking affirmation.

"Make for Allpoints," Ellyella agreed. "The only safe place for us. Then figure out what to do." She looked at Matt. "What do you reckon?"

Matt was focused on his plate. Not looking up he said, "You're asking me? I thought my opinion didn't count anymore." He sighed, then added. "Sure, that's probably best."

"Do you have a better idea?" Ellyella said frowning.

"What about our new ship-mate?" Breel asked.

"Yeah, it will certainly attract attention," Kaemon agreed.

Matt pushed his plate away. "What about the Emissary and this whole place?" he asked. "The reason we came here?"

"You're joking, right?" Ellyella said, her colour rising. "What do you think we can do? We gave it our best shot and we failed." She looked around at the others. "No, I say we pass the problem on to the authorities at Allpoints. This ship and the alien machine should certainly prove our story."

"The Church will not allow that to happen," the Deacon said. "Even at Allpoints, they have their methods and supporters."

"What about the 'changing-the-value-of-the-fundamental particle' and the 'the-end-of-all-life in the universe' thing?" Abiel was looking at the Deacon as she spoke.

"We don't know how long it will take the Emissary to open up the portal, or even if it's possible. Its ancient alien tech," the Deacon said. "How is he going to do that?"

"He'll be able to," Breel said, "in the same way I can pilot this ship."

"What does that mean?" the Deacon asked quickly.

All eyes turned to Breel.

Breel sighed. "I have something to tell you. When I was alone with the Emissary, he took off all his clothes."

"He what?" Matt exclaimed.

"Wow, Breel, you didn't tell us he had a thing for you," Ellyella smiled uncertainly as she said this.

Breel shook her head. "He wanted to show me his body…"

"I bet he did."

"Just shut the fuck up a minute," Breel snapped. "This isn't a joke." They went quiet.

"He wanted to show me his body… because… because he has the same patterns I have, etched onto his skin."

"You mean something similar?" the Deacon asked.

"No, I mean the same. Exactly the same."

The crew went silent.

"So, that means…" Ellyella said.

"It means that you and he, are…?" the Deacon said.

"You mean that bastard was spawned on an alien ship, like, Breel?" Kaemon exploded.

"I don't understand," Abiel said. "That would mean that you are… that you are also an agent of the Light?"

"I don't know what it means," Breel said. "But I'm not like him, that's for sure. He showed me the Light's grand plan for the universe, and it's not what he thinks it is."

"I thought there wasn't any plan, that it was unknowable things from beyond sucking us dry for energy," Matt said.

"What the truth is doesn't matter," the Deacon said. "It's what the Emissary believes that counts and its clear he believes he is leading humanity, those chosen at least, to some transcendent future.

"If we are to assume the Emissary has the same ability to connect to… you called it 'the Network' Breel, that might enable him to close down the Doomsday machine. It might not, but think about it. Even if he does and it starts an effect that will change the laws governing the universe, those effects can only propagate at the speed of light. We don't know how far we are from human occupied space, but it must be a long way, possibly hundreds or thousands of light years. At the very least, humanity will be safe for centuries, plenty of time to figure something out."

"Pity you didn't tell us that before, Deak. You could have saved us a whole lot of grief," Kaemon said.

"We didn't know before. We didn't know where the *RIP* led; we didn't know what the Emissary might find; and we never intended to go through. The whole point of the mission was to deny the Emissary whatever was this side of the *RIP*, and it seems our instincts were sound, on that point at least."

"We know something that does have answers," Kaemon nodded in the vague direction of the alien ship. "Why don't you ask it, Breel?"

"That's my plan, but I don't trust it. It's not been honest with us so far."

"Why do you think that?" The Deacon looked at her intently.

"Ask yourself," Breel replied. "It went to all the trouble of changing the orbit of the moon to force us to do what it wanted, but what leverage would that have been if we had trucked up with a fully functioning spacecraft?"

"You think it brought the shuttle down deliberately?" Ellyella said. "But we might have died on that trek. That would have defeated its objective, surely?"

"I think it's little envoy brought us down prematurely," Breel said. "It said it had limited control over the 'minions' until we freed it."

"Did it disable *Scavenger* as well?" Matt asked.

"I didn't think so at the time," Breel said. "We took a real hammering during the transit, but now… it makes sense don't you think? It would only have needed a small push to tip *Scav's* already compromised systems over the edge."

Ellyella shrugged. "Whatever the truth of that, going forward, there's nothing more we can do. The original plan was to close the *RIP*. We failed. Let's just get back to Allpoints."

Breel nodded. "I don't think you'll be getting any argument," although she noticed Matt was staring down at the table again, resolutely refusing to engage in the discussion.

"And you, Abiel?" Breel asked. "What will you do now?"

Abiel and Kaemon shared a glance. She said, "I don't know. What is there out there for an ex-crusader to do?"

"There has never been one, to the best of my knowledge," the Deacon said.

Matt looked up finally. "First things first," he said. "We aren't done here yet."

Kaemon sighed. "Yeah, you're right." He pushed his plate away.

They all did the same. The Deacon reached across to a flatbread still in the middle of the table.

"Anyone want this?" he asked.

"Go for it, Deak," Kaemon grinned. "Let me get my stuff to the airlock and I'll give you a hand with yours."

"I'll help the Deacon," Abiel volunteered. "I don't have anything to collect."

"Okay then. See you on the other ship." Ellyella placed a palm on the bulkhead as she walked out. "Bye old gal, I'm going to miss you."

Until only Breel and Matt were left.

"Here we are again," Matt said.

Breel folded her arms, staring at him expectantly.

"Ever since we met, Breel, all I seem to have done is apologise," Matt began slowly. "Honestly, I don't know how to say sorry in a way that will mean anything to you, but know that I am. I was backed into a corner and the only thing I could think of was to play along, but the deeper I got in, the harder it became to get out."

"Matt, the whole point of your deception was to rescue your girlfriend. But then *we* slept together. Did you *forget* about her?"

"No, Breel." Matt sounded a little exasperated, like he was getting tired having to explain himself. "But I'm only human. I was desperate for comfort, some kind of normality and, well, if you're honest, that's what you wanted as well, wasn't it? I felt as guilty as hell after, but Masaleya was dead so I was hardly cheating. And then I fell in love."

"You do that a lot?" Breel asked bitterly, then realised she was echoing the words of the Emissary.

He looked down at the remains of his meal. "I let everyone down. You, Mas and the crew. My friends."

She walked over to him, placed a hand on his cheek. It felt hot and dry, as if he were running a fever.

"No, Matt, you let yourself down. I could have forgiven you almost anything. If you'd been honest with us. Told us what was happening. But you didn't trust us enough to back you. That's what really hurts. If you can't trust us, how can we ever trust you?"

He took her hand in his, held it fiercely. "One day I'll make it up to you Breel. You and everyone else."

They stood unmoving for a second, then she pulled her hand free, turned her back to him.

"We need to get our stuff and get away, while we still can."

As if to emphasise the point, the Machine chimed in from the alien ship.

"Guys, it pains me to spoil your party, the one I wasn't invited to, but you really need to see this."

An image appeared, fuzzy from over-magnification. A Second Light ship accompanied by something else, large and rectangular, topped with what looked like a complex radar dish. The two spacecraft were rising from behind the river of rock and ice that was the decimated remains of the shepherd moon.

"Looks like they're neither forgetting nor forgiving." The alien said.

THIRTY-ONE

Breel, suited up, waited patiently in *Scavenger's* airlock. A bag containing her few scant belongings, mainly clothing, was secured to her suit. It drifted lazily in the now weightless conditions. Shutting down the EMD for the last time had been an emotional moment. Everyone else was back on the alien ship, only Breel and Matt left aboard.

There was still no sign of Matt.

She spoke into the suit mike. "Are you coming?"

When there was no reply she said again, a little impatiently, "Matt? Where are you? We need to go."

"I'm here, Breel." He appeared suited and ready. The inner door closed after him, making the tight space feel even more cramped, forcing them to press against one another. They waited for the lock to cycle.

Breel ran a hand over the hull. She had lived on *Scavenger* for such a short time, but it had become her home and sanctuary.

"I'm going to miss this old rust bucket," she said.

A chime told them the air had evacuated. The outer door slid open. The alien ship's weird geometry dominated the view, its own airlock open and waiting. Then Breel felt a sharp impact before she was tumbling out into space. She fired her manoeuvring thrusters to regain control, twisting around until she faced *Scavenger*.

"What the hell, Matt?" But *Scavenger's* airlock was closing. She had a last glimpse of Matt retreating back into the ship. She was left floating outside on her own.

Her private comm channel hissed into life.

"Get back to the others, Breel. They need you."

"What the fuck? Matt? Matt!" She jetted back to *Scavenger* and thumped her gauntleted fist against the airlock door.

"Matt, open the lock, what are you doing?"

She thumped the door again.

Matt must have reached the control room because the ship's manoeuvring thrusters suddenly fired. *Scavenger* moved away, slowly at first, until it was a safe distance from her. Then the main engines fired, one quick burst to accelerate the ship quickly away. Breel could do nothing but hang there and watch it recede.

"I need you," she said quietly to herself.

"What the hell, Breel?" Ellyella helped Breel strip off her suit. "What's happening? Why isn't Matt with you? Where is he going?"

"I don't know, El. He shoved me out the lock, then took *Scav* and ran."

"What do you mean, 'ran'?" Kaemon asked.

Breel pushed past him. The Mech standing in the doorway, moved aside to let her pass.

"What're you planning, Breel?" it asked.

"We have to go after him," she said.

The machine grabbed her by the arm. She had a moment to wonder at how it had calculated just enough force to stop her. A tiny misstep and it would have effortlessly ripped her arm off.

"What is that going to achieve?" it asked.

Breel glared at the huge machine undaunted. "Take your fucking claw off me," she hissed.

The Machine released her, raising its palm in a frighteningly accurate parody of the human gesture.

"Sorry," it said.

"The 'thing' is right Breel," Kaemon put his arm protectively around Breel's shoulders, glaring at the alien. "You'll just be handing us over to the Church."

Breel looked helplessly around at the others.

"What's he think he's doing?" Ellyella's voice was thick with emotion.

"Maybe he's gone back to his own," Kaemon said bitterly. "Scuttled back to stay alive."

Breel shook her head, "I can't believe that."

"Why? Would you have believed he had sold us out all this time?"

"He didn't sell us out," Breel said, voice pitched barely below a shout. "He just... got in over his head."

"There might be another reason," Abiel said.

They all looked at her.
"Redemption," she said simply.

Matt sat at *Scavenger's* controls. He still had his suit on and was breathing from its oxygen reserve. He moved the spacecraft high above the river of churning rock and ice that had once been a world, then accelerated towards the Second Light ships. He imparted an erratic twist from random thruster bursts before he expelled all the air in the ship which added more random movement to his flight. He shut down everything apart from one nav computer. Immediately he cut the drive he was thrown from side to side as inertia reasserted itself. Bangs and crashes thudded throughout the ship as objects not secured were similarly flung around. Finally, silence fell as everything found its place and he and his ship were as one and it was the universe that spun crazily outside.

The ship would cool rapidly, but there would be enough power in the suit to keep him comfortable, at least for the time he needed. A passing glance and *Scavenger* would look like just another chunk of debris, the same temperature as all the other chunks. The small amount of heat that he and the suit radiated would be difficult to detect through *Scavenger's* hull. This high above the ecliptic he wouldn't be an object of attention. The Second Light ships would be focusing their sensors on Breel and the debris around the alien starship.

He hoped.

He settled down to wait, a small spark of heat and light in a rapidly cooling, frigid, metal tomb.

An ululating cry sounded throughout the ship. *Proximity alarm* guessed Breel. She watched the energy pulse narrowly miss them. Viewed at the wavelength of x-rays it was beautiful.

"This is Captain Corlezea of *Burning Rapture*. By order of his most holy, the Lord of Second Light, you are to begin deceleration immediately. This is the only warning you will receive. Failure to comply will result in your total annihilation."

Although *Burning Rapture* and its accompanying weapon were several million kilometres away, the energy pulse it generated travelled at the speed of light. There was no time to manoeuvre to escape in the few seconds it would take the devastating energy to reach them. The rest of the crew and the mech were gathered in the room they were calling the lounge.

"Doesn't this thing have some of that force field tech?" Kaemon asked the machine.

"Won't stop that from turning us into barbecue fricassee." It looked them over. "You guys, anyway. Me, it will just EMP my ass."

"Can we get down amongst the rubble from the moon?" the Deacon asked. "Hide down there?"

"You must have been watching Kaemon's entertainment feed," Breel said from the bridge. "Try to match velocity with that lot and we'd get mashed to pulp."

"We couldn't get to it before they hit us anyway," Kaemon said. "They'd fire as soon as they realised what we were doing."

"If we hand ourselves over, we're dead," Abiel said. "Apart from Breel and the robot. It would probably be worse for them."

"Thanks Abiel," Breel said drily. "It takes the MPG thing time to recycle. Until then, we put as much distance as we can between us and it. After that we won't have a choice but to decelerate. It will be hours before they can catch up. Maybe we'll think of something."

The Second Light captain's voice sounded through the ship P.A. "Since we haven't heard back, I'm going to assume you are foolish enough to keep running. Our next shot will not be a warning. *Burning Rapture* out."

"How long does the MPG take to recycle," Ellyella asked suddenly. "How far can we get before they're recharged and ready to fire again?"

Breel thought about this for a moment. Finally, she said, "Good point El. Running will probably gain us very little, a couple of hours at most. We'll have to think of something else." She addressed the pursing ship. "*Burning Rapture*, stand down, we are decelerating now."

She spun the ship one hundred and eighty degrees, bow to stern, so that the drive was now pointing in the direction they were heading, slowing them down.

"We will still have some time," she said.

"Your Grace, we have the insurgents targeted and they are now well within the kill range of the MPG," Captain Corlezea reported. "They are decelerating as instructed."

The Emissary stared at the blurred image of the alien ship. How many times had he been in this situation only to have Breel and her friends escape to continue to be a thorn in his flesh? His thoughts drifted to poor Maliesh again—Maliesh went from 'poor' Maliesh to 'traitorous' Maliesh, depending on his mood—who had constantly beseeched him to end them once and for all.

He really coveted the technology the ship could avail him, the knowledge the machine entity could give him. And Breel. Could he kill the only thing like him alive in human space?

But what difference would it make now? He was so close to the Light where he would finally have all the answers he craved and all the time in the multiverse to mull them over.

"Yes," Maliesh whispered, "now's the time. You know it's the right thing to do."

"End it," he told Corlezea.

"As you wish, my Lord."

The Emissary broke the connection.

"I'm reading a really big energy spike from the MPG," Breel reported.

Magnified from a distance of several million kilometres, the MPG's dish looked like a small silver moon rising above the dark remains of the shepherd moon. Display artefacts generated from the magnification made it shimmer, as if it were rising through a heat haze.

"Burning Rapture," Breel said into the comms, "we are decelerating as requested."

There was no reply and the energy build-up continued.

"What's it doing?" the Deacon asked.

"I think they've had enough," Kaemon said. "Should have run."

"Wouldn't've made any difference," Breel said. "Secure yourselves. I'll do what I can."

A new heat signature suddenly sprang into existence.

"What's that now?" She increased the magnification to its limit.

"It's *Scavenger,*" Kaemon said, watching from the lounge.

Astonishingly, Matt had fallen asleep; utter exhaustion had overcome him. He awoke to see he had covered much of the distance to the Second Light ship with its weapon in tow. It was approaching fast. It was time. He switched on *Scavenger's* systems. Aboard the enemy ship alarms would be sounding, but it was too late for them to do anything about it. Their relative combined acceleration was tens of thousands of kilometres per hour.

He tuned in to communications. Breel was decelerating the alien ship, giving in to their demands, but the energy continued to spike in the MPG. They were going to kill them anyway. He would have to change his plan. He steadied the rolling and tumbling of the ship, pointed it directly at the Church weapon and lit the drive.

He noted hot flashes of light bursting from the Second Light command ship. They had fired a missile salvo at him. But it was too late, even if one of them hit him. The kinetic energy he was about to unload would be more than enough to do the job.

"I'm sorry, Mas. Sorry I couldn't keep my promise to you," he said out loud, "and I'm sorry I let you down Breel." Tears ran down his cheeks. "Maybe this will go some way to make it up to you." The scarred mass of the MPG filled his screens and proximity alarms announced the arrival of the torpedoes.

"There," the Deacon pointed. "That's Matt."

The sudden glow of igniting engines revealed his location. *Scavenger* was above the MPG, itself above the rubble. *Scavenger* accelerated into a collision course with the MPG.

"Missiles!" screamed Ellyella. Burning sparks raced to meet *Scavenger*. They seemed to be absorbed by the ship for a second before blinding light erupted from its flanks, but only seconds later the burning sphere *Scavenger* had become punched into the Church's energy weapon. It exploded with kinetic force equivalent to a thousand nukes, briefly giving the system a second sun. The MPG vanished into a blinding glare that blanked the screens.

When the image came back, the MPG was still there, but it was clearly dead. It drifted, responding to the imparted momentum of the impact, trailing a line of glowing debris as it moved ponderously down into the churning river of rubble.

Bright flashes erupted from the lower edge of the dish as it was ripped to pieces by multiple impacts. It continued on its now inexorable course, bright flash joining bright flash, pulsing into a continuous curve of light as the Church's once mighty weapon shredded into fragments and joined the remains of the moon to become part of the developing ring system.

The conserved energy that had been building within it, that had been intended to end them, was now released in a new dazzling pulse. It expanded outwards in a phenomenal globe of destruction ejecting smaller chunks of rubble out of the ring plane entirely, while sending larger pieces into new trajectories. The disturbance rippled out from the point of impact before the partially formed ring settled down once more. The only thing left of the MPG was a river of fading glowing fragments, spreading out into a thin line as they slowly cooled.

"Fuck me," the Machine said to the silent humans around it.

Breel, although in symbiosis, was still aware of the tears coursing down her cheeks.

Somehow *Burning Rapture* had survived. She detected new energy spikes as it launched a fresh salvo of missiles. It brought her back into the moment. She spun the ship once more, back to its original heading and accelerated toward the *RIP*.

She dropped out of symbiosis. There was nothing more she could do on the bridge. She joined the others in the lounge.

"The bastards aren't letting us go," she announced, voice thick with emotion.

Kaemon had a consoling arm around Ellyella who sat, eyes closed, trembling. His own eyes were moist. The Deacon and Abiel sat in silence.

Breel sat next to Ellyella and placed a hand on her shoulder.

"I'm sorry, El." Breel's voice betrayed her own battle to keep her emotions in check.

Ellyella looked up. "Why did he do that?" She gave up the fight for self-control and openly sobbed. "He didn't have to do that."

"I guess he did. He said he was going to make it up to us, whatever it took." Breel said. "I never imagined…" She hugged her friend.

"Why did he sacrifice himself to destroy the weapon?" Kaemon asked. "They'll just bring another out."

"I don't think he set out to destroy the MPG. I think he was going after *Transcendent Light*, to take out the Emissary. But then he saw the situation and took out the MPG instead, to save us."

The Alien-Machine came in. "So, I didn't know the guy, or like him much, truth be told, but, hey, that was a hell of a thing he did. I guess I should express my condolences, so, sorry for your loss, you guys."

"Delivery needs work," Kaemon said, "but thanks for making the effort."

"What's happening now, Breel?" Abiel asked.

Breel, struggling to keep her voice even said, "We are powering to the *RIP*. *Burning Rapture* along with a salvo of missiles are on our tail."

"We can deal with the missiles," the alien said. "Check out our weapons and defence systems. You'll be impressed."

"Yeah," Breel acknowledged. "I saw. I'm waiting for the missiles to get closer. I'll need some guidance. You need to walk me through everything I need to know."

"Why are they chasing us?" the Deacon asked. "We'll get to the *RIP* before the torpedoes catch up to us, won't we?"

"Well before," Breel affirmed. "I don't know is the short answer. I can't think why The Emissary would send that fucking thing after us, his most powerful weapon. You'd think he would want all his resources to do whatever it is he's planning to do."

"Pure spite," Ellyella said.

"How long to the *RIP*?" Abiel asked.

"About two weeks, even in this ship." Breel said. "There's nothing more we can do except sit and wait."

They sat in silence, lost in their own thoughts or staring out at the stars. After a while Breel went back to the bridge.

THIRTY-TWO

The object was an absence, lording over the remains of this dead system, but completely indifferent to it. It was spherical, they had measured it, but to the naked eye it was a featureless flat disc occluding stars and dust. The symps had viewed it through many different wavelengths, but even they failed to report anything.

The Emissary, in communion with the Light, however, was seeing it all. The physical sphere was simply its manifestation in this universe. Its true shape extended into a configuration that made his mind ache in its complexity and beauty, extending through multiple dimensions.

The Light was talking to him now. This close to the source, it was deafening and glorious. He felt it soak into his being, enabling him. He understood that to unlock the Light, to allow it back, he would have to construct a key. There had been one, but it had been lost to this reality along with the shepherd moon. He could and would recreate it, although it would take considerable resources. He would prepare himself for any resistance he might encounter from the Church High Council. Maliesh's insubordination would still cast a shadow.

He wondered if destroying the key had been the entity's plan all along, the thing that had enabled Breel's escape. If only she had opened her mind to the possibilities, she would be here to share this experience with him now. Together they would be unbound, unbeatable. She hadn't, though, and she was still alive and still running.

He hadn't anticipated such a move from Harken Court. He had thought the man much too weak for that. He had underestimated the insurgent captain – like Maliesh, who had underestimated his Messiah. His second in command had thought the Lord of Light would be bound by the same laws of physics that bound everyone else, still dependent on mere technology. This close to the Light, he was not so diminished.

He became aware of a nagging intrusion, like the buzz of bothersome insects. Such creatures he could crush with barely an effort, but now was not the time. He came out of his communion and his room aboard *Transcendent Light* materialised around him.

The coms buzzed for his attention. Captain Hannathon's image materialised.

"Yes, Captain."

"My Lord, the insurgents are approaching the *RIP*. *Burning Rapture* is still in pursuit but is too far behind to meaningfully influence the outcome. Captain Corlezea has asked if he should continue."

The Emissary was silent for a moment, then said, "Yes, tell him to continue."

"My Lord, if I may, the resources of *Burning Rapture* and its compliment of men would be very useful at this juncture, especially after the loss of the MPG and its crew."

The Emissary rubbed his chin thoughtfully, controlling a need to wince where Breel's blow still showed as a discolouration.

"Tell me Captain Hannathon, at what point did I suggest we were in a debate? Moreover, a debate where your opinion might be of consequence?"

"I beg your forgiveness, my Lord, I did not mean –"

"Just convey my instructions to *Burning Rapture*." He snapped and cut Hannathon off mid-sentence.

"Despite everything, you still can't catch or stop Breel," Maliesh whispered, *"She is making you look weak and foolish. If you had only acted sooner, as I had requested... Are you sure now?"*

"Yes, Maliesh," he said to the empty room, "I am sure. Although she may think otherwise, Breel and her companions are not yet safe."

Breel was getting to know and understand the peculiarities of the alien ship. She was running simulations for the *RIP* transit over and over. It was the only way to take her mind off Matt. If she let herself think about him, she would find herself so weighed down with grief she would be unable to function. Too late now to wish she hadn't shunned him, that she had been more conciliatory in those last moments aboard *Scavenger*. She worried for Ellyella's state of mind. Her history with Matt had gone much deeper than her own.

There was something else she was doing her best to shut out. The nagging voices. They were getting louder all the time, pushing against the periphery of her awareness. Insistent, urgent; battering at her consciousness. She wanted to let them in, to feel the thrill the connection undeniably gave her, but that final image of horror she had witnessed in the Communion was never far from her mind. That and the experience at the chasm where she had thrown herself out into the void without any regard to her friends or herself. She was afraid if she did allow the voices in, her very nature would change, that she would lose herself and become something alien.

She was afraid that she might become like the Emissary.

The vessel they were making their escape in was astonishing and she had explored perhaps only ten percent of its capabilities. Its weapons and defence systems were, as promised by the mech, impressive. When the missiles from *Burning Rapture* were close enough, she deployed a flack system into their path *that had winked them out of existence*. That was the only way she could think to describe it. It had twisted space-time in some unfathomable way, sending them... *somewhere else*. There were other systems, anti-matter pellets, multi-dimensional grid weapons, degenerate-matter shells, that were far beyond anything her civilisation had. She had only the vaguest idea what these might do and most weren't online yet. There was no time to enable them or manufacture anti-matter or degenerate-matter ordnance in their current situation.

In the end, she hadn't had to ask the Machine-Entity for help. She had figured it out herself, through her augmentation.

Where was the Deshi-damn thing anyway? She was aware of the others, she could detect their body heat, local increase of carbon dioxide from exhaled breath, a slight occlusion in the lattice of reality. She could even guess at their mental or physical state. It was why she was worried for Ellyella.

The machine, though, disappeared from her view from time to time. When she was aware of it, its signature was bright, its occlusion dark and deep. Was it screening itself deliberately, and if so, why? What was the Deshi-damn thing anyway and did it have some other agenda, beyond simply to escape its aeons-long imprisonment?

By now, they had all gotten used to its nightmarish appearance and had even largely accepted it as part of the crew. Maybe some of that was the way it talked. She was sure that wasn't an accident, but a way into their psychology, to put them at ease and maybe underestimate it. What she did know was that she didn't trust it as far as she would be able to throw its considerable mass in a four-gee gravity field. She wanted answers. She dropped out of symbiosis. Now was the time to get them.

They had dumped the cooking facilities in the lounge and printed out a table and chairs more their size. It might become the equivalent to the galley on *Scavenger*, a new communal meeting place. The crew had also sought out rooms to make their own. There was no shortage of space.

They gathered now, but the mood was sombre. Breel looked around the room. "Here we all are," she said and looked at the machine. "Mech, you want to provide some answers? Now's the time."

The machine stood impassively near the door. It stroked the end of its nightmarish head in a passable copy of thoughtfully stroking its chin. The thing settled its weight.

"The Quin'Ratha," he began, "or the *Firsts* as you call them, they went through pretty much the same shit you guys did. A lot of coincidence happening in exactly the right way to give them a planet life could evolve on, then spent a lot of time dragging themselves up from the slime. They only just made it, almost wiped themselves out through pointless wars, greed, and stupidity and then almost fucked the planet, but they survived and went on to develop *RIP* drives and a star-spanning civilisation. Whoo, ooo. They had the whole frickin' kit and caboodle and it was dandy when the reality-rift opened and rained on their parade."

"The *RIP* tech made them a target," Ellyella said.

"Yeah. The Quin'Ratha used it to circumvent the light speed limit, the same as you. It's the only way as far as I know. As they expanded through the galaxy, the sheer amount of *RIP* usage created an instability that allowed the portal to be opened. That's what the *Others*, the things across the rift, whatever they are, seem to home in on."

Kaemon said, "So that would apply to every advanced civilisation using *RIP* tech. Are they a target too?"

"See, here's the thing," the Mech said. "The chances of all the cards landing just right are so small you might as well say life is statistically impossible, never mind life that'll last long enough to build a civilisation capable of star travel."

"Are you saying we are alone in the universe?" Abiel asked.

"No," the Deacon said "I don't believe it's saying that, but the chances are so unlikely, when it does happen, the civilisations are going to be a long way apart, not only in space, but time as well. You might be right and it could be that other rifts are out there, but they are so far away we may never know. The universe is expanding, the light from the event, the effects from that event, may never reach us." He paused a moment, then added thoughtfully. "Maybe that's why the universe is expanding at an accelerating rate. Maybe that's what Dark Energy really is, new energy pouring in from far-flung reality-rifts."

"So, anything over-using *RIP* technology could become a target," Breel said a bit impatiently. "What about the seed ships, what are they in all of this?"

"The Doomsday machine, you've seen it but it's more than that sphere. That's merely its intrusion into this reality. Building that fucker cost them everything. They closed the rift and for good measure generated a barrier that would stop any emerging civilisation over-using *RIP* tech.

"Knowing they were going out, they seeded their bit of space with something that would detect and warn other emerging civilisations, should one evolve. They knew the chances of one appearing in the same neck of the woods were small, but they weren't infinitely so. They thought it was worth doing, to make their sacrifice a legacy, so there would be some point to the death of their civilisation and to stop the new one making the same mistake."

The machine waved a hand over them all. "They had no idea what that life might be like, of course, so the seed ships were designed to recreate a life-form using the aliens themselves as a blueprint. That would give the Network something it could monitor the new civilisation through. Figure out what it was dealing with. When the time was right it was meant to reach out and make contact."

"So, Breel is a kind of message in a bottle?" Ellyella said.

"That still makes no sense," Breel said. "I had no idea what I was supposed to do. What about the Emissary, he's doing the exact opposite."

The machine made another impressive copy of a human gesture: it shrugged. "What can I tell you? It didn't work. Too much time, like the Complex on the shepherd moon, it all failed. Nothing lasts forever."

"Except you, it seems," Abiel said.

"No, I didn't either. I evolved into something else." It pointed a twisted nightmare of a finger at Breel. "Your seed ship was compromised; it didn't complete its task properly. You were an imperfect tool for the Network so it ignored you. As for the preacher, it looks like the Network did reach out to him, but he thinks it's some kind of deity. I think he fell for his own hype."

"But he's trying to reopen the rift," Abiel said. "Isn't that the opposite of what it was built to do?"

"The Network is complex and multifaceted, but it will do what it's told to do, if it believes it is being instructed by the right authority. At the end of the day, it's a servant."

"It's sentient?" Breel asked. "Like you?"

"No, not like me, but not totally unaware either."

"So, none of it is true? The Light, transcendence, everything so many people believe in?" Ellyella said.

"Yeah, well, who the fuck knows actually? Maybe, maybe not," the machine said. "But for this specific thing, no. Sorry."

"The actual truth is irrelevant," Breel said. "It's what the Emissary and his followers believe that counts."

"You said you saw something else," Ellyella said to Breel. "When you were in Communion. Something malignant, you said. Could it be the things across the Rift, manipulating the Emissary through the Network?"

Breel looked at the alien.

"Interesting idea." It ran a hand over its head. It made a thin rasping sound, like someone filing metal. "I don't know."

There was silence.

Breel didn't know what else to say. She felt empty and lost.

"Well," Ellyella said finally, "what now?"

Breel stood abruptly and headed back to the bridge.

"Settle in," she said. "I'll get us through the RIP and then I guess we'll think about what to do next."

Ahead, the unreal radiation from the *RIP* seeped into their universe. They had settled into a routine quickly, spent a good amount of time sleeping and eating. Time to recover and heal battered bodies and minds. When she wasn't asleep, Breel spent the majority of her time on the bridge, running simulations. They still gathered to eat and Breel felt she needed to be part of that, but it was an effort. Since the machine's explanation of her existence, she felt divorced from the others.

She felt more and more at home with the universe, through the symbiotic relationship with the ship. She began to understand how symbiont pilots could lose themselves, the way Cross had. The universe following its course through immutable laws of physics made much more sense to her than the petty squabbles of humanity.

Now they were almost upon the *RIP*. It filled space ahead, huge and implacable. It glowed to her augmented senses. She, Matt, and the crew had fought to close it forever, but The Emissary and his scientists had reopened it. That act of reopening had somehow changed its nature. It felt different.

Just as long as it takes us where we need to go, away from this gods-forsaken place. That's all that matters.

She measured its energy flows and began to correlate the approach vectors she would need. For a moment she missed it, given the anomaly's transformed nature, but then she noted a change in the flow of the radiating forces. A swirl like a tiny whirlpool, then more, many more, like pebbles dropped into a pond, sending ripples across the fabric of the portal. She recognised it for what it was. Something was coming through; not just one thing, but many.

The time had come. The Emissary watched as his fleet burst through the tear in reality that was the *RIP*. Before they had made the transit to follow Breel and her friends to the shepherd moon, he had sent a message via the many repeat relays they had left behind. He couldn't know how quickly he might get a response. He couldn't know what damage Maliesh might have done, how the man might have undermined his authority, but they had heeded his commands and now they were here. An armada sandwiching Breel between them and *Burning Rapture*.

He had seen that the alien ship was equipped with a formidable defence system, but even that advanced technology could surely not engage so many ships. If Breel turned, both *Burning Rapture* and *Transcendent Light* would be waiting. He smiled as beautiful petals of energy blossomed from the spacecraft pouring through the anomaly, heralding a swarm of missiles from which there could be, finally, no escape.

THIRTY-THREE

"Strap in," Breel communicated to the rest of the crew from the bridge. "We got trouble."

The Deacon groaned.

"What's happening, Breel?" Abiel asked.

"Looks like the Emissary called for reinforcements before he followed us through and now they're here."

"How many?" Kaemon wanted to know.

"A lot. Get ready." She cut the contact so she could concentrate. At least four battleships equivalent to *Transcendent Light*, with more coming through, and four heavy destroyers along with a swarm of ancillary and support vessels. Energy spiked from the approaching spacecraft, a barrage of missiles heading their way. She checked the status of their defences. Not nearly enough to take out the torpedoes and she was too far away to deploy against the spacecraft themselves. There were too many and too powerful anyway.

To continue towards the *RIP* would be suicide. She sent a flak array anyway, because she felt the need to assert herself and had the satisfaction of seeing the leading weapons vanish to Deshi-knew where. She turned the ship in as tight an arc as she could, given their phenomenal speed. It would give them a few more seconds. If whatever this thing used as inertial dampers failed, they would all be reduced to a molecular-thin bloody film on the nearest bulkhead. She was aware *Burning Rapture* had let loose more missiles.

She couldn't go back in that direction, obviously. She tracked a course between the two, flying at right angles to the closing enemy ships, looking for something, anything that might give her a way out. The missiles turned, tracking *Scavenger's* vector like a pack of wolves closing on their prey. It had been a naive thought, but the notion that the two sets of torpedoes might annihilate each other in a head-on collision was gone.

She couldn't outrun the torpedoes. Even this ship wasn't that fast. They would catch up eventually, whichever direction she ran in. There was nothing else left to do. She sent a tight beam to *Burning Rapture*.

"*Burning Rapture*, you win, we will stand down and prepare to be boarded." She waited as the signal travelled the light minutes to the attacking ship. Long seconds, then minutes crawled by. They should have received it by now. The warheads were almost upon them.

"*Burning Rapture*, do you copy? We surrender. Call off your attack, disable the missiles and we will decelerate."

"*Burning Ra —*"

"We copy, Breel."

Her heart turned to ice. It was the voice of the Emissary.

"But I'm afraid you have had your last chance. I have wasted too much time and too many resources. I have to call an end to it." There was a pause filled with static. "A pity, really."

"Listen to me," Breel said. "I'm ready to open to the Light. I made a mistake. I understand now what it is, what you have to offer. I'm ready to join you now. You said it yourself, together we would be invincible. Call off your attack, let my people go and I'm willing to do whatever you want."

Static.

The accelerating bombs were almost upon them. She sent another flak volley. More bursts of unreal radiation as the leading torpedoes were displaced. A quick check showed she could deploy one more time. She searched through the rest of the weapons inventory, but there was nothing she could get online in time to help.

The Emissary's voice came back. "Such a pity," he repeated, voice thick with sorrow. "I'm almost tempted to give you the benefit of the doubt, but I don't believe you are sincere and there is too much at stake to allow you to be a distraction any longer. Goodbye, Breel."

The connection was lost.

"Fuck you too, you piece of shit," she muttered.

The swarm of deadly projectiles had been depleted by about half. She waited until the leading ones were almost upon them, then deployed the last of her flak. She took direct control of the proximity deployment, waited until the flak was well into the pack of hunters before allowing them to detonate, if that was the right word. Reality blinked and another half vanished. The remainder rushed forward, undeterred, eager to replace their fellows.

She searched the ship for signs of the mech but it was nowhere to be found.

"Hey," she shouted ship-wide through the comms. "Alien-machine-thing, Mech, whatever you want to call yourself, any ideas because I'm out of them."

"I'm here, Breel." She realised the Deshi-damn thing was on the bridge. How could she not know that? "I think you know what you have to do," it said.

"Cut the cryptic bullshit for once. A straight answer would be good, given we are all about to die," Breel snapped.

The machine made a noise emulating a sigh. "The information is waiting for you. They have been trying to tell you what to do for weeks."

She knew of course, she just didn't want to admit it. The voices had been building all this time, battering at the borders of her awareness and all this time she had been resisting their insistent call. What was there left to lose now? She let them in and was overwhelmed by the torrent of information that flooded her mind. Although she was a conduit for the Network it was also a conduit for her, amplified and facilitated by the exotic tech in the alien vessel they flew in. She had accessed the Network's power before, in a very limited way, but now she was being granted more, much more.

In this new state time slowed, seconds became minutes, then hours. She began to see, although she found it hard to believe, that there was a way, a very slim chance – if she could enable it. If she had time.

She'd almost waited until it was too late.

The Emissary watched Breel's last moments play out. The dot on the display suddenly magnified to the device's limit and the alien ship's strange configuration was displayed, blurred and distorted by the unthinkable distance. So far away that when he finally saw the light from her destruction, the event would have already taken place several minutes in his past.

Tiny sparks appeared in the lower right and flashed across the gap separating them from their target in a micro second. And then...

Nothing.

The Emissary stared uncomprehending. "What happened?"

"Your Grace, we are collating information from the fleet."

He couldn't believe it; it just wasn't possible. Not again.

"I told you." Maliesh sounded gleeful.

"My Lord, we are having trouble… making sense of the data."

"What just happened?" he shouted, banging his fist onto the console in front of him.

"We are detecting unreal radiation from the insurgent's last position."

"What does that mean? What are you saying?"

"Your Grace, there is no evidence of wreckage. Only a fading sphere of energy. It is as if…" the man paused as if he was having trouble accepting the evidence. "It is as if a *RIP* opened and closed."

The Emissary stared at his underling. Captain Hannathon waited, face studiously blank.

"Did the missiles strike, before the ship disappeared?"

"We can't say for sure, your Grace, but some of them are unaccounted for. They may have followed the ship through the transit."

The Lord of Light stared at the empty display.

"Your Grace," Hannathon said, "what are your orders?"

"Yes," Maliesh whispered, *"what are your orders now, your Grace?"*

The ghost of Maliesh laughed.

The RIP formed, raw and ragged, chaotic, unlike any RIP she had known before. Every transit she had made, every transit anyone had ever made as far as she knew, had been instantaneous. There had never been any experience of the journey itself, although many had sought to see something, a glimpse behind the curtain of reality.

She was no longer aware of the ship or her friends. She was an infinitesimally small spark of consciousness, falling through a vast structure of bright nodes, connected by filigrees of energy that curled around dark interstices. The structures folded through angles that she hadn't the language to describe, that strained her mind.

On and on, without end.

She realised that she was seeing the other side of reality, the underpinning structure of it all, although she wasn't 'seeing' in any normal sense of the word. There was nothing to see in a conventional sense, no photons of light falling onto light receptive cells. This was experience on some kind of fundamental level. Her brain was attempting to parse perception of a reality it had no comprehension of, simply hadn't evolved to understand.

It was overwhelming. It crushed her. She fought to hold on to her awareness, to hold on to the idea of 'self' as she felt her being shredding, simultaneously existing and dissipating through aeons of time and light years of distance.

And now she became aware of something else. In that lattice of dark angles twisting through higher and lower dimensions, there was something that watched and calculated.

She reached out to it, to them, trying to communicate, to ask for help, but if they were aware of her existence, they showed no sign of it. She was too small, too insignificant, a mayfly fluttering on the far side of the windows of reality. She was losing herself, her essence shredding and sublimating. She screamed a silent scream...

...and then smashed back into her body. The shock of the transition left her completely disorientated, left her trying to remember who and where she was and what she had been doing, trying to gather the tattered fragments of her personality back into a whole.

The shrill sound of the proximity alarms dispelled the last of her stupor. She remembered – she was Breel – Deshi-damn them all. She was Breel!

The missiles!

She locked into symbiosis with the ship, searching local space and felt despair. Some of the Emissary's mechanised agents of death had been so close when they made the transit they had been sucked though the *RIP* along with the spacecraft and were now bearing down on them to complete their mission. A manifestation of the Emissary's hate and spite made concrete, reaching across the light years with fatal intent.

THIRTY-FOUR

Breel didn't know what to do. She was out of ideas. There was no way to avoid the torpedoes as they bore down on them. But she had to try. She took hold of the ship, swinging it up in a great arc. The missiles duly followed, closing incrementally. They were in a triangular formation, staggered so that their exhausts didn't interfere with each other, but fusion-powered so their fuel was finite. She tracked the missiles, calculated their relative speeds. If she could stay ahead of them, their fuel would eventually run out. They would stop accelerating, but *Scavenger*, using its EMD, would continue to accelerate and leave them behind. She did the calculation. The missiles were moving too fast. No way they wouldn't impact before their fuel ran out.

An idea occurred to her, desperate, but she could think of nothing else. She could wait until the lead bomb was almost upon them, then light her own fusion fire, exploding the head of the pack in the hope that it would take out the others. But the missile would have to be close, very close, so close that, even if its detonation didn't take them out, it would still inflict severe, possibly terminal damage to their ship.

What the hell! They were dead anyway; she had nothing to lose.

She got ready, waiting. Even in symbiosis she was aware of her heart pounding. Then the lead bomb detonated. Expanding plasma rocked the ship, heating the outer skin to a dangerous level. What had happened? She still had her figurative symbiotic finger hovering over the fusion drive but had not enabled it.

A second later, another missile went off, adding to the flood of radiation rocking the ship and then finally the third burst into what was, to her symbiotic vision, magnificent, nested shells of labyrinthine glowing energy.

The radiance cleared, revealing nothing more than starry space. She searched their immediate environment for any danger she might have missed and then searched the ship's outer skin, to check for damage there.

She switched her perception to infrared as there was nothing out here in interstellar space to light the ship. With a start she saw something moving over the hull. It was bright, radiating copious amounts of heat energy into the vacuum. She focused in on it and saw another dark mass moving alongside the brighter one. The new mass was smaller and almost invisible to her. It was only slightly warmer than the ambient temperature of the universe. Whatever it was, it was headed for an open airlock, a bright block to her enabled vision. The moving object became a dark silhouette against the glow of the hatch and she realised it was the alien mech. It was moving carefully, gripping the hull in some way that wasn't clear to her, fighting the constant acceleration of the ship, a force which, given a misstep, would hurl it into interstellar space to be lost forever. It shouldered something bulky, about half its height again. That was the source of the bright energy visible to her infrared vision. A weapon of some kind, cooling rapidly now.

The com system crackled into life.

"I love the smell of plasma in the morning," it said.

Abiel was already in the galley; had been for some time it seemed. She had stripped Matt's gun down to its smallest components and was polishing them methodically. She looked up at Breel's approach.

"Keeping my hand in," she said. She put the part she had been cleaning down on the white surface.

Kaemon sat next to Abiel. Ellyella sat at the end of the table, the Deacon next to her.

"What happened, Breel?" Kaemon asked.

"I opened an *RIP*," she said simply.

"You did what," the Deacon gaped at her. "You can open *RIPs* at will now?"

Breel shook her head. "I didn't do it, I instructed, or asked. The Network did the work."

"But you can open one anywhere, take us wherever we want to go?" Kaemon said.

Breel shook her head again. "Back there, so close to the –" she looked at the Deacon "– the reality-rift. But here, no."

"Where are we, anyway?" Kaemon asked.

"Falling towards Allpoints. I didn't plan it but it must have been uppermost in my mind. The Network delivered us to known coordinates one jump away from the Allpoints system."

"And what did we see, when we went through?" Ellyella wanted to know.

"The network," Breel said, "The other side of reality."

There was silence.

Ellyella said finally. "So, we made it. Where does that leave us? What's our next move, when we get to Allpoints?"

Breel shook her head, to bring herself back from the mind-numbing experience of the fundamentals of creation, back to the mundanity of the galley. "We can't just truck up and dock at Blue Haven. Not in this ship. The Emissary knows we survived. All his agents will be on the lookout for us. We won't be safe, even at the station."

"Yeah, and I didn't just escape a half billion years in hokey to end up in a lab," the machine said. It looked meaningfully at Breel.

"We don't have anywhere else to go," the Deacon said.

"Cavalacro," Kaemon tapped the tabletop with his index finger. "He owes us. *Scavenger* was compromised under his watch."

"I think we have enough stuff left to print out something to overlay the outside of the ship," the Mech said. "To make it a bit less conspicuous."

"And you?" Breel asked the machine. "You'll have to stay aboard. You can hardly go swanning around the habitats at Allpoints."

"Well, I'm not going to run off. I can't pilot the ship, remember? But there might be a way to go swanning, if I can swing it."

"And then what? What will we all do?" Breel was almost afraid to ask.

"I can't stay at Allpoints," Abiel said. "I have unfinished business on New Chincharry. I have to find my daughter, find out what happened to her. I have to let her know who her real mother is and why I had to leave her behind."

Kaemon put his hand over hers. "I'll be going with her. She'll only do something stupid without me to look out for her."

Abiel scowled at him before breaking out a grin.

"I thought you had a bounty on your head," the Deacon said to Abiel.

Abiel shrugged. "I do. I'm not protected by the Church anymore. I'm on my own. I'll take my chances."

"What about you, Ellyella?" Breel asked.

"If I can stay with you –" she began.

"Of course, why wouldn't you?" Breel said quickly.

"– for a while," Ellyella finished. "I just need a chance to get my act together. I've got unfinished business as well, on Blue Haven. My father and what really happened to him. I need to address that."

Breel looked at the Deacon.

"Like El, I'll lodge with you for a while if I may. Perhaps Mr. Cavalacro can help organise a new identity for me. Then I'll be able to carry on my research, on New Haven, or maybe one of the smaller habitats. There must be a way to make the authorities listen. Even if humanity is safe for centuries, the day will come when we will have to address the issue of the reality-rift. And Ellyella's idea of something reaching through the rift to manipulate the Emissary is worthy of further investigation."

Breel felt her heart sink. They were all going to leave her. Eventually she would lose the only family she had left.

The Mech shifted its weight again and turned to Breel. "Hey kid. Looks like it'll be just you and me," it said cheerfully.

When Breel didn't respond it added, "Babe, why so glum? C'mon, it'll be a riot."

The white dwarf was cresting the right limb of the red giant. Like a powerful spotlight glowing through red fog, it turned the giant's crimson atmosphere a bright pink. It climbed higher. A fountain of star-stuff poured from the huge star to splash and burst against the super-dense surface of its tiny companion.

"To absent friends."

"Hello, Corlezea." Hannathon said without turning. A glass of wine appeared in Hannathon's hand. "Yes, to absent friends." He raised the glass to the sky before taking a sip. Back in his cabin his brain was fooled into thinking it was a Montalcino appellation, from Siena on old Earth. It could never be of course. There were only a handful of men in human space whose fortunes would enable them to bear the astronomical, in every sense of the word, shipping costs. Honestly, he thought, why didn't we all just live in these sims when it's so hard to tell the difference and where everything is under control? Of course, even though his brain might tell him he was sipping fine wine and eating the best steak, he would still ultimately starve. Men cannot live on fantasies alone.

"What do we do now?" Corlezea asked.

Hannathon turned to the other captain, who had not conjured a glass to Maliesh.

"There isn't much we can do, except what we are told to do. For the time being, anyway. And hope his holiness doesn't get wind we were part of Maliesh's little insurrection. Have you impressed secrecy on your men?"

Corlezea nodded. "I didn't need to. They are terrified of what could happen to them if the Emissary finds out they were involved. The Emissary is so erratic and unpredictable, there's no telling what he might do. Offering up information might end with the Emissary rewarding them with a kiss, rather than what they might hope for."

Corlezea took two steps and stood next to Hannathon, following his gaze into the sky. Hannathon looked sideways at him. "You were lucky back there. The Light clearly shines on you," he said.

"Yes," Corlezea's face hardened. "Harken-Court almost took us out. I didn't anticipate that."

"Love is a dangerous emotion. The Church is right to suppress it. It can make men dangerous and unpredictable," Hannathon said.

"How do you think he did it?" Corlezea asked. "The Emissary escape Maliesh, I mean?"

"Who knows? Maybe The Emissary has found a way to transmit his nanites through the air," Hannathon guessed. "Until we find out, we have to be very careful if we don't want to end up like him."

Corlezea said, "Damn the man! He should have been more careful who he groomed. Now we will all have to live with the consequence of his bad judgement."

"Still, all is not lost," Hannathon said, looking back to the sky. "After everything, it was worth this journey. If we can unlock the secrets here, we will be the most powerful men in known space, and who knows, perhaps beyond. But it cannot be left in the hands of the Emissary. The man is unhinged."

"Who then? You?"

Hannathon sighed. He walked away from Corlezea and sat on the same rock he had sat upon the last time they were all here.

"Us, Corlezea. Us. We don't need to compete, but control from behind the scenes. Maliesh may have turned out to be incompetent, but his methodology was sound. We need to find a replacement for the Lord of Light, one that will do what he is told. That's all."

"That's all?"

Hannathon took another sip of the really excellent wine. "Maliesh's network in the High Council is still intact and at the moment, still in control. All we can do from here is stay alive. When we get back there will be a reckoning. Or, you never know, an opportunity might still present itself out here. We need to liaise with the other captains, the ones newly arrived and see if any might be amenable to our point of view. After all, they say what happens in space, stays in space."

"We will have to do that very carefully," Corlezea said.

Hannathon sent an instruction to the sim software and the white dwarf suddenly ignited. Seconds later, following a physically accurate model, a shockwave of matter blasted out into the universe at an appreciable percentage of the speed of light. The sky burnt out, completely white. An instant later the ruined city on the horizon began to smoke and glow, followed by the crust of the planet they stood and sat upon. An instant after that, the planet evaporated, leaving them floating in space surrounded by tortured matter. Hannathon still sat incongruously on his rock.

"We need to start again," Hannathon said.

He looked back to Corlezea, brightly lit on one side with shadows as black as the Emissary's soul on the other. A drink had appeared in his hand. It looked like whiskey. Corlezea raised it to the burning, multi-coloured filaments of twisting matter filling the sky.

"Farewell, Maliesh," he said. "You always were a dick."

Hannathon raised his own glass again.

ACKNOWLEDGEMENTS

Despite long, lonely hours tapping at a keyboard, a book is always a collaboration. There are so many people I need to thank that it would require an extra chapter to include you all. If you're not in the list below, know that I am still very grateful for all your help and encouragement.

There are some who need a special mention, however.

Dr. Robert Runté, whose actions above and beyond helped me get the books into a publishable state. Without him they would still be languishing on my hard drive.

Patrick Mahon, whose encouragement and belief in the book was vital to it seeing the light of day.

Marvin Harding, beta reader extraordinaire, who has been reading *Dark Shepherd* as long as I've been writing it.

Sheila Harding who convinced me it was worth carrying on with.

Eric Peterson, who did his best to make sure I got the science bits right in *Reality Rift*. Any errors you may find are wholly mine.

Ian Whates at NewCon press, who edited and believed in *Dark Shepherd* enough to publish it.

And last but not least, Jenny, my partner in crime, who has walked alongside me this whole journey.

ALSO FROM NEWCON PRESS

ANIMALS – Geoff Ryman

A powerful new novel from the multiple award-winning author of *HIM, Was* and *The Child Garden* The chilling tale of a family caught at the heart of a terrifying and transformative epidemic; an astonishing fusion of beautiful writing and pure horror as the world we know falls apart.

The History of the World – Simon Morden

To return his precious human cargo, PurLeeDah, to her home, Corbyn, a sentient ramship, must slow from near lightspeed – a process requiring thousands of years. Little does Corbyn realise that below him, on PurLeeDah's homeworld, his regular orbital passage has been noted and he has come to be worshipped as a god, inadvertently shaping the emerging culture.

The Essence – Dave Hutchinson

Michael's troubles start with the breakdown he suffers on his wife's death. He learns there's a phenomenon – a force, a spirit, a flaw in Reality – known as *the Essence*. A small group of people have been trying to study it for centuries without success. Now, some very powerful people believe Michael may hold the key and they will stop at nothing to claim it.

Cities are Forests Waiting to Happen – Cécile Cristofari

A stunning new novella from the British Fantasy Award winner. Decades after a catastrophic collapse, Rossana, a professional urban explorer, discovers that a rogue artificial intelligence threatens the communication system her world depends on. She heads to the former metropolis of Toronto, intent on isolating and destroying the AI.

Blood in the Bricks – edited by Neil Williamson

Tales of the city redolent with ritual and drenched in dread. Our cities have been around for a long time, their histories built layer upon layer, their secrets long kept and buried deep. Who knows what goes on behind locked doors? These nineteen stories, from award-winning and emerging authors alike, expose the dark secrets of urban life and the chilling traditions that shaped them.

www.newconpress.co.uk